KU-483-740

At the Boss's Command

DARCY MAGUIRE

MADELEINE KER

NATASHA OAKLEY

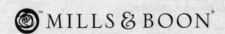

MILLS & BOON

All the characters in this book have no existence outside the imagination of
the author, and have no relation whatsoever to anyone bearing the same name
or names. They are not even distantly inspired by any individual known or
unknown to the author, and all the incidents are pure invention.

First published in Great Britain 2010
Harlequin Mills & Boon Limited,
Eton House, 18-24 Paradise Road, Richmond, Surrey TW9 1SR

AT THE BOSS'S COMMAND
© by Harlequin Enterprises II B.V./S.à.r.l 2010

Taking on the Boss, The Millionaire Boss's Mistress and *Accepting the Boss's
Proposal* were first published in Great Britain by Harlequin Mills & Boon
Limited in separate, single volumes.

Taking on the Boss © Debra D'Arcy 2005
The Millionaire Boss's Mistress © Madeleine Ker 2004
Accepting the Boss's Proposal © Natasha Oakley 2006

ISBN: 978 0 263 88096 0

05-0210

Printed and bound in Spain
by Litografia Rosés S.A., Barcelona

TAKING ON THE BOSS

BY
DARCY MAGUIRE

Darcy Maguire spends her days as a matchmaker, torturing tall, handsome men, seducing them into believing in love, and romancing their socks off! And when she's not working on her novels she enjoys gardening, reading and going to the movies. She loves to hear from her readers. Visit her at www.darcymaguire.com

CHAPTER ONE

Aries—Your love life has been in a lull. Expect to meet someone new who'll stir your passions.
No, thank you, I'll pass.

'It's every girl's dilemma.'

Tahlia Moran pushed open the front door to their office building, turning and holding it for her friend. 'What is?'

'The right timing to get seriously into finding one's life's partner, of course,' Keely said, pushing her handbag strap up her shoulder.

The words hammered right through Tahlia. First the horror-scope and now Keely. Did she have 'seriously single but feel free to cure me' tattooed on her forehead?

'You know,' Keely offered. 'It has to be soon or there won't be any single, straight men left for you. All the good men are getting snapped up.'

Tahlia had to admit her two best friends were doing their bit, going from seriously single to seriously taken in what seemed like a snap. 'I'm fine. I don't need anybody just now.'

'Tahlia—' Keely moved slowly through the doorway, resting her arm on her protruding belly, full of arms and legs. 'I know a lot of women just wait for him to appear, like magic. But we do encourage him to turn up by dating, pitiful though it may be, every single man around.'

'Just in case he doesn't,' Tahlia stated dryly, glancing down at her friend, who was a good six inches shorter than her now that Keely had traded in her heels for flats that didn't add to the swelling she seemed to be experiencing in more places than just her belly.

'Mr Right turned up for me and Em. He will for you too, but you have to date. It's a given, an unwritten agreement with Cupid.'

Tahlia let the door go. 'I'm thrilled for you both, you know that, but I have things to do right now and those things have nothing to do with arrow-wielding midgets or men.' While a partner was on her to-do list he wasn't a priority just now. And when it came to relationships she was in uncharted territory—a place she'd rather not be.

Keely sighed. 'Okay, but he *could* just appear out of nowhere and sweep you off your feet.'

She didn't want to be swept; she was thinking more of being quietly and calmly romanced into a sane and sensible partnership that would prove companionable and satisfying for the long term, some time in the future.

'What does your horoscope say?'

Tahlia tucked her bag tightly under her arm. She'd had quite enough of horoscopes. It wasn't as if they were always right. In fact, they were hardly right at all…so it didn't really matter what it said today.

'Oh, look, there's George.' Tahlia veered towards the guard's desk, sneaking a quick glance at her friend to see if she'd successfully avoided discussing her horror-scope and its nebulous prediction of a certain stirring someone entering her life. 'I've got to thank him for letting me out last night.'

Keely continued across the large marbled foyer towards the lifts. 'Locked in again, eh?'

Tahlia nodded, straightening her suit jacket. There was only one way to guarantee being the only choice for the position of Marketing Executive and that was to out-work and out-perform everyone else.

There was no doubt she'd get the position when the big boss, Raquel, stopped running around the place trying to tell everyone how to do their jobs, and do hers by finally filling the position.

Tahlia couldn't help but smile. Raquel's job would be so much easier once she gave Tahlia the promotion, if only Raquel would get over her fear that Tahlia wanted her job next, rational or not.

'You know, you've got to get out there to find him,' her friend called across the foyer.

Tahlia stared after her, shaking her head and glancing around her. Trust Keely to share her singledom with the world.

She was well aware of the fact that she wasn't just going to bump into the perfect man, that she had to go out and find him, eventually, but there were so many more pressing things to deal with first.

First and foremost, she had to secure that promotion. She needed to have job security before mucking around in the dating scene and possibly finding a partner, just in case it didn't work out.

She wasn't going to go into any relationship blind,

unprepared, naïvely optimistic, or with silly ideas like love was enough.

Her mum had put her career on hold while she had concentrated on motherhood. When things had come crashing down her mother had been left juggling it all, finding out just how hard life was if you neglected sense and relied on love to see you through.

Tahlia was going to wait.

She wasn't going to be pressured into something she wasn't ready for just because Emma and Keely were no longer single. She'd wait until after the announcement of her promotion, after she had everything sorted and under control—all bases covered, then she'd handle the man-in-her-life challenge.

Tahlia pulled up at the guard's station, rubbing the muscles knotted in her neck. 'Hey, George.' Tahlia slapped her hand on the counter, shooting him a smile. 'Thanks so much again for last night.'

'No problems.' The greying guard shifted his formidable weight in his seat. 'Any time for you. They must give you that promotion soon, eh?'

Tahlia nodded, the buzz of her imminent success in climbing another rung coursing through her. 'Absolutely. It's so close, George, I can smell it.'

George smiled up at her, his cheeks creasing in full waves of doughnut crescents. 'Better not to be late, then.'

'Have a great day.' She swung around, glancing at her watch, striding forward. George was right. If Raquel was looking for a reason not to promote her there was no way in the world she'd give her the satisfaction.

The job was so hers.

She connected with a wall of warm flesh and the scent of soapy clean male engulfed her.

Tahlia looked down, finding her footing and the guy's shiny black, very expensive-looking shoes. His suit trousers were black, stretching up long legs that tapered to a nice flat waist.

His soft blue shirt was covered by a black suit jacket that was tailored to perfection, emphasising just how wide the guy's shoulders were.

His tie was the colour of sapphires...she lifted her gaze...as were his eyes, that met hers with a casual assurance that touched his lips, firm and sensual and full of promises.

Tahlia's breath caught in her lungs.

She shook herself. She was going to stay focused and on track, no matter how short-back-and-sides, clean-shaven, suit-obsessed, white-collar-cute he looked.

'Hello,' he offered, his voice rich and deep, flowing over her like liquid Swiss chocolate. The world tipped.

The man caught her arm, holding her steady, a flash of concern in his gaze. 'Are you okay?'

His hand was strong, hot and muddling. Blood rushed to Tahlia's face, filling her head with a blurring that she couldn't afford right now.

She forced her knees to straighten, strengthen, to not fall for a ridiculous weakness that only happened in a twelve-year-old girl's dreams.

'Yes. Of course. I'm fine,' she managed, lifting her chin and shooting him a smile of cool assurance. 'Loose heel, that's all.'

She cast a glance downward to her black heels, willing that one would fall off gracefully and save her from this embarrassment.

His gaze followed, coursing over her suit jacket, down her simple white blouse, over her short black skirt that stopped a good six inches above her knees, down her bare legs to her feet.

His eyes glinted and she had the sudden urge to cross her arms. She felt naked, as though he'd just seen far more of her than he should have. And liked what he saw.

Butterflies swarmed in her belly.

Tahlia jerked her hand up to her face, pushed back her blonde-streaked long fringe and pointed to the lifts. 'Must go. Love to…' Die on the spot. 'But can't be late for work.'

The cute-suit raised an eyebrow, his blue eyes flashing. 'That's it?'

She froze. What? Did he mean to suggest that he was well aware of her disgusting weak-kneed reaction and was expecting her to fall into his arms again? What arrogance!

'*It?*' she enunciated clearly, crossing her arms. What else could he want? 'As opposed to, *what?*'

'An apology.'

'Oh.' The sound escaped her throat. Of course he did. Obviously. Manners. Why hadn't she thought of that instead of jumping to erogenous conclusions? 'Sorry for—'

His mouth quirked, fighting what looked to be a smile.

She stiffened, her blood heating anew. 'Sorry

for…running into someone who was obviously not looking where *he* was going.'

'Either,' he added, his voice an octave deeper.

'Either,' she echoed as casually as she could, hating to concede a point, and more than infuriated at her body's total lack of sense. 'Fine, but since you agree that you weren't looking where you were going *either*, you could apologise…'

His eyes sparkled. 'You're absolutely right, but I was brought up to believe in "ladies first".'

'I think that relates to entries, exits and queues, not to apologies.' She glared up at him. 'And you have to admit that men need all the practice they can get.'

The man put down his case. 'Apologising?'

She nodded. 'It's really something they don't do enough of.'

'Bad day?' He slipped his hands into his pockets. 'Has your husband upset you?'

She shook her head, a smile jumping to her mouth. 'I'm not married.' Gawd, no. She wasn't going anywhere near *that* challenge for a long time.

'Your boyfriend, then?'

'No—' Tahlia took a step back, her stomach fluttering as though there were a thousand butterflies in it. Was he interested, in *her*? 'Look, I have to go or I'll be late and you don't know my boss—'

He didn't know *her* either.

'She doesn't let you forget any transgression, no matter how insignificant, and it's not like she'll be sympathetic to my bumped-into-a-cute-guy-in-the-lobby excuse, even though she is seriously in need of a good—'

'You think I'm cute?'

She touched her lips. Oh, damn. That couldn't have been her. She never babbled, let alone incoherently. She never put her feet anywhere except where she wanted to go.

She pointed to the lifts, opening her mouth, but no words would come out. What in blazes was going on with her?

'See you around then?' he offered, his warm mouth fighting a smile that promised to be as amazing as the rest of him.

She nodded, swung around and forced herself to get as much distance between them as possible, counting her steps, measuring her speed to look as little like the hasty escape it was as possible.

What was that?

Tahlia shook her head. She wasn't going to even think about it. So, the guy was cute and lust was a natural response. She didn't have to concern herself about a bit of lust and there were so many reasons to lust for that guy.

Deep sexy voice, gorgeous body, tall, commanding and handsome as hell, but she wasn't about to listen to inappropriate primal urges.

She needed a list of criteria for the most appropriate partner, a conservative, safe plan to dating, a timetable that would fit in with her commitments and work demands. This was not the time to get distracted or fall for anyone willy-nilly.

She stepped into the lift, taking a deep slow breath. What was she even thinking? One thing she was sure of. She was never going to *fall* for anyone, especially someone like that.

She was not going to make the same mistakes as her mother. No way in hell.

Case Darrington punched the lift button, unable to stop the smile that had crept on to his lips at meeting the most beautiful woman he'd ever laid eyes on.

It wasn't just her looks. It was everything about her.

The way she'd pulled her short chestnut-brown hair up and back into a wild and spiky knot intrigued him, suggesting a conservative layer covering something untamed underneath.

The large chunk of hair that she left loose could be called a fringe, hanging down and cupping her cheek like his hands itched to.

Her skin had beckoned to him, creamy smooth. Her lips, full and plump like peaches just begging to be tasted. Her eyes, deep dark green, pinning him to the spot.

So much to explore…who was she?

He should have asked her name, should have skipped getting exact directions from the guard and just followed her. He should have kept her talking instead of letting her have her escape without even getting her name, her floor, a glass shoe.

Case put his attaché case by his feet and tried to stop smiling. Hell. She'd floored him, with her eyes, her lips, her words…

Case couldn't say when he'd last been so flattered so simply. Had watched such a beautiful display of…innocent reaction.

He stiffened. What was he thinking? He wasn't about to get carried away with any unusual aches in the heart that he'd thought had died on him.

He'd grown wiser the hard way.

The doors opened on the lift and he snatched up his attaché case and stepped in. He wasn't here for anything but work.

He gripped his case tighter, the woman's face leaping into his mind, her green eyes sizzling and her full lips taunting him.

Dammit. Why couldn't life be as straightforward as figures on a balance sheet?

A woman with deep red hair swept into the small space. 'Hello, handsome,' she lilted.

Case turned to find fluttering lashes on dark eyes that were drinking him up.

He stepped back. That tone…that look…sent memories flashing through the gashes in his heart.

'Are you visiting or are you planning to stay around and make all my dreams come true?' she asked softly, her smile widening, showing teeth.

'I work here,' he said bluntly, staring at the lift doors, willing the thing to get to his floor faster. He'd have to look into that. The lift was too slow. Employees needed to get to their floors much faster, especially when accompanied by predatory females.

She waved a hand laden with gold jewellery, the bracelets tinkling. 'I think I'd remember you unless you have that whole Clark Kent-Superman thing going,' she purred softly, sidling closer to him. 'So are you Clark, or are you my Superman? I do love games.'

'I'm new.' And he hated games. He'd seen enough

games to last him a lifetime. Hell, his ex had been a master at them, playing him in ways he'd never believed possible.

She ran a hand along his jacket sleeve, leaning closer, affording him a generous view of her low-cut blouse and the assets heaving there. 'I could show you around.'

'I don't think so, Miss—?' He stared at the panel—the floor he wanted was the only one lit. Please let it be a mistake, let her not be working with him… The last thing he needed was a constant reminder of his biggest failure in life to date.

She giggled softly as though she hadn't heard his denial. 'Call me Chrystal. And you are?'

The lift chimed.

'Darrington,' Case blurted, striding forward.

The doors opened just in time and he kept moving. He couldn't wait to get as much distance as possible between himself and that man-eater.

He only wished he could escape the memories of his failed marriage as easily.

CHAPTER TWO

The Beatles say all you need is love...
I say give me bug spray.

TAHLIA slapped her handbag on to her desk and swept up the files in one deft move, taking a deep breath and lifting her chin, the echo of her babbling bombarding her senses. What was that?

She was never like that. How embarrassing. She cast her eyes to the ceiling. Please let her not be so stupid again.

She glanced around her office, one wall full of filing cabinets, one with potted plants and paintings, one covered in current jobs and timelines and one made of glass with a great view of the lifts.

She shook her head and swept out of the door, striding down the aisle between the cubicles, replaying that débâcle over again in her mind. The floor could have done her one little favour and swallowed her up before she'd made such a complete and utter fool of herself. Cripes. How old *was* she?

She was far too old to be acting like a schoolgirl, that was for sure. Thank goodness that Emma and Keely hadn't seen that deplorable display. She had a reputation to uphold. Cool, calm and always in control Tahlia Moran, soon to be Marketing Executive.

She swung into the last cubicle. 'Morning, Susan,'

she offered, handing the young woman who was just sitting down a file. 'Could you put some ideas together for this client? They want to change their look to reflect the new season.'

'Sure.'

Tahlia nodded, striding down the row, doling out the updates for existing clients wanting changes to their websites and the assignments for potential clients.

She juggled the files in her arms. There were things a would-be executive did not do, and one was running off at the mouth in emotionally charged situations. Not that she was admitting there was anything but an overactive imagination and a neglected personal life at the root of that particular encounter downstairs.

Two years since her last real date wasn't *that* long, not when she was ensuring a successful career for her future.

She clutched the files remaining. It didn't matter anyway. Downstairs had been nothing but an anomaly. She wasn't going to have to deal with *that* guy, or that abhorrent lack of control again.

'Hey, you,' Tahlia offered Emma, stepping into her friend's cubicle and dropping the files on her desk. '*Flirt* magazine's next issue—they want their update to match the theme and want another competition page designed and put on the site.'

Emma took the file. 'Sure thing.' The glow of love was bright in her eyes. 'Did you hear? It's time. Your day.'

Tahlia shook herself. 'Em?'

'Haven't you logged on yet?' Emma shot her a quizzical look. 'Raquel just sent out a mass email to everyone for a meeting in the conference room at half past. Sounds like it could be *it*.'

Tahlia shook her head, kicking herself for not going through her normal routine—checking her voicemail, SMS and inboxes, both cyber and deskbound.

'And?'

'And the whispers suggest it's about the Marketing Exec position.'

Tahlia's belly fluttered. 'She's made a decision? Finally?'

'Yep, it sounds like the Rottweiler has come through. So you'd better get spruced up.' Emma tossed her blonde bob, her smile widening. 'Now you don't have any excuses not to get out there.'

'Out there,' Tahlia echoed, the words ricocheting down her spine, making her skin gooseflesh and the image of that cute-suit bounce around her brain.

'Out there dating. Sheesh, Tahlia, anyone would think from the look on your face that you're not keen to find Mr Right.' Emma clapped her hands. 'I've asked Harry and he has a couple of single mates and Keely says Lachlan is thinking about the possibilities for you too. It would be just perfect if you had someone special to come to my wedding with.'

Tahlia opened her mouth and closed it. What could she say? She had wonderful, interfering, matchmaking-maniac friends who were dying for her to find happiness like they had.

'May I?' she asked slowly, gesturing to the keyboard. Could the promotion really be hers today? Could she dare to believe it finally had come?

Emma rolled her chair away from her desk. 'You have to see it to believe it, right?'

Tahlia stepped forward, clutching the mouse and logging on, clicking her way to her inbox. 'The wording, the tone, the undertones could all mean so much...'

'You're still worried about the rumours that the company isn't going so well?'

Tahlia glanced at her friend. 'You know as well as I do that the whispers suggest jobs are to be axed and no one can deny the fears spreading are of a major shake-up or shake-down.'

'And the latest gossip is that the owners have drawn too much of the cash flow out of the company to fund their overseas romps and WWW Designs is going down, down, down,' Emma said dramatically.

'That's over-exaggeration if ever I heard it.'

Emma nodded, her eyes wide. 'I know.'

TO: *TahliaM@WWWDesigns.com*
CC: *allstaff@WWWDesigns.com*
FROM: *RaquelW@WWWDesigns.com*
SUBJECT: Meeting
All staff,
Be advised that the meeting at 9am in the conference room is mandatory for all staff to be advised of the latest developments.
Don't be late.
Raquel Wilson
General Manager

Tahlia sighed. 'It doesn't say anything regarding my promotion.'

'What else could it be?'

'The possibilities are endless, Em. It could be a new client coming on board, it could be about the rumours, it could be anything.'

'But it could be your promotion. The Rottie always holds an all-staff meeting for changes in personnel.'

Tahlia straightened Em's files on her desk. Was there a reason to get her hopes up? Was it about the position for Marketing Executive?

If it was, there was no one else suitable for the job *so* it had to be her. A bubble of excitement rose up in her chest.

Emma stood up, slapping her on the shoulder. 'Come on. It is *so* about your promotion. It has to be.' She grinned. 'And now you have no excuse to get serious about that part of your life you've put on hold while you got your career *all solid and stable*.'

A chill raced down Tahlia's back.

She smoothed down her suit jacket, shaking off the feeling. It would be fine. 'Yes, not a problem,' she stated casually to her friend. A relationship didn't have to mean disaster, as long as it didn't involve rash decisions, irrational emotions or incredibly embarrassing interactions with too-cute guys.

'You don't sound so sure.'

Tahlia raised her eyebrows, forcing a smile to her mouth. 'I'll handle it like I've handled everything—with criteria, a plan of action and safeguards.'

You could never have too many safeguards, as her mother had shown her. Her mother hadn't considered any were necessary, that love was enough...and it was *so* not enough.

'O-kay,' Em offered, shooting her an odd look, moving out of her cubicle. She glanced at her watch. 'So are you ready for the meeting?'

'Absolutely.' She *was* ready for her dream to come true and Em was right—what else could it possibly be about?

Nothing she couldn't handle.

Tahlia pushed open one of the conference room doors and slipped inside with Emma behind her, weaving through the throng of people, keeping to the wall side of the large room.

She concentrated on the acceptance speech that she'd been practising for months and not on the expanse of glass and views of Melbourne on the far side.

She looked behind her but couldn't see Emma.

Her stomach churned with butterflies. This was going to be the highlight of her year and she damned well deserved it. Why Raquel had waited until now was beyond her.

This was it.

She smiled and her mind filled with all the congratulations that everyone would offer, the sweet proof that Raquel acknowledged her skills and her potential, the incredible thrill of telling her mother she'd finally made it another rung up the ladder.

Raquel cleared her throat, dropping a large folder on the table.

The room fell silent.

'Okay. Thanks for coming, staff,' she said in her trademark nasal bellow. 'Of course you all know that the position of Marketing Executive has been open for some time and is long overdue being filled. I am pleased to announce that a decision has been reached—'

Tahlia held her breath, searching the crowd for her best friends, finding friendly faces with smiles as wide as her own must be.

Emma had been right. This was it—her dream realised, her goal achieved, vindication for endless overtime and a landmark achievement that would ensure that she'd never have to do it hard like her mother.

So what if Emma was getting married and moving to New York to a new job with the love of her life and Keely was taking maternity leave—*she* would have her promotion.

She swung her attention back towards Raquel.

Sapphire-blue eyes caught hers.

Her heart missed a beat.

It was him.

The cute-suit looked taller, dwarfing the staff around him at the head of the table near Raquel the Rottie, standing out all the more in that tailored black suit, the strong lines of his face resembling more a Greek god than…was he an employee of WWW Designs?

What was he doing here? She hadn't heard of anyone being taken on lately, especially a tall, dark and devastating thirty-something.

'Let me introduce to you our new Marketing Executive…' Raquel paused for effect, shooting Tahlia a tight smile, sweeping her hand past Tahlia to the cute-suit. 'Case T Darrington.'

Tahlia's heart slammed against her chest and sank

to the pit of her belly where all the butterflies dropped dead, adding to the weight.

Her vision blurred, her throat closing over. It couldn't be. No. It wasn't possible. There had to be a mistake.

Not him.

Not anybody.

It should have been her!

Raquel put up open arms, her smile wide, avoiding meeting Tahlia's gaze. 'Welcome to the great team here at WWW Designs.'

Tahlia dragged in a slow ragged breath, fighting the sting behind her eyes. How…?

The man behind Raquel sidled out into the open, putting his hands up and rotating slowly like a prize-fighter who'd just knocked out the competition. And he had. Effortlessly.

Her.

CHAPTER THREE

All men are created equal.
But what about women? And are we talking sexism here or feminism-gone-crazy? Has Raquel hired this cute-suit because there are just too many women in the company? Or just because she doesn't want me?

CASE moved to the head of the table, smiling at the new faces around him, taking in the pause after Raquel's announcement, the hesitant applause, the expressions being cast from face to face.

It was to be expected. They had probably figured the position would be filled in-house by someone they already knew who wouldn't question or threaten their way of doing things. And he'd just thrown them out of that comfort zone by being thrown into the mix.

A new face. A loose cannon. Someone who they weren't sure of. *If only they knew.*

'Thank you, Raquel,' he offered the woman who the vision-from-the-lobby had mentioned earlier.

And then there she was, in the audience. He tore his gaze from her, the fact that she worked for him sending warning signals.

'Hello, everyone,' he said smoothly, moving up beside Raquel. 'I'm thrilled to be here and look forward to working with you all. I hope in the coming days to meet you all personally.'

Case glanced towards the beauty again; her face was a mask of professional curiosity. He straightened his tie. Yes. It was time to get serious. He wasn't here to get distracted by a pretty face. He was here to sort out one-hell-of-a-mess.

The challenge was what he needed, had needed since his marriage breakdown, and he'd excelled at finding them. He'd gone out of his way to be involved in the most complicated business deals, play the most exacting sports and pursue the most beleaguered companies.

Since his marriage, women were the one area where he went for simple. Easy, light liaisons with pretty socialites thrilled to be on his arm.

Case scanned the room. WWW Designs was in a perfect mess too. Enough to keep him in busy excuses for not having time for a personal life. And enough to redeem himself for the tragedy his marriage became.

Hell, the look on his parents' faces when he had told them it was over had been the worst part of the whole affair. They prided themselves on their thirty-five years of respectable and spotless marriage, had wished him the same fortunate alliance—the only blemish now was their only child's marital failure.

It was years ago now, but he still hated the feeling of disappointing them.

Case shook his hands out from the balls they'd curled into. He fixed a soft smile to his face and took a breath. 'I've heard great things about the team here at WWW Designs and I'd like to say that I'm very keen on hearing *your* ideas on making improvements, not only in your department, but to make this company even greater.'

Raquel moved forward. 'Thank you, Mr Darrington. I'm sure everyone can't wait to share their thoughts with you,' she barked, shooting a hard look around the room. 'And I'm sure you're eager to get started.'

'That I am,' he said, running his eyes over the crowded room, resting on a pair of very fine green eyes.

'Wonderful. Great. Then let's get on to housekeeping. Tahlia, where are we at on hooking the contracts for the private schools' websites? Mr Darrington, this is Tahlia Moran, Director of Sales.'

Tahlia Moran, aka The Beauty, stepped forward, her shoulders thrown back, her chin high, a chilling blankness in her green eyes that pierced his own for a moment.

Case tossed her name around in his head. It suited her…sweet like her voice and her reaction to him, and strong like the way she held herself and that look.

What was with that look?

She swung her focus to Raquel Wilson. 'We've submitted our ideas to the various schools that were looking and are awaiting their respective decisions,' she said in a cold, lifeless monotone.

His gut tightened.

The woman he'd bumped into downstairs had glowed with such passion that he could imagine clients swarming towards her like bees to spring blossoms.

What was going on in the office to cause such a turn-around in her? Case scanned the room. How many others here were having their enthusiasm sucked out of them? And by what?

He had to find out.

The company's future success could hinge on him sorting it out—and he knew just where to start. With a tall, dazzling mystery that begged to be explored.

He just wasn't sure whether he should.

Tahlia stared at her computer screen, willing the words to clear so she could read her mail and get on with the job she still had.

TO: *TahliaM@WWWDesigns.com*
CC: *KeelyR@WWWDesigns.com*
FROM: *EmmaR@WWWDesigns.com*
SUBJECT: A crazy crazy world

Missed you at the end of the meeting. I expect you needed some space. Gawd, Tahlia. I'm so sorry.

There must be some reason the Rottie chose that creep over you. Maybe there's something going on with them—he is rather cute for a creep.

I think the world has gone crazy. First your promotion goes to some total stranger and then Chrystal. I just had the weirdest talk with her about men. No. Not about size. Or quality. Or quantity. She was asking my advice on how to land Mr Right! Freaky, huh? I guess our office nymph has decided, finally, that she wants more than just sex from men.

What do you think Darrington's T stands for? Tyrant?

Em

And if you need to talk, or scream or yell or cry, I'm here for you, sweetie.

Tahlia threw herself back in her chair, staring at the ceiling. Yes, the guy was a creep, sauntering into the building, flaunting his good looks, great suit and that sexy mouth and sharing that oh-so-deep voice.

Acting as if he was just anybody when innocent hard-working employees bumped into him was wrong, and totally inappropriate behaviour in the circumstances.

The nerve of the guy to meet her gaze in the meeting, all warm and soft, as though he was naïve and innocent and ignorant to the fact that it was her promotion he'd stolen.

He didn't need the job. With a suit that expensive it was surprising he was working at all. *He* probably had a silver spoon stuck well and truly up his—

She slammed a fist on her desk. He probably wasn't even qualified, had probably figured there was nothing wrong with using his wealth and connections to jump over hard-working employees on his ruthless climb to the top.

She'd hardly heard his acceptance, but had seen him smiling at her, as though his stealing her job wasn't enough, that he had to rub salt deep into the wounds of her dashed hopes and dreams.

Bastard. After she had been so stupid and babbling and stupid downstairs.

Gawd. He was her boss now. He was probably going to sack her...especially after what she had said about Raquel...unless he had already told Raquel. Then that was it, she was dead—the Rottie would eat her alive!

How could she have messed this up so badly?

How could she have failed?

Everything had been going so well. She'd had everything under control... How could she not have twigged that the Rottie was interviewing other candidates for the promotion she desperately wanted?

Tahlia cringed. How could she have let her mouth run away with her with the one person who should have seen her as absolutely together?

At least she'd reported the update without revealing a shred of the turmoil that raged within her. She was well practised at keeping it all deep inside.

Dammit. Her mother hadn't let anything get in her way to the top—not her grief, the rumours, motherhood, her limited education, nothing.

She straightened the photo on her desk of her mother in her favourite power suit with her arms crossed and chin up.

It had taken her mother over a year to save up enough for that suit. Tahlia had watched her come home from the supermarket every day, take off her uniform, make dinner and then iron, and study and iron, and go to night school and iron.

Her mother had said her power suit was forged by iron, and was therefore even more charged to give her the boost in business she needed.

Her mother had taught her about goals and strength

and determination and, dammit, she wasn't going to just give in.

She was a professional, like her mother, and she was going to hold her head high and deal with what life threw at her. Hell, she was used to it. Life had thrown a few big ones their way and they'd not only survived, they'd got stronger.

Even the rumours about Tahlia's dad hadn't stopped her mother—if anything they had driven her. Her mother's passion had inspired Tahlia...and Tahlia was not a quitter like her father. She was a winner, a survivor, and totally in control of her own life...and its surprises.

She'd survive this like she had survived everything else in her life to date—she just didn't know how to tell her mother...

Tahlia picked up a pen and stabbed the notepad in front of her. Damn that man. Damn Raquel. Damn the world.

How could this happen...right when she was going to prove that she'd be okay, that she was somebody too, that she'd made it?

Life wasn't fair.

Who was that man?

Sammy's, their local coffee shop, was busy in the afternoons but perfect for the quick after-work drink Tahlia and the girls had before they headed home.

Sammy's was mandatory to catch up on the weekend goss if they hadn't got the chance at work. Most days they'd go the entire day and not get to talk, depending on their work commitments, like the rest of today.

Although Tahlia had to admit she hadn't been so much working as hiding in her office, smothering her thoughts with work rather than trying to make sense of this disastrous turn of events.

She pushed open the coffee shop door, glancing at her watch. She was late. Maybe late enough for the girls to be totally focused on the wedding or the baby shower and to have forgotten entirely about her lack of promotion.

She didn't want to talk about it. She wanted to forget it had happened, try to recapture that naïve innocence and faith she'd had this morning that it was imminent, not an 'if' but a 'when' and she was the success she wanted to be.

Tahlia weaved through the tables. She definitely didn't want to talk about it until she knew what in heavens she was going to do about it.

Keely and Emma were leaning over their usual table, looking up at the same time, as though they'd picked her up on some radar.

'I'm so sorry, honey,' Emma said, gathering up the photos of wedding cakes and a couple of dozen letters that were probably more of the RSVPs she'd been checking off her guest list for the last week. 'About the promotion.'

Tahlia slid into the seat at the booth, gesturing for Andy, their usual waiter. 'It's nothing. A slight hiccup. I'll be fine.' She wished she could feel as fine as she hoped she sounded.

'Darrington is one hell of a hiccup.'

Tahlia shook her head, swallowing hard. 'So your baby shower is next week—' And then she'd be abandoning work for putting her feet up and focusing on her future, her baby, her husband and her new house.

'And you're avoiding the subject. What are you going to do about the new suit in the office?' Keely asked, tipping her head.

'Nothing,' Tahlia said as casually as she could, shrugging. 'I'm going to ignore him.'

Emma tapped her pile of stuff into symmetry. 'That may be a bit difficult seeing as he's your boss.'

'And he's cute as,' Keely added.

'I'm a professional.' And there was no way she wanted to see the guy again after their mortifying first meeting, let alone the fact he'd destroyed her dream.

Keely leant forward in her seat, her hand resting on her bulge. 'So you're telling us that you haven't noticed how nice-looking he is?'

She shook her head vigorously. 'No.' She wished she'd known who the guy was from the start so she hadn't allowed her body to buzz around in flights of fancy. 'I don't find that sort of clean-cut chiselled features, tailored-suit sort of guy attractive at all.' *Now*.

Today was just another good reason to avoid men altogether—they were trouble. They took what you wanted and ruined your life.

Emma drained her cup. 'So what now?'

'I get on with my job,' Tahlia said coolly, raising her eyebrows and giving a soft shrug. What else could she do?

'If we still have one,' Keely offered, flicking cookie crumbs from the table in front of her. 'Rumour has it that the owners are selling up WWW.'

'That one has been going around for ages,' Tahlia retorted, fighting the ache in her belly. It couldn't happen, not to her workplace, *her* future…

Keely got up, picking up her coat. 'I've got to go…home to Lachlan—gosh, I still can't believe my luck.'

'You deserve it,' Tahlia offered, grabbing her friend's hand and giving it a quick squeeze. 'And more.'

Emma shoved her wedding stuff into her large bag. 'You know you could start looking around for another job?'

Tahlia shook her head. 'I've got too much invested here.' And she'd rather walk on hot coals than admit failure, especially to her mum. She was going to get that promotion even if she had to wait another year for it.

'But don't feel bad that you're running off to the Big Apple.' Tahlia slapped the back of her hand to her forehead dramatically. 'Leaving me all on my own to battle the Darrington disaster.'

Emma laughed. 'You'll do just fine.'

Tahlia nodded, forcing a smile to her face. 'Of course. Always.' She was always fine. She had been fine when her father had died, fine when her mother had gone to work, fine when she'd come home to an empty house, fine when her mother hadn't made it to her graduation, her birthdays or their lunch-dates, and she was fine now.

She could handle Darrington all on her own. She'd find out who the man was and what he'd done so that she could explain how he could get her job promotion—to herself and to her mother.

Maybe he just had better luck than her. She bit her bottom lip. Maybe she should get a few charms to be on the safe side, to cover all bases, to ensure her success.

She'd do anything to get where she wanted to go. She was a professional.

CHAPTER FOUR

Everything in life has a price.
And I never know what it is until it's too late.

CASE sat in the large leather chair and surveyed his
new office again. He couldn't quite believe he was
here.

He'd spent all yesterday calling in employees, talking to them, encouraging them to tell him just how
much they did in the company and how much more
they could do, given the right incentives.

Work was going well.

This was going to be good for him. It reminded him
of where he'd been six years ago, took him back to
simpler times, when he still believed in so many things,
including love and marriage.

Framed prints hung on the walls, large ferns sat in
the corners looking as if they were in need of a water
or a wax—he never could tell if indoor plants were
fake or not—the sofa in the corner was cream with tan
cushions that matched the rug under the glass and
chrome coffee table.

The place could do with a makeover, as one of the
employees had suggested, to improve morale. He'd
have to look into it. And Miss Tahlia Moran.

Case snatched a pen from the desk, slapping it into
his palm. No. There was no mystery to unravel.

Nothing to explore except how to get this office dynamic working to its highest potential.

The only responsibility he had was to the company. So what if she'd vanished during the meeting yesterday, somewhere after her report and the general housekeeping.

He stabbed the pen into the file on his desk. He wished she'd left his thoughts as easily. He couldn't stop wondering about her and that lack of light in her eyes.

He'd half thought of calling her into his office yesterday but had caught himself. There was no rush here—he could take his time to investigate the office politics, the hierarchies and issues at WWW. Besides, he would run into her eventually. They were on the same floor.

But he hadn't yesterday.

Was she avoiding him? He rubbed his jaw. She could easily be. Women were strange creatures. She could be put out that he hadn't mentioned his position to her when he'd bumped into her. But dammit, he hadn't wanted anything to interfere with her first impressions of him. It was so rare for him to have people see him as himself.

For once in his life he just wanted to be Joe Anybody.

Much good it had done him. He was her boss now, and the cool professional look she had cast him across the boardroom yesterday had said it all.

'Mr Darrington,' Miss Moran offered, tapping on his door. 'You wanted to see me?'

She stood tall with high black heels, black trousers

that held her curves and a white shirt with the top buttons undone, giving the hint of a lace undershirt.

His blood heated.

Her hair was in the same wild knot as yesterday, her lips were pursed, her green eyes cool and assessing, a finely arched eyebrow quirking as though she was not impressed to be here.

'Yes.' Case cracked his knuckles. He'd spent the last twenty-four hours trying to work out *why* it mattered so much what she thought of him...

He moved around his desk, extending his hand, offering it to her. 'Case.'

She nodded.

'And you are Tahlia Moran, Director of Sales,' he suggested lightly.

She raised her eyes to meet his. 'Guilty,' she said, striding forward and taking his hand.

Heat sizzled up his arm. 'Nice shake, Miss Moran.'

She pulled her hand from his smoothly. 'Ditto, Mr Darrington.'

'Call me Case.'

Tahlia stepped back. 'I have to say...before... downstairs...you caught me off-guard. I'm usually quite...sane.'

'O-kay,' he murmured, watching the rise of colour in her cheeks. Was she embarrassed?

His body buzzed at the thought. *Did* she like him? Had she felt the heat between their palms too? Had she felt that buzz yesterday when they'd collided?

Was that why she was so upset that he was her boss—because she felt the electricity between them but maybe had her own rules for not getting involved with workmates?

Hell, he had the same ideals. But if there could be one person he'd compromise his rules for it would be her, and that incredibly sweet innocence that she'd just bubbled with yesterday morning.

Now he'd never know…anything she said would be sugar-coated for 'the boss'.

Case straightened his tie. He was giving himself a headache. There was only one way to find out what was going on with Tahlia Moran and put his mind at rest…

He just hoped he liked the answers.

Tahlia glared at the man standing behind *her* desk in *her* office with *her* title as casually and comfortably as though he owned the place. 'If we could make this quick, Mr Darrington, I have work to do.'

He lifted an eyebrow. 'Would you like a coffee?' he asked, reducing the distance between them. 'I'm just on my way to the kitchenette.'

'Fine,' she bit out, stepping well back for the man to pass by. She didn't want to be anywhere near the guy, let alone touch him again.

She swiped her hand against her thigh, trying to dispel the tingling in her palm.

He stopped beside her. 'Ladies first,' he said smoothly, gesturing the way for her.

'Fine.' She sauntered down the hall, her breathing short and shallow, her hands clenched tightly at her sides. The promotion-stealer *had* to remind her of yesterday morning's embarrassment!

Wasn't it enough that he'd started throwing his weight around? Meeting everyone under him and convincing them he was interested in their ideas.

Jerk.

So, it was a great idea, not only to meet his staff but to get friendly and supportive…especially since he was a stranger coming in, but if he was thinking it was going to be easy to get on her good side he had another think coming.

Tahlia pushed open the door on the kitchenette and stalked across the room to get as much distance between them as she could. 'So what can I do for you, Mr Darrington?'

'Call me Case,' he said again smoothly, striding to the coffee pot and picking it up with one hand, plucking a mug from the rack with the other. 'How would you like it?'

She crossed her arms over her chest, resisting a reaction to his casual friendliness, his supposed humility in the face of his superior position, the ease with which he brandished the coffee pot as though it was natural to him to make his own.

Tahlia stiffened. 'How would I like it?' Pretending to be just another workmate was *not* going to get him anywhere with her. 'I think honestly and straight down the line,' she said evenly. 'No sugar-coating or fluffy padding would be nice.'

'I meant your coffee, but okay…' He smiled, his blue eyes gleaming at her.

Tahlia swallowed down the flutter in her belly. Snap out of it. So he was in a kick-arse deep blue suit that hugged his body like silk to pillows. So his eyes smiled as sexily as his mouth. She was *not* going to make any mistakes today. 'Black, no sugar.'

Darrington nodded. 'I need to know all about my staff. My team. I'm reliant on them to make or break this company,' he said, splashing the coffee into her mug and sliding it down the bench to her.

She halted its progress, cupping the mug in her hand. 'It sounds like you're aiming at Raquel's job next,' she said slowly. He couldn't take that off her too... 'A little ambitious for the first week, aren't you?'

He put the coffee pot back, poured some milk in his mug and added three spoons of sugar. 'I like to aim high. I like to push my staff to their potential and I like to succeed.'

She nodded tightly. WWW Designs sure needed that sort of attitude, that optimism and drive...but from her, not some interloper!

Case Darrington sipped his coffee. 'So what do you have to offer, Miss Moran?'

She paused, her nerves rippling their response down her spine and settling deep in her belly. 'My track record speaks for itself, Mr Darrington,' she bit out. She'd be damned if she was going to spell out her worth to a man who had undermined it.

He leant against the counter, his attention fixed entirely on her. 'I want to hear it from you.'

Tahlia took a deep breath. 'Well, that's all well and fine but I'm a busy woman. I really don't have time to list my skills, my achievements and my worth to this company to somebody who can't be bothered reading my file.'

His mouth fought a smile. 'You're not scared of me?'

She took a gulp of the coffee and looked pointedly at her watch. 'No.'

'Not even wary?'

'No.'

He crossed his arms over his wide chest. 'Aren't you worried I'll fire you for your lack of respect for authority?'

Tahlia shrugged. 'If you can't see my worth from reading my file, by what I do around here, then I'm better off somewhere else.'

He nodded slowly, his mouth fighting a smile. 'You are absolutely right.'

She met his sapphire-blue eyes warily. 'I am?' What was he up to? It had to be something…

'Yes.' He picked up his mug and walked to the door. 'Maybe we can discuss any ideas you have…over lunch some time?'

'Ye-es,' she said slowly. She had a lot of ideas to improve the place that Raquel hadn't seemed to want to hear despite numerous discussions, letters, memos and slip-anonymous-suggestions-on-to-her-desk attempts.

It would be nice to have someone who was actually open to improvement rather than just wanting to keep doing things the way they had always been done because it was *her* way.

Tahlia surveyed the man in front of her. Did the Rottie have any idea what this new guy was up to? She couldn't wait to see her face when Darrington brought her his recommendations to change her system.

She caught herself. Darn it. He wasn't meant to be like this, all competent and businesslike and friendly.

He was meant to be an insensitive jerk who didn't really care about anything but his own career.

He was…nice, and behaving like one hell of a good boss—if she could trust him. Huh. Like that would ever happen. Tahlia Moran was never going to trust a man.

She wasn't about to weaken, not when so much depended on her being strong, sensible and in control.

'So I'm guessing you'll want to meet to discuss new markets, existing clients and what my team's ideas are to advertise our services?'

Case Darrington shook his head. 'Not a priority for me just now,' he offered casually, and left.

Tahlia stared after him. Not a priority? He didn't want to know about it? What on earth was wrong with the guy? Didn't he have any idea what his job was?

She swung to the sink and tipped the rest of her coffee down the drain and rinsed her cup. This was such a stuff-up!

How could he have been put in that position, *her* position, if he wasn't going to do what was needed?

She strode to the door, her blood hot, her body tense.

This wasn't her failure; it was Raquel's. She was the right person for the job…a mistake had been made. She just had to prove it.

So the new guy thought he was God's gift to the office with his smooth deep voice, friendly act and dazzling blue eyes? So he enjoyed toying with her and watching her embarrass herself?

So Case *Thieving* Darrington liked playing games? She could play a few of her own to find out what she needed.

He wouldn't know what hit him.

CHAPTER FIVE

They say it's lonely at the top.
I say it can be lonely anywhere.

CASE glanced at his watch. What time did they take lunch here? He ran a hand through his hair. He had no idea.

He'd tried to play it cool by waiting, taking his time, attempting to talk himself out of taking the woman to lunch over the last two days, but it was impossible. Everyone he talked to had something to say about Tahlia Moran's dedication and commitment to her work...

He'd cracked and sent an invitation to lunch to her this morning.

He had to know more about her than the snippets he'd picked up in conversation around the office.

It wasn't enough.

There was enough information to go either way. Her dedication to her work intrigued him, her confidence teased him and her beauty tortured every inch of him. But he could be wrong...like with Celia, his ex...and Tahlia's dedication could well border on obsession, her confidence narcissistic and her beauty only skin-deep.

Tahlia's reluctance to pander to him or his ego fascinated him. Her forwardness, her bluntness, her total lack of pretence appealed to something in him. What, he didn't know…

He couldn't afford another mistake. For his parents' wavering belief in him as much as his own reluctance to go through anything like Celia ever again.

So what was he doing? Playing with fire…

He stood up and strode to the floor-to-ceiling window and stared out at the Yarra river and Melbourne's city sprawl on the other side.

Hell, he needed a breath of fresh air in his life. He deserved one after what Celia had put him through.

Celia had been amazing in the beginning, sweeping him off his feet with her calm assurance and big smiling eyes into a whirlwind marriage that had torn through his savings, his illusions and his heart.

He could have gone on for years, trying to make it work, pushing her to see a counsellor with him, attempting to recapture the magic of those early days. Her spending hadn't mattered. He had been making enough to fund her passion for designer clothes, shoes and jewellery.

All he had wanted was for her to love him again.

He hadn't known what he'd done wrong.

Hadn't known what to do next.

He'd gone home early that day to beg for her help in saving their marriage, rekindling the magic, sharing in finding the solution that eluded him. What he'd found was Celia sharing herself with some bronzed stud in their bed.

Case closed his eyes, the image scored in his mind. He was a fool. Even then he would have tried again, would have burdened the blame, just to get her to want to save their marriage as much as he had wanted to.

She hadn't. She'd wanted a divorce, half of what was left of his assets and to be rid of him.

Thanks to several savvy lawyers involved in their pre-marital agreement, she'd only got two out of three.

Case ran a hand through his hair, cringing. It was nearly a year since the divorce had finally been settled. Logic suggested it was long enough to get on with life, but the wounds he bore still ached deep in his chest.

The betrayal was going to take longer to get over and he was strong enough to ignore Tahlia's lush peach lips, those dazzling green eyes, her sweet voice and intriguing focus on business.

The knock startled him. Case turned. Tahlia Moran stood at his door in a short black skirt that showed just how long and shapely her legs were, the slight curve of her hips and her narrow waist.

Her hands were on her hips, her lips pursed. 'Ready, Mr Darrington?' she lilted, her voice sweet as apple blossom.

Maybe not. Case swallowed hard, pulling at his tie and straightening it, his blood roaring hot and fiery through him.

He couldn't deny he was attracted. But he didn't need to take any risks. He could keep it light. Keep it simple. Get to know the woman, with no strings and no complications.

He wasn't going to get distracted from WWW Designs, no matter what Tahlia Moran made him feel.

*　　*　　*

Tahlia stood in Case *The Target* Darrington's doorway, her cheeks heating under the warmth of his gaze and the way his eyes caressed her.

She could feel everything traitorously warming.

'So?' she offered, crossing the files in her hands over her breasts, lingering in the doorway, grinding her teeth, glaring at the man who had stolen the only thing that really mattered.

Her work was her anchor and the darned waters had changed on her—she was no longer tethered to rock, she was drifting and she hated it.

She'd even emailed the girls an SOS in desperation to get them over to her place tonight to help her with this dilemma.

How was she going to get the information she needed out of the guy? It was one problem she could do with help with.

Tahlia bit her bottom lip. She didn't like asking for help…would play it down tonight and smoothly draw their wisdom without sounding needy.

She didn't need anyone.

He cleared his throat. 'So you're here.'

She nodded, looking away from the window to his paintings on the walls. 'Ye-es.' Did he suspect she was going to give the note a close encounter with the shredder and plead ignorance of receiving it rather than accept his invitation?

But she was a professional who was going to use the opportunity of lunch to find out exactly what was on Case's CV that entitled him to her job.

He stood up. 'Ready for lunch?'

'Sure, but *why* are we going to lunch?' she asked

carefully, keeping her eyes on him and not on the view.

'I really need to come up to speed fast. Find out about the office dynamics as quickly as possible to maximise my position here.'

She couldn't help but smile. He sounded just like she would if she was dropped into his situation, although she would never crush the dreams of someone else who'd earned the promotion through damned hard work.

Darrington straightened his suit jacket, the fabric looking even finer and more expensive as he got closer to her. It must have cost a fortune to have it made from a fabric like that, and to hug his wide shoulders, taunting everyone in the vicinity...

Who was this guy?

She had to find out and then do something about him...

'What?' he asked, his voice deep and husky, his gaze on her mouth.

She shook herself, trying to stop the smile.

His blue eyes glittered. 'Your smile is—'

'Hungry. I'm hungry.' She cast a look at her watch. 'I'll meet you at Sammy's, the coffee shop, in half an hour, okay?'

He nodded, his gaze still on her lips.

She tried to smother the smile, tried to think of something else other than sweet revenge for every thwarted nobody who'd been stomped on by a rich somebody.

She didn't want him to guess what she was up to.

She hoped he liked surprises.

CHAPTER SIX

'I deserve the best and I accept the promotion now.'
Because I'm willing to do whatever it takes, because
I'm worth it, because he's an arrogant, wealthy
sexy-as-hell annoying man who doesn't deserve it.

'So.' TAHLIA handed the menu back to the waitress. 'Apart from being partial to fish and chips, what titbits do you have to share about yourself so I can spread them all over the office by the end of the working day?'

Case put down his lemon squash, trying not to smile at the woman's amazing frankness. Was she for real? He wasn't sure what to make of her or the incredible feeling he had deep inside whenever he was near her.

And she'd said yes. She'd agreed to lunch with him, which could be construed as an indication that she may like him. She had to know as well as he did that they could have discussed anything at the office.

And she was asking a lot of questions. He probably shouldn't see her wanting to know about him as anything more than face-value gossip for the office, but he couldn't help feeling it was more. 'For the record it was a fillet of the finest deep sea dory, garden salad and fries.'

She fixed him with her sea-green gaze. 'So you *are* a snob.'

He leant back in his seat, considering her challenge. 'And you're against snobs?'

'Isn't everyone?' she lilted, raising a finely arched eyebrow at him.

'Well, not the snobs, obviously,' he murmured, his gaze on her glistening peach lips, which were as mesmerising as the words coming from them. No one had challenged him on this level before. Because he was too rich to be a snob or too rich to be called one to his face?

She straightened the cutlery in front of her, her long fringe falling over her right eye. 'Right. Snobs stick together.'

'I'd say so.' He clasped his glass tightly, the urge to smooth that lock of hair back from her face excruciatingly tempting.

'You don't sound so sure. Don't you know a snob, maybe intimately?'

'If you're asking me if I'm a snob, then no, I'm not,' he said as casually as he could, the buzz that she was interested enough to want to know filling his head, and other places.

'Well, a snob *would* say that.' She crossed her arms over her full breasts. 'Where were you born, where did you grow up and where did you go to school?'

Case stared at the dazzling woman opposite. Blunt and forward, like he'd never experienced before. And he wanted to give her all the answers she needed, as honestly as he could, as long as she didn't find out why he was really at WWW.

He took a sip of his drink and placed it down gently on the small round table between them. 'Born to John and Marie Darrington in Melbourne. Was raised modestly in Toorak by said parents. Went to school first at Stott's College then did a business degree at Melbourne University.'

He put up his hands. 'All snob-suggested but, despite my parents' success and standing, I was raised just like a regular kid.'

'Really? And a regular kid is raised how?'

He offered her a smile. It was way too early to get into how much worth his peers and parents had put on money, possessions and connections as he had grown up, especially on how to keep the family 'up there' after his father's new money had got them out of what they called middle class mediocrity. 'How about you?'

'About me?'

'Yes.' He leant forward, tipping his head, trying to catch her gaze from behind that lock of hair. 'I'm interested in knowing all my staff's background.' And hers in particular.

She gave a shrug. 'As I've already said, you could read my file.'

'There's a lot not in a file.' He'd already looked, twice. 'I'd like to hear it from you.'

'Not much to tell. Born and raised in Sydney. Moved to Melbourne after university. My first job was here, and here I still am. I've been with WWW Designs for just over four years, working my way up, putting in the long hours, doing that extra bit to make an impression.'

Case nodded. She'd made an impression on him all right. 'I did the same.' He'd been determined to make his career on his own, refusing his father's help, and putting in the hard work. 'Long hours and that extra commitment is the trick.'

Tahlia cringed. Sure, there was a trick all right, in stealing other people's promotions, and she was going to find out exactly what his was and shove it down his throat.

And he'd missed *her* point entirely. Gawd, a woman would have to put up with a lot being interested in this guy. 'Your someone at home must be very patient with your hours,' she bit out.

'Yes, he is.'

'He?' She froze. Did he live with his father or a room-mate? He looked like a confirmed-bachelor-playboy in a penthouse apartment on the North Shore sort of guy, the sort that liked his own space to do all the entertaining he desired.

'Yes. Couldn't do without him. Fetches my paper, shoes, even finds my car keys when I mislay them,' he said, his deep voice washing over her.

She had known it. A butler. He was a total snob then and the title was especially earned if his money and connections had got him *her* job promotion.

Andy arrived with their orders, slipping the plates in front of them, shooting her a wink.

'Thank you,' she said, straightening her plate in front of her, arranging the grilled chicken burger with salad for easy access of her right hand to maximise efficiency and minimize this lunch with the enemy.

'Thank you,' Case offered Andy, rotating his plate, glancing at Tahlia. 'And he likes bones.'

'Bones?' Tahlia echoed. *What?*

Case grinned. 'My dog, Edison. He's a Border Collie… You're in such a hurry to label me, aren't you?'

A dog? Sheesh. She pushed back her fringe, tucking it behind her ear, feeling the annoying heat in her cheeks. 'You can't say you haven't labelled me.'

'That's true,' he said softly, his gaze coursing over her.

Her blood heated at the thought of what the label was… She didn't want to know, or think about it. 'I have goldfish myself. Low maintenance,' she blurted. 'I did think of getting a cat but then she would have eaten Bert and Ernie, the fish, and although they don't fetch sticks, papers or shoes they do listen very patiently when I get home and need to—'

She pressed her tongue against the roof of her mouth in an attempt to still it. Was she babbling?

'Please, don't stop.'

She lifted her burger and took a large bite, filling her mouth with food instead of a plethora of personal stuff that had no business in her mouth, let alone pouring out.

What was wrong with her?

He watched her.

She chewed, swallowed and sighed. Was it her horoscope messing with her again? 'You're a Leo, right?'

'Sagittarian, I'm told. You?'

'Puzzled at how you came to WWW Designs. I didn't see you come in for an interview for the position and I see most people who come to the floor, not because I'm a busybody or anything, just that my view is of the lift—'

Case swallowed his mouthful. 'I noticed.'

'And?'

He shrugged as though it wasn't important. 'I was out-sourced. Head-hunted. Appropriated by Ms Wilson. I think you're right, by the way. She does seem in need of a good—'

'Mr Darrington…' she rushed in '…you must have met Raquel previously, then, for her to get such a good impression of you to go and steal you from another firm—which one, by the way? One of our rivals?'

He smiled at her. 'I met her…at a…party.'

She was getting nowhere. The man wasn't giving much away at all! Tahlia leant close. '*Are* you the enemy?'

'No.' His mobile rang. 'Sorry, but I have to get it.' He pulled the small handset from his belt. 'Yes… Hello, Simon, everything okay…? Oh…right.' He glanced at Tahlia, then swung to one side of his chair, gazing at his shoes. 'It's not exactly a good time… Fine. I'll try… Go ahead with that… No, not yet on that… I'll get back to you regarding that… Okay… Yes… Look, I'll talk to you later.'

He grinned sheepishly at her, putting the mobile phone down. 'Where were we?'

Tahlia took another mouthful of her lunch, forcing the chicken down her tight throat. Whatever that had been about…she didn't like it. 'What was that? Were you picking horses?'

She mentally prayed. Let him be a gambler, let him be an alcoholic gambler, let him be an alcoholic reckless gambler. That would prove to Raquel what a terrible mistake she'd made.

He shook his head. 'No.'

Tahlia stared at him. 'So it would be—?'

He smiled at her, shrugging. 'Companies.'

'So Simon is your broker?' she asked slowly, trying to match it to what she'd heard. It could have been, but something didn't quite fit.

'For someone professing not to be a busybody you ask a lot of questions.'

'Self-preservation.'

'Oh?'

She took a sip of her water. 'I like to know what I'm getting into, in the office, with the new boss,' she stumbled, the words sounding too...suggestive.

'Oh?' he murmured deeply.

She put her drink down, taking a breath. 'And you haven't told me one thing that supports the fact that you're any way qualified for the job,' she said in a rush. 'Or that your personality would complement the working environment or that there's anything about you that *doesn't* scream silver-spoonfed life, apart from your dog.' And that smile, and those eyes and that deep warm voice.

'Lucky you weren't the one hiring, then.'

She glared at the man opposite, but he was focused on his meal, carefully avoiding her gaze.

Tahlia finished her salad, forcing the food down on to a stomach busy doing somersaults at his every sapphire glance. This wasn't the plan.

She wiped her hands on a serviette and arranged the cutlery carefully on her plate. She was getting nowhere. 'Look, I represent the busybodies of the office and I demand some incredibly personal information that I can share with them that will ensure that you're not only human but approachable, sensible and on-the-whole nice.'

She crossed her fingers under the table. If that wasn't an invitation for him to arrogantly sing his praises and convince her once and for all that he was exactly who she hoped he was, then she didn't know what was.

He stared at her.

His gaze dropped to her mouth.

Visions of his firm, sensual lips smothering hers rocked through her, setting alight every nerve that hadn't already realised he was sitting barely a metre from her.

Hmm, a kiss. That would be personal all right, but not something she could share with the office... She shook herself. Or wanted. She didn't want his mouth on hers, at all, ever.

She dropped her gaze to his mouth, which was firm and enticing.

Kissing the boss would prove that he was a playboy, after short skirts and a good time and not focused on the company's best interests...

Was a kiss what he was thinking of or was she being stupid?

He jerked to his feet. 'You don't think I'm human? Approachable? Nice?' he asked, dropping some money on to the table to cover the meal.

She sucked in a long slow breath, rising from her seat. 'Nothing you've said or done suggests any of the latter,' she said in a rush.

'I've answered every question...' he offered, turning and walking to the door.

She nodded. He had, as easily and openly as though

he were just any other guy, but she knew he wasn't…
There was something that didn't add up with Case
Terrorising Darrington.

'I've just had a very pleasant lunch with you…' He
opened the coffee shop door and held it open for her,
watching her with steady blue eyes.

'Ye-es,' she managed, striding through the door,
smoothing down her skirt, counting her heartbeats with
the clack of her heels on the ground.

She couldn't deny that he was *being* friendly and
nice but that didn't mean he was anything but a good
actor.

Tahlia lengthened her stride, pushed open the door
to their building, holding it for Case this time. The air
was tense between them. 'And—?' she had to ask.

He strode alongside her as they crossed the foyer. A
lift was waiting, its doors open.

Case strode in, punched their floor number and
turned to her. 'Now what can I do to show you I'm
only human?'

Tahlia's glance went straight for his mouth.

Case fought every impulse in his body to reduce the
distance between them, take her into his arms and crush
his mouth to hers.

It was insane.

He'd thought he'd got his instincts under control.
After the disaster that his marriage had turned into, he
would have thought he'd have learned.

He took a deep breath. He wasn't going to rush into
this, no matter what this was.

If he hadn't been so young and naïve four years ago

he wouldn't have ended up with a two-year sentence for stupidity with Celia.

He'd been in such a rush to get married and complete his well-rounded success in all areas of his life he hadn't stopped to think.

The fact that she'd been married once already to another blinded-by-love well-off businessman should have given him fair warning of what he was in for.

He pulled his attention from those lips that were taunting him and those sea-green eyes that seemed to be daring him to take the plunge. 'Tahlia, Miss Moran... I...don't have a personal assistant or secretary.'

She blinked. 'She went when the Executive went, sir,' she said smoothly, her sweet voice hardly registering the look of surprise that showed in her eyes.

'Really?' He cleared his throat, pushing down the heat in his body. Talking shop would dull the senses. 'Why was that?'

'Yes. I believe Raquel can explain your predecessor's departure more appropriately than I can,' she said slowly, staring at the lift doors, her sweet perfume circling around him and taunting him.

It would be so easy to lean over and hit that stop button, sweep her into his arms and taste those lips and feel the passion that lay there, simmering just beneath the surface.

'I want to hear what you have to say,' he asked tightly. Any sort of office history may serve as a distraction to the desire coursing through him.

'He and his secretary had a hot and heavy affair.'

Case stared at the ceiling. Cripes. Just what he

needed to hear. 'And that was frowned upon by company policy?' he asked slowly. And maybe he'd find out Tahlia's policy.

She smoothed down the fabric of her short skirt over gently rounded hips. 'Well, yes. The powers that be don't want office harmony going to hell because of spats between exes and all those favouritism issues that become a factor in intimate relationships, not to mention issues of harassment.'

'That makes sense,' he said softly, forcing his feet to stay where they were and not take him any closer to the woman who was calling him like a siren to the rocks. 'But what do *you* think?'

She moistened her lips and jerked her gaze back to the lift door, holding her hands tightly in front of her. 'Me?' she asked tightly. 'In the end, the staff are all adults…mostly,' she rushed on. 'And it's impossible to police—more a guideline, really. You know, don't mix business and pleasure.'

'Right.'

She sucked in a breath. 'And in that particular instance the pair involved were doing more of the pleasure than business, and not just in his office—'

'O-kay,' Case said, adjusting his belt and taking a step back from Tahlia. 'I get the picture.' Vividly. And his mind filled with all the places they would have gone and visions of him visiting such quiet nooks with the incredible woman next to him.

'Basically it's to dissuade secretaries of the young and idealistic variety from thinking that a fling with the boss is going to help the career,' she blurted, twining her fingers together.

Case couldn't help but smile at her rush of words. Was she nervous?

'Well,' he offered, his voice low. 'You can inform the office and any young and idealistic staff that I'm single. But I can assure you that I will not give my assistant any illusions about climbing the ladder through sexual favours.'

The lift doors opened.

Tahlia stepped forward. 'You don't have to assure *me* anything, despite your lack of assistant,' she shot over her shoulder.

He wanted to assure her of so many things, but the scars still ached from Celia. 'Well, that's the thing,' he said slowly, following her. 'Until I get one, I'll need some help.'

She swung to face him. 'Of course. You've met quite a few of the staff. Have you anyone in mind…maybe from the copy room or mail room on a temporary basis?' She touched a flushed cheek; her nails, long and rounded, were painted the same peach as her lips. 'Until we get someone else in, you know, advertising and interviews take time.'

Case shrugged, slipping his hands deep into his trouser pockets. 'I'm thinking of someone who's very aware of who's who and what's what and how the place is run.'

She looked towards her office, pointing in that direction, avoiding his gaze. 'Great. Look, I'd love to chat on and on but I do have work to do, as you well know. And I'm sure you do too. Having such a senior position and all. If that's all? Let me know what you decide…how you want to do it…*who*.'

Case rocked back on his heels, taking in her tall, shapely body, her neat black skirt and jacket, her white sleeveless shirt. Her all-business appearance covering the all-enticing challenge that gleamed in her eyes like burning embers waiting for his breath.

He knew exactly who he wanted. 'Actually, I'm thinking of you.'

CHAPTER SEVEN

'What does not destroy me, makes me stronger.'
Yeah, right, Nietzsche. *And who does not drive you crazy, can't steal your job and make you act stupid?*

TAHLIA sat at her desk, staring at her computer screen. Case *Taunting* Darrington couldn't mean *her*, want her, as his assistant—that was just wrong, humiliating and wrong, and stirring and sexy and wrong.

As if she was going to accept a job helping out the competition, the man who had stolen her job, her promotion, her rise, her nice safe rung that she was going to conduct the next challenge of her life from.

Hell, the man had taken so much from her he didn't deserve anything but the same confusion and pain he was putting her through.

This was her life he was messing up, her feelings he was messing with and her anchor he'd cut loose with no concern for the weather.

She gripped the desk tightly. Just because her life was fraying at the edges didn't mean she didn't have her act together and couldn't handle anything that came her way…no matter who her father was or what he'd done.

Tahlia lifted her chin and clicked on her inbox.

TO: *TahliaM@WWWDesigns.com*
CC: *KeelyR@WWWDesigns.com*

FROM: *EmmaR@WWWDesigns.com*
RE: SOS

Still okay for tonight? Can't wait to hear about your mysterious SOS.

I'll bring a couple of my favourite romantic movies to soothe your soul. And chokkies.

Have you seen Chrystal? She's acting weird and standing in quiet corners with the pot plants. It's truly freaky. Do you know what's going on?

Em

Tahlia sighed. Chrystal was the last thing on her mind. She wasn't just the office date-a-holic, she was the resident drama-queen.

As one of the receptionists-cum-fix-it gals Chrystal was all over the place. It could be anything or anyone that had disturbed Chrystal, from a new male in the building to a new female too-good-looking for her comfort to a resident female wearing the same outfit, jewellery or shoes.

Tahlia's only surprise was that they all hadn't heard the latest development in Chrystal's life firsthand, at least twice.

Actually, she wouldn't mind listening to one of Chrystal's adventures rather than dwelling on Case Darrington.

TO: *TahliaM@WWWDesigns.com*
CC: *EmmaR@WWWDesigns.com*
FROM: *KeelyR@WWWDesigns.com*
RE: SOS

You can count on me being there too. The SOS
sounds very mysterious. And I'm coming with
wine—to enjoy vicariously through my mates—and
doughnuts!

Re Chrystal: Do you think it could be Liam, that shy
programmer downstairs, who's caught her eye finally? Sure, he's nothing like Chrystal. He's as shy
as a monk and as nerdy as hell. But he's cute and
he must be the only fresh meat left.

She's had to have done every single straight guy in
the place, and then some. Except Liam and
Darrington, but he's way out of her league. Tahlia,
is he married? I heard you two had lunch—is he the
reason for the SOS?

See you tonight where you must tell all!

Keely

Tahlia stared at her screen. She'd love to tell all, but
she wasn't sure she could tell her friends anything if
she wasn't sure what was going on, least of all with
herself.

Where was her usual together self? Would her
friends even recognise this babbling bimbo she'd
turned into and help her resolve her current angst?

Should she even try or, as her mother said, deal with
it on her own because the challenges in life were to
make *us* grow, not to leech off or lean on others?

She scrolled through her inbox of business memos.
At least her friends would help her wipe her mind of
every annoying trace of Case *Taxing* Darrington with
their movies, their treats and their company.

Maybe she shouldn't have invited them. How would

she survive hours with them and not blurt out her incredibly stupid attraction to Darrington, despite his snobby-arrogant-potential-playboy-jerkdom? They'd think she was an idiot.

Maybe she could distract them by getting them to help with her criteria for a partner instead, to narrow down her prospects, help her pick the qualities in a man that she could live with for the rest of her life.

Tahlia snatched up a pen. She wasn't about to get into dating without a plan. She didn't want to be responsible for hurt feelings, crushed dreams or unreal expectations. She didn't want to be anybody's last straw.

She closed her eyes against the wave of memories that crashed against her heart. How had her mother picked herself up, carrying all those burdens, after her father had died?

Had she been haunted by questions, wondering what it had been that broke her husband's will to live? Had she been tortured by their last argument over unpaid bills, her need for him to be there for her, for him to be a good father?

Had she wished she could take back her last words, the last time she saw him, time itself? Tahlia's throat tightened. Like she did.

She jerked straight-backed, blinking away the ache, and picked up a file and flipped it open. Business was safer to think about, deal with and be involved in than all that personal stuff, except where Darrington was concerned.

She chewed on her bottom lip. She didn't like being

as out of control as she was around Case Darrington, and feeling way too much.

It just wasn't professional and the sooner he was gone the better. And if she had to be the one to show him the door, so be it.

It would be a giant step in the right direction.

Case dropped his attaché case and knelt down on the polished timber floor and hugged Edison, nestling his face in his neck, breathing in his heavy doggy scent in an effort to douse the haunting memory of Tahlia's perfume.

'Hey Edi, you miss me, boy?' he crooned, slapping Edi's back and standing up, loosening his tie and kicking off his shoes. 'It's been one hell of a day.'

He'd driven himself insane all afternoon, trying to rationalise his impromptu request for Tahlia to be his assistant. Was it logical or a knee-jerk reaction to her story about the last Marketing Executive?

Running into that Chrystal woman in the lift again had just topped off his agony. At least they hadn't been alone, but that hadn't seemed to deter her.

Evading her probing, very personal questions had been one challenge, avoiding her pushing herself up against him a whole other dilemma.

Case shrugged off his suit jacket and tossed it over the black leather recliner. He was supposed to be the Marketing Executive, not some mouse for the woman to toy with. Hell, if she only knew who he really was!

One thing he was going to outlaw was desperate women. They freaked him out.

'That you, Mr Darrington, sir?' Luciana's heavy accent laced every word and echoed around the high ceilings of his open-plan loft-style apartment.

The designer had got a bit carried away with the stream running down the hallway under glass and the waterfall in the lounge, but Edi didn't seem to mind it. Better than the toilet bowl.

His Italian house-fairy heaved her ample frame from the hallway that accessed the laundry room and kitchen, wiping her hands on her canary-yellow apron. 'Dinner is in oven. Timer dings, you eat. Yes?'

'Yes, thank you,' he said, smiling at the woman who liked to think she'd adopted him. He couldn't live without her. She cleaned the house, cooked and kept Edison company while he wasn't around. He should have discovered his housekeeper phenomenon before he married Celia; he may have decided he didn't need the anguish.

Luciana snatched up a heavy cane bag from the floor, beside the black steel and smoked glass dining table, shoved her apron deep inside and straightened the greying coil of hair at her nape. 'You good boy. Nice boy. You need good woman.'

He shrugged. It was a familiar conversation he had with her, and a sure-fire way of having all the single young females of her family tree described to him. 'I have you.'

She laughed. 'I help you find,' she sang, opening the front door, pausing, taking out a cloth from her bag and wiping down the ochre wall beside her. 'If you not finding.'

'I don't need help, but thank you anyway, Luciana,' he said, lurching forward and ushering the most valuable employee he had to the lift. He punched the button. 'See you tomorrow?'

The doors opened. She stepped in and turned. 'Yes. What you want for dinner? I could cook special lasagne, secret recipe?' she said, eyeing him carefully.

Case could read the gleam in her eyes. Probably lining up a whole meal that she planned him to share with someone she knew.

'No dinner. I have a date,' he rushed on. Better to eat out alone than endure Luciana's umpteen single relatives' profiles again and be asked to pick one. Maybe Simon would be free.

She nodded, her smile wide. 'Good. You need a good woman.'

The doors closed and he wandered back to his penthouse suite, closing the double doors behind him and looking out of the floor-to-ceiling glass windows that stretched the entire wall at the view of the northern shore of the bay.

He didn't need any help in finding a woman. He found plenty. Finding one who liked him for who he was…was the hard part. Who wanted to know him, be with him, for him.

How to find said woman was the biggest dilemma in his life. He couldn't help but question a woman's motives if she knew all he had. He wondered how he'd broach protecting his assets from another bad choice, how he could downplay his portfolio and try to assess whether it was him she liked or his money.

The phone rang and Case answered.

'So what was with today?' Simon asked in his best

lawyer-cum-best-mate tone of inquisition. 'A desire to play undercover agent?'

'A desire to make everything I own into a resounding success, actually,' Case stated drily. And he sure needed the challenge of taking his newest acquisition back into the black.

He had needed to distract him from himself. 'I was out with my Director of Sales.' And her very fine green eyes.

'Why didn't you just go there—no lies? You *are* the new owner of WWW Designs.'

Case sank into a recliner chair. 'Because of all the airs and graces that are always put on to muddy the truth.'

He'd already seen the myriad attempts of the General Manager at WWW Designs to flatter him into keeping her on; the woman was practically dripping with greasy compliments—on his clothes, his business acumen and his plan to be put on the staff incognito.

Case knew the best way to maximize the company's efficiency was to get in there and see how it was being run firsthand and nothing was going to stop him, especially a small thing like a few white lies. The fact that he needed to escape the monotony of his routine didn't come into it. Much.

'So you're after the truth by telling lies.' Simon made a guttural noise deep in his throat. 'You know you don't have to keep on with it—you could get someone else to do it.'

Case loosened his tie. 'No. I like it there.' And liked being surprised by a certain member of his staff and her lack of hesitation in speaking her mind.

Simon groaned. 'Come on, get serious. Your time is far too valuable to put into this. Just employ an efficiency expert, or *I* could go.'

Case rubbed his smooth jaw, loath to put words to the hollow feeling in his chest at the thought of backing down from this challenge. 'I don't see it that way.' This was an opportunity just begging for him to conquer it…and maybe, hopefully, fill that void for just a little while.

And what a challenge. WWW Designs was the biggest firm of its type in the state and he was itching to turn the company around and shove its success in all the biggest rags and in a few faces who had failed to see how much more he was than just a suit and a bank balance.

'What about the ethics of it?'

Case smiled. 'What ethics would they be? As the new owner I could have sacked them all but I'd rather find out how they're doing things and where the problems lie. I'd hate to get rid of valuable staff.'

'Right, sure, that's what it is. And the fact that you were getting bored doesn't come into it?'

Case stared at the modern painting on the wall. Simon was too smart. 'Okay, I admit it. I wanted to do something new. There's no crime in that. I'm sure you're holding the fort.'

He was so sick of presiding over a clockwork company, being obliged to attend one function after another and kissing arse to every prestigious alliance in the business.

'Sure, I can take care of the company, if I can call you to make the decisions without using some damned code.' Simon cleared his throat. 'But come on, be serious, what are you expecting to find there?'

'I'm looking…' Case rubbed Edi's chin with his foot '…for something…' To wipe out the empty feeling that had been eating him up inside. Ignoring it hadn't helped. Dating hadn't helped. Work hadn't even helped, until now.

'Well, I can tell you you're not going to find it at WWW Designs. But are you sure about what you're getting yourself into?'

'Not a problem; nothing there that I can't handle.' Case rang off, Tahlia Moran's sweet face coming to his mind.

Tahlia Moran didn't know what he had, the companies he owned, the properties that were his, the people that he rubbed shoulders with or the five cars parked downstairs in the garage.

She hadn't questioned him on choosing companies to buy out today at lunch—had probably accepted that he was playing the stock market, not playing Monopoly.

Was this his chance?

She was all he could think about since lunch, and he'd acted impulsively. He'd made that reckless phone call before leaving work. The one that had tortured him all the way home.

It was way too early for gestures like that.

Hell, was he being silly entertaining the thought that he could have a relationship with the woman? Could he be incensed by lust into making another mistake that could not only cost him dearly, but break what was left of his heart?

The trouble was that she was incredible. A man didn't meet incredible often in his life... How could he ignore incredible?

Edi sat by his feet, his tail pounding the floor.

Case glanced down at the big dark eyes of his best friend and companion. 'I'm being an idiot, aren't I? Getting carried away, just because I feel something more than what I normally feel. It's nothing, right?'

Edi's tongue lolled out of his mouth.

'Time for a walk, hey?'

He knew exactly what he had to do. Stay away from the incredible woman, at least while he had a job to do that involved being near her.

He could plead ignorance if she mentioned his brash action... What had he been thinking? He knew more than anyone that nothing could be built on lies.

Case hauled himself up out of his chair. Maybe she wouldn't even guess it was from him. She probably had a heap of men in her life anyway. A woman that beautiful...

Case raked both hands through his hair and back over his face, slapping himself on the cheeks. This thing between them was probably nothing anyway.

Staying away would prove that his attraction was nothing more than convenience, just because Tahlia and her hot body and fiery eyes were there, and nothing more.

How hard could it be to avoid her?

She wasn't about to take up his incredibly rash invitation to be his assistant...and he'd be flat out assessing employee performance, sifting through personnel files and meeting them all, one by one. And it was a big office.

Case swung around, striding to the hallstand and taking out the leash. Edi followed, his tongue wagging, panting his eagerness.

There was no reason to see her at all.

CHAPTER EIGHT

What I want in a man on a good day:
1) Tall, dark and reasonably good-looking
2) White collar professional
3) Sense of humour
4) Reasonably sane in-laws
What I want in a man on a bad day: space

'YES, Mum. I am looking after myself.' Tahlia threw herself on to the couch, a nuked bowl of low-fat noodle dish in one hand and the phone in the other.

'And the promotion?'

She stared at the ceiling. 'No news yet.' There was no way she was going there with her mother, least of all admitting how the new guy had not only taken her job but had turned her world inside out and wanted her to be his assistant—glorified or not. Her mother would go nuts.

Her mother figured Tahlia had her life together, under control and on plan like hers was. Usually, she'd be right. Today she was so far from it, it made Tahlia's belly fight the noodles.

She couldn't tell her.

Her mother would demand the entire story and every detail so she could bestow her wisdom and advice to remedy the problem.

Tahlia was used to it. As a child she'd listened with

her mother to motivational tapes, had filled out goal sheets and dream journals and said affirmations just like her mum.

She knew the drill and knew exactly what her mother would say and she couldn't bring herself to share the sorry news and hear the disappointment in her mother's voice.

She'd tortured herself enough for one day with Case's request to be his assistant.

Maybe it was just another way to torture her into submission. Damn the man. Wasn't it enough that she was tortured by his smile, his eyes, his very fine-looking body? And thoughts of him being all too human with his shaggy little dog and all.

'I'll let you know—' she said carefully, watching her tone.

Her mother tsked. 'Still nothing? And you're home this early? Couldn't you have found something to do at the office to show them that you're keen?'

Tahlia sighed, pushing the red velvet cushions around beside her. 'I have been, Mum. But I do have to have a life too.'

She took a mouthful of noodles, staring at the newscaster on the muted TV in the corner, the pile of business management books on her coffee table and the fashion magazine laid open to the latest in-office wear for kick-arse professional women.

'Are you sure you've done everything you can to make your boss see your assets?'

'Yes, Mum.' Tahlia couldn't help but smile. Her new boss seemed very aware of her assets…and the thought of his blue gaze coursing over her body made her nerves tingle anew.

There was a long pause. 'Are you dating?' her mother asked in a whole different are-you-running-your-life-right? tone.

Tahlia swallowed the lump of food that threatened to choke her, putting the bowl on the coffee table beside the wineglasses and empty bowls set out for the girls. 'Dating the boss?' She coughed. 'No. Of course not.'

'I meant dating in general, honey. Of course you're not dating your boss.'

Tahlia shook herself. 'Right.' Of course the thought hadn't crossed her mind; it probably hadn't even crossed Case Darrington's.

'You know you shouldn't let anything distract you from what really matters.'

'Yes, Mum. I know.'

'You know the risks involved in relationships, how messy they can be…' Her mother sighed heavily. 'You know how important it is to get your life right first.'

'Yes, Mum. I'm getting that promotion first, Mum.'

'That's a good girl. I'm so happy that you're learning from my mistakes and you don't have to go through what I—'

Tahlia cringed. 'Yes. I'm so lucky to have you.' There were some lessons she could do without, even if it meant settling for someone safe rather than someone who was trouble. 'And don't worry, I will get that promotion.'

'Of course you will.'

She shifted in her seat. Some time, after she figured

out where Darrington came from and what he was up to. 'Look, I have to go. My dinner's getting cold and I have a ton of work in front of me.'

'That's the girl,' her mother gushed. 'You make it so they can't do anything but give you the promotion. *You just have to do more.* Bye now.'

Tahlia rang off, a cold ache in her chest. She *had* thought she'd done everything, but obviously it wasn't enough. Yet.

One thing was for sure; Raquel couldn't help but notice soon that Darrington wasn't getting the job done—he was spending far too much energy on the staff and neglecting the rest of his work.

All she needed to do was wait…

She gave her neat apartment a slow assessment. She had only one bedroom to minimise rental costs and maximise her saving capability, a small kitchen to make her own food rather than rely on take-aways, a large fridge full of water, fruit and vegetables and frozen meals for one.

It was all about moderation. Why hadn't her father seen it? Moderation and control was the key to life. If he'd mastered it he wouldn't have needed to have lied to her mother about the poor state of business, their financial difficulty and his state of mind.

He wouldn't have needed time to himself so much, wouldn't have drunk so much and wouldn't have been on the balcony that night…wouldn't have leant so heavily on that loose rail.

Sirens still made her body chill and every part of her freeze and listen, for the sound of her mother talking with her father at the table as though he was there, safe, as though they were there, together, as though life was all okay again and her father hadn't fallen to his death leaving all those problems they said he couldn't face for her mother.

The doorbell rang.

She put down her bowl and strode to the door. At last. Her friends. She couldn't have done with her own company a moment longer, especially when her mind was filled with images of Case and his wide shoulders, slim hips, cute tight butt and those incredible sapphire-blue eyes.

She swung the door wide.

Roses. Plump crimson blooms filled the doorway, with soft sprays of baby's breath at the edges and deep green leaves intermingled amongst the rich vivid flowers in front of her.

She froze, her breath stuck in her throat. Was Case on the other side of the veritable garden? Were his eyes going to be sparkling with promises his lips couldn't wait to fulfil, his blood rushing as fiery hot as the colour of the roses, just waiting to sweep her to him...?

The flowers moved aside. 'For Miss Moran,' said the delivery man, thrusting a clipboard under her nose for her to sign, his face beaming as though he was giving them to her himself.

The chill of reality cooled her body.

Idiot. As if he'd come over. Sure, the guy looked at her and was nice but it didn't mean anything except that it had been far too long since she'd been on a date.

He was her boss! As if the guy was going to send her flowers—but if not him, then who?

She signed and gave the man his pen and board

back. Why had she neglected her personal life so badly? If she hadn't she wouldn't be so at a loss every time she was in the vicinity of Case.

If she was a dating veteran she probably wouldn't even register Case and his attributes, she'd be used to men and attention and wouldn't be tortured thinking about a man so obviously unsuitable for her.

Tahlia took the roses and held them close to her chest, breathing in their sweet scent. Nice. She hadn't had roses since…too long.

It was a lovely thought. Her mother? No way. Emma and Keely, maybe…

She closed the front door, flipping open the card tucked amongst the stems. *'Thinking of you.'*

Case, or a secret admirer? 'Yeah, right.' It had to be him. Logic suggested there were no other viable options for the sender. *He liked her.*

She closed her eyes and let the realisation wash over her. Did he want to get to know her better?

The thought wasn't entirely unattractive, especially the part where she and Case would be in each other's arms, tasting each other's lips, their bodies pressed together, exploring the amazing chemistry that was making her act insane.

Was life about compromise?

She glanced at Bert and Ernie. She could put a glass lid on top of their fish bowl and get that pussycat that her mother had never let her have.

No.

She held the bunch of flowers away from her, shaking her head. She was not going to waste valuable time with stupid fantasies about the boss.

She was not going to entertain thoughts like that about the man who stole her job, flowers or not.

She was *not* giving up. She was a professional and that was *her* promotion, no matter what he made her feel.

The doorbell rang again.

She flung open the door, steeling herself. If Case Darrington thought that a bunch of flowers was going to romance her into his way of thinking…

Emma and Keely filled the doorway. 'We're here.'

They bustled in, arms full of bags, the pizza wafting cheesy garlic aromas around the room.

'Who's your admirer?' Keely asked.

Tahlia tossed the flowers on to the hallstand. 'Work…from work. Condolences on my promotionless week.'

Emma picked up the flowers, cradling them in her arms. 'We should have thought of that. Who did?' She plucked the card. 'Who's thinking of you?'

'Raquel,' Tahlia blurted.

'Yeah, that you're not breathing down her neck. Two-faced Rottie that she is.' Keely drew her into a hug, juggling pizza and packages. 'She should have given you the job, not that jerk.'

Emma waved the card. 'Hang on. How dumb do you think we are? Raquel wouldn't spend a dime on sending you anything, let alone flowers.' Emma took the flowers into the kitchen. 'Fess up.'

'Fine.' Tahlia slipped the pizza from Keely's hands, strode into the lounge, dropped into her favourite deep-cushioned chair and opened the box. 'I'm pretty sure they're from Case Darrington.'

Emma whistled, pulling a vase out of the cupboard below the sink and filling it with water. 'He is rather cute and if I didn't have my wonderful Harry I would consider pushing him into a cupboard and ripping his clothes off.'

Tahlia stared at her friend, trying not to let the image infect her, her stomach holding on to the thought and pushing it low.

'And?' Emma unwrapped the bunch and slid the stalks into the vase. 'He glanced across the crowded office,' she said dreamily. 'Saw you standing there with your freshly pressed jacket, white shirt that struggled to contain your throbbing heart and a short skirt showing off long, long freshly waxed legs that he couldn't wait to have wrapped around him—'

'No,' Tahlia snapped, pushing down the heat in her veins. That girl had been watching too many romances.

She looked away. She couldn't tell them everything now and confess what she was feeling. It was just too embarrassing. 'Not exactly. I think he's an ass. A jerk. An office playboy just toying with me.' She shook her head with vigour. 'I don't want to talk about him.'

'Okay,' Emma said, stifling a smile, whipping her fingers across her lips. 'No more talk about the playboy.'

'All right.' Keely nestled herself on the sofa. 'But then what was the SOS for?'

'I need help…with my list for my perfect man,' she rushed on. As if that would ever happen. 'Like you had, Keely. I figure if I had a checklist I think I may be better equipped to find someone to settle down with.' Somewhere in the distant future.

Emma placed the vase of roses on the hallstand. 'Really. Truly? You're finally going to do it? Even without the promotion?'

Tahlia cringed. There was no way, but she had to get them off the promotion and Case subject. 'I know I've used that job as an excuse not to get into dating and maybe I used it a bit much. You know, all those eggs in one basket thing. I think I need to work on another basket while I mop up the broken eggs in my other one.'

'Sure. I get it.' Keely nodded slowly. 'You need time to grieve…and all. What have you got so far?'

Tahlia pulled out the scrap of paper she'd been doodling on this week, paused and folded it, tucking it tight under her thigh. It was already all wrong.

She ripped open a pack of M&Ms Keely had unpacked on to the table and tipped them into a bowl, snagging a couple of strays and popping them into her mouth. 'I haven't got much so far. Short, blond and…' Not handsome. She'd had enough of handsome. 'I don't mind if he's had a close encounter with a brick wall.'

Tahlia scooped a large handful of M&Ms into her lap and leant back, tucking her legs up on to the seat. 'I think that sort of broken nose, scarred face, thinning hair sort of look is one that screams character,' she blurted, shoving half of the load into her mouth.

Emma flopped on to the sofa, ripping open a bag of sweets, shooting Keely a look. 'And his job?'

Tahlia chewed hard and swallowed. 'His job—something where he gets down and dirty.' She rushed on, trying to rid pastel shirts and silk ties from haunting her mind. 'None of this intellectual shirty-suited sort of person. I want someone rugged, calloused and... rugged.'

Tahlia took a breath and shoved the rest of the M&Ms in her mouth, glancing to the bottle on the table, crunching them up. She needed something stronger than sweets...

Emma popped the cork on the wine, grabbing a slice of the cheesy pizza. 'And this man's hobbies would be—?'

'Collecting bottle tops maybe, tattoos or beer bottles or sandals lost on the beach,' Tahlia said in a rush. There. As totally opposite to *that* man as she could possibly get. 'Well? What do you think?'

'I think you'll find him at the local pub, swilling down beer and chewing glass.' Keely laughed. 'Are you setting yourself up for disappointment or just afraid of dating?'

Tahlia jerked to her feet. She didn't like where this was going. She wasn't afraid of dating or men, not in general anyway. 'No. I'm being practical.'

Emma poured a glass and slid it in front of Tahlia and picked up a pen. 'Right. I think you ought to start fresh. What have you got—?' She lurched forward and snatched the piece of paper from her chair. 'This is more like it. What's wrong with this tall, dark and handsome white-collar intellectual—? Oh.'

'What oh?' Keely leaned forward, holding her stomach. 'What have I missed?'

Finishing off her slice of pizza, Emma opened a bag of popcorn, balancing it on her lap and waved the paper at her. 'I think our Tahlia has already fallen for someone but is in denial.'

Tahlia slumped back into her seat and crossed her arms. 'I'm denying nothing.' And she wasn't admitting anything either. 'I have not fallen for anyone. I do not fall. I make lists and plans and stay aware of all contingencies at all times.'

Emma tossed a piece of popcorn at her. 'Right. Sure. Liar.'

'I'm not lying. There is no way I'm interested in Case Darrington as anything other than my arch nemesis that I need to crush like a bug.'

'That doesn't sound healthy.' Keely poured cola into her glass.

'You should have heard him. He expected me to be his assistant until he hired someone. Me!' She touched her chest, feeling the rage anew. It felt far safer than those other feelings she didn't want to have. 'After he had the nerve to steal my promotion, he wants to make *me* his assistant.'

Emma tipped the popcorn into a bowl and pulled out some more packages. 'Sweetie, take the job, play the secretary-cum-assistant role—it would be great for you to get to know him, wouldn't it?'

'You guys are crazy.'

'Go on, email him now and tell him you'll help him out with the job. It doesn't have to be for long.' Emma took another slice of pizza. 'It will resolve, once and for all, whether it's displaced animosity that you feel for your new boss, lust or something else entirely…'

Keely waved a chocolate-covered jam doughnut. 'And thank him for the flowers.'

'And you could tell him you're thinking of him too,' Emma lilted, casting her gaze to the incredible bunch of red roses on the hallstand.

She was, but she wasn't thinking straight. She was considering her friends' advice, but sense would suggest it was extremely flawed and terribly biased in favour of her associating with a cute-suit instead of focusing on her career.

Could these strong feelings be caused by her anger? She nodded. Definitely…it made far more sense than considering she'd let anyone touch her heart, let alone someone who'd taken something so precious from her, or someone who could make her feel so vulnerable.

That had to be wrong.

Tahlia took her glass. Maybe she *could* spend some more time with the boss, get beneath that tailored exterior of his, past the sweet soppy dog-at-home thing and reveal the true jerk underneath.

Tahlia knocked back her wine and settled back into her chair with a slice of pizza in one hand and an iced doughnut in the other. She'd give the matter some serious thought and maybe check out her horoscope in the morning to see if the stars could shed anything on the matter.

She bit into the sweet powdery softness of the doughnut. One thing she did know was that she was not going to rush into anything, least of all him.

CHAPTER NINE

***They say all things good to
know are difficult to learn.***

*Especially when it involves alcohol, romantic
movies, too much sugar and way too helpful friends.*

TAHLIA strode through the foyer, every step a challenge
to the fragile head on her shoulders that still didn't feel
like her own.

They'd drunk far too much on Friday night, or at
least *she* had, but she was sure they'd all be suffering
the morning-afters for days.

Keely had polished off every last doughnut, citing
the extra mouth she had to feed, and Emma's chocolate
consumption would've put a ten-year-old to shame.

Tahlia had spent most of the weekend tucked up in
bed with the weekend papers and the *Business Review*,
nursing her hangover, her promotion failure and an addled brain full of Darrington fantasies.

Why had she drunk so much?

She waved to George, tucking the newspaper tighter
under her arm. She'd deliberately avoided reading her
horoscope this morning because she didn't want to
know, and especially didn't want to be tempted to
check for what Sagittarians were up to today—as if she
cared. Did it matter what Case's was? It did not.

Sure, she'd emailed him under the influence some

time in the wee hours of Friday night, taking up the offer to be his assistant, but it didn't have to be the disaster she'd first thought it was when she'd realised what she'd done.

Sure, she'd let herself get talked into it by Emma and Keely, but after two days analysing the pros and cons she had to say it was the right thing to do.

There were too many question marks around Darrington. It was time to resolve some of them, once and for all, and spending time in close proximity seemed a perfect opportunity to do just that.

He was up to something, she was sure of it.

She was a professional, after all. What could it hurt to take the opportunity to see just what he was up to and harden her heart to feeling anything for the man?

So he had probably sent her the flowers. It didn't mean anything, except that he was looking for more distractions from doing the job.

Marketing Executives weren't usually so obsessed with the staff right down to the copy kids temping while in uni, let alone the mail clerks.

She had to find out what Case Darrington was about, then expose his failings to Raquel and get the job that should have been hers in the first place.

Her fantasies would be squashed, thankfully—they were taking too much of her time, torturing her with memories of imagined glances, warm smiles and soft words that couldn't possibly exist anywhere except in her addled brain. And in unexplainable flower deliveries.

She punched the lift button.

'Good morning, Tahlia.' A familiar nasal bark.

Tahlia turned to look Raquel Wilson in the eye. She was the same height as Tahlia but solid, wearing crimson trousers with hot red stilettos and a black cotton top that clung to her like a second skin.

'I'm sorry you had to find out about the position of Marketing Executive the way you did.'

Sure she was. Tahlia forced herself to keep a straight face, to keep the raging heat churning up inside from bursting from her mouth. The Rottie's cool regard for Tahlia when she was just another employee had turned to chilling after she'd become Director of Sales.

Raquel waved her Rolex-clad arm, her diamond rings glinting. 'I know how much you wanted the job.'

'Yes,' she said and shrugged. Best to pretend it didn't matter than admit weakness in the face of power personified. Raquel could rip her throat out professionally, if given half a chance and even less of an excuse.

Raquel forced a laugh as fake as her nose. 'Just wanted to clear the air between us so there's no hard feelings.'

Tahlia nodded. 'Right. Sure.' As if. The woman was paranoid about Tahlia's slow and steady climb up the corporate ladder.

'I'd hate for you to take being overlooked for the promotion personally.' Raquel tossed her jet-black dyed hair back from her shoulder. 'And I really don't have much time spare to write you out a reference, but if you insist…'

'No. I'm not taking it personally at all.' She forced a smile. If only Raquel knew just how personal the whole thing was getting, the scent of the roses coming back to her, with a pair of sapphire-blue eyes that turned her world upside down.

She took a slow breath. 'I'm sure your decision was taken with the utmost care and Mr Darrington is *far* more qualified for the position than me.' At least as far as Raquel had been concerned at the time, but showing her how wrong she was would be incredibly satisfying. 'Where on earth did you find him?'

Raquel's grin faded. 'Oh, around.'

Tahlia raised her eyebrows—the Rottie had to guess she'd put the wrong person in the job. 'And around would be?'

Raquel's eyes narrowed. 'Well…look, sometimes the best people come through unexpected channels.' She stepped towards the doors. 'You understand?'

'I think I do,' Tahlia said slowly, her mind churning.

The doors opened and Raquel alighted. 'You will be nice to the man, won't you?' she tossed back at her. 'He is new and isn't familiar with the job and its requirements and will need all the guidance and assistance that you can offer him.'

Tahlia gave a light shrug. 'Of course,' she said strongly, gritting her teeth. She couldn't wait to help him do the job he had been hired for.

The doors started to close.

'I'd expect nothing less from you,' the Rottie shot back.

Tahlia stared after the big boss, every part of her wanting to scream, yell and cry at the injustice. She took a deep breath, willing her blood to cool.

She was in control. So the man *had* got her promotion on the sly. She'd damned well be *his* assistant and give him the helping hand he needed, right out the door.

CHAPTER TEN

Keep your friends close and your enemy—
Case Taker *Darrington closer still—as close as I can*
handle…and more. I'm going to know more about his
skeletons than my own and then I'm going to bury him.

TAHLIA dropped into the desk outside Case's office.
Getting romanced out of a job sucked, Case expecting
her to be romanced into being his secretary was a joke,
and she was all for making hers the last laugh.

She was so going to prove her point, no matter what
small furry animals the guy had at home.

Tahlia stabbed the keyboard.

> TO: *EmmaR@WWWDesigns.com*
> CC: *KeelyR@WWWDesigns.com*
> FROM: *TahliaM@WWWDesigns.com*
> RE: Men

You two were wrong. Looks like Case *Treacherous*
Darrington is a jerk. Just spoke to Raquel, who ex-
pects me to babysit the guy into being a competent
Exec in lieu of me. Sounds like no experience and
potential leech. Crap.
Life sucks.
Keely, sure, Liam is cute and shy and looks at
Chrystal a lot but could it be possible that she could
be interested in a real relationship?

No, Case is not married. No girlfriend, but I'd say he's had quite a few. Not that I care.

And no, don't you two start on this stupid attraction thing again—it absolutely does not exist.

Have to go through being his PA thanks to two particular sugar-inebriated friends and emailing under the influence.

I tell you this interaction with this sub-human job-stealer is for the good of the company and all aspiring employees everywhere, nothing personal.

T

Tahlia stared at his office door. She'd yet to knock and tell the guy just how personal this wasn't.

She stood up slowly. He was trouble to her and the company and it was her duty to sort him out before he caused any damage to the already-hampered WWW.

She needed to find out more about him, and straight from the source. She had to get the guy to lighten up, to open up, to reveal his secrets.

Tahlia had got some advice, in a roundabout way so as not to highlight her goal. Keely had suggested beer to get a guy to open up. Em, being Em, had suggested seduction.

Against her better judgement but for the good of the company, she'd decided to act nice and flirt the guy into dropping his guard.

If he could use his connections to procure her promotion, she could use her God-given wiles to get what she needed.

Her blood fired at the thought of playing with the fire in Case's eyes.

She smoothed down her jacket. For the future of WWW Designs, home to her friends and many a talented person who deserved a far better boss, she'd make the sacrifice.

She owed it that.

TO: *TahliaM@WWWDesigns.com*
CC: *EmmaR@WWWDesigns.com*
FROM: *KeelyR@WWWDesigns.com*
RE: Men

I think you protest too much, honey.

And Chrystal wanting a relationship? Why not? She's human, isn't she? I think eventually we all need something more in our lives. And I'm so glad I've found it.

K

Well, bully for her.

Tahlia pushed away from the desk and rapped on Case *Test-time* Darrington's door and swung it wide. 'Good morning, Mr Darrington.'

'Tahlia,' he offered, smoothly rising. 'I got your message. I…I was surprised, to say the least…'

Case wasn't wearing his suit jacket, just a baby-blue shirt sitting as enticingly around those wide shoulders as his tailored jacket had been. His trousers were dark and his deep aqua silk tie brought out flecks of dazzling light in his eyes.

Gawd, he looked good. Too good. She shifted on her black heels. 'Me, too. Surprised, that is.' At the roses, at herself, at her email accepting this assistant job and at her tenacity.

He shot her a sheepish grin. 'I figured you'd think it was below you…'

'Not at all,' she said smoothly, flicking her fringe back. 'You're my boss and I'm quite happy to do whatever you feel best serves the company.'

'Yes, well…'

She stepped forward, her fingers flexing, a crazy desire to run her hand over his smooth clean jaw rushing through her. 'And thank you for the flowers.'

'Flowers? Me?' He cast a look to the windows. 'Sorry, I don't know anything about flowers.'

Tahlia paused. 'You didn't send the flowers?'

'Look, about you being my assistant—'

Didn't he still want her as his assistant? Didn't he want to admit he had the finest taste in roses? Or that he'd been thinking of her…?

'Is there something wrong?' she asked slowly, trying to make him out—just standing there looking incredibly gorgeous. His blue gaze pinned her to the spot, making her heart clatter in her chest. 'I can procure you a secretary from somewhere else in the office if you think I'm unsuitable in any way,' she said in a rush, running through the possibilities of stealing someone from somewhere for him if that was what he wanted.

Case stood immobile, his brow furrowed as though he was having some war of his own.

Tahlia flicked back her fringe, standing taller. What was she thinking? *She* had to do this. It didn't matter how cute or hot or serious he looked. 'But I do think that *your* idea of me helping you out and acclimatising you to the office is a great one. Save you a lot of time and it's not like it has to be for ever, just a few days or so. I can help you out and do my job, just from the desk here.' She jabbed her thumb behind her.

That should be enough. It wasn't as if he would pose much of a challenge, not when he was looking at her like that, running his gaze down her black trouser suit that was tailored perfectly around the soft curves of her hips, the jacket contoured perfectly to shape her waist, the lapels small but angled low, highlighting the lace chemise-like top she wore like a shirt and the view of the valley of her breasts it afforded.

It was a great choice for suggesting a softer, gentler side, a side that was all ears to whatever he wanted to share.

'Great. I'm glad you agree…' He ran a hand through his hair, pulling his gaze to her face and her Peach Passion lips '…with my idea. That's great… I'm sure this will be great. Thanks.'

She sauntered to the chair by the wall, gripping the back tightly, avoiding the windows. How long would she have to endure this extreme torture at the mercy of those incredible blue eyes and deep voice and steamy looks?

Tahlia slid on to the chair, crossing her legs carefully. 'So where do we start?' she said softly.

Case sat down, holding his hands tightly in front of him. 'How about we start with you? How about you tell me a little about your history, your aspirations and what the company needs to do to help you fulfil those goals?'

'My goals?' She couldn't help but stare at the guy in the big black leather chair that was going to be hers, the office that ought to have her name on it, the walls she was going to hang her photos and qualifications on and the bank of windows that she'd been ready to hang vertical blinds on. What could she say?

He leant forward, his eyebrows rising slightly. 'You do have goals?'

'Of course I have goals,' she bit out. How dared he? 'I've had goals since I was twelve, when I decided I was going to run a kick-arse company like this one, and not for one minute have I ever questioned that I was going to make it. My aspirations? To sit at the head of this company and run it properly and squash all the rumours.'

'Rumours?'

Tahlia bit her lip, breathing slowly, willing her blood to cool and her heart to slow. 'There have been a lot of rumours about the company lately,' she said more carefully. Had she messed up? 'You know, about how much financial trouble they're in.'

'Oh?'

She shrugged. 'I'm surprised that a man as smart and as finger-on-the-pulse as you would want to get on board with a company obviously in trouble. There's even a lawsuit going because Raquel messed up.'

'That's been settled.'

Tahlia frowned. 'How do you know?'

'I…' Darrington rubbed his jaw '…heard it on the grapevine.'

'Okay,' she said slowly. 'And why did you come here?'

He leant back in his chair. 'I like a challenge.'

'You're not worried?'

He shook his head and stood up. 'No. Are you?' He moved around the desk and leant on the edge, looking down at her, his arms crossed. 'Why would you stay on if the company is in trouble?'

Tahlia looked up at her boss, appreciating his move to that of dominance, and his wide shoulders. He was looking down at her with his dreamy blue eyes, his profile all power and his lips so enticing… It was a good move, to show who was boss.

'I've got friends here,' she said evenly. 'They need their jobs and I figure I'm helping by staying, you know.' She shrugged and stood up. Had she been too honest? 'I've put a lot of work into this place; it would be hard to walk away.' Incredibly hard, but if she had to go she was determined on doing her bit first.

She was close, just having the height advantage due to the fact he was leaning his cute butt on the edge of his desk and she was wearing heels.

She took a step closer, her brain stumbling for what she could do to soften the guy up. 'So I'm here and eager to do whatever I can to get the company back on track, on plan, on the path to success and happiness for all.'

Case stood up. 'Well, we'll do our bit as best we can then, yes?'

Tahlia looked up into his face, fixing her gaze on his sapphire-blue eyes that were looking down at her, slightly narrowed as though trying to make her out. 'Sure, but there's one thing I have to know first,' she said.

'Yes, what's that?' he asked, his gaze dropping to her mouth.

Her mind went blank.

He was so close.

Her heart thundered in her chest. She moved, stumbled, reached out and touched his smooth silk tie and his hard chest underneath, looking up.

Their lips met.

His mouth quivered beneath hers, softened, yielded, and danced with hers.

He tasted as sweet and spicy as he smelt, like cinnamon toast and coffee…and his lips weren't firm, they were soft, hot and intoxicating.

Heat rushed through her body and the urge to deepen the kiss, wrap her arms around his body and drown in the man almost swamped her.

Tahlia pulled back, letting the silk slide through her fingers. 'O-kay,' she breathed. 'Thank you.'

His eyes glittered. 'What was that?' he croaked, his voice husky.

'I'm…I'm pretty sure it was a…kiss,' she offered softly, staring at his mouth, her own tingling with a need for more. The crazy desire to push up against his body and try that again throbbed deep inside her.

'Yes.' He straightened his tie and tightened the knot, smoothing the silk flat against his shirt. 'Why?'

Her mind clambered for an answer. She had no idea how it had happened. Who had kissed whom? Oh, gawd. How had that happened?

'Just checking,' she said as casually as she could, swinging around and striding to the door on legs that felt spongy. She had to save this embarrassing situation and turn it around to her advantage.

'Checking what, may I ask?'

Her mind spun. What? How he kissed? That he was willing? That she could rise to any challenge for the job? That she was a babbling klutz around the man? She touched her tingling lips. *That he liked her?*

She couldn't help but smile. 'That *you* sent the flowers.'

TO: *KeelyR@WWWDesigns.com*
CC: *EmmaR@WWWDesigns.com*
FROM: *TahliaM@WWWDesigns.com*
RE: Men
Rub your good luck in, why don't you? And I'm not protesting, I'm explaining. A girl's gotta do what she's gotta do.
Tahlia

CHAPTER ELEVEN

Sagittarians—watch out,
you may get more than you bargained for.

CASE sagged on to the edge of the desk, gripping the edge of the timber tightly. What in hell—or heaven—was she doing to him?

He rubbed his jaw. Reading his mind? Doing what he'd decided wasn't a good idea? Taking the plunge and finding out if the feeling was mutual?

Hell, yes.

He had no idea how that had happened... Had he kissed her? Hell, he'd wanted to. He may have leant that bit closer, made it happen.

What a kiss!

She was more than a breath of fresh air—she was a spring breeze, warm and sensuous, encouraging a clean break from the past, the promise of something new and exciting.

He stared at his office door, his heart still pumping hard, his blood hot, his whole body still in reaction to those sweet soft lips that had teased him with a hunger that he longed to sate, slowly and sensually through the night with her.

And what a night it would be...exploring the magic that sparked between them like electricity, short-circuiting sense and setting off fires.

Case stood up, raking his hands through his hair. Dammit. This wasn't the time.

He tried to laugh. That kiss had been one hell of a surprise. And he'd brought it on himself. He should have learnt by now that rash actions, like sending those flowers, led to trouble. Beautiful, radiant, curvaceous and irresistible trouble. A woman who he shouldn't be engaging until after the staff assessments were done.

A relationship was built on honesty and how could he be honest when he was pretending he wasn't himself?

Sure, she saw him as an almost-equal, saw him as he was…him. Hell, she would probably be perfectly suited to take over this position herself once he was done here.

He loved the way she talked to him—no airs, not a grace in sight and enough blunt barbs to sink a ship.

Would she be the same if she knew who he was? That he owned this company and several more? That he was so much more than the executive-on-the-way-up that he pretended to be? Would it matter to her?

It had mattered to Celia. She'd totally conned him into believing she loved him. That she couldn't get enough of him, that she'd die if she wasn't his for ever.

He'd never had anyone feel like that about him before, had been convinced it couldn't happen if he didn't have that same intensity and commitment. Had married her anyway and had done all he could to live up to her adoration.

He had been such a fool.

The fax machine bleated. Case ignored it. He knew who it was from, same time every day.

He hadn't had a clue with Celia. Not when the 'simple' wedding to seal their love had turned into a three hundred guests media extravaganza because it was her 'special' day. Not when the Melbourne penthouse hadn't been big enough and a twelve-room mansion on the park was what she wanted, because they did want to start a family. And not when her desire to see the world didn't include him, because he had to stay at home and work for their future.

He had been an idiot. He'd rushed into Celia because she hadn't wanted him to think straight. He wasn't about to make the same mistake again.

This time he was older, wiser and in control.

Case moved to the fax machine, plucked the paper from the tray and went back to his desk, sitting down in his large leather chair, running his tongue across lips that begged for more.

Was the ball in his court? Did he want to return it? Hell, yes. No matter what had happened with Celia, there was no way he was going to miss out on discovering what lay beneath Tahlia Moran's captivating layers—in due course, after his work was done.

He laid out the fax in front of him, forwarded from his head office. Since his mother had discovered the fax machine she'd committed herself to keeping him informed of the entire Darrington family tree via the fax.

She knew he was hard to catch, always on the go, busy-as-hell with his businesses and she'd given up on trying to talk to him 'like normal people' did on the phone and had found an alternative.

It was endearingly crazy. It wasn't as if he needed

to know what operation his father's sister's mother-in-law was having, who his cousin was dating or what the cook served for dinner last night, but he had to love her.

The curse of the only child, he guessed. Who else was she going to tell? His father was always busy—too busy for much except eating and sleeping and, of course, work.

His mother was still waiting for him to retire, so that they could have some time together, and his father could live life...only business came first.

Case jerked to his feet and strode to the door. He'd made enough mistakes where work was concerned. He wasn't going to wait until business fell into place to live... And at this moment living meant Tahlia...and discovering everything about her.

Case couldn't wait.

He gripped the door handle and paused. He'd have to be careful. He'd romance her in a leisurely way, with deliberate style and elegance, ensuring this staff assessment was done before he let himself drown in those sea-green eyes and luscious lips.

He wasn't going to mix business with pleasure.

Tahlia couldn't stop smiling.

Oh my God, she'd kissed her boss! And he'd been incredible.

She'd never considered an office romance before—old, crusty executives not being her thing—but right at this moment an office romance didn't seem such a bad idea.

She bit her lip. The guy could kiss and was more

than easy on the eyes and made her feel things in places she hadn't known existed.

Darn it, but this was all wrong.

She was here for a reason and she hadn't ever failed to complete a goal.

Darrington seemed to know nothing about doing the Marketing Executive job and had even less interest in finding out how to do it. How could he manage the whole design and sales team if he didn't want to know what they were doing?

She sighed. He could be a nice guy but the fact remained that she had to do right by the company.

She punched Raquel's extension. It was almost a shame to have to 'out' his failings to Raquel. Maybe Raquel wouldn't have a total hissy-fit when she found out she'd hired a guy who couldn't do the job and seemed more interested in the staff than doing what he was hired for.

Maybe she wouldn't fire him but demote him. She could put him on as Tahlia's assistant, or somewhere in Personnel…he seemed to be interested in people.

'Wilson.'

'It's Mr Darrington's assistant here,' she said in a meek soft voice. 'Would he be able to schedule a meeting with you at, say…eleven on Thursday?' Tahlia held her breath. The week should be enough to gather the evidence that would support her case, if the Rottie agreed to the timing.

Raquel was notorious for messing people around just to make sure they knew the hierarchy—she was the boss and could do what she wanted. Tahlia would probably have to beg and grovel to get an appointment with her any time this month.

'Mr Darrington. Yes. Of course. Not a problem.' And she rang off.

Tahlia put the phone down in the cradle, staring at it, her stomach leaden. What was that? Raquel never just accepted a time without argument. Something was up...

'Hey,' a familiar deep voice said.

Tahlia's skin rippled as though a thousand butterflies had brushed her body. She looked up at Case. 'Hey.'

'I need to talk to you.'

She stood up, trying to suppress a smile. Couldn't he get enough of her? She sobered. What could possibly have Raquel bowing to him? His good looks, his playboy eyes or that smile?

She narrowed her gaze, running her eyes over the man again, from the tip of his shiny black shoes to the tip of his spiky haircut. It didn't matter.

By the end of the week she'd know every inch of this guy, inside and out. She'd discover all his secrets.

Tahlia's gaze moved to Case's mouth. She probably should avoid those lips. 'What can I do for you, Mr Darrington...Case?' she lilted.

He paused.

She watched his brow furrow. Oh, gawd. Had she got her signals crossed? Had the flowers been from someone else entirely? Had her clever saving-face parting proved she was crazy and she'd just made the biggest fool of herself for no reason at all or had she just scared him off with that incredibly stupid and impulsive kiss that had come out of nowhere?

She tipped her head. He didn't seem like the sort of guy who would scare easily.

He moved closer. 'I don't mean that I'm not flattered or that I didn't enjoy—'

Heat rushed to her cheeks. Oh, gawd. How could she have been so stupid? 'So you didn't send the flowers?'

'I did, actually.'

She tapped the pen on her chin. She had known it! He *was* interested in her, at least enough to send her flowers on Friday—and by goodness that kiss had said as much. He hadn't been exactly bone-cold beneath her lips—far from it.

He was putty in her hands.

She stared at his mouth again. It would just be so easy to lean forward, take a step, tiptoe and kiss him once more, wrap her arms around that firm, hard body.

She froze. To soften the guy up for an interrogation of his motives, not for anything else.

Her whole body ached. 'Then?' she blurted. 'What? It was a mistake? The flowers were sent to the wrong address and it wasn't me you were thinking of? It was someone else entirely and I took it to mean that you were as interested as your amazing blue eyes said you were and—'

Case stepped forward, the distance between them gone. He lifted his hand and touched her lips with his finger, stilling the words rushing from her mouth. 'The kiss *was* amazing.'

The echo of her embarrassing jabbering faded in the wake of the look that shone in his sapphire-blue eyes, the incredible intimacy in his touch, the flames that scorched through every nerve in her body.

She couldn't look away and couldn't move.

He drew his finger back, watching her mouth, the tip of his finger brushing her bottom lip sending bolts of desire through her.

'So?' she whispered.

He dragged in a deep slow breath. 'I…I don't think it's appropriate for me to—'

She stood taller. 'Of course.' Tahlia nodded tightly, trying to fight the surge of heat in her veins.

She would never have considered crossing the line herself under normal circumstances. How could she have thought a man like Case would cross it just because of her?

Had she really thought he'd be some office playboy looking for a quick roll in the copy paper? That the man could be flattered into blurting out his background and connections so she could use them against him?

She shook her head. 'I understand. I am your personal-assistant-cum-glorified-secretary and I'm sure you don't want any scandals on your CV.'

'It's not that.'

She stiffened. 'It's not? You're not worried about what an affair with your PA could do to your future?'

'An affair?'

She bit her lip. Oh, darn, where had that come from? How could she say so many stupid incriminating things around him? 'Well, I guess I could be thinking along those lines,' she said more carefully. If he wasn't sitting in her chair and messing with her workplace. 'And

I wasn't going to be so forward to suggest anything as threatening as a relationship.'

He crossed his arms over his chest. 'Why would you think I'd be threatened by a relationship?'

She shrugged. 'Most men are.'

He dropped his arms to his sides. 'I'm not most men.'

She swallowed hard. 'I can see that. So, if it's not your employment future you're worried about—'

'No.'

'Then?' She looked towards the ceiling. Please let there not be an unrequited love, a dead girlfriend, an ex with a brood of kids. She caught herself. She didn't care.

He slipped his hands into his pockets. 'I already guaranteed you that I wouldn't get too personal with my assistant.'

Relief washed through her like spring rain. 'I'm sure I could overlook that under the circumstances,' she said softly, smiling. Back to Plan A—flirt him into making a fatal mistake.

'And those circumstances are?'

Tahlia looked at her heels, wishing she didn't feel quite so much for the idea. 'That your assistant is me.'

CHAPTER TWELVE

Too many cooks spoil the...bachelor?

'HELLO, handsome.'

The redhead stepped out from behind a large fern in the hallway, her modest attire doing nothing to dampen the gleam in her eyes.

Case stopped. 'Good afternoon, Chrystal,' he offered casually, looking past her to where he wanted to go.

'Case,' she lilted, fluttering her lashes and looking up into his eyes.

'Is there something I can do for you?' he asked, cringing. He had a fair idea what the woman wanted and there was no way he was going there.

'Actually, yes,' she purred, leaning into him as though she still had her revealing top on. 'I was wondering if you'd like to go out with me some time, you know, like on a date.'

Case swallowed hard. 'I'm flattered by your offer, but I—'

She touched his arm, pouting. 'You want to get to know all your staff, don't you? Well, some of your staff are worth getting to know better.'

Tahlia's smiling eyes leapt to his mind.

Chrystal stroked his arm. 'And there's only so much you can find out about a person by working with them.'

'Ye-es,' he said slowly, the idea tumbling through his mind.

She sighed deeply. 'I understand that it's just so much easier for some people to open up to others after hours, away from the workplace.'

He nodded slowly. 'Look, it's been lovely talking to you but I have to get back to work.'

'Don't you think I'm pretty?'

Case froze. He was on dangerous ground. He knew more than anyone what a woman scorned was capable of. 'Yes, but—'

She reached up and stroked her fingers down his cheek. 'So don't you think you should give "us" a chance?'

Us? Case stepped back. 'I'm sorry, but I can't.' His mind spun. 'I'm just not…up to it.'

The woman's forehead creased. 'Okay, but whatever the problem is, I think I could help.'

He sucked in a deep breath. 'It's something that only time can heal, I'm afraid.'

'Oh?' She touched her palm against his chest.

'Yes,' he rushed on, extricating himself from her hand. 'I'm not ready. I can't. I've just been divorced, only a few months ago…and I can't. It was tough. Nasty. You know, bad.'

Chrystal's eyes widened. 'Oh.'

'So thank you for your kind offer, but—'

'I understand,' she said softly, patting his shoulder. 'Sure. I get it. Just know I'm here for you…for anything, even talking, if you need to.'

He sighed. 'Thanks.' He sidled past her, shaking his head. He couldn't believe he'd said that to her. It *was* the truth. He'd been divorced…nearly twelve months ago. And although he'd dated on and off, he wasn't dating anyone manipulative and self-serving like Celia. No chance in hell.

Case detoured via Sales. She had been right about one thing, though.

He glanced into the Sales Director's office, at Tahlia, bending over her desk, gathering files, juggling coffee and balancing a pen between her lips. Was he asking too much of her?

Doing her job and helping him was a big ask. But by the gleam in her eyes she seemed to be enjoying the challenge.

He was glad she thrived on it. He liked being near her. Had enjoyed the day with her, having her leaning close to him, her perfume sweeping around him, her warm body close, her sweet voice explaining patiently the ins and outs of the place.

He knew enough about WWW and what a Marketing Executive did; now all he wanted was to know about her.

Any time he managed to get her mind off the business at hand she started asking questions he couldn't possibly answer about himself, yet.

She was driving him crazy.

She swung around.

'What are you doing for dinner tonight?' he blurted.

She lifted an eyebrow.

Case moved forward and plucked the pen from her lips, searching her eyes for the answer. 'I'd like to take you to dinner.'

She hesitated.

'Somewhere nice.'

'O-kay. Sure. Why not? We can get to know each other a bit better. You know, you could tell me all about yourself,' she rushed on.

'Yes.' He smiled. 'Ditto.'

'Ditto it is.' She shot him a smile, sweeping out of the door, her eyes glittering.

TO: *TahliaM@WWWDesigns.com*
CC: *EmmaR@WWWDesigns.com*
FROM: *KeelyR@WWWDesigns.com*
RE: Baby shower

Gals,

Re my baby shower on Saturday. No strippers—my mother is coming. (This is not a hen night, that's for Em. Save stud for then. My mum is not coming!) Have you met our born-again virgin, Chrystal? Yes, she's taken a vow of…da-da da-dum…celibacy. Is the world still the right way up? Chrystal is a virgin wearing a skirt that covers not only her thighs but her knees! And has a blouse *covering* her breasts. Who said the impossible isn't possible?

K

'How do you get a good guy?'

Tahlia stared at Chrystal's reflection in the mirror. 'I don't know. I'll let you know when I get one.' Her mind tripped to Case and she shook her head. She wasn't sure he was a good guy and he wasn't hers. 'You should probably ask one of the others.'

'True.' Chrystal nodded slowly, brushing her wild hair back and tying it at her nape, doing a good imitation of a school marm. 'You're as messed up as me, only more socially acceptable.'

Tahlia shot her a look. 'Gee, thanks. Why do you say that?' Did she have a 'Romantically Challenged' label stuck on her forehead?

'You're not caught up in the must-haves.'

She swiped her lips with her Peach Passion lipstick. 'I have a career, an apartment, a car and investments. What else could I possibly need?'

'You're joking, right?' Chrystal's eyes widened. 'Even I've worked out that it's not about material things. It's about the people in your life. And sure, I know, I've had a lot of people in my life, men mostly, but it's about keeping them there, you know, people that care for you.'

Tahlia stared blankly at the woman she'd known had hidden depths, but had never realised just how deep.

Chrystal sighed heavily. 'And you need a good man to give you a good—'

'I don't think so. I've done very well without a man in my life, and I don't intend to get one until I get my career all sorted out,' she rushed on. Which, if all went to plan, shouldn't be long, right after she sorted out Darrington.

Chrystal shrugged. 'Could be too late. All the good ones will be gone.'

Tahlia felt the words echo down her spine, and down, settling heavy in her toes.

'All I'm saying is, don't leave it too late,' Chrystal said softly, collecting her handbag.

'Is that what this makeover is about? Finding someone to share the rest of your life with before it's too late?'

'Yes,' Chrystal snapped, flicking a stray strand of her hair back. 'And there's nothing wrong with it.'

'Of course not. If that's what you want.'

'And you don't?'

Tahlia moved towards the door. She did not. How could she? Most people went into relationships blindly, not realising the cons. She'd seen the cons close-up and it was not pretty. She didn't want that.

A fling here or there she could do, but that was it.

'I have to go,' Tahlia said softly. 'I'm still at Mr Darrington's office, so send anything or anyone after me there, okay?'

'Absolutely.' Her eyes shone. 'You know all you have to do is ask and I'll be there. I don't know why you're looking after Case Darrington when you could be looking after your own stuff in the comfort of your own office…'

Tahlia interrupted. 'I know, but I have to do this.'

'Like closure for that promotion that you didn't get?'

She paused, holding the handle to the ladies' room. 'Something like that.'

'Well, when you've had enough closure—'

'Absolutely.' She yanked open the door. It wouldn't be long and she'd close the door on her Director of Sales position and be in her rightful one, with Case somewhere far more suitable.

Chrystal sashayed towards her. 'What do you think about mixing business with pleasure?'

Tahlia swung to face Chrystal, her mouth open. Did

she have that 'Lusting after the Boss' label on her fore-head too?

'Don't look so shocked. I know I've dated nearly everyone in the building—'

She was asking for herself? 'In general, not a good practice, but sometimes it's unavoidable.' Like flirting with Case. 'Why?'

Chrystal sighed, clasping her bag to her chest. 'Just this guy I really really like. He's sort of conventional and uptight like you.'

'Thanks.' Tahlia moved through the door.

Chrystal followed. 'Although he did say that he was still getting over the wounds of a really nasty divorce and couldn't entertain a relationship…he's a real wounded soul…and I want to help heal him.'

Tahlia sighed. Poor girl. The last thing she would ever want to get was tied up with a guy with those sort of issues. 'Don't get your hopes up. A guy like that…' Could seriously be a problem. 'Will have so many is-sues you may not have a chance for happiness.'

'Maybe, but he's so handsome and hot. I think he's worth a try.'

'Good luck.' Tahlia sighed. At least her parents had started out well, without lies, without issues that would destroy what they had. Her father had managed that on his own.

She would never go near a guy like that. Too much to deal with, too hard to wade through the baggage, too much like asking for trouble and disappointment.

Chrystal fluttered her fingers at her. 'Good luck to you, too.'

Tahlia didn't need luck. She had Case to practise her

arts on tonight and a list of criteria for her ideal mate. She had nothing to worry about.

TO: *TahliaM@WWWDesigns.com*
CC: *KeelyR@WWWDesigns.com*
FROM: *EmmaR@WWWDesigns.com*
RE: Baby Shower

Of course all the studs are booked for my hen night. Only the cakes, clown (joking) and cocktails (non-alcoholic) are for your shower. Can't wait. Counting down the days.

Saw Chrystal. Will all her work on herself pay off? Dunno. But Liam can't get enough of Chrystal… he's breaking and losing stuff all over his cubicle so he can put in acquisitions to her. At least twice a day…and she *hasn't* noticed!

I think it's someone else who has caught her eye. But who? Maybe someone from outside work.

Em

CHAPTER THIRTEEN

Tahlia's rule number 103: when in doubt,
wear black and show a lot of leg.

TAHLIA threw another dress on to the bed. She had to get exactly the right outfit for tonight—one that said she was cool, calm and collected.

The phone rang.

Tahlia dropped the coat hanger, the outfit dropping to her feet. Please let it not be Case. She didn't want him to cancel…

She snatched up the phone. 'Tahlia, how may I help you?' she chimed.

'Hello, honey, how is everything with you?'

She swallowed hard, the butterflies in her belly subsiding. 'Mum. I didn't expect to hear from you again so soon.'

'Can't a mother ring her daughter to find out if she got the promotion?' There was a pause. 'Surely they've made a decision by now.'

Tahlia dragged in a deep breath. She couldn't do this a moment longer. She couldn't lie again, not even to spare her mother's feelings, or to save herself a lecture on how she should have got it. 'I didn't get it.'

A long pause. 'You're kidding, right?'

'No, Mum. Truly. They got someone else.' And what a someone else he was.

'Oh, honey…' Her mother tsked.

She shrugged. 'I did the best I could. I put in the hours. I did the extra mile but the General Manager just felt some new blood was better for the company at the moment.' And hopefully her moment would still come.

'Of course you did.'

She sat on the only edge of the bed not covered in clothes. 'Don't worry, I'll keep working for it.'

'Tahlia, honey. I know I've pushed you to make something of yourself but you can't just focus on work; you need a life too.'

She froze. 'What?' This couldn't be her mother.

'You can't leave it too late,' her mother warned. 'You're not getting any younger.'

'Mum,' Tahlia gasped. She didn't want to hear this. She'd done everything to live up to her mother's aspirations for her; she couldn't change the rules on her now. 'What's going on?'

Her mother sighed heavily. 'I know I haven't exactly been a great example to you with men. What with your father—' Her voice got tighter. 'Then with ignoring the whole species. But I figured I'd already had love, my time, my lessons—'

'So, *now* you want me to find a man?' Her voice broke into a high-pitched squeal.

'Honey, I want you to be happy.'

She shook herself. 'I'll be happy when you're proud of me.'

'Oh, baby. Of course I'm proud of you. I've been proud of you since the moment I saw you.' Her mother's voice thickened.

Tahlia nodded tightly, her chest warm.

'You know that, right? But look…I didn't call about your promotion… I went out at the weekend…with a friend of mine…'

'What is it, Mum?' Her mother didn't usually beat about the bush.

'And I'd like you to come around next week for dinner,' her mother asked tentatively.

'Why? What's going on?' she blurted. She hadn't had a meal with her mother since…for ever. She was always too busy.

Her mother sighed. 'I want you to meet someone.'

Tahlia swallowed hard. 'Your friend? You've met someone?' Her blood ran to her toes. How could her mother do it? How could she let herself take another risk? When the last one had cost her so very much.

'Yes, he's been asking me for ages and I finally just went out with him and it was…so nice. Will you come and meet him, honey? It would mean a lot to me.'

'Of course I will,' she said in a rush and she rang off, placing a hand on her chest.

What in heaven's name could induce her mother to want a man in her life again? How could she trust one? It was just not possible.

Was it?

Case was losing it. He had to be. He had meant to take the romancing of Tahlia Moran slow and steady, not ask her to dinner.

It had been a spur of the moment thing, and he had to admit that it felt great. For the first time in a year he wasn't beating himself up about Celia. His mind was totally absorbed elsewhere.

It was crazy how one woman could haunt him while another one pushed so many buttons he felt as if he was going to short-circuit if he didn't drag her to him and taste her lips.

His blood stirred at the thought…

He sobered. No. He'd pushed those thoughts down to work with her today and it had worked. He'd survived her perfume, her soft looks, sweet voice and that long fringe that begged to be brushed back so he could see her emerald-green eyes.

Hell. It was bad enough at work. What had possessed him to further the torture? He couldn't trust himself around her, let alone out at night.

He'd wanted a challenge…

He rapped on Tahlia's door. The building was well located on a good side of town, with great street appeal. It wasn't too old, but old enough to have established gardens and that lived-in homeliness about it. All in all, a good investment. She'd do well with it, despite it being on the first floor and liable to be lacking the requisite view of the city for optimal capital gains.

Case reached for his tie. Not there. He was going casual…and the fact that he truly liked this woman was terrifying. The other women he'd dated over the last six months were all predictable, uncomplicated and easy to be with because they were no threat to him.

He couldn't say the same about Tahlia.

He'd survive tonight, take it slow. It wasn't a hot, brief, passionate affair he was after but something more serious, something he wanted to think about, something to take time over…something that was going to last. That couldn't happen until he could tell her all she wanted to know, and more.

He wanted to tell her how he had started his first business at twelve, how he had invested money in the stock market at eighteen, how hard he had worked in college to buy into his first business.

He straightened the collar on his mauve shirt, tucking it in tightly against his black trousers and adjusting the fit of his black jacket. For now, he'd have to play this cool.

The door opened.

Tahlia stood like a vision in the doorway. Her hair was in another spiky knot at the back of her head, but her make-up was darker, richer, highlighting the colour of her eyes, the silky creaminess of her skin and the deep red lips that beckoned him.

A black dress clung to every luscious curve of her body, plunging low over her breasts, delighting his mind and hands with their gentle softness. Thin straps held the slip of fabric on her, straps that looked so easy to slide off her smooth shoulders…

His body ached.

His heart thundered.

His blood fired to her call.

'Case,' she said, her voice sweet and soft. 'You look great… It's great… I'm so glad you came…' She paused. 'I'm happy to see you.'

He couldn't help but smile. She looked so together… The staff at WWW Designs had only praise for the woman and her competence. Did he make her nervous? 'You thought I wouldn't come?' he asked carefully, trying to slow his heart and regain control. 'How could I stand *you* up?'

'The thought crossed my mind…like the flowers. That tonight was an impulse that you weren't going to follow through on.' She gave a soft shrug. 'I don't want you to be here if you don't want to be here.'

He straightened tall. Dammit. He'd never failed to follow through on anything in his life; he damned in hell didn't want to give her the wrong impression. 'I assure you there's no other place I'd rather be but with you tonight.'

She smiled, her cheeks flushing softly. 'Shall we go?'

'You're not going to invite me in…to meet your fish?' Case cast a glance behind her, up a polished timber hallway to where he could just see a cream sofa. He could tell a lot from a person's home and he wanted to know everything about this bewitching enigma.

'*Would* you like to come in?' she offered carefully, glancing up at him with her sea-green eyes and a coy smile on full red lips that he couldn't afford to taste again, just yet.

His body ached, impatient for more of her. He swung his attention to the landing. 'No. That's okay. Reservations and all. Maybe later.' He cringed. That sounded as if he wanted to—do all the things to her that had running through his mind all day.

'Maybe,' she said softly, her mouth twitching as she pulled the door closed.

Was she playing with him? Teasing him? She sure as hell was hitting the mark. He wanted to pull her into his arms, smother those red lips with his mouth and strip off the layers that she wore.

'Case,' she whispered.

He pulled his gaze from her sweet mouth. 'Yes?'

'Dinner?'

'Yes.' He urged his feet to move, despite every inch of him wanting to stay, somewhere quiet, somewhere where he could explore Tahlia Moran, Director of Sales, with the utmost care and attention.

He followed her to the lift, watching her hips, her shape, her body move in that incredible dress, an incredible amount of smooth leg flashing with every step.

A split ran up the right side of the dress to her thigh, affording him far more than he could cope with seeing of her very nicely shaped, very smooth-looking leg.

Blood rushed southward, hot and fiery. His hands itched to swing the woman into his arms and show her just what sort of danger she was toying with.

He clenched his fists by his sides, breathing deep and slow, pulling his gaze from her mesmerising sway and tantalising show of flesh, watching the floor in front of him.

So much for staying in control...

Tahlia waited in Case's silver Saab for him to come around to her. She needed the space to catch her breath. She wasn't sure who she was kidding, who was playing who— The man was driving her wild.

The way he looked at her set her ablaze, his deep voice echoing through every nerve, his touch...almost too much to bear.

How could he be so calm?

Yes, the man had reacted to her dress. Thank God. It had taken her long enough to pick it out. Tonight had to be just right to gather the info she required to highlight Raquel's mistake.

Her heart had leapt up her throat at Case's suggestion that she invite him in. She had been sorely tempted, her mind throwing up some crazy idea of getting him out of her system.

She accepted that exploring what Case *Tantalising* Darrington had to offer wouldn't just be educational, recreational and inspirational; it would prove that he was an office playboy and deserved the consequences of stealing her promotion with his good looks and connections.

Tahlia touched her lips, closing her eyes and imagining what sort of havoc the rest of Case would have on her body when his kiss had wrecked havoc on her senses.

It was probably a good thing he hadn't accepted her invitation… A public place was far safer.

Case opened the door, holding out his hand for her to alight, his strong clean-shaven jaw close enough to touch, run her fingers down, trail her lips over.

Tahlia took a sharp breath, more than keen to exit from the enclosed space that was filled with the scent of new leather, hot male and his sexy cologne.

She'd think more clearly in fresh air.

His fingers folded around her hand, sealing her palm against his in a connection that felt so good—too good.

Her hand burned where it met his, making her nerves buzz, the cascade of electricity flowing upwards and then sinking deep into her belly. 'Thank you.'

Case drew her close to him, closing her door, looking down into her face with an intensity that sang to her body.

'We're here,' he said suddenly, stepping back.

'Yes.' Tahlia swung to face Bohemia, one of Melbourne's top restaurants. It boasted the best chefs, the best service and the heftiest prices. She wouldn't have expected anything less of the guy. 'Showing off, are we?'

'What do you mean?' he asked, his voice tight.

'I'm sorry. I don't mean to suggest that snob stuff by you bringing me here,' she rushed on. 'Just that your tastes befit a Marketing Executive, that's all.' Even if he didn't know the job and would take far too much time to learn the ropes to help the company now, when it needed help most.

'Oh. Yes. The wage does offer its advantages,' he said casually, catching her hand and drawing her to the entrance.

'I see.' She tried to stir up her resentment again, but failed. She couldn't feel straight with her hand in his— her body was all sensations, all reactions, all tingling for more of Case's attention.

He pushed open the door, letting her hand slip from his other hand as he held it open for her to pass, his gaze going to the slit in her dress. The light in his eyes and the flicker of a muscle in his jaw sent pulses of excitement racing through her.

Tahlia rubbed her palm against her thigh to expel the charge still tingling there. What she could do about the tingling in the rest of her body, she had no idea.

Case weaved through the line of people in the foyer,

beckoning her to follow. 'Reservation for Darrington,' Case said smoothly to the maître d'.

The balding man in a tux smoothed his thin moustache and nodded. 'Your usual table, Mr Darrington?' he asked, sweeping up two menus and swinging around.

'Yes.' Case glanced at her sheepishly. 'That'll be fine. Thank you, Louis.' Case placed his hand in the small of her back, guiding her after Louis.

'So you bring all your women here, do you?' she asked, biting her cheek, fighting an unusual ache around her ribs. 'Not that I mind,' she blurted. 'Or care. I'm sure a man like you must get around and wouldn't be short of offers and it's not like this isn't a nice place to bring dates to show them not only how much you're making but your taste in wine and food, and your style—'

'That's not my intention,' Case offered.

Louis stopped at a small round table which was nestled in the corner of the room. A deep red leather bench-seat curled around the table, against the coffee-coloured wall and a print of a modern artwork with bold strokes and even bolder colours.

A candle flickered under a textured glass shade, the crystal wineglasses gleaming in the light, the wine bottle all too obviously chilling in the ice bucket beside the table, at the ready.

It was one thing to suppose the man was a career Romeo, another thing entirely to see it, feel it, know it. Tahlia glanced back across the busy room towards the door.

Was she just another distraction from doing his job properly?

'You don't like?' he asked, moving closer to her. 'We can go somewhere else if you're not comfortable, if you don't want to stay…'

She lifted her chin, stifling her concerns. This was business, nothing personal. 'Why mess with something that obviously works for you?'

She slipped on to the bench, sliding a little on to the seat in front of the setting on the table, twining her hands together on her lap. 'Nothing wrong with being organised, regulated, into an efficient routine and all that.' Sounded a lot like what she'd do if she was a guy and was dating regularly.

Tahlia glanced up at Case, who was settling himself at the other side of the small table, his knees brushing against hers. 'Doesn't mean this is contrived,' she blurted, blood rushing to her face and southward.

She stared at her place setting and straightened the cutlery. 'That I'm just another woman to pass a meal with and try on for—'

'Hey.' Case reached across the table and held her hand. 'I'm here with you because I want to find out more about you, because I'm interested in who you are, why you're who you are,' he said slowly, his voice deep and his sapphire-blue gaze on hers. 'I'm sorry I didn't make more of an effort with the dinner arrangements but it was short notice and I have a rapport here.'

'That's okay—' she waved her other hand '—you don't have to explain.'

'I want to.' He gave the hand captured in his a gentle

squeeze. 'I don't want you to think for a moment that this isn't special.'

Tahlia frowned. He couldn't mean that. It was just a spiel. He was an expert, after all. A tall, handsome, amazing Casanova. 'Really?' she asked as innocently as she could.

'Yes. I've brought dates here, but no one as inquisitive, observant and amazingly frank as you.'

She couldn't help but smile. 'Sorry. I'm not usually like this.'

'Don't be sorry,' Case said, leaning closer to her. 'I like you just the way you are.'

Tahlia's chest warmed, filling her with a soft heat that radiated outward, making her whole body light and tingly.

She glanced at where his hand covered hers in his warmth, his strength, and she couldn't help but like the feeling, like him.

No, not a good idea. She knew where liking a man got you—into loving a man, trusting a man and depending on him and she wasn't going to experience that sort of vulnerability and loss, ever.

Sure, she respected the way he dealt with the staff but she'd confirmed his total lack of application to the Marketing job and all it entailed.

He had secured her promotion through dubious connections.

'Case…that's an odd name,' she blurted, extracting her hand as slowly and as casually as she could before she did something she'd regret.

'My father's a lawyer,' Case said, drawing his hand back and straightening his setting. 'I think it was my mother's way of tackling his workaholic nature. She's a psychologist. Decided all she had to do to get him to switch on to giving me attention was to say my name. Case wants you. Spend some time on Case.'

'Did it work?'

'Yeah, pretty much.' He shrugged, picking up the bottle of wine from the ice bucket. 'Unless there was a case more important.'

'Case priorities?' she said softly, fighting a smile. She was glad her mother wasn't the only strange one in the world. 'I'm sorry... I do know the feeling.'

'Your dad's into work in a big way?' Case asked, filling her glass.

'Yes. He was.'

'Was? He's retired?'

She glanced around the busy restaurant—the tables all full, the soft murmur of couples doing little to ease the tension that pounded in her chest. 'Deceased.'

'I'm sorry. How did—'

'So am I.' Tahlia gripped her glass. 'Is *your* dad retired?'

'No. Still working, much to my mother's dismay. She's got a list a mile long of all the places she wants to go to, all the things she wants to see, and still he keeps on working.'

'That's sad. Does she have hobbies?' she rushed on, eager to get as far from the issue of her father as quickly as possible.

'Yes. Me.'

Tahlia couldn't help but smile, relief washing through her at his dropping the subject of her father. 'Let me guess... You're her only child and she's trying to get you married off so you can give her grandchildren, probably contacts you…almost daily…to ensure her plight is foremost in your mind at all times.'

Case laughed. 'Spot on. How did you know?'

'I'm an only child too.' And she'd been hoping for years that her mother would start behaving like everyone else's and care about that stuff. Now she was… Tahlia wasn't so sure she liked it.

'And your mother is after grandkids?'

Tahlia took a sip of the deep bold claret. 'Always on my back.' He didn't have to know it was all about work, at least until tonight.

'I guess it's part of the job description. You'll be just the same when you have kids.'

'No way. I'm going to be nothing like my mother,' Tahlia bit out. Visions leapt to her of her mother curled into a shattered ball on the bed she'd shared with her father, the days of tears, the weeks of silence, the haunted look in her eyes, still.

'That's what they all say,' Case said lightly, but he couldn't help but notice the stricken look on her face. 'What? Have I said something…anything to—?'

'Nothing,' she said lightly, picking up the menu. 'Let's order. I'm starving. Chefs in places like these take for ever in getting food to the table.'

Case nodded, picking up his menu, casting his eyes over the list of cuisine his restaurant offered. She may have guessed he brought all his women here, but not why. And she wouldn't be able to fault the service. Everyone knew who he was…and no one disappointed the boss.

He gripped the menu, the words blurring. He was bursting to tell her.

Case took a gulp of the red wine. For the first time since Celia he wanted to tell a woman all about himself, all his assets, all his achievements, including making this struggling enterprise one of the top five restaurants in Melbourne.

He wanted to impress Tahlia, see her awe, hear her praise, see a warmth in those sea-green eyes that was just for him. 'You do want kids, though?'

Tahlia glanced up, her eyes wide. 'Ye-es, at a later stage I would like to have a couple of children,' she said carefully. 'But I wouldn't bring them into a relationship that wasn't absolutely totally stable and loving.'

'Me neither.' He lifted his arm and a waiter arrived at the table at the ready. 'I'd like the quail entrée, Piper's Peppered Steak with the Chef's Best Salad and the Raspberry and Apple Pie with cream.'

The waiter turned to her.

'Quail,' she said, nodding to Case, her eyes bright. 'The chicken breast with garden salad and a chocolate cheesecake.'

'Is your mother local?' he asked, watching her take a sip of the red wine, her lips almost as dark, looking as rich and sweet as cherries, just begging to be tasted.

'Ye-es,' she said slowly, her gaze on him. 'My mother took a job here just after I first moved to Melbourne to work with WWW Designs. I don't blame her for coming too. I wouldn't want to be all alone and she is all alone and I understand that I'm all she has and all—'

Case heard the flood of sweet words from her mouth, saw the shine in her eyes as she dropped her gaze to the setting in front of her, and wanted her. Desperately, totally wanted her...never to be alone.

He swallowed hard. 'God, you're beautiful.'

Tahlia glanced up at him, a soft flush on her cheeks. 'You don't have to resort to flattery to get me to talk,' she said casually. 'Shoe size? Seven and a half. How I take my coffee? Black with no sugar. Where I go on holiday? Anywhere that has a seminar that can help my career. So what do you want to know?'

Case shook his head. 'Can't a guy make an honest comment about his date's extraordinary beauty without it being taken as a means to an end?'

She shook her head. 'No.'

A waiter moved between them brandishing their entrées, the sweet scent of the freshly roasted delicacy wafting around them.

'You seem dedicated to work.' Case stripped the small quail of its meat, the prized morsels melt-in-the-mouth soft. 'Your file is impressive. You've done a lot in a few short years.' He glanced at her, trying to make her out.

She placed her hands in front of her. 'So you finally read my file.'

Finally, for the twentieth time. She was twenty-six years old and had worked diligently, pursuing her career, yet still seemed so young and innocent in so many ways. 'You mustn't have had time for much of a personal life.'

Tahlia put down her fork, staring at him. 'No, not

much of one, but I've had my fair share of boy-friends…if that's what you're asking.'

Case shook his head. 'You are amazingly frank, Miss Moran.'

'You are incredibly nosey, Mr Darrington. Anyone would think you have an ulterior motive.'

'I do.'

'Oh?'

'I'm seriously interested in all my employees, but I don't usually take them out for dinner.'

'And why am I so different?' she asked softly, watching him with narrowed eyes.

'Because you fascinate me.'

She stared at her plate. 'I—'

He'd scared her away. He could see the hesitation in her eyes, hear it in her voice, feel it in every aching muscle in his body.

'Not that I don't usually bend my principles for a pretty woman,' he blurted. 'Or go after something I want…' Dammit, he was digging himself deeper.

She glanced up at him, a soft gleam in her eyes and a knowing smile just touching her lips. 'I know.'

Case leant back in his seat, watching her. Whatever she thought she knew, it made her happier and more relaxed. Who was he to argue?

Whatever she was thinking had put a smile on her face that glowed with a vibrancy that tantalised him.

It couldn't be bad.

CHAPTER FOURTEEN

Emma's rule number two: make love, not war.

TAHLIA chewed on her bottom lip, walking slowly to her front door, every footfall thundering through a body too alert, too aware of Case so close behind her, the warmth of his suit jacket around her shoulders smothering her with his spicy cologne mixed all too enticingly with pure male scent.

Their third date, in as many days, had been wonderful, the food almost as incredible as the company.

It wasn't that she *wanted* to date him, but she found that at work she was so busy with finding files for Case, setting up interviews and doing her own job that she hardly had time to do anything more than admire his dedication to the employees. And he did keep asking her out so she had the opportunity to find out more about him.

Who was she to decline?

At least the plan was working. She was getting to know Case, although she was discovering more about his pets, his parents, his hobbies and his childhood than the details of his career.

Now he was being incredibly tortuous by doing the chivalrous escort-the-girl-to-the-door thing that drove her mind mad with the should-she or shouldn't-she invitations for coffee, inclinations to kiss him, and intense desire to do more than show him the door after the coffee and kiss.

'Thank you for another wonderful evening,' she offered tightly, opening her bag and scrabbling for her keys, pushing the silly notions from her mind.

He was a professional and her boss. Much as she wanted him to be the office playboy, after spending the last few days with him she had serious doubts. He was simply wonderful.

'My pleasure, Tahlia,' he said, her name a mere whisper on his breath.

She shivered, plucked out her keys and fought the jumble for the right one. 'It was great. The mousse was so rich and sweet and smooth—' She glanced up at him—like his voice, like his jaw, like his lips…

'It was,' he said, inching even closer. 'Can I help?'

She watched as he took the keys from her hand and poked the one she'd labelled 'front' in the lock and turned, pushing the door wide.

'Thanks.' Tahlia swept his jacket off her shoulders, the moment when he'd wrapped her in it scored in her memory, his body heat still lingering around her, her heart hammering against her ribs.

She tried to keep that comment he'd made that first night she'd gone out with him, that she was just another date, foremost in her mind, but the rest of the week pressed in on her, smothering her senses with a kindness and a warmth a shallow Romeo just shouldn't have.

She wanted to tell him everything, stay close to him, talk to him all night…and more.

Was this what her mother was feeling? Was this crazy feeling the reason she'd risk so much on a man?

Tahlia looked up into Case's sapphire-blue eyes. 'I lied, you know,' she said softly.

'Oh, yes?' he said, lifting an eyebrow and taking a step back. 'About what, exactly?'

'I haven't exactly had my share of boyfriends.' Tahlia bit her lip. 'No serious boyfriends at all, really.'

'Oh.'

Her belly tightened. 'But don't get me wrong. I have had boyfriends. Plenty. Just no one special, you know, someone who made me feel like—' She caught herself. 'What about you?'

He shook his head. 'No serious boyfriends either,' he said softly, a smile teasing the corners of his mouth. 'But I did… I was…in a serious relationship.'

'And—?'

'And it didn't end well,' he murmured, moving closer. 'But I believe in second chances. Do you?'

She hadn't thought she ever could after what her father did… Hadn't believed she could ever trust a man again, but this feeling, and Case, was special.

She looked up to hand him his jacket, catching his blue gaze and holding it, the gleam residing there fixing her to the spot. 'Yes,' she whispered.

Case lifted a hand to her face, brushing her cheek with his knuckles, pushing back her long fringe, hooking his fingers around her neck and drawing her closer.

His gaze dropped to her mouth.

'Case—' she croaked, moistening her lips instinctively, her whole body aching for him. 'This may not be a good idea—' There was still so much to say before anything happened between them.

He leant down, brushing his lips over hers.

Oh, gawd—yes. Sensation sizzled along her lips, cascading down her body, nestling deep in the pit of her stomach where a yearning ache flared.

He tasted her mouth, teased her lips with his own, drawing up his other hand to cup her face.

Oh, hell, yes.

Tahlia pressed her hands against his hard solid chest, his heart thumping beneath her touch, his warm skin beneath just one thin layer of cotton, all that hard muscle and flesh so close…

He drew back, tasting her lips again. 'You're probably right. Not a good idea…' He brushed her lips with his mouth. 'Not a good idea at all.'

She backed into her doorway, her hands clenched tightly in his shirt. 'Colleagues and all.'

Case followed, his gaze on her lips, his hands on her shoulders. 'Absolutely. Not a good practice.'

'Practise is good,' she whispered, flicking open his shirt buttons and sliding her hands against his warm skin, revelling in the heat of him, the hardness of him, the incredible smoothness.

He sucked in a deep breath, pushed the door closed with his foot and kissed her soundly.

Case's lips caressed hers, soft and sensual. He drew her closer still, running a hand down over her waist, down her hip, down her thigh and up again, moulding her against him.

Oh, by all she'd denied too long, yes.

She popped the rest of his buttons, running her hands

up his hard chest and over his wide shoulders, pushing the shirt from his body.

Case lightened the kiss, as though the cool air of the room had subdued his desire. He dragged in a deep breath.

'We're professionals,' he murmured, trailing kisses along her cheek, over her ear and down her neck. 'We should look at the bigger picture. Not make rash decisions…'

Tahlia pressed her lips against his shoulder, his skin sweet and salty. 'What are the cons?' she whispered. 'Career suicide?'

'No.' Case slipped his hand behind her back, his breath exciting the pulse in her neck. 'Office gossip.'

'Hierarchy complications?' Tahlia suggested, trailing her fingers down the bare flesh of his back and up again. 'Impartiality issues?'

'Not being able to keep my hands off you at work,' Case murmured in her ear, coaxing the zip down at her back. 'In the lift, in the office, on my desk.'

Fire erupted deep inside her. She twined her fingers in his hair. 'What are the pros?'

Case brushed her shoulders with his large hands, sweeping off the straps, letting the dress fall to the floor. His eyes glittered, his gaze travelling up her long legs, over black lace panties to her matching lace bra. 'You.'

She couldn't help but smile, pushing everything from her mind except this moment, with him. It didn't matter who he was, what he really wanted, as long as he wanted her.

She took a step towards him, reaching up and touching his cheek, running her palm down his jaw. 'And this,' she whispered, brushing his lips with hers on tip-toe.

Case swept her into his arms, crushing her mouth.

Tahlia opened herself to him, welcoming the hunger, the heat of his kiss that was only matched by the flames of lust leaping up inside her.

He lifted her into his arms.

She pushed open the bedroom door behind him.

He strode into the room, placing her on to the bed reverentially, drinking in the sight of her. 'Oh, God, Tahlia,' he groaned, tracing her curves with his eyes, his hands following. 'I'm lost. You drive me wild.'

Tahlia ran her hands down his chest, hooking his belt and unclasping it, drawing it slowly from his trousers. 'And crazy?'

'And crazy,' Case whispered hoarsely, unclipping her bra and peeling it from her full breasts.

'I want you too,' she said softly, drawing him down and claiming his mouth. And she did. She burned for him. Wanted him so much she could hardly breathe.

'And practise makes perfect,' she whispered.

Tahlia watched Case sleep in the soft light from the streetlights outside. Wow. She couldn't believe this—how nice he was, how amazingly lucky she was to wake up next to him.

She trailed her fingers down his chest, wondrous at the ripples of muscle, the light scatter of chest hair, the perfection of him.

He caught her hand. 'Hey, that tickles.'

'Sorry, did I wake you?'

'Yes, but it was the nicest way anyone has ever woken me.'

She couldn't help but smile. Gawd, she felt amazing… He'd given so much, shared with her so much. She wanted more, so much more, craved to be closer, know *everything* about Case Darrington. 'Last night was—'

'I know,' he said, his voice deep.

'No regrets?' she whispered.

'How could I have regrets?' Case leant up on his elbow, looking down at her. 'Not a chance.'

'So, can I ask you something?' she asked tentatively, tracing his jaw with the tip of her finger. 'About your last serious relationship—you mentioned it last night.' She needed to know how long ago it had been, that she wasn't a rebound girl to patch some wounded ego.

Case cupped her face. 'It wasn't just a serious relationship… I was married.'

Tahlia froze. Oh, gawd.

'It's okay. I'm divorced—' He frowned. 'I'm not defective… Okay, maybe I am, but I can promise you I won't make the same mistakes again.'

'Should I ask what they were?' she whispered softly, drawing her hand back and placing it on her chest over her heart.

'I wasn't blameless,' Case forced out. He needed to face it, needed to say it. He'd spent far too long blaming Celia for the whole disaster. It was time he accepted his part in it. Needed to, so he could move on and embrace a future with Tahlia.

'I was away a lot, working my butt off to reach my

dreams, my goals, and I lost sight of the fact that Celia had dreams and goals too.'

'Celia was your wife?'

Case swallowed hard. 'Yes. Much as I didn't want to be a trophy husband, my neglect and my obsession with work made her feel like a trophy wife. I regret the pain I put her through. I regret that I turned into my father.'

'And?' she said softly, looking up at him with wide eyes. 'Are you still your father?'

'No, thank God.' He pushed her long fringe back from her face. 'I learnt.'

'Too late,' she whispered softly.

'Yes. While I worked like a maniac she filled her life with things, jewellery and men. By the time I realised what I'd done it was too late; nothing I tried could fix it.'

'Did you love her?'

Case ran his hand down her cheek. 'I thought I did. It was a kind of love, but nothing like—' His voice broke. Like what he was feeling for the woman in his arms.

'I'm sorry.'

'I was too, for a long time, but not now.' He shook his head, drinking in Tahlia's creamy smooth skin. It was time to come clean. He couldn't keep anything from her now. 'Tahlia, I—'

She touched his mouth with her fingers. 'Enough talking.' She drew him down to her, taking his lips with her own, smothering the memory of Celia with the magic of her kiss.

It could wait. They had plenty of time. It was probably something he shouldn't just blurt out anyway. It was something to prepare her for.

At least now he knew for sure. His heart wasn't broken. It was finally alive with the magic of love. He'd found exactly what he had been looking for. Tahlia.

CHAPTER FIFTEEN

Keely's rule number seven: face your fears and seize the moment.

TO: *TahliaM@WWWDesigns.com*
CC: *KeelyR@WWWDesigns.com*
FROM: *EmmaR@WWWDesigns.com*
RE: Chrystal and that look on your face

First, tell all. You haven't looked like this since… ever. What's up? Are you in love? Has it got something to do with that man in your chair who fits your original criteria or have you found a tattoo-wearing, glass-munching man to turn you on?

And Chrystal is floating around extolling advice about wounded men like a Florence Night-in-love. Has Cupid hit?

Em

IT WAS ALL Tahlia could do to sit outside Case's office and not go inside and taste the magic of his lips again and again and again.

He was like a drug and she couldn't get enough of him. Last night had been magical in so many ways and she couldn't believe she'd been so stupid to deny herself this.

Thank heavens that Case had come along and opened her eyes to life, to sharing, to him.

Was this what Chrystal was after by chasing every pair of trousers in the building and what her mother had found in the man she wanted her to meet?

TO: *EmmaR@WWWDesigns.com*
CC: *KeelyR@WWWDesigns.com*
FROM: *TahliaM@WWWDesigns.com*
RE: Chrystal and that look on your face.
I'm not saying anything that will later incriminate me, especially where the 'office playboy' is concerned. I will figure out what I'm feeling and in due course share my adventures with my two closest friends.
Definitely *not* shot by arrow-wielding midget.
T

No way was this love. Her mother and father had had something far more sensible than this craziness she was feeling. Besides, she couldn't be in love. She wasn't going to love anyone.

She'd decided when she was twelve that love wasn't for her—about the moment her mother had told her what had happened to her father, that he wasn't ever coming home again.

Love was for suckers, for young, naïve romantics. She was a professional and this was just another necessity to attain her true goal in life—a perfect career, because you could rely on work, you couldn't rely on men.

All men were liars; they didn't share their feelings or their fears and consequently left the world thinking they had jumped, when they could just have befallen a tragic accident.

So Case had shared his failed marriage with her—it didn't mean he was the one that she'd risk everything for... Or was he?

She chewed on her bottom lip. He was divorced... What did that say?

She was never going to subject herself to pain, no matter how amazing Case *Tantric* Darrington was in bed, or how warm his lips were, how safe his arms were or how nice it had been to hear another human being's heartbeat when she had woken up this morning in his embrace.

Chrystal rushed up the hall towards Tahlia. 'Is this a good time?'

Tahlia nodded and waved her closer, anything to distract her from the love issue. So Case was incredibly, wonderfully nice—it didn't mean she liked him. So the guy was great in bed—it didn't mean she wanted him. So she wanted to spend every moment with him—it didn't mean she loved him.

Chrystal sauntered up to the desk, her plaid knee-length skirt doing nothing to hide the exaggerated sway of her hips. 'You won't believe what I just heard.'

Tahlia sat taller and picked up a pen, spinning it in her hand. 'What? Tell me.'

The receptionist leant forward, her blouse not as demure as the D cups she owned beneath it. 'I heard on the grapevine that WWW Designs has just been sold.'

Tahlia gripped the pen tighter. 'Oh, God. No.'

'Yes.'

She dragged in a ragged breath. It couldn't be. It was a mess. Who would want a mess like WWW? The only workplace she'd ever known could be ripped apart, her workmates scattered to all corners of the city, her secure future torn to shreds. 'To whom?'

'Some conglomerate, they say.' Chrystal straightened and examined her nails. 'I'll let you know if I hear what's going on, but someone said it's one of those companies that owns a company that owns another one.'

'But who?' If she knew who was behind it all she'd be able to work out whether they meant to revamp the place and run it, or chop it into little pieces and sell it off to make a nameless profit for a bunch of rich fat-arsed shareholders.

'I don't know, but the guys in Programming said that the first thing these big guys do is bring an expert in and turn the place upside down, weed out the inefficiencies and re-haul, or dissect, depending on the value.'

'I know,' Tahlia said softly, pulling her jacket tighter around her. She hadn't put everything she had into WWW Designs, years of her life, just so that they could sell it off, chop it up and destroy it. *Please, no.*

Chrystal shrugged. 'Nothing to do but give everyone the heads-up so they're all working to top form. Slackers get the sack.' She paused. 'And I'll let you know if I hear anything about the new owners from the rumour mill.'

'Okay. Good, thanks,' Tahlia said, her body numb.

Chrystal swung her attention to Case's door. 'Should *I* tell him?'

Tahlia shook her head. 'I'll do it.' The poor guy was going to be out of his new job if an efficiency expert came in. He'd done nothing except get acquainted with the staff under him, which was all well and good, but if an expert came in they'd want to see him doing the job that he was at least a few weeks off knowing the ins and outs of.

She chewed on her pen. An expert coming in would be perfect to get rid of the Rottie, what with the mistakes she'd made lately, but Case was like a sitting duck.

She stood up. Her promotion would be available again, for sure, if the new owners decided to keep the place running, and poor Case didn't have a clue.

She tossed the pen on to the desk and picked up the file that she'd been making on Case. Some things were more important than her promotion, like doing the right thing for someone she cared about.

Tahlia froze. *Was* she falling in love?

TO: *TahliaM@WWWDesigns.com*
CC: *KeelyR@WWWDesigns.com*
FROM: *EmmaR@WWWDesigns.com*
RE: Chrystal and that look on your face.

Poor Chrystal—if she had her sights on Case she's out of luck. Case is interested in someone else… (Hey, Tahlia—how's it going with lover boy?). After all the work she's done too. Hope she doesn't fall off the virgin-wagon when she finds out… She's so much nicer like this. Liam certainly thinks so. He's kicked those nerdy spotty shirts and gone for pastels and got contacts and a haircut.

Em

Tahlia froze at Case's doorway, looking out through the full-height windows to the balcony, the existence of which she usually managed to block out.

The sliding door was open.

Case was out there.

Fear ripped through her like cold steel. 'Case,' she croaked, her voice closing over.

Case turned. 'Miss Moran. Come to share the glorious morning with me?'

'Yes,' she breathed, dragging her feet like lead weights across the floor, focusing on the amazing man who had awakened her to so much. Not the windows, not the height, not the balcony. 'But inside, okay?'

His brow furrowed. 'What is it?'

'Please.' Tahlia glanced around her, dropping the file on a chair. It was so high up she could see cars in the distance that looked like toys ants would play with. 'I don't like heights.'

Case walked back into the office, sliding the door closed behind him. 'Do you want to talk about it?'

She shook her head, the memories pressing in on her, the scream, the silence and the sirens.

He took her hands and directed her to the chair closest to the wall. 'I did notice you didn't have a window in your office.'

Tahlia nodded, fighting the logic of how many people could guess her fear, and hating herself for it. Her father's face leapt to her mind.

She lifted her chin, meeting his warm gaze. 'It's not something I talk about.'

'Sometimes it helps to share problems.' Case knelt in front of her, holding her hands in his warm ones. 'I'm here for you.'

She couldn't help but smile. How could she not share this with him after he had shared so much with her? 'My father…died.' She sucked in a deep breath. 'He fell from a balcony…there was a loose rail.'

'Oh, God, Tahlia.' Case's voice broke. 'I'm so sorry. I had no idea.'

'Losing my father was tragic for me, for my mum and me, but listening to the whispers was shattering.'

'Whispers?'

'He'd been drinking. He had financial problems. And he was fighting with my mum.'

Case rubbed her hands. 'It *was* an accident.'

'But you wonder… I wonder…if I could have been a better daughter. If I had better marks at school. If I hadn't nagged him to play checkers with me, then he wouldn't have been up there—'

Case swept her into his arms, holding her against his chest. 'Oh, hell, Tahlia.' He stroked her hair back from her face. 'It was an accident,' he said quietly.

'Yes,' she whispered. 'That's what they all said, but—' She had heard the whispers.

'Hey, of course it was an accident. He loved you and your mother very much… He probably just wanted to protect you from his business worries; he didn't want you to think he wasn't the strong, capable man you thought he was.'

She nodded. 'He fell.'

'Yes, and anyone who says he jumped is a fool, who doesn't know how beautiful and loving you are…who doesn't know how much he was loved.'

She nodded. He was right. It wasn't what happened. It was the meaning she placed upon it. She'd spent far too long listening to whispers that didn't matter. She had loved her father and her father had loved them and it had been an accident, a tragic accident that had stolen her father from her.

'Has anyone told you how wonderful you are?' she asked, sucking in a deep breath. Or how easy it could be to fall in love with him?

'Not lately.'

She rested her head on his chest, which held a heart so warm and loving to offer her such understanding and kindness about her father.

Case held her close, staring out of the window, breathing in her sweet scent, feeling her breath slow down, become deeper, her body relax.

He'd never felt so close to another human being than at this moment. Tahlia had finally let another layer slip away. She'd let him in. He'd never known a feeling like this.

It was incredible.

What he'd thought had been love with Celia had obviously just been infatuation, followed by a hefty dose of ego-induced denial. He had never liked admitting mistakes. And marrying Celia had been a whopper.

Working so hard to save their marriage had probably been more for the sake of the marriage than for them—to show himself and his mother that he wasn't his father. He could change.

He had changed. Now he knew what love was. Sure, it was early days, but he knew, deep in his chest, that he couldn't live without Tahlia. She was air to his lungs, reason for his being, the future mother of his children.

It was her.

He should tell her the truth about why he was here, who he was and exactly why he'd lied, before this went further.

'Tahlia,' he murmured softly. Was now the time? She was obviously vulnerable just now.

Hell, to lose her dad in that way… He ached to fix the past, go back and save her father, so she didn't have to deal with it, feel that pain.

She stepped back, sucking in a deep breath. 'Oh, gawd, I totally forgot why I came in,' she said strongly, sounding more like the Tahlia he knew.

'Understandable.'

She shrugged, swiping down her white blouse and short office skirt, taking his attention to her legs, firing his body with memories of the feel of her wrapped around him, of making incredible passionate love to her.

'I need to talk to you.'

He nodded, watching her move to his desk and sit down opposite his chair as though nothing had happened, all cool and collected. She glanced at him and the soft look in her eyes clawed at his gut.

It was time to tell her. There was only one person who knew who he really was and he wasn't about to let Raquel come between them.

There was no reason to wait until after this little assessment was done. Waiting wasn't worth the risk of enjoying anonymity any longer.

Sure, before he would have said he needed assurances before he risked telling her the truth. Assurances that she wasn't another Celia to run knives through his heart. But that wasn't Tahlia.

She was special. Amazing. His.

Case moved to the desk and propped himself on the edge in front of her. It would probably be a good idea to solve her concerns first. 'What is it?' he asked. 'Is there something I can do? Something wrong?'

A shadow flitted across her face. 'Yes.'

Case's gut tightened. He'd do anything to make things right for Tahlia. What else could be wrong?

'WWW Designs has just been sold to some conglomerate,' she said softly, looking up into his face, her eyes wide.

'Oh?' He watched her carefully. Did she know who he was? Please let her not have found out from anyone else.

Tahlia crossed her legs. 'Odds are they'll send an efficiency expert in to assess the way the place is run.'

'They probably will,' he said, breathing out. He'd have to tell her, before this went any further. Better the truth came from him and not from someone else.

'No. I know they will.' She jerked to her feet and paced the floor in front of him. 'Don't you get it? I *know*.'

Case's gut tightened. *'You know?'*

'Yes. I know that Raquel hired you because you knew someone that knew someone and that you're very easy on the eye.'

'I'm easy on the eye, am I?' He couldn't help feeling a thrill when she said it, or the heat that ran through him at the look in her eyes, her sweet voice.

She threw up her hands. 'You are, I assure you, but you're not getting it. It's not about you being a tall, dark, handsome hunk of a guy—'

'Is that all I am to *you*?' he asked slowly, tongue in cheek. He wanted to be so much more than that to her. Was he kidding himself that there was more to this? She had said she wanted an affair... Could he get her to want more?

She stopped in front of him and kissed him on tiptoe. 'No, idiot. Listen, you have to get up to speed and fast. I don't want you to lose your job.'

'Lose my job?' he echoed.

'Yes, you idiot.' She slapped his shoulder. 'You're not exactly the most qualified person for the job, if you hadn't noticed. And sure, you had connections to get you into the position, but with an expert coming in you're going to have to do a lot more than sit in that chair and look at personnel files.'

He pulled her closer, tucking her fringe behind her ear. 'You don't want me to lose my job?'

'No.'

'Why?' he asked, pulling his knuckles back across her smooth cheek to her lips, which were just begging to be kissed.

Tahlia slapped him on his chest, glaring up at him, her heart pounding. 'Because…' Was it too early to say? She knew she felt it—it pumped through her entire body, filling her chest with a warmth to rival the sun. 'Because I think I like you. Okay? Is that what you wanted to hear?'

'Yes. Actually.' He caught her chin in his hand and tipped her face up, wondering whether there was more she wasn't admitting to. 'How can we find out for sure?'

'I can tell you all the things you need to know about the job if you'll let me help you—'

'Tahlia—'

She shook her head, picking up the file she'd made on him and propelling him back to his desk. 'No. You may think you know it all, but truly an expert will wipe the floor with you. You have to know everything.'

Case perched himself on the edge of the desk, holding both her hands. 'Tahlia—'

Tahlia shook her head. 'Just listen. Liam is our top programmer, distracted at the moment by the opposite sex, but the best. He's being poached by our biggest competitor and if thwarted in love will go somewhere else if he doesn't get the right incentives to stay on.'

Case frowned. 'Does Raquel know this?'

'The Rottie? She's so out of touch.'

'The Rottie?' Case echoed, stifling a smile. The woman would certainly be livid if she found out that was what they called her but, he had to admit, it suited her.

Tahlia waved a hand dismissively, slapping the file on to the edge of his desk. 'Keely is heading out on maternity leave in a fortnight and needs to be assured her job will not only be there when she gets back but that she can create website designs at home until she's ready to come back full-time.'

'She could.'

'Emma has accepted an offer from a firm in New York and she's leaving. She brought in *Harold's House* and is marrying the owner of *Harold's House* so it's in WWW's interests to have an open invitation for her to return.'

Case pulled her closer to him, tucking her between his legs, drawing her on to his lap. 'Tahlia, I need to tell you something—'

She smiled. 'I know…' She loved him too. It was crazy but she was going to do this right, unlike her mother. 'Chrystal is a valuable asset but needs far more to occupy her; she's under-motivated and finds herself trouble, a lot.'

'Short frizzy redhead on the prowl?'

'Yes.' Tahlia hooked her arm around his neck, snuggling closer to him. It was time to tell him what she'd been thinking and doing for the last week. 'And me; you need to know something about me. That I was—'

Case smothered her with a kiss that washed away the tension knotted inside her. It was a soft, dreamy kiss, a kiss for a tired soul to melt into.

She finally pulled back, her lips tingling. 'What was that for?'

'To get you to shut up for a minute. I have something important to tell you.'

'Uh-huh.' She sighed, running her tongue over her lips.

Case's gaze dropped to her mouth. He leant closer and brushed his lips over hers again, slowly deepening the kiss, a hand sliding up her waist to cup the fullness of her breast.

She'd never felt so amazing before, so complete, so totally and utterly safe. Nothing could go wrong.

The door burst open.

'What in hell is going on here?' Raquel's nasal whine echoed through the room.

CHAPTER SIXTEEN

The best-laid plans of mice and women.

TAHLIA froze. She broke away from Case and straightened her jacket, casting a look at the Rottie, who looked as if she was about to break some capillaries.

What could she say to save this situation? She had slipped and fallen on her new executive, or just that she was falling in love with him? 'First aid,' she said in a rush, making the space between them larger.

She lurched forward and picked up the file.

Raquel strode into the room. 'Right, Ms Moran. First aid,' she bit out, swinging her gaze to Case, looking as if she was trying to swallow a melon.

Case stood casually where she'd left him, as though being caught by the boss was nothing to him, his eyes still shining and his mouth curved sensuously in her direction, as though all that mattered was her.

Tahlia's chest ached. He was amazing. He had no idea who he was messing with but he was about to find out all about the Rottie's bark.

Would she sack him? Both of them?

She bit her lip. This couldn't happen to Case. He was innocent, a decent guy who'd just happened to get the job she'd been obsessed about.

She had been crazy to care so much about that promotion. Her mum loved her for who she was, was proud of her no matter what she did, was okay with her living her life just the way she wanted to.

She didn't have to be afraid any more—her mother wasn't.

Tahlia moistened her still-tingling lips. She didn't care what happened to her now, but Case couldn't be punished for her stupidity. She loved him.

She touched her chest where her heart echoed her thoughts. She loved him. How it had happened, she had no idea, but she knew there were other jobs but there was only one Case.

She stepped towards the General Manager, who had terrorised the entire office for years, holding the file close to her, her heart thundering in her chest.

She couldn't let Raquel know she'd made a mistake employing Case; she wanted to keep him, no matter what chair he was sitting in.

'It was my fault,' Tahlia blurted. 'Don't blame any-one but me. I was the one who kissed him—he's been nothing but the nicest guy.' She glanced at him. 'De-cent and caring and keen to get to know the staff like a good manager of people should—'

'Right,' the Rottie snapped. 'If you'll excuse Mr Darrington and myself, we have business to discuss.'

Tahlia glanced at her watch. Of course that was why the woman was here. It was eleven a.m. and Raquel was right on time.

She should have remembered the Rottie was coming and, dammit, she'd proven Case's weaknesses all too well.

'We do?' Case asked, straightening his tie.

Raquel swung to him. 'Yes. Your assistant arranged for me to come in.'

Case stared at her blankly.

'You didn't know? Where's your assistant? I'll have a few words to say about interrupting my very busy schedule for fictitious meetings. Everyone knows how busy I am keeping this office running smoothly.'

Case swung his attention to Tahlia, the light in his eyes fading. 'Tahlia?'

Raquel stared at Tahlia. 'You? No way. You'd never take a step backward...'

Tahlia's blood chilled. This was not good. 'I need to talk to you,' she offered Case, mentally crossing everything she had that this stopped here.

'*You're* his assistant?' Raquel crossed her arms over her chest. 'I know I said to help the man out, but I never expected you to do *that* much, especially considering...'

'Considering what?' Case asked, his voice deep and cool, his face a mask of stone.

No. This couldn't be happening. She stepped forward, brandishing his file at the man she loved. 'Case—'

Raquel snatched the file from her hands. 'Considering that she's been after the Marketing Executive job for months.'

Case swung to face her. 'Why is Raquel here?'

Tahlia tore her gaze from the incriminating file in the Rottie's hands and fixed her eyes on Case. What could she say?

Would he ever look at her again with those warm blue eyes, whisper sweet words with his deep, smooth voice, touch her lips again with his or hold her in his arms if he knew how crazy mad she had been at him for taking her job?

Raquel flicked through the file and cleared her throat. 'Well, Mr Darrington, I believe I'm here to see just how committed Miss Moran is to her job.'

Tahlia stared at the Rottie, her calm tone sliding down her spine. She wasn't upset? How could she not be barking blue murder at the repeat performance of the last executive, of having a file full of evidence supporting her very questionable decision to employ Case?

'This is fascinating.' She shook the file. 'Documented evidence that you, Mr Darrington, aren't qualified for the position she feels she should have got.' She shook her head slowly. 'And what was that intimacy in aid of? I'd love to hear how you thought *that* could help your cause, unless you've discovered—'

Raquel swung to Case, lifting an eyebrow.

He turned to her, piercing her with a chilling look. 'Tahlia?'

Her name slid from his lips like poison from a broken glass. No. How could he believe that she'd wanted anything other than to be with him after the week they'd spent together, after last night, after they'd shared so much, after she'd surrendered her heart to him?

Tahlia felt the rattle in her chest, staring at the file she'd filled to justify being his assistant, spending time with him, going out with him, wanting to know him.

A tearing ache ripped through her chest as the enormity of what was at stake hit her. She'd been an idiot, making a mess of the one thing that mattered.

She couldn't lose him. She didn't want him fired; she needed him.

'I was stupid.' Tahlia sighed.

Case couldn't be hearing this. There had to be a mistake. There was no way that Tahlia was the sort of woman to manipulate her way up the ladder. Not a chance. Not with all he knew about her, unless it had all been lies.

Could she know who he really was? Had her revelations of all the ins and outs of the employees just been a ruse to ensure she kept his attention when it came to the hirings and the firings?

Raquel swung to face him, tucking the file under her arm. 'Mr Darrington, I'm sorry about this. I take full responsibility,' she said sweetly. 'I just didn't think Miss Moran would go to such lengths to ensure her promotion.'

His gut tightened. Raquel was certainly going to great lengths to ensure *her* position and rightly so; she'd been on shaky ground from the start.

He turned to face the woman he had thought he knew. '*I* was placed in the position *you* were after…so you had to prove there'd been a mistake.' He took the file from Raquel, flicking through the pages, his blood going cold in his veins.

'I was angry. It meant so much to me—' Tahlia blurted, her eyes wide.

Her words hit him full force in the chest. It was true. The only reason she had wanted to be near him was to prove her point.

Celia's face lurched to his mind, her memory a dull

ache to the darkness tearing through his chest. He swung to face the window.

He couldn't have walked right into a relationship with a woman just like his ex-wife, couldn't be attached to a manipulating liar who was just after what he could give her, couldn't have given his heart away to someone who didn't love him for who he was.

He couldn't have done it again.

CHAPTER SEVENTEEN

Tahlia's rule number one: don't fall in love.

TAHLIA crossed her arms in front of her. 'So are you going to fire me?' she asked Raquel, forcing herself to keep her tone soft, really only wanting one answer from the woman with the power—was she going to fire Case and punish him for Tahlia's stupidity?

Raquel smirked.

Tahlia knew the answer. The Rottie wouldn't hesitate to fire *her*. She hated having Tahlia breathing down her neck, spouting ideas on improvement, undermining her authority, especially when Raquel had messed up that contract.

'Fire you?' Raquel snorted. 'Why in heavens would I do that when you're hammering all the nails into your own coffin?'

Tahlia glanced at the Rottie, her mind trying to subdue the storm of emotions to make out what the woman was saying. What was going on?

'That file is interesting reading,' Raquel said, lifting her sculpted nose. 'But I think that little interlude I witnessed takes the cake. Case Darrington isn't a fool.'

'Of course he isn't,' Tahlia said, straightening tall and looking at him by the window, the urge to go to him and hold him, wrap him in her arms and tell him it was all okay burning in her.

Did this mean the Rottie wasn't going to fire him? A bubble of hope rose in her chest. He'd be okay? If she was fired, would he be safe?

Tahlia shook her head, trying to clear it.

'Look, I'll let Mr Darrington explain why he's really here sitting in the Marketing Executive's chair, sorting through the personnel,' Raquel simpered, swinging around and heading out through the door. 'If you really need it spelt out to you…but you're an intelligent woman and, judging from your behaviour when I walked in, I'd say you know already, don't you think, Mr Darrington?'

What? She turned back to Case, who stood at the window, stiff like a tin soldier, his arms crossed tightly across his chest, his brow heavy.

The Rottie closed the office door.

Tahlia shook her head. 'Case, I feel there are a few things I need to say.'

'Likewise,' he said, his voice a monotone.

Tahlia sucked in a breath, a cold chill clawing at her belly. 'I have to say I was incredibly put out by your getting the position I'd coveted and I may have had ideas to rectify the situation, but that all changed.'

'I can imagine.'

'Case, look at me.'

He turned and faced her, his gaze steel-blue, his mouth pulled thin. 'And then you decided it was more in your interests to seduce me with your beautiful body, your sweet voice and your innocent damsel-in-distress act?'

'Yes. No. I didn't mean to,' she said softly. 'It wasn't an act.' How could he think that? She'd never enjoyed being with someone as much as she loved being with him, knowing him, loving him.

He shook his head. 'Not an act until you heard that the new owner *had already* put in the efficiency expert.'

Tahlia's blood chilled. Someone was already here going through the staff files? Who? Surely she'd have noticed, but she had been so busy focusing on her own problems, her loss, the frenzy of strange emotions she was having for her new boss.

She froze, ice seeping into her toes. 'You,' she said, her voice devoid of the emotion that rocked through her.

Oh, gawd. She was an idiot. Of course it was him!

He'd waltzed in, distracting everyone with his good looks and charm, diverting her attention to him and not to what he was doing.

She shook her head. What would he think of her? Raquel was right—she'd proved to him, one hundred and fifty per cent, that she was a fool.

Did he always test the staff this way? Sweep them off their feet and into warm arms that weren't safe at all, that weren't to be trusted, that weren't meant for her and for her alone.

Tahlia's eyes burned. She had been an idiot to think she was ready for a relationship...ever!

She blinked hard and lifted her gaze. The coldness in his eyes burned through her.

How could she have let herself love him?

'Of course, I knew that all along,' she blurted, her voice rough, hoping he'd believe the lie. 'You being so obviously out of your field of expertise, put in a position of power and yet…wanting to spend all your time trawling through personnel files. Not something a new executive would put first on his list, not what I'd do, and I figured you'd like games.'

'I should have guessed.' Case clenched his hands by his sides. 'It was a chance to ingratiate yourself and secure the position you coveted, I'm guessing.'

Tahlia nodded tightly. 'I knew exactly who you were from the start,' she forced out, every word gouging holes in her heart. She had to save some semblance of pride in all this. 'The rumour mill, you know.'

Case looked away. 'Right. Of course. So you knew that I could give you exactly what you wanted, if you played me right?'

She forced a smile to her mouth. 'Of course. I figured if I put together a file on you…I'd prove that I was executive material…and really was passionate about the job and…' the words were like bile '…then I figured why not guarantee my promotion—'

'Right, of course. You knew,' he said, his voice devoid of all emotion. 'I'd hoped I had a few weeks before the news of my purchase was heard here.'

His purchase? *He* was the owner? Tahlia stared blankly at him, the word ricocheting through her. He was the man behind the company that had bought WWW Designs? And he was here, pretending to be just anyone?

'A couple of weeks to get the job done,' Case said casually, '…and I…I usually…entertain myself on the job. Life can be so boring…and since you seemed more than keen to—'

Tahlia's chest ached, right down to her toes. He *was*

a class A playboy snob looking to entertain himself until something better came along and she'd been used. 'Glad to be of service, sir,' she bit out. 'Just doing my bit. For you…the office… Me.'

She backed away from the man who was a stranger to her. And she'd given him everything on a platter—the staff, her friends, her father, and her heart.

How could she have trusted him?

He turned to face her. 'Just wanted to let you know that I enjoyed the game. Thanks. I especially enjoyed the sincerity with which you shared all the pertinent information you wanted to get across about the staff. I'll take into account the tainted nature—and your possible ulterior motives—in that discourse when I make my decisions.'

Tahlia moved behind the chair and gripped the back, holding herself up on legs that wanted to fold underneath her. How stupid had she been to share all that with him? The enemy.

She stared at his handsome face, just made to woo women into madness, fighting the ache in her throat.

If only she could take back the last week and keep her distance, her cool, her fears and dreams to herself. 'I should imagine you would take everything I said with a grain of salt.'

She glanced at the door. 'So—' That was it then. There was nothing for it than to skulk back to her office and pack her desk, knowing that the first man she'd let in had not only stuck a knife deep in her career, but had also twisted it deep in her chest. And she only had herself to blame.

'So—' Case strode to his desk. 'You get the promotion that you wanted, Marketing Executive. I think you're just the sort of ruthless career-minded person we want to have leading the charge.'

Tahlia shook her head, her vision blurring. She couldn't have heard right. He was giving her the job thinking that she was some manipulating ladder-climber?

'You have the promotion, Miss Moran,' he said in a monotone voice, not looking at her. 'You can start as Marketing Executive on Monday.'

She lifted her chin. He was giving her the promotion she'd wanted, the dream she'd coveted, and it felt so very very wrong.

She didn't want to be a part of a business that employed the sort of person he thought she was.

She took a step backwards. She'd been an idiot to open her heart, leave herself vulnerable, show her weaknesses to him…to trust him.

'Great, thanks,' she shot out coldly. 'I'm so glad we don't have to continue this farce—a bit much of an effort, yeah?' She held herself tight. 'I appreciate it.'

He nodded tightly, a muscle in his jaw flicking.

'And I'm guessing I'll get the generous rise that goes with the job,' she bit out. 'Seeing as I did such a good job entertaining you and all, not that I didn't enjoy you a bit.' Too much. Way too much. 'You were a great change from the hulking suits that usually are in a position to give me a boost in my career.' She inched backwards, her heart thundering protests. 'That I couldn't possibly get on my own merits,' she forced out, every word scouring her throat.

Case stood like a statue behind his large desk, staring

at her, his face grim. 'I have to say you were the smoothest operator, the best I've...the—'

She shrugged, heading for the door, dragging in a deep breath, blinking the moisture from her eyes. 'I'm surprised you didn't guess that a cutthroat career woman like myself would be dying for that chair, would do anything.'

A shadow passed over his face. 'Yes, I should have,' he said, his voice deep and husky.

Tahlia paused at the door, her throat aching with screams. 'What prompted you to come in yourself, by the way, rather than send someone else?'

'I was bored.' Case shrugged and sat down in the leather chair. 'Thanks for breaking the monotony. And, since I've given you the promotion, I'd appreciate you continuing to keep the fact that I'm the new owner to yourself.'

'Glad to do my bit,' she said strongly. 'But how do you know that I haven't told everyone already?'

'Believe me, I'd know. I can recognise flattery and posing a mile off.' He gave her a cold, hard look, as though looking at her for the first time.

'Right, okay, then. I'll go then and leave you to decide the fate of the rest of the office without me distracting you with my games,' she said in a rush.

'Appreciated,' Case said, shuffling the papers on his desk. 'Goodbye, Miss Moran.'

'Goodbye,' she whispered, her voice failing her. She strode through the door and down the hall. She should have stuck to her rules, her list, to business and not personal.

She had been right to avoid a personal life. She

didn't need it or to have her heart ripped out and crushed.

She touched her lips and her vision blurred. She'd never kiss his lying mouth, hold his playboy body close, hear his traitorous heart again…

How could she have been so stupid? She should have known he'd let her down, betray her trust, believe what he wanted to believe and do what he wanted. He was just like her father.

Tahlia stopped at the desk and pulled out her handbag and shoved her favourite pens, a stapler and a few rubber bands in. At least she had her promotion.

The thought made her feel ill; as if she'd take anything she hadn't earned. This was all so wrong. It wasn't meant to be like this.

He was meant to be wonderful. He was meant to be the one. He was meant to be her perfect partner who was there to support her, not break her heart into little pieces.

Tahlia fought against the chill in her veins.

She hooked her bag on her shoulder and strode down the hall. She'd email a resignation. She couldn't ever see the lying jerk again.

Although there was one more thing to give him before she left.

TO: *allstaff@WWWDesigns.com*
FROM: *TahliaM@WWWDesigns.com*
RE: WWW Designs' newest employee
Please be advised that Case *Trustless* Darrington is in fact the new owner of WWW Designs and is in the process of making staff evaluations.

All those interested in keeping their jobs, please note
Mr Darrington is currently using the Marketing
Executive office, where all reports, visitors and any
gifts, donations and flattery will be gratefully re-
ceived. (NB: he has a sweet tooth)
Thanks to you all for making my work days satis-
fying and special. My thoughts and good wishes are
with you all.
Tahlia Moran
Ex-Director of Sales

CHAPTER EIGHTEEN

Sagittarians—Think before you make big decisions.

CASE still heard the door shutting after Tahlia left yesterday, haunting him with its finality. He hadn't watched her leave, couldn't bear to see her or let *her* see the pain in his eyes, the crushing weight on his chest.

His worst nightmare had come true and the sequel hurt far more than the original ever had—how could that be?

Dammit. How had he let her under his radar? When he had known she was trouble from the first moment he'd laid eyes on her.

Hadn't he learnt anything with Celia?

How could he have believed that he'd get it right by being naïve and stupid like last time? He should have investigated her and known more about her than she knew herself. Then he wouldn't have to feel this way.

Tahlia's confession had said it all. She was a player. She hadn't even denied it. Had revelled in it. Had yanked out his heart and crushed it under her sharp truths, shattering what he'd held so dear, so close, so incredibly beautiful to him that morning, with the dream of spending for ever with her. Of her having his children, of sharing his heart, his dreams, his life.

He pulled at his tie. He had been a fool. Again.

When was he going to learn not to give in to the optimistic organ in his chest and rely on his head?

He couldn't even fire her. He should have, but if that job was what she really wanted then he had to give it to her...if that was all he could ever give her.

Case raked his hands through his hair, glancing at his watch. Time to play the executive again. Hell. Could he pull it off now, with Tahlia's game playing over and over in his head, trying to put together the skewed logic she'd had in playing him.

Why had she bothered when she'd known who he was from the start? All she had had to do was be competent and efficient and she'd have had her precious promotion...

He rubbed his face; he couldn't make her out. He'd spent all night tossing, trying to fit the woman he knew she was to the one she had said she was.

Nothing made sense.

A knock on the door tore him from his thoughts. Was it her? Had she changed her mind and decided she wanted to share a bit more with him before he left, that he wasn't so abhorrent and she could stand his company even when it didn't serve a means to an end?

'Come,' he barked, his voice hoarse.

Chrystal poked her head around the corner. 'Is it safe to come in?'

'Yes,' he said with a sigh. 'But leave the door open.'

'I'm here to help,' she said smoothly, striding into the room, her hips swaying in her knee-length tweed skirt.

'Help?' He put a pile of papers between him and the

woman in front of him, feeling some comfort in her demure outfit but not in the look in her eyes.

'Yes. I'm here as a shoulder to cry on, or an ear to listen to your angst, or to answer whatever questions you have about the office.'

'Cry? Angst?' He straightened in his chair. Was he that obvious? He hoped not. There was no way he wanted Tahlia to know how much she'd meant to him. 'Would you please explain yourself?'

She plucked out a plate of cookies from behind her back. 'These are for you. And just in case you don't remember, I'm Chrystal from Reception, the one who'd love to have a chance to mend your broken heart.'

'Right.' He waved a hand. 'Thank you so much but I have to be honest and tell you there's no chance for you and I at all. I'd be doing you a disservice if I led you to believe otherwise. I'm not attracted to you at all.'

Chrystal leant heavily on the desk, leaning over towards him. 'Okay, if you're sure. And, just so you know, it's so nice to work with someone as clever, handsome and incredibly intelligent as you.'

Case tugged at his tie. 'Thank you.'

A tap at the door jerked him from the gleam in the woman's eyes. A pretty woman with dark hair stood at the door, her hand resting on the bulge of her pregnancy. 'Is this a good time?'

'Absolutely,' Case said quickly, standing up. 'Thank you, Chrystal.' He watched Chrystal leave, every step she took a relief to the tension in his shoulders and neck. 'What can I do for you, Miss…Rhodes, Mrs Brant or—?'

'Keely is fine.' The young woman moved into the office. 'Just thought I'd drop in some doughnuts,' she said, sweeping out a box of iced doughnuts from behind her back and putting it down on his desk. 'And to find out if you could tell me what's going on with Tahlia.'

Case swallowed hard. 'Miss Moran. Yes. She's a very strong-willed young woman who obviously knows what she wants and has no hesitation in going after it.'

Keely nodded, her eyes narrowed. She tilted her head, opened her mouth, then closed it. 'That she is,' she said. 'We'll all miss her.'

Miss her? As Director of Sales, he guessed. Despite her ruthlessness, she did seem to have a warm rapport with the staff.

'Just a minute, Miss…Mrs…Keely. One question.'

She glared at him. 'Yes, Mr Darrington?'

'Is Tahlia…Miss Moran…afraid of heights?'

'Is grass green? Absolutely. She's terrified. Has been since…' She trailed off.

He clenched his hands. That at least had been real. 'Her father died,' he murmured.

Keely's brow furrowed. 'She told *you* that?'

Case's gut tightened.

'She doesn't tell anybody that.' Keely swung around and waddled back to the doorway, weaving her way through a crowd of employees milling in the hallway, all brandishing plates, bags, bows and flowers.

What in hell was going on?

He punched the computer he'd ignored all morning in favour of staring morosely at Tahlia's file.

Case stabbed his computer keys, logging on.

TO: *CaseD@WWWDesigns.com*
FROM: *TahliaM@WWWDesigns.com*
SUBJECT: Resignation.

Please be advised that I, Tahlia Moran, hereby give my notice to my smart-arsed sexy-as-hell boss who I wouldn't want to work for because he didn't fire me for unethical behaviour.

I'd like it noted that I will not be returning to WWW Designs, due to the accrued sick leave and the holidays that I didn't take due to my commitment above-and-beyond to the company.

Please note that I am a professional, Mr Darrington, and hope that both my dalliance with you and my impromptu absence has not put you to any convenience.

Tahlia Moran

Case jerked to his feet, a hot warmth spreading through him. She didn't want the job!

Oh, hell. Could this mean what every inch of him wanted it to? Or was this another chapter in her game?

Was she for real?

Could he slap his heart back in his chest one last time and take a chance?

He pushed back his chair, replaying that moment in his office, knowing the job didn't matter...

Oh, hell, he'd made the biggest mistake of his life.

CHAPTER NINETEEN

Dear Diary,
Some idiot said it was better to have loved and lost
than never have loved at all—load of crap. If I didn't
know love, I would never know this pain or care about
an arrogant jerk that didn't deserve anything,
least of all my love.

TO: *Tahlia007@hotmail.com.au*
CC: *KeelyR@WWWDesigns.com*
FROM: *EmmaR@WWWDesigns.com*
RE: Case Darrington

I can't believe you're resigning. Not possible.
Whatever happened? And Case is the owner? How
did you find out? What happened with you two? You
looked so happy.

I saw Case today. He doesn't look happy, although
all the gifts that are flooding in should at least satisfy
that sweet tooth.

Hope you're going to be there for the baby shower.
Do you need soup? Company? Chocolate?

Just found out. Chrystal is after Case. Saw her gush-
ing all over him. And for the office playboy you
thought he was, he wasn't looking all that thrilled
about the attention.

Why aren't you answering my calls?

Em

Tahlia chewed on the end of her pen, staring at her home desktop, stabbing the computer keyboard. Served him right to have Chrystal after him.

> TO: *Tahlia007@hotmail.com*
> CC: *EmmaR@WWWDesigns.com*
> FROM: *KeelyR@WWWDesigns.com*
> RE: Case Darrington
>
> Just heard Liam asked Chrystal out! And she said yes, as long as he understood she wasn't going to have sex with him. So, virgin still she may be, reluctant to be blunt, no way.
>
> Liam is head over heels. Hope Chrystal realises how nice he is and doesn't break his heart.
>
> How's your heart, Tahlia?
>
> K

Tahlia pushed away from the desk she had in the corner of her room, hauling herself out of the chair and weaving her way through the books that couldn't take her mind off him, clothes that didn't feel right on her skin and take-away boxes on the floor.

She'd binged all yesterday, had tried to smother the ache in her belly with pizza, Chinese, doughnuts, ice cream and chocolate, to no avail.

She'd spent the morning in bed with the phone off the hook. She couldn't face talking to anyone, let alone her mother.

How could her mother tempt fate and trust a man again? The thought made her stomach toss… It was just a matter of time before she was hurt again.

How could she be such a fool?

Tahlia slapped her cheeks. She had to shape up. She couldn't miss Keely's baby shower, no matter what she felt.

Tahlia pushed open her bedroom door. She ought to find something to wear, have a shower, drag her sorry-arse out and pretend to be happy.

At least she could be happy that her two best friends had found love, and even Chrystal. Fancy that it was Case that Chrystal was keen on, who she'd done the incredible makeover thing for, who she'd reclaimed her virgin status to entice.

Tahlia kicked yesterday's clothes out of her way and stopped. That meant that Chrystal's guy, the one who was still getting over the wounds of a really nasty divorce, was Case. Great.

What did the man do? Deliberately torture unwitting females into falling madly in love with him and sacrificing everything for him so he could get some revenge on the species for his pain?

She swiped at her cheeks, damp again. She wouldn't put it past him. Rich, lying, manipulating snob that he was.

How could he be that guy?

She shook herself. It didn't matter anyway. She knew what he thought of her and he'd shown her just how much love could hurt, and she didn't want it.

She was better off with a glass-chewing bartender covered in tattoos.

The doorbell rang. She glanced at her watch. Probably Em or Keely. She'd pretended to be out, hiding deeper under her blankets when they'd come by last night.

She knew she couldn't avoid them for long, especially when she was expected at the baby shower tonight.

Tahlia traipsed to the door, straightening her T-shirt over her jogging bottoms, and trying to comb her loose hair with her fingers.

She pulled open the door.

Case *Traitor* Darrington stood in her doorway, almost filling it, his dark suit sitting perfectly on his body, his hair ruffled, his jaw slightly shadowed.

He cast a glance over her as though drinking in the sight of her. 'Hey.'

'Hey,' she echoed, willing herself to slam the door closed in his handsome face so she didn't have to hear what mean thing he was going to reveal to her next, but she was frozen.

'I came over to find out why you resigned when I gave you the promotion you were desperate for. And also why everyone is bringing me sweets.'

She tried to smile. 'Oh. Haven't you read the email?'

Case nodded. 'You spilled the beans, then, which I find incredibly odd seeing how hard you worked for the promotion.'

She shrugged. She couldn't do this. She wasn't up to this. 'The beans are spilt. The news is out. I've resigned. Let's leave it at that, okay?' She tried to close the door.

Case put his hand up, holding the door. 'Not okay. I think we have a few things to discuss.'

Tahlia swung the door wide and retreated to the lounge, throwing herself into her favourite chair, tucking up her legs and staring at her fish, who were swimming around the bowl as though nothing was wrong at all. 'Fine. What?'

Case closed the front door behind him and leant against the wall. 'Tell me why you resigned.'

'I told you, I didn't want to work for a place that would hire me even after what I'd done.'

'Really?'

'Would you? If the boss saw you as a manipulative career-climbing user,' she blurted, holding herself tightly, swallowing the burning ache in her throat.

He strode to her chair and squatted, holding the arms to steady himself. 'Tell me why you'd go to all that trouble finding out all my flaws as a Marketing Executive if you knew who I was from the start.'

She glanced at the man with the sapphire-blue eyes who had torn her heart in half. How could she trust him again? She knew what trusting a man got you. Pain.

'Please, Tahlia, tell me.'

Tahlia lifted her chin and looked at the man and knew deep in her heart that this was her chance to move on. To open herself and tell him like it was, not because he deserved to hear it, not because her mother said so, not because it was a good career move, but for her and her alone. It was time to let the past go and make her own future, and all her own mistakes.

'I didn't. I didn't know who you were,' she blurted, her eyes stinging. 'When I bumped into you in the foyer I felt things I didn't want to feel. When you took my promotion I decided to smother those feelings with anger. When there was no anger left I covered those feelings with all the reasons you shouldn't have got my job.' She sucked in a deep breath, fighting the ache in her throat. 'And when I found out how nice you were I gave into them, for you.'

'Tahlia.' Case sighed. 'And when did you find out who I was?'

She looked away, her cheeks heating at her stupidity and ignorance of his role at WWW. 'When *you* told me.'

His brow furrowed. 'Then—?'

'I'm not that person,' she whispered, 'that you think I am. I can't be. I earn my own way, through hard work, intelligence and commitment, not—' She glanced at the bedroom door.

'Hell, Tahlia.' Case dropped to his knees on the floor in front of her. 'I'm so sorry. I've been the biggest jerk. When I heard that you were only interested in your career—what you could get out of me—everything that went wrong in my marriage came back to haunt me.'

She stared into his face. 'It's okay. I'm fine. I'll be fine. There's plenty more jobs around.' She lifted her chin defiantly.

'Tahlia, I need to explain.'

'What's to explain?' She shrugged. 'You just lied about everything.'

'I was there to do a job.'

She nodded tightly.

'The job is all I've ever had to hang on to when my life wasn't working, all the more so in the last few years. I've been so burnt in the past I wasn't willing to let myself have a future. I wanted you to like me for me, not because of what I owned.'

'I don't care what you own.'

'What do you care about?'

Tahlia stared at the man she loved so much it hurt. 'I did want that promotion and I did want to prove to Raquel she'd made a mistake in hiring you instead of me.'

'I would have done the same.'

Tahlia leant forward, cupping his face in her hands. 'I had to spend time with you to prove my point…but then I realised I wanted your kisses, your touch, the magic you offered, just for me. All me.' She bit her lip. 'And I wanted more.'

'The job?'

She shook her head slowly, her gaze glued to his. 'You. I wanted to keep you.'

Case's eyes brightened. 'Why?'

Tahlia stared at her hands in her lap. She knew it was time. She had to say it out loud. Sure, she had no control over what his reaction would be, what would happen next, but she owed this to herself. 'Because I love you, Case T Darrington.'

Case touched her chin with his finger, lifting her gaze to meet his. 'Hell, Tahlia, I've never met anyone like you.'

'And that's good?'

'Of course it is.' He drew her into his arms, brushing his lips against hers. 'I love you too, with all my heart and soul. Can you forgive me for being an idiot?'

'I think I can.' Tahlia couldn't help but smile. Sure, there were going to be risks in loving someone else but she couldn't imagine living a day without Case in it. 'By the way, what does the T stand for in your name?'

Case wrapped her in his warm, strong arms and held

her close, swamped by the incredible turn in his life. He'd learned all right, how to love, and he would never let anything be more important, ever.

'My middle name,' he murmured, pulling her closer and breathing in her sweet scent. 'Trustworthy.'

EPILOGUE

*They say that love's what makes the world
go round. I say keep me spinning.*

EMMA strode back to Keely's lounge chair and dropped on to Harry's knee, pulling a stuffed giraffe on to her lap and an arm around her fiancé. 'Phew. That was the last guest.'

Tahlia scooped the rest of the mountain of wrapping paper into a rubbish bag, surveying the pile of presents on the coffee table—baby rugs, bouncers, bottles, nappies and teddies galore. 'You've got everything you need now, Keely.'

Keely smiled, snuggling into Lachlan's arms, cradling her big belly with both her hands. 'I sure have. And you know what, I think you guys do too.'

Tahlia glanced to Emma, who was caressing Harry's face with the giraffe, her eyes shining.

'I do,' Em piped, tossing the giraffe behind the sofa and using her lips instead.

'I can't believe you'll be saying "I do" in a couple of weeks,' Tahlia offered softly. 'In front of your family and your friends.'

Emma laughed. 'I can't wait.'

Tahlia turned to the amazing man behind her, the man who had touched her life in so many ways, the man *she* was taking to the wedding. She moved closer to where he sat in the chair.

Case leant over, brushing his lips over her cheek. 'I like your friends,' he whispered, his breath hot on her skin. 'And I love you.'

Tahlia stood up, the warmth of his words filling her, glancing around at the wonderful people who were her colleagues, her friends, her family. She loved them all, needed them all, wanted them all to stay in her life, but one in particular…

She looked down at Case, his eyes shining with his love for her.

'Hey,' Keely said. 'Six months ago did any of us think we would be *here*?'

'Nope.' Em laughed. 'Not a chance.'

'No way,' Tahlia said, dropping into Case's strong, safe arms, her heart full of love she'd never thought could be hers. 'But there's no place I'd rather be.'

TO: *TahliaM@WWWDesigns.com*
CC: *KeelyR@WWWDesigns.com*
FROM: *EmmaR@WWWDesigns.com*
RE: Love and promotions

Saw Liam and Chrystal down at Sammy's, all over each other—it was so beautiful.

Can't wait to receive my orders from my very own best friend, the new Marketing Executive, Tahlia Moran, woman in love.

Can't believe you didn't accept the position of General Manager—yippee, the wicked Rottie is gone—although I have to admire your dedication to working your way to the top on your own merits.

How's Case going? Is he getting a work-out? Does he like your merits? And is that a ring on your finger? Tell all.
Em

THE MILLIONAIRE
BOSS'S MISTRESS

BY
MADELEINE KER

An English Literature graduate, **Madeleine Ker** has been writing for over two decades. Her first romance novel was titled *Aquamarine* and was published in 1983. She describes herself as "a compulsive writer," and is very excited by the way women's fiction is evolving. She is also a compulsive traveller and has lived in many different parts of the world, including Britain, Italy, Spain and South Africa. She has a young family (whom she has "relentlessly dragged around the world") and a number of pets.

CHAPTER ONE

SHE had never been so late in her life. And it wasn't even her fault.

As the airliner banked over the bay, Amy got a good look at the city where she had been expected hours ago. Many hours ago. She checked her watch. Yesterday, in fact.

The rising sun was slanting low over Hong Kong, making the millions of windows in the skyscrapers glow like gold. It was a breathtaking sight. With the thoroughness that marked everything she did, she had already studied the city in detail from guidebooks, and now, from several thousand feet up, she could pick out some of the major landmarks.

She did not have much time to practise her geography. It all swept past her window in a few seconds, the harbour, the Peak, Kowloon, the dense grid of streets that, even at this early hour of the day, already twinkled with innumerable cars.

She hunted urgently for the glass tower that was her destination. The plane was going fast. There it was! She managed to catch a glimpse of the tower, its hundreds of blue glass windows glowing in the morning sun. Then it was gone. But at least she had seen it. She was supposed to have been there, ready for her interview, at lunchtime yesterday.

Amy Worthington felt her stomach swoop in unison with the airliner's descent. She checked her watch. It was coming up for eight in the morning. Her interview with Anton Zell was history. So was the job it should have led to.

He would already be in another country. It had been made very clear to her that Mr Zell was only in Hong Kong for one day. And wherever he was, Anton Zell was not renowned as a man who accepted excuses. She had been given her great chance and had missed it. It had been up to her to make sure she was present for the interview on time. For various reasons, she had chosen a flight that would have got her to Hong Kong with four hours to spare. Instead it had got her there eighteen hours late.

Had there ever been an unluckier flight? The misery had begun in London, as one delay after another to the flight had been announced; infinitely worse had been the pilot's laconic announcement that, due to engine trouble, they would be landing for repairs at an Asian airport whose name she couldn't even pronounce.

Amy felt like bursting into tears. This job was vitally important to her. It represented a quantum leap upwards. She knew she was capable of doing it, and doing it very well. It offered wonderful things—a spectacular salary, company accommodation in Hong Kong, travel, excitement.

But it also represented a major challenge. Whatever her capabilities were, she had not worked at this level before. She had everything—the intelligence, the confidence, the training—everything except the experience.

She needed to convince Anton Zell, known as one of the most demanding and powerful men in business, to give her a chance. And that meant persuading him to take a risk on her, an unknown, young and relatively inexperienced person, when there were many others, with a lifetime in industry behind them, who would also be queuing for this post.

Exactly how she was going to do that was a subject that had occupied her thoughts almost every hour of the past two weeks. Technically, she felt she knew the answers to almost any question Zell might throw at her. She had studied every scrap of information that had been released about his current projects and she had researched every possibility diligently.

She was adaptable and she felt ready to assimilate anything that might come her way.

That wasn't the problem.

The problem would be in persuading Anton Zell that someone of her youth was capable of standing up to the relentless pressures of the job.

The man who had helped to arrange this interview for her, her uncle Jeffrey Cookson, had put it succinctly: 'Zell moves at a pace that would burn most human beings to ashes. The interview is going to be hell, my dear. But get through it, and you'll be working in the next dimension.'

Nor was her physical appearance going to help. Her looks had often been described as 'angelic'. That, presumably, referred to her soft blonde hair and soft grey eyes, matched by fair skin and a sweet face. That there was more than a bit of devilry in her make-up did not appear on the surface. Nor did she look a month older than her twenty-eight years. Though her life had been no bed of roses, the sorrows and struggles she had been through had left no mark on her beauty. But there were occasions—and this was one of them—when she would have liked to look a little sterner and older.

She recalled the other thing Jeffrey had said. 'He's based in Hong Kong and does a lot of work all over south-east Asia. He'll have his pick of PAs who can speak the local languages. So you'll have to offer him something special, Amy.'

The jet engines roared deafeningly as the plane came in for landing at Kai Tak Airport. Staring out of the window, Amy saw the rooftops hurtling past, apparently only a hand's breadth beneath the wings. She had heard about this famously low landing approach, but she had never anticipated how stomach-churning it would be in real life!

She had no idea whether a Zell Corporation employee would be waiting to meet her. Perhaps they had given up on her. Her only hope—and it was a very faint one—was to see whether another interview could be arranged at short notice, somewhere else in the world. But it was a given that her failure had put her out of the running, and that Anton Zell had already appointed someone else to the job.

Getting from the plane to the terminal was a long shuffle along various claustrophobic, grey tunnels. It seemed interminable. Restlessly checking her watch, Amy saw that it was by now almost ten o' clock. On top of everything, she had probably also lost her hotel booking in this furiously busy city. She longed for a meal, a quiet room, a shower, and perhaps even an hour or two of sleep.

At last she retrieved her suitcase, which looked a lot more battered than it had done when she'd last seen it in London, and trudged through Customs to the arrivals hall, pushing her trolley ahead of her. As she emerged through the sliding doors she scanned the crowd anxiously, hoping to find a hospitable figure, perhaps holding up a sign with her name on it.

She did not seem to be in luck. A sea of faces stared back at her incuriously. Signs were being held up, but, since they were in Chinese, Arabic, Hindi and languages she did not even recognise, they only confused her.

She came to a standstill, hunting through the jumble for a single welcoming note. Impatient passengers jostled past her. She heard an exasperated comment in Chinese. A heavy trolley rammed painfully into her calves, making her gasp.

'You're blocking the exit.' The deep voice was accompanied by a strong hand which closed around her arm and pulled her inescapably forward. 'Lao Tzu said, "Swim against the current, but do not be a boulder in the stream".'

Amy looked up in bewilderment. The tall man who was hustling her away from the exit was wearing jeans and a dark blue silk shirt. But the lean, tanned face—the most handsome face in the world, according to a recent *Vogue*— was deeply familiar to her.

'Mr Zell?' she said in astonishment.

'Miss Worthington, I presume,' he replied laconically.

'Oh, I'm so sorry to be so late,' she panted, trying to keep up with his pace as he steered her through the crowds. 'My flight was delayed and then—'

'I know all about your flight,' he cut in. 'Take my advice and don't use that particular airline again. Their planes are old and they don't pay their ground crew enough.'

'I didn't expect you to meet me in person!'

'There's nobody *but* me, Worthington,' he retorted.

'I'm sorry?'

'It's Sunday morning,' he said. His strong hand was in the small of her back, pushing her relentlessly onward. 'I expect my staff to work hard six days a week. I don't ask anybody to work on a Sunday.'

'Oh, I'm so sorry,' she babbled. 'I really didn't mean to cause you so much inconvenience—'

'This is where we have to leave your trolley.' With effortless strength, he scooped up her bag and abandoned the trolley in his wake. 'Please don't get your coat caught in the escalator.'

She snatched her trailing coat up hastily as they got onto the escalator. 'Mr Zell, I do apologise for all this—'

He turned to her. His eyes were a deep cobalt blue. Their gaze hit her like a jolt of electricity. 'You have apologised four times now,' he said. 'Don't you think that's enough?'

'Yes, Mr Zell.'

'Then stop.'

'Yes, Mr Zell.'

She studied him covertly as the escalator rumbled upward. He looked formidably fit, broad-shouldered and flat-stomached in his casual silk shirt. And she thought she agreed with *Vogue*—he was probably the handsomest man in the world by a long way. His eyes and mouth were devastatingly sexy. He was in his early forties, and silver had appeared at his temples, but the rest of his hair, neatly cut—but not slicked back in approved zillionaire style—was black as jet.

Nor was there anything about his clothes that suggested he was fabulously wealthy and powerful. His watch was a steel sports model. No diamond glittered at his neat ears and his lean, tanned fingers were bare. The most expensive thing about him seemed to be his phone, a hi-tech titanium wafer into which he was now talking, telling his driver to meet them at the main entrance.

He snapped the phone shut, then turned to meet her eyes. 'Something wrong?'

'I—I understood you were only going to be in Hong Kong for a day. I hope you didn't have to change your plans on my account.'

'I'm planning to fly out to Sarawak this afternoon at two,' he replied. 'I'd like to get this interview over with.'

'Of course.'

'We're going to go to the office to do it.' He raked her with an up-and-down glance. She was suddenly acutely aware of the crumpled state of her clothes; her fawn trousers and jacket had been elegant when she'd set off, a lifetime ago. Now they proclaimed that she'd slept in them, woken in them, writhed in them, squirmed in them, wrestled a bear in them.

God alone knew what her hair looked like.

'I'm sorry, I'm not very smart for an interview!'

'I'll make allowances. Do you insist on changing? Want to go to your hotel?'

'Oh, I'm fine, thank you,' she said quickly. Her heart was pounding hard. She could not believe her luck. She was going to do the interview after all! She was getting a second chance!

'How about breakfast?'

'No, thank you, Mr Zell.'

'You're not hungry?'

'Breakfast is for wimps,' she said bravely.

'Many people consider me a monster,' he said curtly. 'Would you want to work for a monster, Worthington?'

'No, Mr Zell.'

'I am not a monster. If you are hungry or thirsty, please feel free to say so.'

'Well, actually—'

'Come.'

That powerful hand in the small of her back drove her out through the doors into the full, humid heat of a Hong Kong morning. A sleek black limousine nosed through the traffic and headed purposefully towards them. A chauffeur in a green uniform jumped out and hefted Amy's suitcase into the boot. Anton Zell propelled Amy into the interior.

The door thumped shut, cocooning her in a world of opulent luxury. Every surface was upholstered in cream leather and smelled delicious. She sank into her seat, blissfully feeling the air-conditioning starting to soak away the muggy heat.

Opposite her, Anton Zell was talking into his phone again. 'I'm running late, Lavinia,' he said in a clipped voice. 'A small but unavoidable calamity. I'll be in touch as soon as I can.'

The limo oozed out of the parking bay. 'To the office, Mr Zell?' the driver asked over his shoulder.

'Yes, Freddie. Stop at Choy Fat on the way.'

'Yes, sir.' The partition slid shut, sealing them in privacy.

Zell snapped his phone shut. His hands were strong and fine, she noticed. 'So what brings you to Hong Kong?' he demanded of Amy.

'I beg your pardon?'

'Why do you want this job?' His deep blue eyes were

piercing hers. The abrupt questions were unsettling her. She tried not to stare at him like a hypnotised rabbit.

'Is the interview starting now?' she asked.

'It started yesterday at noon,' he retorted. 'Aren't you happy at McCallum and Roe? Do you have some trouble there?'

'No, of course not.'

'"Of course not"? Then why have you flown all the way to Hong Kong to look for another job?'

'Because I'm capable of very much more than McCallum and Roe ask of me,' she replied.

'Does that mean you expect me to pay you very much more than McCallum and Roe pay you?'

'It means that I need a greater challenge in my work,' she rejoined. 'I'm not the sort of person who likes to coast along, doing the minimum. I like to be stretched. I need to feel that I'm always giving of my best. At the end of each week I want to look back and see that I've broken new ground, achieved things of substance—not just kept a chair warm.'

He watched her carefully as she spoke. 'Are you a risk-taker?'

The question flummoxed her for a moment. 'I am not a reckless person,' she replied slowly. 'But I am prepared to take risks when the reward seems worthwhile. And where what is risked is mine, and not someone else's.'

'You enjoy responsibility?'

'Yes,' she said candidly, 'I do.'

'Can you deliver projects on time?'

'Yes,' she said decisively.

'But you couldn't deliver yourself to this interview on time,' he pointed out silkily. 'You've arrived—' he checked his watch '—exactly nineteen hours late. You chose a flight that gave you too little margin for delays, Worthington. You took a risk. But what has been lost is mine, not yours. My time. People who take risks with my time do not last very long in my employment.'

'I understand,' she said in a low voice, stinging from the rebuke.

'Do you know why I need a new PA?'

'I have heard that your old PA had a sudden illness.'

'Marcie developed a heart murmur. She didn't tell me the full truth. She was trying to keep going until I found a replacement, but she collapsed,' he said. 'She only got out of hospital yesterday. Right now, I need someone urgently.'

Amy tried to smile. 'Well, here I am, Mr Zell.'

His answer was a grunt.

They had been driving along a freeway towards the stupendous collection of towers that was Kowloon. The driver now took an exit and entered a road that ran alongside the harbour. The blue water was crowded with boats, from huge cargo vessels to small shabby junks with their characteristic bat-wing sails. The quayside was strewn with piles of crates, coils of ropes, huge mountains of rusty chain and forests of multicoloured barrels. It was an exotic, chaotic world.

The limo pulled up at the kerb opposite a mooring where a large, dun-coloured houseboat was crowded in among smaller craft. On the congested deck, a family had set up a food stall and were serving a group of longshoremen. A smiling boy ran up to the car. Anton Zell slid the window down, letting in a fragrant smell of cooking.

'Boiled or crispy?' he asked Amy.

'I beg your pardon?'

'You wanted breakfast,' he replied patiently. 'In Hong Kong that means noodles. Do you like them slippery or fried?'

'Crispy,' she said determinedly, trying not to notice just how shabby-looking the junk was. It was probably unwise to look surprised at anything Mr Zell came up with, no matter how freakish. He gave the order to the boy, who scampered back to the boat.

'You come highly recommended by Jeffrey Cookson,' Anton Zell went on, studying her with his penetrating gaze. 'But then, he is your uncle.'

'He's been very kind to me,' she replied.

'So it seems. Apparently he brought you up after your parents died.'

'More or less.'

'So we should not be surprised that he thinks the world of you,' he concluded drily. 'But he is not the only one. Your first employers, Charteris Industries, gave you a glowing commendation, too.'

'I'm glad to hear that,' she said stolidly.

'So did McCallum and Roe. But people with glowing commendations are sometimes being hurried from job to job because they're unemployable.'

'That isn't the case with me,' she said.

The boy returned to the limo with two china bowls of noodles and two sets of chopsticks. Amy took the bowl gingerly. It was scaldingly hot. Praying she would not end up with strands of fried noodle hanging off her buttons, Amy dug the chopsticks into the food. It was surprisingly delicious.

'This is wonderful!' she exclaimed.

'These people are Hakka—boat people. They're good cooks. You looked as though you thought I was trying to poison you.'

'I thought it might be part of the stamina test,' she said innocently. 'Make the interviewee eat street food and see if she dies of dysentery.'

'You think you're too good to eat street food?' he asked, lifting one black eyebrow.

'Not at all,' she replied hastily. 'But in my experience

it's unusual for multimillionaires to eat breakfast with ste-
vedores.'

'Nothing in life is free,' he replied calmly. She studied
his face as he ate. All faces, in her experience, no matter
how beautiful, had their weak points, angles from which
they lost their beauty. But not Anton Zell's. No matter what
angle you took, he was perfect. And the photographs had
not even begun to show the vivid life that animated his
expressions. 'But some of the best things are very cheap,'
he went on. 'The food is good here and the view is wonderful.'

She had to agree. The view across the bay to the sky-
scraperscape on the opposite shore was magnificent. 'I'll
remember that.'

'So you have already left McCallum and Roe?'

'I've been with them for four years. I never took any
leave in that time. I had twelve weeks' accumulated leave
built up. I asked if I could take that. It seemed an ideal way
to go job-hunting.'

'Young Martin McCallum has something of a reputation
with female colleagues.'

Amy felt her face flush. She swallowed a mouthful of
crisp fried noodles. 'Yes, that's true.'

'Is that why you're so eager to leave?'

'No, it isn't, Mr Zell. And I resent that implication,' she
added angrily.

His eyelids drooped slightly. 'You're a beautiful woman,
young and single. Are you telling me that Martin McCallum
failed to notice these things?'

'He noticed,' she said shortly. She had had her share of
that particular problem. Female employees who had affairs
with the boss's son and heir were not unknown. 'I have no
problem keeping my private life and my job separate.'

'Did he make a pass at you?'

She was on the point of telling him that was none of his

business; but a glance at those dangerous eyes warned her not to avoid the issue. 'Yes, he did.'

'And how did you deal with it?'

'I told him I wasn't interested.'

'I hear that's not so easy.'

'I managed.'

'What would you do if I made a pass at you?'

She felt her stomach swoop, the way it had done in the plane coming in to land. His eyes were holding hers inexorably and she would have given anything to know the thoughts that lay behind them.

'I would turn you down, too,' she heard herself say.

For a moment there seemed to be a gleam of amusement in his eyes, but the passionate, deeply chiselled mouth did not smile. 'Why?'

'I told you, Mr Zell. Because I know how to keep my private life and my work separate.'

'What if the two were the same?'

'I don't understand.'

'Ever heard the expression "Sleeping your way to the top"?'

'If I thought you were that kind of man,' she said coldly, 'I would not have come all the way to Hong Kong for this job.'

'So what kind of man do you think I am?' he asked.

'I only know what I've heard.'

'And what is that?'

'That you're one of the most dynamic, creative men in your business. That working for you is an unparalleled opportunity to learn and grow. I know nothing about your private life, Mr Zell. That doesn't interest me.'

At last he broke the eye contact and finished off his noodles deftly. 'People on my personal team don't have a private life, Worthington. There isn't time or space for one. As my personal assistant, you'd be at my side for days at a time, weeks at a time, sometimes in very remote places. If you have a family, they will suffer. If you have a boyfriend, he will leave you. You will certainly learn and grow. But you won't have a private life.'

'Not even on Sundays?' she asked bravely.

'What?'

'At the airport you said you didn't expect your employees to work on Sundays.'

'You are not applying to become an employee,' he said. 'A personal assistant is not an *employee*.'

'What is she, then?'

He laughed softly and she saw that his white teeth were like everything about him—beautiful. 'You ought to know. You're applying for the job.'

'Well, I know that I'm to have no private life and no Sundays off. And your previous secretary was driven into the ground by overwork.'

'You're getting the picture. Now, let's see if we can build up a picture of *you*.' He rapped on the partition. 'To the office, Freddie.'

CHAPTER TWO

THE blue glass tower which she had glimpsed from the plane was infinitely more impressive from the ground. No logo was emblazoned on the exterior to proclaim that it was the headquarters of the man beside her, but its unique architecture had made it famous.

Freddie, the chauffeur, drove them down into an underground parking area beneath the building. Apart from uniformed security guards at the booms, the cavernous space was empty.

They got out at the brushed-steel doors of an elevator. Anton Zell entered a code on the key-pad and the doors opened. They went in, Anton carrying her bag. As the elevator whooshed upward, Amy felt her stomach dip for the third time that morning. A sense of unreality came over her. Whatever she had expected from this interview, the last thing she'd anticipated was spending a whole morning with Anton Zell himself!

They went right to the top floor and emerged from the elevator into a plushly carpeted reception area. This level, too, was eerily deserted. The doors to all offices stood open; in some, computer screens glowed and machines hummed, but not a human presence stirred. From this height, the views from the huge windows were astonishing, taking in the sprawling city below and the dazzling blue of the harbour.

Amy had expected he would lead her to his office. However, the room he led her into looked like the sickbay. Glass-fronted cabinets with medical supplies inside, a large double sink and a high steel couch completed the image of a doctor's surgery.

'Why are we here?' she asked.

'Your medical,' he replied succinctly. 'You signed the forms.'

Her jaw dropped. Of course she had signed the forms, agreeing to undergo a medical examination as part of the job interview—it was pretty much standard procedure for a job with this level of confidentiality.

'There's nobody here!'

'Except me. How observant of you.'

'*You're* going to do it?'

'Absolutely,' he said with a glint in his eye that might have been amusement.

'But—but that was supposed to be conducted by a doctor,' she gasped.

'By a Zell Corporation medical officer,' he corrected. 'Glynnis Prior. She's not a doctor, she's a nurse. And right now, our Glynnis is in Singapore, visiting her married daughter there. She was here yesterday—when you were supposed to arrive.'

'You're not qualified to do a medical on me!' she said, her face scarlet.

'I'm not going to give you a kidney transplant,' he said. 'Anyone with first-aid training can conduct the test. And I have plenty of first-aid training. I've done everything that's needed here many times. Of course, you can refuse to take the tests,' he added, watching her from under those formidable, dark eyebrows.

'And what would happen if I did refuse?'

'It would be taken as a sign of bad faith. That you have something to hide. The interview would end immediately and you would not be considered for the job.'

Grimly, she stared back at him. 'You mean—I would just go home?'

'At your earliest convenience.'

She thought furiously. She had not come all this way to back out now. But everything in her rebelled at the thought of letting Anton Zell perform a medical examination on her!

As if reading her thoughts, he picked up the blood-pressure cuff. 'None of it is a big deal, Worthington. Let's start with your blood pressure, shall we?'

Reluctantly, she rolled up her sleeve and sat on the couch. He wrapped the cuff around her arm and secured it. At the first sign of any funny business, she decided, she would walk out of here.

But where would she walk to? She was on the top floor of *his* building, all alone except for a bunch of *his* security guards, and no way back to the airport except in *his* limo, driven by *his* chauffeur.

He was already pumping up the cuff. She felt it bite into her arm. Listening carefully to the stethoscope pressed to her arm, he did not look like any doctor she had ever known.

'Do you speak Chinese?'

It was her weakest point and she tried not to wince. 'No, Mr Zell. I speak French and German and I can get by in Spanish and Italian.'

'Your blood pressure is a little high,' he commented, pulling off the Velcro cuff.

'I've been squashed up behind a family with young children on an airliner for twenty hours,' she retorted. 'And not much has happened since I got off to bring it down again!'

His fingers were biting into the sensitive inside of her wrist. 'And your pulse is rather fast, too.'

'Hardly surprising, either.'

'Any history of heart problems?'

'No,' she said.

'Do you suffer from high blood pressure? Hypertension?'

'No! Everything is usually normal. I'm suffering from the effects of a long flight, Mr Zell, nothing more.'

He noted the readings in a dossier. 'How did your parents die?'

Amy was looking out of the corners of her eyes to try and see how thick the dossier was, and what might be in it. 'My father died first,' she said. 'He had cancer. And no, before you ask, it wasn't a hereditary type. My mother nursed him to the end. But I think the experience shattered her. She was very frail. She died of pneumonia two years later.'

'How old were you?'

'I was eight when my mother died.'

He looked at her intently, but without any appearance of compassion. 'And this is when Uncle Jeffrey stepped in?'

'He was my mother's younger brother. He took me into his house. I grew up with his kids, my cousins.'

'And he put you through school?'

'Yes.'

'And then through college?'

'That's right.'

'Very altruistic of him.'

The suspicion of irony in his tone made her angry. 'Yes, it was, as a matter of fact. He wasn't very pleased to have an extra mouth to feed, but he did what he thought was his duty!'

He was washing his hands in the sink. Now he opened a sterile packet which contained some kind of kit. He pulled on latex gloves and began preparing a squat syringe. 'How did you repay your uncle's kindness?' he asked, watching what he was doing with narrowed eyes.

'I won scholarships all through school. And then all through college, too. What are you doing?'

'I'm going to take a blood sample,' he replied calmly. He probed the tender inside of her elbow with his fingertips and found the vein. 'Have any disabilities?' he asked, swabbing her skin with icy alcohol.

'No. Ouch!'

The needle slipped adroitly into her vein. The body of the syringe filled steadily with blood. She bit her lip. He was very close to her. She could feel the warmth of his skin, could smell a trace of some expensive cologne.

A sudden wave of perilous dizziness washed over her. She swayed, afraid she would fall.

'Am I hurting you?' he asked, steadying her with a strong hand.

'I'm fine.'

'You look pale. Does the sight of blood disturb you?'

'No. What is this blood sample for?'

'Well, it's the full moon, and I need a snack,' he replied. He slipped the needle out of her vein and pressed a pad of cotton wool to the spot. 'Hold that there for a moment, please. It'll be used for drug screening, Worthington. Do you use recreational drugs of any kind? Anything I should know about?'

'No!'

'Cigarettes?'

'No.'

'Alcohol?'

'A glass of wine now and then.'

'What sort of wine do you like?'

'Dry white, mostly.'

'Champagne?'

'Yes, very much.'

'I need you to sign this sample,' he said, giving her a pen. She wrote her name on the package and he put it in the fridge. 'The lab people will pick it up in an hour. Now I need a urine sample.'

'Well, you're not going to get one,' she said firmly.

'You don't have to do it here, you can go next door.'

'And you can go a lot further!'

He frowned. 'You're refusing to give a sample?'

'Yes, Mr Zell,' she said sweetly. 'I'm refusing to give a sample. You can take that as bad faith, good faith, or any kind of faith you choose. You've got my blood and that's as far as it goes.'

He sighed. 'Are you diabetic? Do you suffer from hepatitis?'

'No to both questions.'

'Then I suppose we can skip the urine sample.'

'Thank you.'

'You're very squeamish,' he said, writing in the dossier. 'If you're lucky—or unlucky—enough to land this job, you'll look back on this moment with a bitter laugh.'

'Thanks, I'll remember that.'

'OK,' he said, shutting the folder, 'we can continue the rest of this in my office. Let me put a plaster on that arm.'

He planted a small sticking plaster on the little red dot on her arm where his needle had gone in and led her down the corridor.

His headquarters were a corner office with magnificent views. Placed around the office were several scale models of recent Zell projects—complex masses of piping and tanks that made up the specialised oil refineries that he had pioneered and made his fortune out of. She recognised several of them—they were dotted all over the world, many here in south-east Asia.

Directing Amy to a chair, he opened an icebox and took out a champagne bottle and two frosted glasses. 'Is this what, in your experience, multimillionaires have for breakfast?' he asked.

'I suppose it's more traditional,' she said cautiously. 'Are we celebrating already?'

'No. But you look as though you could do with a drink. And you did say you loved champagne.' He poured the foaming Roederer into her glass. 'I thought you were going to pass out back there.'

'I did feel a momentary qualm,' she said. 'It was a long flight. A glass of Cristal might help, at that.'

'I need to ask you a few more questions,' he said, clinking his glass against hers.

'Of course.'

'Have you ever been arrested?'

She almost choked on her champagne. 'No.'

'Ever been convicted of any crimes or felonies?'

'No.'

'Can you tell me what the Laminate Plate System is?'

This time she did not stumble. 'LPS is a steel-elastomer-steel composite that Zell Corporation developed for building storage tanks. It's stronger and lighter than conventional steel. It's also much tougher, and that has obvious implications for marine construction. You've just leased the patent to a Korean shipbuilding company. If the system works out it may eventually earn you even more than you're currently making in the petrochemical industry.'

He was standing by the window, watching her over his glass of champagne. The morning light revealed the perfection of his figure—long, muscular legs, taut waist and powerful shoulders, supporting a neck and head that would have graced a Greek god. He seemed to smile slightly.

'You say the words "petrochemical industry" as though you really are fascinated by it.'

'I am,' she said. She indicated the scale models of refineries that stood around the office. 'I'm fascinated by complex engineering projects like these, Mr Zell. I like everything about your work. I especially like the environmental dimension you've started adding to everything you do. I like the care you take not to contaminate the ecologies where your refineries are located. I like the fact that you've used your brilliance to develop systems to refine used oil. Even your Laminate Plate System could have a beneficial impact on the environment. If it's used for the hulls of supertankers, oil spills from holes in the hull could become a thing of the past.'

'Commendably ecological sentiments,' he commented. He did not appear to have been flattered by her words; indeed, she had not been attempting to flatter him, only to express her genuine feelings.

'Yes, ecology matters to me,' she said. 'I want to hand something down to my children.'

'How many children do you have?' he asked blandly.

'None! It was a figure of speech.'

'Have you ever been married?'

'Never.'

'Do you have a current boyfriend?'

'I don't think that's relevant!'

'It's very relevant. I warned you, Worthington, your work schedule is not going to allow much in the way of a love-life over the next months. If you're in the throes of a great romance, planning a family some time soon, anything like that, then this is not the job for you.'

'I have nobody,' she said in a quiet voice. 'I'm not planning a family and there is no great romance in my life. I am happy to put the Zell Corporation first and foremost. Mr Zell, I may look young and flighty to you, but I can promise you that you won't find anyone more prepared to throw herself into this job than I am. I'm prepared to eat, drink and breathe Zell Corporation business from now on.'

He considered her from under brooding lids. 'You're starting to frighten me,' he said drily.

'I frighten myself sometimes,' she agreed. 'Would you like to hear about the greater vibration damping and improved thermal insulation offered by your new copolymer pipe linings? Or about how your unique solvent extraction system eliminates the need for thin-film evaporators as well as the costly hydrotreating step that makes your competitors' systems so expensive?'

'No, thank you.'

'Then perhaps I can tell you about the remarkable success Zell Corporation has had in the Marseilles plant, removing water, additives and contaminants at ambient conditions, so that the resulting oil can be handled with traditional distillation equipment?'

'All right, you've shown that you've done your homework and have a retentive memory.'

'I have an IQ in triple figures, too,' she said helpfully.

'I don't mean to patronise you,' he replied. 'Since Marcie's illness, I have been in desperate need of a new assistant. Look at this.' He tossed something into her lap. She picked it up. It was his slim titanium phone.

'Your cell-phone?'

'Satellite phone, Worthington. It works anywhere. I switched it to silent at the airport. Take a look at the screen.'

She obeyed and saw the blinking announcement: 37 missed calls, 44 new messages.

'I see your problem,' she said.

'Good. Do you want to start dealing with those?'

'Me? Now?'

'We don't have a lot of time. We're flying to Borneo at two.'

'"We"?'

'You and I. Us. We have a plant to inspect.'

'Does this mean I'm hired?' she said breathlessly.

'Unless your blood test shows you're a dope fiend or pregnant.'

'But I—I wouldn't know where to start!'

'For now, all I need you to do is answer that phone. Work out who is urgent and tell all the others I'm not available.' He indicated the huge teak desk in the corner of the office. 'That used to be Marcie's. When we get back to Hong Kong you'll start working out her systems. She won't be coming back to the office, but the secretaries will help you.'

'Mr Zell, I didn't expect to be starting work right now! I was planning to fly back to London tomorrow. If I'm really hired, I have things to arrange.'

'You've messed with my schedule. I think that gives me the right to mess with yours. I need you in Borneo this afternoon. When we get back, I'll make sure you have time to return to London and organise your life.'

'But I only packed clothing for three days!'

'What you're mainly going to need in Borneo,' he said succinctly, 'is a raincoat. It's the monsoon season.'

CHAPTER THREE

HUDDLED under the raincoat she had bought at Hong Kong Airport, Amy was still answering calls as they toured the Bandak refinery. It was late afternoon, but the wild weather made it almost as dark as night.

It was a panorama of rain in all its most turbulent manifestations—slashing down in curtains and beating on the buildings, driven up, down and sideways by the wind, pouring from the refinery's vast but as yet half-finished system of pipes in waterfalls, ploughing muddy torrents in the red dirt. Beyond the construction site, the jungle trees flailed wildly. Palm fronds and branches had broken off, and littered the earth.

The flight from Hong Kong, though made in Anton's private jet, had been rough, with lightning and high winds to contend with. The landing, at an airstrip near the construction site, had been hair-raising. On the ground, the rain, driven by gusts that were alternately warm and cool, was like nothing she had seen before. For the first time, she understood what the word *monsoon* meant. That sense of unreality washed over her again. She had not dreamed, as she flew into Hong Kong that morning, that by nightfall she would be in Borneo, Anton Zell's newest and rawest employee!

'We're ahead of schedule, despite the monsoon,' the site manager was telling Anton. She was listening to the conversation with one ear whilst taking a call with the other. They were standing with the engineers in the shelter of a cabin. The rain was pounding on the roof, a ferocious as-

sault on all the senses. 'The first phase will come into production two months early.'

'Have the seals been tested?'

'They all hold up. The new system looks good.'

'What level of production are we looking at for phase
one?'

'We've got the preliminary calculations here,' the man
said, holding out a folder. 'We should be refining two thousand tons a month by next May.'

'Give those to my PA,' Anton commanded.

Amy accepted the folder from the site manager with a
smile, never interrupting her conversation. She was already
carrying a great wedge of information. And the woman to
whom she was talking on the satellite phone was determined
to speak to Anton, even though he had given her strict instructions that he was incommunicado.

'I'm so sorry,' she murmured, 'but Mr Zell is in a meeting
and I cannot disturb him.'

'I can hear his voice, damn it,' the sharp, aristocratic
voice snapped. She had identified herself as Lady Carron,
and Amy was getting a vision of someone at the other end
twirling an ebony cigarette-holder a foot long. 'Where is
he? Propping up some bar, surrounded by floozies?'

'He's touring a refinery,' she replied evenly, 'and he's
surrounded by engineers.'

'Who the hell are you, anyway? You're not Marcie.'

'That's correct. My name is Amy Worthington and I'm
Marcie's replacement.'

'Well, what the hell has happened to Marcie?'

'Mr Zell worked her to death, Lady Carron. Can I take a
message?'

'Yes, you damn well can. Tell Anton I will be waiting
for his call.' The line clicked, but Amy was already taking
the next call.

Anton came up to her and took her arm. 'We're just about

done here. The pilot says the weather is getting worse. I don't think it would be wise to try flying back to Hong Kong tonight.'

'I would rather be torn to pieces by piranhas.'

'Piranhas are South American, Worthington. We'll spend the night in a hotel in Kuching.'

'A Lady Carron keeps calling. She's expecting you to call back.'

'One of the more troublesome shareholders. We had our annual general meeting a couple of weeks back and she raised merry hell. She can wait. Let's get back to the Jeep.'

The road into Kuching was not so much a road as a shallow river. The Jeep made heavy progress, lurching in the thick mud. She relayed the other messages she had taken on his behalf. He seemed to listen with half his attention. Amy could see that his mind was still focused on the refinery with laser-like intensity, making calculations, projections, estimates.

They reached Kuching, a sprawling, picturesque town on the Sarawak River. Despite the monsoon, life was going on, and the streets were crowded. Everybody simply accepted the downpour.

The Jeep made its way through the evening traffic to the hotel, which was on the riverfront. It was a charming old place, full of old-world colonial glamour.

The room she was given had a balcony overlooking the river. She undressed, finding all her clothes, despite the raincoat, soaked through. She had a change of clothes in her bag—the outfit she had planned to wear for the interview. It was going to have to do.

The shower was modern and the water hot. She let it soak away the tiredness of the day. There had never been one like it in her life before. She had fixed on Anton Zell, the business genius, as a means to escape from England. But Anton Zell, the man, had entered her life like the monsoon itself, lifting her off her feet and blowing her thousands of miles off course. She wondered when—if ever—her feet were going to touch ground again.

She smoothed a cooling skin lotion all over herself, trying to convince herself that none of this was a wild dream. With a towel wrapped round her hair and another plastered round her torso, she emerged from the bathroom.

She stopped dead when she saw that Anton Zell was sitting on her bed, reading through the folders that the Bandak site manager had given them.

'Mr Zell!'

'Anton,' he said, not looking up. 'Nobody calls me Mr Zell. Is your first name really Amelia?'

'Amy.' She was acutely aware of how much of her nakedness was showing below and above the towel. 'And I'm not dressed yet.'

He glanced up and considered her with smouldering blue eyes. 'I've managed to shower and change and read twenty pages while you've been in there.'

'You're a man,' she said pointedly.

'A hungry man.' He was studying her legs unashamedly. 'I've booked a table at the restaurant.'

'I need to dress!'

He rose. Deliberately or otherwise, he brushed past her on his way out. 'You smell like a rainforest orchid. Perfumed and humid. Don't take all night, Amelia Worthington. I'll wait for you in the lobby.'

The dining-room was enchanting, a vast, high-vaulted room whose moulded ceiling was supported by ornate columns. It looked as though it had barely changed since the last century, with lovely old teak furniture and an eclectic collection of sofas and rattan chairs scattered around. The doors were open onto the garden to let in the breeze, though bamboo blinds had been lowered to keep out the worst of the monsoon rain. The tables were lit by candles. By their glowing light, the Iban masks and sculptures which hung on the walls seemed to take on a flickering life.

'None of those things are real shrunken heads, are they?' she asked Anton as they perused the menu.

He snorted. 'Go to the bottom of the class, Worthington. Shrunken heads are South American, like piranhas. The Iban take heads but they don't shrink them. Shrinking heads involves taking out the brain and—'

She interrupted hastily. 'All I want to know is, are they human?'

'I don't know. Some of them look familiar. That one is very like a personal assistant of mine who vanished a couple of years ago.'

'You enjoy tormenting me, don't you?'

'Yes,' he said frankly. 'There has been no head-hunting in Borneo for over half a century. That pretty cranium of yours is perfectly safe. I can recommend the curried fish. The mackerel is fresh and it's quite delicious.'

'All right,' she conceded. She was really too baffled by the strange words in the menu to make up her own mind. 'I love this hotel.'

'Good. I've stayed at the Hilton and the other smart hotels up-town, but this place is my favourite.'

'I hope I'm not letting you down. These clothes were meant for the interview, not going out.'

'Business, not pleasure?' He looked at her with smoky eyes. She was wearing the grey suit she had chosen for the interview, elegant, professional and formal. The feminine touch was supplied by the pearls that glowed against her pale skin. 'Who bought you those exquisite pearls?'

'They were my mother's,' she said, pleased that he had noticed. 'Aren't they pretty?'

'They're perfect for your wonderful complexion. Pearls and an English rose.'

She smiled. If he enjoyed teasing her, she enjoyed being

teased. It was a long time since she had felt this light-hearted. The rain was still pouring outside. Above them a fan rotated slowly, keeping the air cool. A waiter clad in snowy white except for his mustard-coloured turban took their order and then brought them the drinks they'd ordered.

'So,' Anton said, watching her with amusement in his eyes, 'whose idea was it to call you Amelia?'

'What's wrong with the name?'

'It's painfully Victorian. Amelia Worthington sounds like a virtuous orphan in Charles Dickens.'

'Well, I am an orphan,' she said lightly, 'though I don't know about virtuous.'

His expression changed. 'I forgot. I didn't mean to offend you.'

'No offence was taken. It happens to be an old family name. It was my great-grandmother's.'

'Oh, indeed.'

'Indeed.' She sipped her cocktail. He was such a handsome man that just watching him filled her stomach with warm butterflies. It might be a lot harder than she had anticipated to be in close proximity with the best-looking man in the world, according to *Vogue*. 'In any case, you are an orphan too, aren't you?'

'Aha. Still showing me how well you did your homework?'

'I'm just repeating what's written about you.'

His eyes were watching her mouth. 'Did you really tell Lavinia that I worked Marcie to death?'

'Lavinia?'

'Lavinia Hyde-White. Lady Carron.'

'Oh, the person who keeps calling? The one you described me to this morning as "a small but unavoidable calamity"?'

His devastating mouth quirked. 'Did I say that?'

'Yes, Mr Zell. And if you find Victorian names ridiculous, how about Lavinia Hyde-White?'

'Well, like yours, it's apparently an ancient family name.'

'Do you call her "Lavvy" for short?' she asked sweetly. 'Or perhaps just "Lav"?'

'It's always Lavinia.'

'I'm surprised you can keep a straight face at board meetings.'

'I invariably keep a straight face with rich and beautiful women.'

'Is that why you're laughing at me?' she retorted. 'Because I'm a poor, plain orphan?'

'You're not plain, Worthington,' he said, the expression in his eyes making her heart turn over. 'You have the face of...' He paused.

'Please don't say an angel. That would be so unoriginal.'

'Well, coming out of that bathroom in a skimpy towel, you looked like a very young angel who had been playing with an imp, and who'd had to have the brimstone scrubbed off her by the archangels.'

The cocktail had gone to her head and she couldn't help laughing. 'I know where the brimstone came from.'

'You have a lovely laugh,' he said. 'Original or drama school?'

'Don't be so cynical,' she retorted.

Their food arrived. As he'd promised, the curried fish was delicious, flavoured with coconut and ginger and other spices she'd never tasted before.

'I'm not an orphan in the sense that you are,' he said without preamble. 'I never knew my parents, so I did not have the experience of losing them, as you did. What you went through was much more traumatic.'

'It can't have been easy growing up in a series of foster homes,' she said.

He shrugged his broad shoulders. 'Most were good. A

few were very bad. I grew up in a lot of different environments and that made me the person I am. But going to live in someone else's house when you are young, with someone else's children, teaches you many things about life.'

'Yes, it does,' she said soberly.

'I guess that is something we have in common. Maybe your head won't end up on a spike after all. How's your fish?'

'It's wonderful, thank you. I'm glad I took your recommendation.'

'You'll need to be a good traveller in this job,' he said. 'Go any place, sleep anywhere, eat anything.'

'Anton,' she said, using his Christian name for the first time, 'I need to know something. Are you really giving me this job? Or did you just grab me because I was available, and can I expect to be dropped just as quickly when you're in a more serious mood?'

'Let's say that, like any job, there's a probationary period. If you measure up, you stay. If not, then you might be glad to leave anyway.'

'So I could be fired tomorrow? Well, at least there is a way out of your employment other than serious illness.'

'There's also death. Being fired is definitely worse than either of the other two.'

She toyed with her food, her small appetite already satiated by the spicy dish. 'And how will I know whether I'm measuring up?'

'You're asking me for a job description? Now, in the middle of Borneo?'

'Yes.'

He considered her carefully. 'Let me ask you, first. What do you think the principal part of your job is?'

She smiled. 'So far, it's been talking into that little titanium phone. You could replace me with an answering machine.'

'Let me explain some things about my working life. I don't spend much time in the office. Not any more. There was a phase of my life when I spent every waking hour at a computer or in a lab, designing systems to do the things I dreamed of. Now, I pay teams of people much cleverer than I am to do my research for me. I just come up with ideas. New ideas. As you know, this company is on the edge of a major new development based on technology I've been able to develop. But I am compelled to travel between my various projects. If they're being built, like the one we saw today, I make sure they're being built properly. If they're already running, like the one in Singapore that we're going to in five days' time, I make sure they're running properly. That's why I just warned you that you need to be a good traveller. You're never going to be home.'

'Nor are you,' she pointed out.

'Nor am I,' he agreed. 'I'm not married. I've always known that I could never inflict this kind of life on a wife. Not until I'm ready to settle down.'

'And when will that be?' she asked daringly.

'When I meet the right woman,' he said flatly. 'Until then, I'm married to my work. I have no space or time for women—the sort of women who want a commitment from a man. But no man is an island. Which is why I need a PA. And that brings me to the answer to the question I asked you a moment ago. The chief quality I look for in my personal assistants is companionship. Compatibility. Being able to amuse me and get along with me for long stretches of proximity. It's a very special kind of relationship. I hope you understand what I'm talking about.'

She drew back as though she had been burned and stared at him, feeling the food in her stomach start to curdle. 'Let me guess that Marcie was not grey-haired and seventy-ish?'

His languorous eyes widened at the change in her tone.

'What's the matter? You look as though you've seen a ghost—with a shrunken head.'

'Perhaps the curry disagreed with me,' she said shortly.

'I hope not. No, Marcie is not grey-haired and seventy-ish. She's in her thirties, tall and very elegant. In fact, she used to be a fashion model.'

'Lucky you.'

'I beg your pardon?'

'Unusual for a woman in her thirties to have heart problems.'

He was watching her pale face curiously. 'Yes,' he said curtly, 'very sad. It was a great shock.'

'Perhaps there were other complications,' she said, folding her napkin.

'What do you mean?'

Amy pushed back her chair. 'I'm really tired, Mr Zell. It's been a long day.'

He looked irritated, but did not argue. 'If you insist. I suppose we should hit the hay. Let's go upstairs.' He rose from the table with her. They walked out of the dining-room. The Iban masks on the walls seemed to be leering at her mockingly as she left.

On the landing outside her room, exhaustion washed over her. The blood seemed to drain from her heart and she staggered. Anton caught her arm to support her.

'What's wrong with you?' he asked suspiciously.

'It's been a long day,' she said with an effort. 'I just need sleep.'

He reached out and hooked one finger around the string of pearls that hung at her throat. His eyes were locked on hers. He drew her face to his. At the last moment, she closed her eyes involuntarily.

She felt his warm lips touch hers, a contact so sweet, so intimate, so achingly familiar.

So dangerous.

She looked up into his eyes. They were dark and intent. He took the key from her nerveless fingers and opened her door.

'Goodnight,' he said. 'Mind the head-hunters don't bite.'

She shut the door and locked it as though the devil himself were on the other side.

Amy was awakened very early the next morning by thunder.

She opened her eyes slowly, remembering where she was. Up in the vaulted ceiling, a fan chopped at the air languidly. She took in the elegant room lit by a rainy dawn. Yesterday was like a dream to her. It was hard to believe it had all happened. Yet there was a heavy stone in her chest that told her that her heart remembered, even if her mind didn't.

Her lips felt swollen, as though that momentary kiss had seared her mouth, leaving the tender skin burned.

Fragments of yesterday echoed in her mind. *Ever heard the expression 'Sleeping your way to the top'?* That was what he had asked her at the harbour in Hong Kong. *It's a very special kind of relationship. I hope you understand what I'm talking about.*

Oh, yes.

She knew exactly what he was talking about. He had made it very clear. A wealthy man with no wife, married to his work, always on the move. No space or time for women—*the sort of women who want a commitment from a man.* But no man was an island, he had said. That was plain enough.

Thunder muttered overhead. Amy rose and went out onto the balcony, wrapping the sarong around herself that the hotel had provided.

Young Martin McCallum has something of a reputation with female colleagues. When Anton had said that yesterday, her heart had nearly stopped; why hadn't she seen that as the glaring clue it was? Had he heard? Did he know what had happened to her at McCallum and Roe? Was that why he'd thrown the job at her so casually—because he needed someone in Borneo, and knew that she had a *reputation*, too?

The grey-green river swept in a curve past the hotel. Already, though it was just after dawn, the river traffic was building up, sampans and barges drifting through the sheets of rain. She stared at the boats unseeingly. She had wanted so desperately to be out of England; well, here she was, about as far from London as you could get in every way.

Lightning glared, and thunder crashed overhead. Had she really been so dim-witted as to leap from the frying-pan into the fire? How could she be so *stupid*? What had been the point of travelling thousands of miles, just to meet another Martin McCallum? Hadn't she learned her lesson? Hadn't she been through enough pain yet?

In London she had felt that everyone was staring at her, that everyone *knew*. Knew how foolish she had been. Knew that she had been naïve enough to allow herself to be seduced by the most notorious womaniser in the City. Knew that she had allowed herself to be blinded by his promises and dazzled by his charm.

That she hadn't even noticed when they'd all been laughing at her, as she walked around with starry eyes.

That she hadn't taken, hadn't even *understood*, the warnings.

That she'd been so impossibly stupid that, when she'd learned she was pregnant, she'd expected Martin McCallum to be as delighted as she was.

Her eyes blurred with tears as she remembered that terrible day, Martin's mockery turning to fury as he heard her stammering declaration that she wanted to have the baby, wanted the child that had been conceived, so she still thought, out of their love. Martin shouting at her, asking her just how stupid she was. Martin telling her there had been no love, only sex. Martin screaming at her to do something fast.

Do something, you little fool. I'll pay.

Do what, Martin?

What do you think, for heaven's sake? Open your eyes! Get rid of it. Or I warn you, you're on your own. I'll get my father to sack you and you can see how you like being an unemployed single mother!

Amy huddled into her sarong. She had certainly opened her eyes that day. Her illusions had evaporated like wraiths.

And with them had also gone her heart and her soul. Her happiness, her self-respect, her sense of wholeness, her feeling that life was good and that she was good and that her happy future was unfolding.

And that, of course, was why she had found herself here in Borneo, standing alone on a balcony, looking at the dark green jungle. Like a creature on the very edge of civilisation, not sure whether it belonged to the light or to the darkness.

It had taken her so long to recover from the psychological effects and start to believe in herself again. She'd fixed so much hope on Anton Zell. Zell, the genius, the billionaire who cared, the oil-industry captain who protected the environment, the decent human being, the beacon of hope.

If he turned out to be another abuser, who thought a fat salary paid for her body in his bed, then the world was indeed a bleak place.

She could hear tapping at her door. She wiped the tears from her face and went to answer it.

It was Anton. He was already dressed. She had forgotten how handsome he was; his deep blue eyes jolted her.

'I'm glad you're up. We need to make an early start.'

'OK.'

'Make me a cup of coffee, Worthington. The kettle in my room is broken.'

'Of course.' She let him in and fumbled with the coffee things.

'Have you been crying?' he asked.

'It's just rain,' she said, her back to him. 'I've been standing on the balcony. The view is really something. I didn't see it last night, it was dark and—'

He touched her sarong. 'You're soaked! What were you thinking of?' His strong hands closed around her shoulders and drew her round to face him. He looked down into her face. 'Amy, what is wrong with you? Are you ill?'

'I'm fine,' she said. She tried to sound brave, but she was trembling in his grip.

'Is there something you want to tell me?' he asked quietly. 'Something I should know?'

She managed to laugh. 'Oh, no. I think I got a tummy bug yesterday and I didn't sleep very well, that's all. It's over now. Do I look that bad?'

He seemed unsatisfied with her prevarication. 'Don't hide things from me, Worthington. Don't even try. I assure you that I will find out every single thing about you in the end. So if there's something to say, say it now.'

'There's n-nothing!' she stammered.

'What happened last night? One minute we were having fun, the next you were running for cover. What went wrong? Was it something I said?'

Amy took a deep breath. Just looking into that face made her heart pound like a trip hammer. He was a very suspicious man—and a frighteningly perceptive one. She tried hard to give him a more genuine smile. 'No. It was just the bug. Sometimes these things require a fast exit.'

He nodded. 'All right, if you say so. At least you look more like yourself again. Bright-eyed and bushy-tailed.'

'I don't have a tail.'

'You have bright eyes. Usually. They're a lovely shade of grey, but sometimes they go absolutely black.'

'Do they?' she said with a breathless laugh.

'Yes. Then you stop looking like an angel and start looking like a creature from the other place. Still beautiful—but darkly beautiful, not brightly beautiful.'

'Let me make your coffee,' she said, breaking away from the moment in panic. She fussed with the spoons busily. Her heart had lifted for a moment but now it was hard and heavy again. The sense of nightmare was back. Someone else had said things like that to her. Things that made her spirits soar and joy rise in her.

Someone called Martin McCallum.

CHAPTER FOUR

THE job had been offered with 'accommodation in Hong Kong', but that had hardly described the Causeway Bay flat Anton had installed her in.

A fully serviced apartment, decorated in the height of style, equipped with the latest sound and viewing systems, with wonderful views of the bay, close to the most glamorous shopping and possessing—luxury of luxuries in crowded Hong Kong—its own private balcony, it was the most beautiful 'accommodation' Amy had ever been in. Judging by her boss's laid-back style, she doubted whether Anton Zell himself lived in anything more thrilling.

You couldn't even accuse the apartment of being soulless, like most corporate accommodation, because the gleaming Oriental antiques with which it had been furnished exhaled the very mystery of ancient China.

The only problem was that she'd had so little chance to spend time here that, after three whole months, she still didn't know how everything worked.

Taking the initial decision to accept the job had been hard. She'd felt as though she were between the devil and the deep blue sea. The memory of that kiss had almost kept her in London. To tell the truth, it had been a chance meeting with a former colleague from McCallum and Roe that had decided her. The look in his eyes, knowing and somehow smirking, had reminded her that there was nothing left for her in London.

Whereas here in Hong Kong…

She threw the glass doors open and walked out onto her balcony with a glass of freshly squeezed orange juice. The bay was as blue as a sapphire, as blue as Anton Zell's eyes. In the typhoon harbour below her apartment, the luxury yachts of the very rich swayed gracefully alongside the picturesque junks of the boat people, where barefoot children scampered and women hunkered down beside kerosene stoves on the deck.

The great forest of glass towers was backed by a mountainscape of brilliant white cloud, building up into a cobalt sky. It was Sunday morning and she wasn't due back at the office till eight o'clock Monday morning. In the past three months she had worked right through every weekend. That had included almost a whole fraught month in Singapore to visit a refinery which was not meeting production targets due to various system malfunctions.

Solving the problems had taken a sustained effort. She had never seen anyone work as hard, or with such concentration, as Anton had during that month. If there were any doubts in her mind as to exactly how he had become so successful, they had been removed forever in Singapore. He was able to concentrate his mind like a laser, cutting relentlessly through problems until a solution was found.

She had been at his side constantly, relaying instructions, taking calls, scheduling his appointments. But whether she had offered him the companionship, that *special relationship* that he had spoken of, she could not tell; every waking hour had been spent in work and neither of them had had much energy to do anything than grab a bite of food and go to sleep in their hotel when the day was over.

There had been no repetition of that kiss in Borneo, though it continued to haunt her memory like the touch of a jungle flower. What was the phrase he had used? A rainforest orchid, perfumed and humid. That was how the touch of his lips on hers stayed in her mind, something exotic and definitely dangerous.

She shook the thought away. Remembering the way he

had kissed her in Borneo brought back other things, things that darkened her day.

Such as the details she had learned about Marcie, her predecessor, from Glynnis Prior, the pleasant, middle-aged medical officer who had been so happy to talk to her when she'd gone into the sickbay for a plaster to put on a cut finger.

And it was a Sunday and she had leisure to explore this wonderful new world she was in. She did not want to think about Anton Zell and his dark mysteries. The trouble was, she hardly knew where to begin. She drank her juice, watching the sails drift across the busy harbour.

The door buzzer sounded. Wondering who it could be— the building had a strict policy of keeping out hawkers— she went to the entryphone. The figure on the closed-circuit television screen was awfully familiar.

'Anton?' she said, snatching up the phone.

He was standing with his hands in his jacket pockets. 'Are you going to keep me waiting on the street?'

'I'm trying to let you in!' She was frantically hunting for the right button to open the door. She'd never had to let anyone in before! It had to be this one with the red key on it. She pressed it and was relieved to see Anton's impatient figure disappear from the screen.

She ran to the bathroom, her heart beating fast, to try and make herself presentable for this unexpected call. She just had time to brush her hair into shape when the doorbell chimed. Slightly breathless with her haste, she opened it.

Anton walked in. Her efforts to beautify herself were wasted; he hardly spared a glance on her, but looked around the apartment with piercing eyes. 'Damn, I'd forgotten how nice these apartments are.'

'It's beautiful. I'm very happy here.'

'You ought to be,' he said drily. 'You live better than I do. I have a bachelor flat in Wanchai.' He shrugged. 'Oh,

well, I can get to work in fifteen minutes. So—are you settling in?'

'I've hardly had a chance to find my feet,' she said with
a smile. 'The driver picks me up every morning, but I still
haven't really seen anything of Hong Kong!'

'That's why I dropped by,' he said. 'I need to do some
things around town. You could tag along and get an eclectic
guided tour.'

'You mean—come with you?' she asked hesitantly.

He gave her a dangerously lifted eyebrow. 'Since we've
spent the last three months in each other's pockets, I guess
the prospect of yet another day in my company is hardly
appealing?'

'No, it's not that!'

'If I promise not to mention light end stripping, surge
vessels or vacuum distillation, would that help?'

She smiled. 'Actually, I find engineering details fascinating.'

'I see. It's just me you find repulsive?'

Amy gave in. 'I'll get a raincoat.'

'Ah. You're turning into an old China hand.'

The flimsy raincoat, which could be squeezed into a
pocket, went with her everywhere; she had learned early
about the vagaries of Hong Kong weather, no matter how
brightly the sun shone. It was April, a lovely month in Hong
Kong, but that did not rule out rain.

There was no limo today; Anton's car, a sleek black two-
seater, was parked outside.

'Wow,' she said admiringly, 'nice wheels!'

'Well, get in.' He opened the door for her. His hand in
the small of her back propelled her in. She had never quite
got used to that strong hand which gave her those unantic-
ipated shoves in the right direction.

'Fast and furious, but no room for baggage,' she said,
settling into the bucket seat. 'Like her owner.'

He switched on the engine with a throaty rumble and set off. The top was down and it was fun to feel the wind blowing her hair. She settled back, feeling absurdly excited.

'Why did you say that?' he asked after a silence.

She glanced at him. 'What?'

'That I had no room for baggage.'

'Oh, I'm sorry, I didn't mean to be cheeky.' His expression was serious and she was afraid she had offended him. 'It wasn't meant to be a negative comment. Just that—'

'That?'

'Well, it's your style. No prisoners, no passengers and no Sundays off. It's a nice way to live if you have nobody else to consider.'

'And nobody else to consider you.'

'Anton, you are the centre of a whole universe of people who think the sun rises and sets with you. Of course people consider you. They rejoice in your smile and tremble at your frown.'

'More the latter than the former, I think.'

'You should smile more often.'

'I'm smiling now,' he said, baring his teeth like a tiger.

'And I'm rejoicing,' she said. 'Look.' She grimaced back.

'I *am* human,' he said. 'I'll even treat you to breakfast.'

'As long as it isn't noodles. I've tried every combination of noodle for breakfast since I've been here, and I still crave a plain old English fry-up.'

'That can be arranged,' he said. 'I even know where to get English bacon and eggs in this town. I know every restaurant in Hong Kong. I eat out three times a day. What I never do is sit down at my own table to eat a meal made in my own kitchen.'

'Stop, you're breaking my heart,' she said. 'I know how you dream of a wife in curlers, frying you liver and onions, while your three kids tug at your sleeve yelling, "Daddy, Daddy"!'

'Hmm, that does sound awful.'

'Oh, please. With your two-seater sports car and your bachelor apartment? Working till midnight then slurping noodles and whisky in some Wanchai strip club? Everything about you screams "single and loving it".'

'And you?'

'What about me?' she laughed.

'You're working for the single-and-loving-it guy. When you came to me for the interview, you told me there was nobody more prepared to throw herself into the job than you. You said you wanted to eat, drink and breathe Zell Corporation business from now on.'

'Yes, I did. And I am.'

'So what's the difference between you and me?'

'Maybe none, at that. Except I don't complain about it. I'm an obsessive-compulsive loner and happy with it.'

Anton grinned. 'You're only half joking, aren't you?'

'I just think neither of us is ever going to be sitting at that homey table with the three kids and the fried liver and onions. So it's pointless to dream about it.'

'It's never pointless to dream.'

The conversation was quickly getting painful for her, so she changed the subject. 'Where are we going, anyway?'

'Battery Street. I thought you might like to see the jade market.'

'Jewellery? Oh, yummy. Now you're talking.'

'Jade is more than just jewellery, Worthington,' he warned. 'Jade is a way of life. It's the stone of heaven. It's a medicine, a religion, an art form. You rub it for health and worship it for its beauty and take it into the next world. You can even eat it if you want to live for ever.'

'No, thanks. Four score years and ten contain trouble enough. Anything else I should know?'

'Well, many kinds of stone go under the name of jade, and it can be green, white, lavender, red, yellow or even black. But the two most important stones are nephrite and jadeite. Nephrite is by far the most common. Jadeite is harder and more valuable.'

'Which should I buy?'

'Buy whatever speaks to your heart.'

'Am I going to be robbed?'

'Depends if you follow my advice.'

The market, at the corner of Kansu and Battery Street, was crowded and busy. As they strolled, Amy watched, fascinated, as small groups of men, some of them ancient enough to sport long white Confucian beards, haggled over paper packets of the green stone.

The covered part of the market was crammed full of booths and stalls. As Anton had predicted, a bewildering assortment of goods was on offer. There were man-sized boulders of raw green jade; boxes of tiny beads and blobs; carved animals both great and small, realistic and mythical. There was jade of every colour imaginable, from deepest black to snow-white, taking in the hues of the rainbow between.

Threading their way through the crowds, they were assailed by tradesmen offering them jade of every description, extolling the quality, calling on them to admire the colour, holding pieces aloft to demonstrate the transparency. Much of it was astonishingly beautiful to Amy's eyes.

One shop in particular caught her fancy. The owner had arranged a multitude of small carved animals on shelves. Looking closely, she marvelled at the dragons and lions.

'These are beautiful!' she called to Anton. 'And they look really old!'

He joined her, looking at the collection with a critical eye. 'Some of them are genuine,' he said. 'Anything that's claimed to be over a hundred and fifty years old is likely to be a reproduction. But these late Qing Dynasty ones are authentic. They date from the nineteenth century. See how polished they are? They've been lovingly cherished over generations.'

'I adore this piglet,' she said, picking up the fat little creature and admiring its chubby cheeks and pop eyes.

The shopkeeper came forward. 'Beautiful piece,' he enthused. 'Five hundred dollars.'

Amy blenched at the price. 'Too much for me,' she said, putting it hastily back.

'Wrong animal, in any case,' Anton said. 'These animals correspond with the Chinese astrological zodiac. You, unfortunately, were not born a pig.'

'What am I, then?' she demanded.

'It gives me great pleasure to inform you that you are a monkey,' he said gravely. 'This one would be more appropriate.'

She took the carving he was holding out to her, and fell in love instantly. The little monkey was clutching a fruit to its chest with both arms and looking over its shoulder anxiously to see if there was any competition for the delicacy. It was so exquisite that she gasped out loud. 'Oh, what an adorable monkey! I love it!'

Anton's eyes narrowed angrily. 'You've just doubled the price, damn it,' he growled.

'I don't care,' she hissed back. 'What are the monkey's qualities?'

'Well, if you had been born a pig, you would have been a much nicer person to know and I would not have hesitated about employing you.'

'I didn't notice you hesitating about employing me,' she pointed out.

'But as a monkey,' he went on, ignoring the interruption, 'I benefit from your superior intelligence and charm. Though your deep distrust of other people makes you hard to get close to.'

'You're making this up! And what are *you*? A tiger, I suppose?'

'A dragon.'

'Oh, now, why am I not surprised to hear that? And what are your qualities, oh, great dragon?'

'I'm a brilliant perfectionist who makes impossible demands on others.'

'That's frightening,' she said. 'There's something in this astrology stuff after all.'

She let Anton take over the haggling and eventually bought the delightful little monkey for a third of its initial price. Although, as Anton told her sternly as they walked out, it would have gone down even further if she hadn't shown such conspicuous signs of being infatuated with it.

'I'll know better next time,' she said. But she couldn't have been more pleased with her purchase. She unwrapped it and crooned over it happily. 'I suppose I should have asked whether it's nephrite or jadeite.'

'It's nephrite,' Anton said. 'The carving is fine, but the stone isn't particularly valuable. Come, I want to show you something special.'

He took her arm possessively in his strong hand and led her down a dark alleyway where the shops were less crowded and there were no tourists to be seen. At the very end of the lane was a shop with a carved red door. It appeared to be closed but when Anton rapped at the dragon-shaped wrought-iron knocker, it was opened by an elderly man wearing spectacles with flip-up magnifiers on each lens. He greeted them warmly.

'Mr Wu,' Anton said, 'I was hoping you could show us some of your wares.'

'Of course,' the old man said, opening the door wide. Again, Amy was aware of that strong, forceful hand in the small of her back, urging her forward.

Mr Wu ushered them courteously to chairs. 'Please, sit down. Some tea?'

'That would be very nice,' Anton said.

Amy sat beside him in front of the desk where the old man had been sorting through a collection of ancient fragments that looked like dull stone coins, some with holes drilled in them. 'Those are *bi*,' Anton murmured in her ear. 'Religious objects from China's distant past.'

'How old are they?' she whispered back.

'Shang Dynasty,' he answered. 'From the sixteenth century.'

'Wow, five centuries old!'

'No,' he said patiently, 'the sixteenth century BC. They're *thirty-seven* centuries old. The Shang Dynasty corresponds to our late Stone Age.'

'Oh,' she said.

'China is a very ancient civilisation,' he said, deadpan.

Mr Wu came back into the room with a tray. He served them tea in small cups, and, while they sipped the scalding, chrysanthemum-scented brew, began unfolding a carefully wrapped baize bundle.

Amy watched in fascination. The baize roll contained around a dozen pockets, and from each pocket Mr Wu extracted a piece of jade. There were rings, earrings, bangles and necklaces of polished beads. The workmanship was perfect, yet extremely simple. What made her gasp was the colour of the stone—a deep, almost iridescent green that she had never seen in her life before. The pieces glowed with an intensity that was alive. For the first time she believed Anton's tales of how jade was revered and regarded as the stone of heaven.

'There's nothing like this anywhere in the market,' she said in awe. 'I've never seen such an electric green!'

'Burmese imperial jade,' Mr Wu said, beaming. 'As beautiful as emerald!'

'Yes, it is,' she agreed. 'Most of the emeralds I've seen don't begin to match this for beauty. These beads are wonderful. And these rings…I think I would rather have one of these than an emerald.'

'What about this piece?' Mr Wu said gently. He was holding out a bangle. 'This material is the finest quality. And the workmanship is equal to the material.'

She took the bangle. The stone was cool, despite the warmth of the shop. It was, as Mr Wu had said, the best piece in the collection; the stone was a deep and vivid green. It had been carved with a dragon, whose sinuous and muscular body writhed all around the band, his fire-breathing jaws meeting his fiery tail.

'It's marvellous,' she sighed, turning it in her fingers so that the dragon seemed to twist as though alive, his scales shimmering. The thing was so beautiful that she was almost reluctant to hand it back to Mr Wu.

'Try it on,' Anton suggested. She slipped her hand into the cool green hoop. Against her pale skin, it looked wonderful. When she began, reluctantly, to take it off again, he shook his head. 'Keep it on.'

'I might get attached to something like this,' she said with a smile.

'I hope so,' he replied.

'What do you mean?'

Mr Wu rose. 'I will prepare more tea,' the Chinese man said courteously, and disappeared into the back of the shop, leaving them alone.

Anton looked her in the eyes. 'This is yours,' he said.

Amy's heart sank swiftly. 'Oh, no! This is a very valuable piece!'

'It is yours.'

Her face reddening, Amy shook her head. If this was his idea of a joke, it was a highly embarrassing one. She pulled the jade bangle off her wrist. 'Anton, I can't accept this.'

'It's a gift,' he said. 'A way of welcoming you to the Zell Corporation and wishing you luck in your new job.'

'Those are very nice sentiments,' she said awkwardly. 'Nevertheless, I can't take this. Please give it back to Mr Wu.'

Anton's eyes were cool. 'I can't. I've already paid for it. And it does seem to have your name on it.'

She looked at the bangle closely. Its section was in a D-shape. On the smooth inner surface of the jade, Chinese characters had been exquisitely incised.

There were also some words in Roman characters: the date, and the inscription, To Amy from Anton.

She was dumbstruck for a moment. 'You've had it engraved!'

'I knew you were going to like it,' he said, as though there had never been any other option. 'I knew it would suit you perfectly, and it does. I want you to wear it to the office.'

Amy's whole body felt hot and flushed. She had a sensation of panic, of being suffocated in this small, ornate shop with its drawers full of treasures. 'You don't understand,' she said urgently. 'I *cannot* accept this gift, beautiful as it is. Please ask the jeweller if he can polish this inscription out.'

'That's impossible. It's been cut too deep.' He was clearly getting impatient. 'What is the matter, Amy? I don't understand you.'

'Then try,' she begged him urgently. 'New employees don't accept lavish gifts from their employers. I'm not a fool. I know what this bangle must be worth.'

'Amy,' he said shortly, 'I can afford to buy you a piece of jade.'

'The point is not what it means to *you*,' she said, her eyes flashing angrily at his intransigence, 'but what it means to *me*! It would put me under intolerable pressure.'

'Why are you spoiling my day?' he asked, frowning at her.

'You're spoiling *my* day, Anton. Everything was lovely up until now—the drive, the market, helping me choose that little monkey—but this is just awful!'

'You think the bangle is awful?'

'Of course not. It would be a fabulous gift from a man to his wife, but not between employer and employee!'

He shrugged, growing colder as she grew hotter. 'I think of you as a kind of wife, Worthington,' he said with ironic mockery.

'Then stop thinking of me like that,' she retorted.

'I don't understand what the hell is eating you,' he said, his eyes growing cold. 'It's just a gift.'

'Putting thousands of dollars on my arm is not "just a gift". I joined your company to work, not to become a concubine.'

'Have I asked you to be that?' he demanded.

'Not yet. And the day you do is the day I walk out, Anton. You made it very clear what you wanted in Borneo—and you've been dropping subtle hints all morning, about how lonely and neglected you are. Do you think I don't know what you're talking about?'

'What am I talking about?' he asked.

'You've said it again today: "a kind of wife". But what you want is the wife without the marriage.'

He stared at her flushed face in silence for a moment. 'You've misunderstood,' he said brusquely. 'What I want is the marriage without the wife.'

'It's the same thing,' she retorted. 'You're very adept at solving problems, and this is your solution to one particular problem.'

'If I wanted sex,' he said grimly, 'I would get it at those Wanchai strip clubs where you say I slurp noodles and whisky till dawn.'

'I know you go there, because you've thrown the tabs at me to pay the next morning. Whatever you're slurping there does not come cheap!'

Anger made his eyes darken. He took the jade bangle from her and dropped it into his pocket. This time, the hand in the small of her back was almost rough. 'All right, that's enough. Let's go.'

CHAPTER FIVE

SHE felt achingly sick as they drove back to Causeway Bay in silence. She knew she had said things back there in Mr Wu's shop that she should not have allowed to pass her lips. She would be lucky to keep her job.

If he only knew the raw nerve he had touched—that he kept on touching, with almost every thing he did or said. There were moments when a kind of madness took her over and filled her with unbearable anguish.

True to form, the moist banks of white clouds had closed in swiftly and by the time they reached her apartment block, the rain was pouring down, making pedestrians dash to and fro, buried under umbrellas or plastic wraps. Of course, all Anton had to do was touch a button on the dashboard and the hood of the sports car closed over them with an electric whirr. Men like Anton did not get wet when it rained.

He pulled up outside her place. The rain drummed on the canvas hood over their heads. He turned to her with sombre eyes.

'Maybe you can give me an explanation before you go?'

Her throat was tight. 'Anton, I'm sorry I spoke out of turn today. I had no right to say some of those things. But I felt I had to say them. I don't want you to get the wrong impression about me.'

'And what impression would that be?'

She stared out at the rainy forest of masts, unable to meet his eyes. 'Personal assistants find out all sorts of things. It's the nature of the job. You know—like a wife without the marriage.'

'What things?'

57

'My predecessor. The beautiful Marcie. You told me she had a heart murmur and had to leave suddenly.'

'And?'

'Marcie had a medical check-up three days before she left so suddenly. Whatever the report said, there was nothing wrong with her heart.'

'You've looked in her file?' he asked in a dangerous voice.

'No, of course not. Somebody told me.'

'Who told you?'

'It doesn't matter. Lots of people are speculating about Marcie and her heart murmur. But she's not in Hong Kong any more. She was whisked away to a clinic in Switzerland.' She faced him, her mouth twisted in a painful smile. 'There was *some* kind of medical emergency. Something that had to be dealt with urgently. But it wasn't a heart murmur.'

'Why should this concern you?' he growled.

'Why?' She extended one finger. 'Firstly, because she was my predecessor. Secondly, because you lied to me about why she left. Thirdly, because she didn't leave on health grounds—her contract was terminated because you fired her.' She held up three fingers for a moment, then let her hand drop back into her lap. 'That's why it concerns me.'

'I see,' he said heavily.

'Wherever Marcie is now,' she said in a pain-filled voice, 'I don't want to end up in the same place.'

'I hope you won't,' he replied.

'I'm alone in this life, Anton. I have to take care of myself because there's nobody else who's going to do it.'

'I understand,' he replied, nodding. 'More than you can know.'

'If you want to fire me, I'll know why.'

'It sounds to me more like you're leaving.'

'I adore my job,' she said, her eyes filling with tears. 'I don't want to leave.'

'Then you may as well stay.' He leaned across her and opened her door, letting in a warm rush of rainy air. 'Since you're such a big girl, you don't need me to show you up to your apartment.'

She ran across the street, the rain beating into her face. She felt sick inside.

As she dried herself in her apartment, she found something hard in her pocket. It was the little jade monkey, clutching her prize but looking anxiously over her shoulder.

There was a hollow place in her heart. He hadn't even attempted to explain what had happened to Marcie. In a way, she was glad. She didn't want to hear any more lies.

And in any case, she knew exactly what had happened to Marcie. The talkative nurse in the sickbay had been delighted at the chance to gossip.

She adored Mr Zell. Absolutely mad about him. Worshipped the ground he trod on, if you know what I mean. She was a lovely, lovely girl, but then she started to look off-colour. Was even sick a couple of times in the office. Mr Zell ordered her to take a check-up. She wasn't pleased about that, I can tell you. But she couldn't refuse, could she? Next thing she's got the sack, and spirited off to some mysterious clinic in Zurich. I mean, anyone can put two and two together, can't they?

Oh, yes, it was easy to put two and two together. She knew exactly what kind of medical emergencies required instant dismissal and a mysterious visit to an expensive clinic. A clinic which specialised in little accidents. She knew all about that.

She was not going to suffer that pain again. Not even though she knew that she was never going to meet anyone like Anton Zell in her life again. She had once thought she was in love with Martin McCallum, but Anton was teaching her differently.

Because she, like Marcie, was also learning to adore Mr Zell. To be absolutely mad about him. To worship the ground he trod on.

She put the little jade monkey on her bedside table and curled up on the bed, not caring that her wet hair was dampening the pillow. Thunder rumbled across the bay from China.

Amy stared at the delicate green figure. How long was she going to be able to keep clutching her prize and looking over her shoulder?

Six weeks later, they flew back to Europe. The Zell Corporation was a partner in a big refinery project in Marseilles; one of the other companies, Barbusse Resources, had offered to buy out Anton's holdings. It would be a radical move, but it seemed to have found favour with Anton. They were going to hammer out the details of the deal.

They were also going to take advantage of being in the south of France in June to take a break on the Côte d'Azur and visit some of Anton's friends there, including Lady Carron, who had a villa at Cap d'Antibes. Amy was looking forward to seeing whether her surmise about the foot-long cigarette-holder was right.

Anton's private jet had seating for twelve passengers, but on this flight there were only the two of them in the luxurious cabin—Anton's financial team were already in Marseilles, at the negotiating table.

They had been in the air for three hours, having taken off in the warm dusk. It was now dark outside the cabin and they were both hungry. Amy went up to the galley and took the prepared meals—supplied by an aviation catering firm in Hong Kong—from the fridge to the microwave. As the first tray heated, she closed the curtains all down the Lear jet's body.

Anton was engrossed in papers relating to the shares deal that was coming up. She was amused as always to see that he was wearing glasses to read with. And as always when he was concentrating, he was so focused that he seemed barely aware of her presence as she walked past him. He did not even flinch when she opened the bottle of iced champagne with a loud pop. She had to fight down a mischievous urge to flip his glasses off his nose, just to get him to notice her.

For some reason, there was a large and beautiful parrot on board, sitting sleepily in a cage at the back of the cabin. It had something to do with the deal, Amy was not sure exactly what.

The microwave pinged. She took a meal up to the cockpit and gave it to the pilot, who was—disconcertingly—reading a book on trout fishing. Then she put her and Anton's meal in the microwave and took the champagne and two glasses to where Anton was sitting.

'Sorry to interrupt you,' she said, holding out the glass.

He tossed the papers aside. 'I've finished anyway,' he replied. 'What's for dinner?'

'I'm not sure, except that it looks a lot nicer than the usual airline food,' she said.

'And you look a lot nicer than the usual airline hostess,' he smiled.

She was delighted by the compliment. Since the disastrous visit to the jade market in Hong Kong, relations between them had been strained and restricted to work issues. Though she kept telling herself that was exactly what she most wanted, Amy ached for the intimacy that had once existed between them; an intimacy that seemed to have gone for ever.

She ached for his smiles, the way he used to tease her,

the way he used to touch her. But it was as though that had never been. And inside, she felt a terror that mounted every day—a terror that he would grow sick of having her around and would dismiss her and find someone more congenial.

The thought of *that* was unbearable.

'Well, thank you, sir; that has earned you a bottle of our complimentary champagne while you wait for the chef to add the final sauces.'

'Pour away, stewardess. I want to see beaded bubbles winking at the brim.'

'Coming right up, sir.'

Anton clinked his champagne glass against hers. 'God bless.'

'Bless you too,' she said, drinking.

'What are you smiling at?' he demanded.

'I always smile when I see you wearing glasses,' she said.

He took them off. 'I have grey hairs, too. You find the signs of age amusing?'

'You're not old,' she said soothingly, 'you're just in your prime.'

'So kind of you.'

'Think nothing of it.' She indicated his paperwork. 'Have you worked out your thoughts yet?'

'I worked them out long ago,' he said. 'I built the refinery about five years ago for a man named Henri Barbusse, of Barbusse Resources Incorporated. As part of the deal, I own forty per cent of the joint venture company, which is called Zell France. Henri is now a very rich man. He wants to buy out that forty per cent interest, which will make him sole owner of the facility.'

'Doesn't that mean you'll lose revenue?' she asked.

'Henri will offer a very good price,' Anton replied with a smile. 'The plant has a capacity of fifty thousand tons a year—and that's a lot of money. But I can use the cash elsewhere.'

'Such as where?'

'Well, the Marseilles facility is a finished mission. Right now, I'm excited by projects in some developing countries in south-east Asia—countries like Vietnam and Laos. I can use the money there, and they can use the technology. It's perfect for their economies.'

'How come?'

'Because it makes much more sense for them to recycle than to import. And in countries where the environment is especially fragile, reprocessing is a vital step.' He drank his champagne. 'These economies have been held back by politics and wars for decades. But I see them as the Asian tigers of the future. And I want a stake in their growth.'

'So you're not altogether St Anton,' she said drily.

'Not altogether,' he replied with a grin. 'But I do love those places, especially Vietnam. We'll be taking a trip there in a couple of months. You'll see just how beautiful it is.'

'Please tell me—what's the parrot for?'

'It's a macaw,' Anton replied. 'Henri Barbusse is mad about exotic birds. He has an aviary full of them. This is a gift for him. Getting the paperwork sorted out was a nightmare, I can tell you.'

Amy went to get the food. They settled down side by side in the ample seats to eat off the fold-down table. The trays actually contained a variety of beautifully prepared Chinese dishes in pretty little bowls. They both used chopsticks—living in Hong Kong, you soon got used to dispensing with knives and forks.

'This is a *very* superior airline. I've never had a whole plane to myself—not to mention the owner as my fellow passenger.'

'To me, space is the ultimate luxury,' he said. 'The main thing I remember from my childhood is never having any space of my own.'

'I know what you mean,' she said, sipping the icy champagne, which was delectable. 'When you're supernumerary, nothing is yours. You have to share everything. There's no place to call your own.'

'Except the space in your head,' he replied.

'Yes,' she said quietly. 'Except that. And they even try to take that away from you.'

Anton glanced at her. 'At the interview you told me that Jeffrey wasn't very happy to have an extra child to raise. Was he really that mean to you?'

Amy paused before answering. 'No, Jeffrey is a very good person. But he made sure I knew how lucky I was to be in his house. And my cousins took their cue from that. They made my life hell, especially when their father wasn't looking. And I could never complain to him—because I had to be so grateful.'

'And this is why you're such a hard case now?'

'Am I a hard case?' she said innocently.

'Tough as nails.' He selected a delicious sweet-and-sour prawn from his bowl and popped it into her mouth with deft chopsticks. While she chewed it appreciatively, he studied her. In the soft lighting of the cabin, his eyes were impenetrable. 'Tell me how they made your life hell.'

'Oh, I suppose I'm being melodramatic,' she said awkwardly. 'It wasn't that bad. But there were three of them— twin girls and a boy. The girls were much worse. They used to gang up on me and hurt me as much as they could. You know, girl things—pinching, pulling my hair, breaking my things.'

'Girls are expert torturers,' he said gently.

'Oh, yes. Sometimes they really hurt. They knew what they were doing. And I couldn't fight back, because the moment I did, they would tell Uncle Jeffrey and I would be punished even worse. They wanted to make me cry, but eventually I learned how to take it without crying. So as they got older, they started using words, instead.'

'What sort of words?'

'Predictable stuff. Why are you so interested?' she asked with an uneasy laugh.

'I'm interested in everything about you,' he said. 'Tell me what they used to say to you.'

Amy sighed. 'They used to tell me that my parents committed suicide because they knew I was the Devil's child.'

Anton's eyes widened. 'That's pretty good stuff. I had something similar in one place they sent me to. It gave me nightmares for years.'

'Me, too,' she said, half smiling at him. 'I used to dream the most awful things.'

'Gore and monsters. I know. What else did they say to you?'

'Oh, that nobody wanted me, everybody hated me. They told me I was ugly and wicked. That sort of thing. It got really bad when...'

'When?' he prompted as her voice trailed away.

There was a hot lump in her throat. 'I don't think I can tell you about it.'

Anton put his arm around her unexpectedly and drew her close to him. He drew her head gently onto his shoulder. 'Try,' he said in a quiet voice. 'It can only make it better to let it out.'

The warm smell of his skin was like a drug that intoxicated her senses, making it easier to say what was so hard. 'When I was twelve or thirteen and my body changed...'

'I understand.'

'They found out. They said such awful things. The girls were more or less my age but they hadn't started yet. I think they were jealous, in a way. I didn't dare tell anyone, not even Aunt Sheila. I didn't have a mother. I had to cope on my own. But every month after that was a nightmare, trying desperately to hide what was happening. But they always found out and then they would make life unbearable for me.'

He held her close, stroking her silky hair with a gentle hand. 'I'm sorry, Amy.'

'The twins started a year later and then it eased off. They were too busy concentrating on their own adolescence to worry about mine. And around then, they started just ignoring me. They'd done all the hurtful things they could think of. They got bored with the game and started leading their own lives. But I will always remember that as the worst year of my life.'

'But you got through it,' he said quietly. 'And now you know that if you could get through that, you can get through anything.'

She smiled against his shoulder. 'I supposed that's true.' It was heavenly to be cradled in his arms like this, to feel the warmth of his compassion, understanding but not sentimental, surrounding her. 'But I don't want to talk about me any more. I want to hear about you, Anton, about the foster homes you grew up in.'

'Changing the subject, I see.'

'Same subject, different viewpoint. You said some of your foster homes were very bad. Tell me about them.'

'The worst one? They wanted to make me as unhappy as they were. They beat me with a strap and locked me in a cupboard for days at a time.'

She felt suddenly sick. 'Oh, Anton, I'm so sorry. I didn't mean to touch such a painful memory.'

'I didn't mind the strap so much,' he said calmly. 'The cupboard was much worse. Because I wanted so desperately to go to school, you see. In the end, that saved me. The school sent someone round to the house to see why I was absent such a lot. So they took me out of there. I was kept in an orphanage for the next two years before they tried me with another foster family. The rest of my families were all wonderful. But somehow, after that, I always found myself on the outside, emotionally.'

'I'm so sorry,' she repeated. 'What happened to me was nothing like that.'

'It was probably just as bad,' he said. 'Inadequate and miserable people are the cruellest. They want to destroy everybody else's happiness. The worst part is not the insults or the bruises. It's not feeling loved.'

'Yes,' she whispered. 'I feel sick to my stomach, Anton. Poor little boy!'

He laughed. 'Don't tell me there's a weak spot in the armour plating!'

'I'm not armour plated as far as you're concerned,' she said softly. 'Always remember that, when you feel like teasing me.'

'I will. And please don't ever be afraid of telling me things,' he went on. 'I understand you better than you can know.'

'I believe you do,' she said, lifting her head to look at him. 'Thank you for listening—and for telling me about you.'

He kissed her mouth lightly. It was like a touch of velvet, but she drew away swiftly, as though she had been burned. 'Well, we're a couple of hard cases, aren't we?' he said, smiling at her with those amazing blue eyes.

Not trusting herself to reply after that kiss, Amy cleared away their trays and dumped everything in the service locker. Talking to him about her childhood, and catching a glimpse of his, had touched nerves deep inside her. She found that her hands were trembling with emotion. How strange to relive those memories here, high in the dark night, flying to France!

When she returned, Anton had produced blankets and pillows. 'Sleep beside me,' he commanded softly, 'in case nightmares come.'

'I won't have nightmares tonight,' she said.

'I'm not talking about you.' He reached up and turned off the overhead lights so that the cabin was in dimness.

The arm rest between the wide seats lifted up, and the backs went down, to produce a large and very welcoming bed. Amy kicked off her shoes and lay down beside him. His strong arms surrounded her, drawing her close. Though she was fully clothed in trousers and a blouse, and he in his customary jeans and silk shirt, the contact was as electric to her as though they were naked.

'We're the same, you and I,' he murmured, his warm breath brushing the sensitive skin of her throat. 'Always got our noses pressed to the window. Fogging up the glass and seeing things in a rosy, fuzzy glow.'

'I have no illusions, Anton.'

'You like to think you're so tough, Worthington,' he growled. 'Every day you get up and add another layer to that suit of armour you clank around in. I wonder if you can even see out of it any more.'

'It's safe in here,' she said. But lying in his arms she did not feel safe—not very safe at all.

CHAPTER SIX

AFTER the ceremonial presentation of the macaw—which Henri Barbusse seemed enchanted by—the negotiations began in a large, featureless hotel in Marseilles. It commanded panoramic views of the sea and had excellent conference facilities, but was otherwise about as exciting as a shoebox inside.

But the negotiations were fascinating. Sitting beside Anton and making sure he had all the papers he needed, Amy was in a perfect position to observe the subtle and not-so-subtle intricacies of the debate. In another time and place, Anton and Henri Barbusse might have been two generals commanding rival armies, and instead of millions of dollars, the profit and loss might have been in human blood.

As Anton had predicted, Henri Barbusse, a small, square-bearded man in his fifties, was offering a very large amount of money. His style was very different from Anton's; where Anton was relaxed and casual, Barbusse was a dandy, always impeccably starched and cufflinked; where Anton acted and spoke spontaneously, Barbusse was always smoothly produced, something of an actor. He reminded Amy of one of his own beloved birds, small, neat and always preening his feathers.

The main area of debate centred around exclusivity. While buying out the refinery, Barbusse wanted to prevent the Zell Corporation from building any similar plants for anyone else in France.

Anton smilingly conceded that the point was an important one. He seemed so relaxed about it that Amy began to be afraid he would give away too much. But watching how

Anton, with apparent casualness, worked the deal to his favour was an education in negotiation at the highest level.

By the second afternoon, Barbusse had conceded that Zell France would receive a royalty on every gallon for five more years, and Barbusse Resources Inc. had to order at least one more refinery within two years, and discuss the possibility of a third and possibly more plants. The additional refineries were to be installed at locations already belonging to Zell France or its partners, and Barbusse was to compensate Zell accordingly.

The papers were ready to sign and a Press conference was called to showcase the agreement. Media interest was high, and TV cameras as well as a bevy of newspaper reporters were on hand to film the signing and tape statements from both Anton and Barbusse.

To celebrate the conclusion of the deal, the next night Henri Barbusse took the whole negotiating team out to a magnificent dinner which began with Marseilles's most famous dish, *bouillabaisse*, which—as Anton took great pleasure in telling her—was made from the deadly stonefish, proceeded through lobster thermidor, and concluded with an assortment of liqueurs and nougat.

Amy was wearing a stretch dress in dark blue which flattered her figure, and she could tell she was getting a lot of male attention, which pleased her ego. Among the male eyes which dwelled on her curves were Anton's. He had not seen her in going-out clothes, she realised; in Hong Kong she dressed very formally, for the office; and when they were in the field, she wore loose casuals in khakis and browns. By the expression in his eyes, he was enjoying the glimpse of her curves which the blue dress afforded!

After dinner they were taken to a cabaret, which was funny and sophisticated, and then on to a club. It was a delightful evening and she was very taken aback when Henri Barbusse asked her to dance in between numbers.

On the crowded dance-floor, Barbusse was unexpectedly flirtatious. 'Where did my friend Anton find such an angel as you?' he demanded.

'I assure you, he doesn't consider me an angel, Monsieur Barbusse!'

'You are divine, my dear. A symphony in blue and gold! I have been watching you for these past two days. If conditions with Zell are ever less than heavenly, you come straight to me, OK? I will make all your dreams come true!'

'I'll bear that in mind,' she said tactfully.

'You do that.'

Barbusse had gyrated her into a corner of the dance-floor from which there was no escape and now he closed in. Amy found herself enfolded in octopus arms, with an insistent pelvis bumping hers suggestively.

'You do that, little bird,' he said hoarsely into her ear. 'Bear me in mind!'

'I will, I promise.'

Wishing she knew some jiu-jitsu, she tried to evade the amorous millionaire. A scented beard brushed her cheek. 'Do not fly away, my little bird,' he murmured. 'Tell me what Zell pays you. I will double it.'

'I'm happy with my salary!'

'I will make you happier.'

'But I like living in Hong Kong,' she replied, trying to squirm out of the embrace.

A hand closed around her breast. 'You will grow tired of it—come and live in Paris!'

'I'll think about it,' she repeated, jerking the hand away from her breast.

'Take my card, little pigeon,' he murmured, 'you have the most beautiful bosom I ever saw.' He produced a gilt-edged card with his number on it and tried to slip it into her cleavage. She intercepted it as gracefully as she could. She managed to evade both the scented beard and the exploring pelvis at last, and when the number ended scampered back to Anton with relief.

Anton was smiling lazily at her. 'What was that interesting dance you were doing with *cher* Henri?'

'It's called *Dodge the Oil Magnate*,' she said breathlessly, adjusting her dress.

'Or maybe, *Dances with Wolves*?'

'Right. Or *In a Tight Corner with a Tycoon*.'

'And what was he whispering in your shell-like ear?'

'He was offering me a job at twice what you pay me.'

'No, really? It looked like he was demonstrating some of the perks of the job, too.'

'You are a pig,' she said, and he laughed out loud.

'Weren't you tempted by the generous offer?'

'Of course I was tempted. He gave me his card.'

'Yes, I saw him post something down your front. Such a delicious letter box. But I'm surprised Henri's little offering didn't get lost in the recesses of your costume.'

'I'm beginning to wish I'd worn something less *décolleté*,' she said ruefully.

'If you've got them, flaunt them. Especially if they're doubling your salary every time you trot them out.'

'They're not that big, for heaven's sake.'

'Pushing them in Henri's face probably made them look larger,' he said, deadpan.

'I was *not* pushing them in his face!'

'Yes, you were. You can push them in my face now, Worthington. Unless you're too out of breath?'

He took her hand, and, breathless as she was, she went back on the floor with him to dance.

Dancing with Anton was much nicer than dancing with Henri Barbusse. He was graceful and light on his feet and made no attempt to paw her. When the music changed to a slow, dreamy number, he took her gently in his arms and held her lightly but firmly against his strong body. He danced so well that she could almost forget that she had feet at all, and just drift along to his rhythm.

'So?' he asked her. 'Has Marseilles been interesting?'

'I've learned more in the last couple of days than in the past five years,' she said.

'What have you learned?'

'For one thing, that Anton Zell can have it all.'

'What do you mean?'

'Well, you came here to sell your share in a refinery. But it's ended up that you're still going to share in the profits for five more years, build up to two new refineries, and sell some very expensive industrial real estate. You're a very clever man.'

He brushed her cheek with his. 'Flattery will get you nowhere.'

'I'm not flattering you, Mr Fox. Merely commenting on your cunning.'

'Can I comment on your beauty?'

'Flattery will get you nowhere. But go ahead if you must.'

'You are by far the most beautiful woman here,' he said, his breath warm against her neck. 'But that's the least of it. You're probably also the most beautiful woman in France tonight.'

'Only probably?'

'There *are* twenty-five million others. One has to be cautious in business estimates.'

'Oh, so this is a business conversation we're having?' she said, feeling his powerful stomach muscles brushing against hers.

'A wage negotiation.'

'Am I in line for a raise?'

'Well, I don't want you going over to the opposition. I like you just where you are.'

'I don't plan on going over to Henri Barbusse any time soon.'

'But you have kept his card.'

'A girl has to have a back-up plan.'

'I see. So what do you want, Worthington? More money—or more perks?'

Her breasts pressed against his chest as they moved together. 'Tell me about the perks.'

'I tried to give you a jade bracelet, but you turned me down flat.'

'Ah, yes,' she said wryly. 'Don't think I didn't get the symbolism of that particular perk.'

'Symbolism?'

'Oh yes.' Her hair brushed his cheek. 'You wanted to put a bangle carved with a dragon around my wrist.'

'Correct.'

'Giving everybody the message that I belonged to the big dragon himself.'

'Or maybe that the big dragon belonged to you.'

'Hah! That'll be the day!'

His mouth touched her temple, then her cheek, then the corner of her mouth. 'But I was trying to tell you how beautiful you are,' he murmured. 'That dress suits you perfectly. Are you wearing any underwear beneath it?'

'Of course.'

'It doesn't show.'

'It's very expensive underwear.'

'So I'm clearly already paying you too much.'

She lifted her face to his to retort, but he didn't give her a chance. His lips sealed hers with a firm, possessive kiss that made her bones melt. 'Mr Fox,' she whispered, looking up at him with shining eyes, 'you are taking liberties!'

'I am sorry,' he said, not sounding apologetic in the slightest, 'talking about your underwear—or the absence of it—made me lose my head for a second.'

'"I lost my head" is a very feeble excuse.'

'Better than, "I lost my underwear".'

She burst out laughing. Luckily the slow number ended, and the pace picked up, and she was able to beg him to let her go back to the table for a drink.

The party was still going strong in the early hours of the morning, when Amy started to droop and begged for permission to go back to the hotel to bed.

'I'll take you,' Anton said.

'Oh, please don't leave the party,' she replied, 'I'll go back to the hotel on my own, there's no need for you to escort me!'

'I've had enough too, honey bunny. And I think Henri wants an excuse to get back to his exotic birds, *n'est-ce pas, Henri*?'

'It is rather late,' Barbusse said with a smile, 'and you had better get your own bird of paradise back to her nest before she puts her beautiful head under her wing and goes to sleep!' He kissed Amy's hand lingeringly. 'I will see you tomorrow, Anton.'

Five minutes later, after shaking a dozen hands and accepting fulsome congratulations, she and Anton were walking out of the club.

It was a beautiful, clear night. Their hotel was a ten-minute walk away, so they elected to stroll back along the Promenade.

'When Monsieur Barbusse wakes up tomorrow morning and reads that contract, he may have rather more than a hangover!' she commented as they walked.

Anton burst out laughing. He put her arm around her waist and drew her close, so that they were walking in unison. 'Believe me, Henri is a better businessman than you give him credit for. He's going to make a lot of money out of this deal. And I have the capital I need to expand in south-east Asia. Nobody got robbed here.'

'Just remind me never to play poker with you,' she said.

'Look! The moon in June.'

A full moon was hanging over the sea, making a river of silver light along the waves. They stopped to admire it. She rested her head on Anton's shoulder dreamily.

'Here you are, orphan boy,' she said. 'Now an industrial giant, with interests all over the world. What's it like to come from having so little to having all this?'

He stroked her hair. 'There's an old saying—a man only has what he can hold in his two hands. Looked at from that point of view, I have always had what you call ''all this''. And I will always have nothing.'

'You own yourself,' she replied quietly, 'and that's more than most men have.'

'Or most women. And you own yourself, Amy.'

'It doesn't always feel like that,' she said in a small voice.

'You're the most self-possessed woman I know,' he said, smiling. 'The problem is trying to get you to let go now and then.'

'For example?'

'For example, you know that I am mad about you, but you won't let me near you.'

She shivered at his caress. 'You're near me now.'

'True, in a brotherly sort of way. But—for example, if I tried to kiss you now, you would jump like a scalded cat.'

Amy closed her eyes. She was not so sure of that. 'Cats are animals that like things on their own terms,' she said.

'Something that every cat-lover knows,' he said, his voice purring. 'Now, you see, Henri Barbusse is a bird-lover. He likes to put them in cages and admire them in captivity. I prefer you spitting and scratching.'

'I would never leave you to go to Henri Barbusse, even if he tripled my salary.'

'So you are a little bit mad about me, too?' he asked softly, kissing her ear.

Shudders ran down her spine. 'No,' she whispered, 'I just like my job, Mr Zell.'

'That's all?'

'That's all! Now take your wildcat home before she starts scratching and spitting!'

The yellow moon followed them as they walked back to the hotel, holding hands.

With everything concluded in Marseilles, they were free to go to the Côte d'Azur for a short break. They were to be house guests at the Antibes villa of Lady Carron—whom Anton had described as a troublesome shareholder, but who, Amy suspected by her imperious phone calls, might be something more.

Anton rented an open-topped Mercedes sports car—which he claimed was *de rigueur* in the south of France in summer—and they drove in a leisurely way from Marseilles along the coast. She was getting on so well with him lately that everything was like a happy dream.

They drove through a sunlit Mediterranean landscape of vineyards, pine forests and wide beaches, stopping along the way to have lunch in the garden of a country restaurant called La Sirène, where the food and the wine were magnificent.

'So the people we're going to be staying with in Antibes are major shareholders in the Zell Corporation?' she asked Anton over the gooey and delicious *tarte Tatin*.

'It's a complicated story,' he replied. 'To try and simplify it: Sir Robert Carron was a financier who backed me when I started up. The first few refineries I built were financed with loans from him. His firm also steered us through the rights issue when we went public a few years later. He had confidence in us so he bought several blocks of shares. He married Lavinia quite recently. She was much younger than Robert. When he died, she inherited a lot of his shareholdings—so she now has a twenty per cent stake in the Zell Corporation.'

'That gives her quite a voice.'

'Exactly. Hence this visit. Lavinia is young, but very shrewd—and very strong-willed. She has her own idea about the direction the corporation should be taking. So I've got two choices. Buy her out—or keep her sweet.'

'And keeping her sweet is cheaper,' Amy said, her voice a lot more acid than the mouthful of buttery, caramelised apple she had just swallowed.

'Cheaper *and* more fun,' he said with a wicked glint in his eyes.

'I see,' Amy said, even more sourly. 'The dear departed Sir Robert had good taste, did he?'

'She's not particularly beautiful. But she is interesting. As you will see.'

'I can hardly wait.'

'It will be an education,' he promised.

'It's so peaceful here,' Amy sighed, looking up at the cypresses and gnarled olive trees all around, not wanting to leave. It was hot and the chirring of cicadas was soporific. 'I think this must be an enchanted garden. I'm very glad to be out of Marseilles.'

'So am I,' Anton replied. 'At least it's stopped you putting the moves on poor Henri.'

'I was *not* putting the moves on him,' she said indignantly.

'Yes, you were. It was scandalous. You were as bad as *her*.' He pointed to the old stone fountain, in the shape of a seductive and very bosomy mermaid, after which the restaurant was obviously named.

'I was not,' she retorted. 'Henri is a randy old goat, and you know it.'

'He did appear to be ripping your bodice.'

'He was trying to give me his card.'

'Is that what you mermaids call it?'

She glanced at the statue of the mermaid. 'Anyway, I don't have her attributes.'

'Just as well,' Anton said silkily. 'I'm very glad that you're woman from the navel down, and not halibut.'

She giggled. 'You are wayward, dear master. And you don't know much about mermaids.'

'Enlighten me,' he invited, filling her glass.

'Well,' she said, 'mermaids do occasionally mate with mortal men. They lose their fish tails and look just like ordinary women. But it's usually only for a year or two. They pine for the sea. And one stormy night, they change back again without warning. They disappear. Go back to the sea.'

'Leaving a heartbroken mortal man?' he suggested.

'And the bed full of fish scales.'

'So you could be a mermaid after all?' he asked, looking into her eyes

Amy batted her eyelids. 'You never know.'

'Hmm. That might explain some of your peculiar ways.'

'It might, indeed,' she agreed.

'And tell me,' he went on softly, 'what induces a mermaid to mate with a mortal man?'

'When they fall in love.' She rested her chin on her hand, smiling at him. 'But it hardly ever happens.'

'And when they do fall in love, isn't there any way of keeping them from turning back into mermaids?'

'Only one way.'

'Tell me.'

'They have to have a baby. A mortal child. Then they forget the sound of the crashing waves and become human women for ever.'

'So if I want to keep you, I have to make you pregnant?'

She had been lost in the romantic warmth of their bantering, but those words brought a sudden chill into her soul. 'That wouldn't be very wise,' she said, looking away.

'I'm only teasing,' he said gently. 'I just want to know how to get a mermaid to fall in love with me.'

'I told you, it hardly ever happens.'

'Like hurricanes in Hertford, Hereford and Hampshire?'

'That's right, Professor Higgins.'

Anton smiled faintly at her tense expression. 'And the maiden turned back into a cold stone statue. What did I say?'

'Nothing,' she said.

He sighed. 'Well, if we're going to reach Antibes by suppertime, I suppose we'd better get moving.'

Amy felt her heart ache as they left the enchanted garden with the stone mermaid. Why was it that in the most heavenly moments, something always popped up, like an ugly jack-in-the-box, to bring her back down to earth?

CHAPTER SEVEN

LAVINIA CARRON'S villa was not in Antibes itself, but situated in the rocky, sun-baked hills behind the town. It was a very commanding position, with spreading views of the harbour and the old town, with Nice visible in the distance, on the other side of the bay.

The house itself was very large, made of stone, and obviously two or three centuries old. No expense had been spared in its restoration. As they drove along the immaculately gravelled driveway, Amy glimpsed modern sculptures among the surgically pruned flowering shrubs and tall cypresses of the gardens. There was a spectacular rose garden, too, the flowers arranged into geometric beds according to colour and height.

They pulled up in a courtyard with a gleaming and rather magnificent marble fountain featuring three life-sized lions spouting water from snarling muzzles.

'Eighteenth-century Italian,' Anton told her. 'Imported from Florence by Lavinia. It was rather too mossy for her taste, so she had it sand-blasted.'

'How hygienic,' Amy commented.

As they were getting out of the car, they heard the clop of a horse's hooves. A woman on a big bay gelding came trotting into the courtyard. She jumped off lightly.

'Anton! Darling! How lovely to see you.'

Lady Carron was a slim woman with brown hair and a lean, suntanned face, in which large, violet eyes glowed brightly. As Anton had said, her features were interesting rather than conventionally beautiful, with an aquiline nose and a rather thin mouth; but she was certainly a very attractive woman nonetheless. And she looked very good in her boots, jodhpurs and white cotton shirt.

She kissed Anton warmly on each cheek. 'You look wonderful, darling boy. Quite untarnished by Eastern suns.'

'You look like a bowl of choice fruit yourself, Lavinia,' he grinned. 'This is my assistant, Amy Worthington. Amy, Lavinia Carron.'

'Pleased to meet you, Lady Carron,' Amy said, resisting the urge to curtsey like some pre-Revolutionary French peasant.

'Call me Lavinia, please.' She gave Amy a hand which was small, strong, and still encased in a pale cream leather riding glove. 'So you're the new girl! I hope you've been looking after this naughty boy of mine?'

'I have been trying,' Amy said lightly.

'Well, you can have a rest, you poor child. I'll take over from now on.' The glitter in the lavender eyes made sure Amy understood it was an order. Seen from close up, Lavinia Carron was not quite as young as the trim figure would suggest, but she was obviously very fit. She pulled off the gloves and took Anton's arm in a firm brown hand. 'Come and have a drink on the terrace, you naughty boy; you must be parched in this frightful heat.'

The invitation did not include Amy, obviously. Anton threw her a rueful glance over his shoulder as Lavinia marched him off, leaving Amy with the servants who had emerged to take the bags and lead the horse away. She gave him a death's-head grin in reply.

The house had been furnished in the kind of taste that took a large budget and a very competent interior designer. It was also spotlessly neat and clean. Anton had been allocated a large room overlooking the garden and the blue Mediterranean in the distance. Her own room was very

much smaller and darker, and boasted a view of the sta-
bles—where a large pile of manure was being forked into
a cart by a young groom, no doubt destined for Lady
Carron's roses.

She unpacked, trying not to feel resentful at having been
so instantly and efficiently separated from Anton. Though
he treated her as a friend and equal, there was no reason to
expect that his wealthy friends would behave the same way.

Feeling very much the poor relation, she tried to repair
her appearance—her hair had been dishevelled in the open-
topped car—with a quick shower and a change of clothing.
She had just finished dressing in trousers and a deep pink
shirt when Anton knocked at her door and let himself in.

'Come and have a drink,' he said. 'You must meet the
other guests.'

'Are you sure I'm wanted?' she asked. 'I could just go
down the back stairs to the pantry and get a bowl of gruel.'

He laughed, deep blue eyes dancing. 'You'll get used to
Lavinia. She has a certain style.'

'So I see.'

'Nice view,' Anton commented, deadpan, looking out of
her window.

She joined him. Lady Carron's glossy bay gelding was
now being assiduously brushed in front of his stable door
by the same young groom. 'I don't believe that horse has
been ridden at all,' she said grimly. 'In this heat, both she
and it would have been covered in sweat and dust in ten
minutes.'

'Perhaps she was just setting off when we arrived.'

'Or perhaps she wanted you to see how trim she looked
in her Lara Croft outfit. Please tell me she isn't entertaining
her guests in bespoke riding boots from W&H Gidden, with
silver spurs a-jingling?'

'She is not wearing spurs, as you very well know.'

'Now, you see, a *real* lady would never wear jodhpurs to greet her guests. She just wants you to look at her backside.'

'Well, being mistress of the house means you get to choose what view each guest gets,' he said, evidently amused by her ill-temper.

'Which is how you and I both wound up looking at the rear end of a horse,' she said sweetly, studying herself in the mirror. 'I'm ready to go down now, Master Anton.'

The party assembled on the terrace was not very large. In addition to herself and Anton, there were two other couples, one Swiss, one French, and a solitary Englishman named Mike, who attached himself in a rather melancholy way to Amy. The one factor they all had in common was the unmistakable trappings of serious wealth—costly jewellery, watches, teeth and facelifts gleamed in the light of the setting sun.

An unobtrusive maid served the drinks. Lavinia effortlessly steered Anton over to the other end of the terrace, where loud explosions of laughter were punctuating a funny story being told by the Swiss woman, who was a spectacular blonde with a lot of bosom on show. Her husband, a banker, was egging her on.

The Englishman, Mike, who turned out to be Lavinia's neighbour, had evidently already consumed several of the bright-orange drinks which he favoured.

'I live in the next villa along,' he told Amy. 'Can't see my house from here. Lavinia owns practically the whole hillside.'

'It's such a wonderful setting,' Amy said sincerely. 'You're very lucky. Do you live here all the year round?'

'I do. Lavinia doesn't. She also has a house in London and a place in Barbados.'

'Wow.'

'My house isn't quite as swish as Lavinia's,' Mike said,

eyeing the flawless regularity of the stonework with an al-cohol-bleared eye. 'See how smooth the masonry is? When she was doing up the place, she had the stonemason go over the whole house with a fine-tooth comb. Every stone that was a funny shape or colour was ripped out and replaced.'

'She likes all her ducks in a row.'

'Oh, yes. A bit of class, Lavinia is. Asset to the com-munity. You should see her, flying in with the chopper. She got her helicopter licence last year. Orange jumpsuit and mirror shades. Delicious sight.'

'Even better than in jodhpurs and riding boots?' Amy asked sympathetically.

'Just about as good,' Mike said sadly. 'Been trying to get her to marry me ever since old Bob died. Don't suppose I've got much hope.'

'Keep trying,' Amy advised. 'You know the old saying? Nothing propinks like propinquity.'

'Eh?'

'Being a neighbour,' she explained gently. 'You're in a good position.'

'Right,' Mike said, tapping his inflamed nose wisely. 'That's just earned you another drink.'

The sun went down, giving way to a velvety and cicada-inspired night. Dinner was served in the dining-room, which was an impressive chamber furnished with curvaceous ma-hogany Chippendale and what appeared to be real Impres-sionist paintings in heavy frames on the walls.

As on the terrace, Amy had been paired with Mike, who by now was even sadder and more inebriated. But the party was small enough that she could hear all the conversations that were going on.

Lavinia had finally changed out of her tailored riding gear and was wearing a violet sheath dress which intensified her eyes and showed off her slim, suntanned arms and shoulders—as well as two apple-like breasts that might or might not have owed their firmness to a judicious addition of silicone.

'You look wonderful, Lavinia,' Anton said appreciatively, 'like something from a Paul Jacoulet print.'

'Thank you, sweet boy,' she purred in reply. Amy spread her napkin studiously in her lap, hoping she wasn't going to throw up.

The meal started with *moules à la marinière*, succulent mussels cooked in sherry. The main course was a huge baked fish in a rich Provençal sauce. Lavinia was watching with a hawk eye as the maid served each guest in turn.

'Now tell me, you wicked boy,' she said to Anton, smiling at him lazily over her Baccarat wine glass, 'what is all this nonsense about turning the Zell Corporation into some kind of ecological charitable trust?'

'I've never thought of myself as a charity,' he replied with a smile. 'But you know as well as I do that the petrochemical industry doesn't exactly have a shining record on environmental issues.'

'And pray, who cares about *that* apart from a few lunatic fringe groups?'

'Well, we all ought to care about it,' Anton replied, 'since we all have to live in the same world, breathe the same air and drink the same water.'

'Drink the stuff that comes out of the tap?' Lavinia said disapprovingly. 'You bad boy, you know I only touch Vichy or Perrier.'

Anton smiled. 'Well, I hope you don't plan to start buying your own air, too. You wouldn't be nearly so pretty wearing a scuba mask.'

'You're just trying to annoy me,' Lavinia said in a purring voice. She reached out a slender brown hand and began to stroke his arm. It was a gesture of unmistakable possession.

'These projects of yours to refine used oil aren't nearly as profitable as big, old-fashioned refineries.'

'I haven't noticed that profits have dropped lately,' he replied mildly.

'Not yet—but they will do if you let the opposition take over your traditional business while you gallop off on your new hobby-horse.' The slim, tanned fingers curled on his forearm, and the pearly nails dug in hungrily, assessing the springy muscles. 'And *recycling*—that must be the least stylish word in the English language, for heaven's sake!'

Anton laughed. 'It ought to be the most stylish word in the English language.'

'And anyway, what's the percentage in cleaning up old oil that's already been used?'

'The percentage is that we're teaching people to re-utilise a finite resource. When the planet's oil supplies run out, we're going to have to start cleaning up the old oil anyway. But we won't be able to do that if it's all been dumped in holes in the ground!'

'Oh, Anton! Who's interested in all that Doomsday talk?'

'People who care about the environment, for one thing. For another, people who want to offset expensive oil imports.'

Lavinia lowered her eyelids over amethyst eyes. 'But dear boy, don't we *want* the price of oil to go up?'

'Not unless you're happy to see the world caught up in another oil crisis, with all that that entails.'

Heinz, the banker, leaned forward. 'It doesn't do to turn your business into an aid organisation, old boy. You've sold off the Marseilles refinery, which was making a fortune.'

'The deal looks pretty good to me,' Anton replied easily.

'Maybe the stockholders will feel less certain. And launching new technology is a risky business, whatever fine moral principles you espouse. As Lavinia's banker, I have to agree with her. Remember your shareholders. Don't get carried away by a dream.'

'My whole business is built on a dream,' Anton said. 'The day I stop dreaming will be the day I stop living. My latest dream is of a cleaner world where our oil supplies last for centuries longer. But I've made it clear at the last few shareholders' meetings that refining raw stock is an increasingly crowded field. We have to look to new technologies if we're to keep growing. Refining used oil is the way of the future. And as crude oil gets scarcer and more expensive, it can only become more important. To everybody, not just developing nations. It's a new field, yes, but we're going to be dominant in it.'

'Darling boy,' Lavinia drawled, 'I like to see lots and lots of money in my bank account. Nothing else matters to me. I don't care if that means chimneys belching smoke or the occasional oil-spill on some remote coastline—as long as it isn't ours.'

'Hear, hear,' Mike said in a slurred voice.

'We're in the oil business,' Lavinia went on. She was still kneading Anton's arm insistently. 'If the price of Mr Jones filling his gas tank goes up, that just means more profits for you and me!'

'But it *is* on your coastline,' Amy heard herself say.

Lavinia turned cold eyes on her. 'I beg your pardon?'

'It is on your coastline,' Amy repeated. 'That sea that you gaze at may look blue, but it's more polluted than anywhere else in the Mediterranean.'

'That's an exaggeration, to put it kindly,' Lavinia said grimly. 'Everything you have eaten tonight comes out of that sea.'

'Yes, and I'm afraid that this delicious fish we're eating is full of heavy metals like mercury, cadmium and lead. And those tasty *moules à la marinière* contain some very col-

ourful toxins, including polynuclear aromatic hydrocarbons.
It all comes from the oil refineries at Marseilles. Nobody's
doing very much about it, except people like Anton. So it
is on your coastline, you see.'

Lavinia's mouth and eyes showed her anger. 'We have
all heard these scare stories for years. But nobody has actually died yet.'

'Millions of fish and shellfish have died,' Amy retorted.
'Every year, countless tons of used oil just get dumped into
the environment,' she went on. 'With Anton's technology,
all of that could be turned back into a valuable resource and
reused. And his shareholders have no cause to complain.
Profits are well up for the tenth quarter in a row. I think
you should just let him do what he does best, sit back, and
enjoy the profits.'

'Amy,' Anton said in a low, but warning voice.

'I'm sorry, perhaps that was unpardonably rude,' Amy
said, flushing hotly. 'It's a subject I feel strongly about.'

Lavinia's hand was clamped hard on Anton's arm now,
as though she had suddenly become aware of a dangerous
challenge to her authority. In her violet sheath, she resembled some exotic snake about to strike. 'Well, dear Snow
White,' she said thinly, 'having eaten my poisoned apple,
when can we expect you to fall into a deep—and silent—
slumber?'

'Amy is certainly right about the bottom line,' Anton said,
stepping swiftly into the breach as Amy coloured even more
hotly. 'The new technology and its spin-offs look set to earn
us even bigger profits. I'm going to announce expansion
plans at the next board meeting.'

His calm voice seemed to soothe Lavinia's ire as he explained the network of refineries he was planning to build
over the next years, but Amy felt as though a jagged stone
had lodged in her throat. She hadn't meant to get so carried

away, and insult Lavinia Carron at her own table. Or to embarrass Anton by being so obstreperous that her hostess had told her to shut up. He was probably furious with her and she would be lucky to keep her job. Most likely, she would be finding herself unemployed by tomorrow morning.

Truth to tell, perhaps it had been watching those sharp, pearly nails raking Anton's skin that had enraged her so much, not just the conversation.

Whatever her excuse, she was now plainly about as welcome at the dinner party as a pile of horse manure. The best thing she could do was cart herself off as soon as possible and spread herself on the rose beds.

Accordingly, as soon as they adjourned from the table and moved to the salon, Amy offered a quiet apology about feeling tired and excused herself. Lavinia ignored her utterly. Anton, cornered between the hostess and her Swiss banker, was too busy to do more than glance at her as she left. Slinking up to bed, Amy felt tears of mortification pricking behind her eyelids. She was hurried on her way by a comment from Lavinia which—luckily—she did not hear, but which brought a guffaw of laughter from the other guests.

She lay in her lonely bed in a state of misery. Despite the huge size of the house, she could occasionally catch bursts of laughter or music from downstairs. It gave her the sensation of being a child again, exiled to her room for some fresh piece of bad behaviour, eavesdropping on a life which she was not permitted to share.

She was still far from sleep when, hours later, her door swung open and the light flared on.

Dazzled, her eyes hurting, she sat up in bed. A tall figure was towering over her.

'Anton?'

'What the hell were you playing at tonight?' he demanded savagely. 'Have you lost your mind?'

'Anton, I'm so sorry,' she said abjectly. 'I don't know what got into me.'

'Didn't you listen to *anything* I told you on the way up here?'

'Yes, I promise that I did listen—'

'Lavinia holds a twenty per cent stake in the corporation. Can you understand that?'

'Yes,' she whispered.

'And she doesn't like the new direction we're taking. The idea was to reassure her—not antagonise her. *And* her bank manager, for heaven's sake.' Her eyes were growing used to the light, but it did not give her any consolation to see that his mouth was a harsh line and that his eyes were almost black with anger. 'What the hell did you think you were playing at?'

His tone was so angry that she was on the verge of tears. 'I didn't mean to mess things up for you, Anton. When she started talking so callously, I just lost it. Are you going to fire me?'

'Lavinia has specifically requested exactly that,' he replied.

Her eyes welled. 'Oh.'

The sight of her wet eyes seemed to make him pause. 'Don't do that,' he snapped.

'Sorry.' She blotted her tears. 'I've been lying here counting the ways in which I made a fool of myself tonight.'

He sat on the bed beside her. 'It was certainly a spectacular display of foolishness.'

She cringed at the comment. 'I'm so sorry,' she said with a lump in her throat. 'Am I fired?'

He paused before replying. Her heart fluttered like a broken bird. 'If I don't fire you,' he said in a calmer voice, 'Lavinia will be even angrier.'

'Then you'd better fire me,' she whispered.

'I don't take orders from anyone,' he said shortly. 'And I have never fired anyone for speaking their mind. Besides, you said nothing but the truth. I'm going to risk Lavinia's wrath.' His eyes narrowed terrifyingly. 'But if you say or do one thing more to annoy her while we're here, I will personally throttle you.'

'I'll be as silent as a stone,' she said fervently. 'I'm really sorry, Anton. I don't know what got into me.'

'The point of this visit is so I can make sure she doesn't create a fuss at the next board meeting and panic other shareholders. Do you think you can manage to stay in the background for a few days?'

'I'll go for long, solitary walks,' she vowed. 'You can let her squeeze your arm and tell her she looks like a portrait by Paul Jacoulet as much as you like.'

'Good,' he said.

'Who is Paul Jacoulet, by the way?'

'A French artist who made drawings of beautiful women.'

'Oh. How cultured you are. Those breasts aren't real, you know.'

'Amy,' he said warningly.

She cursed herself. This was becoming a kind of insanity. 'Sorry. I will behave, I promise.'

She felt his hand stroke her hair. 'I know it's going to be hard for you,' he said softly. 'You looked like an angel tonight—try and be one for a while.'

She turned her face so that her soft cheek rested in the palm of his hand. 'How far do you intend to go along the path of charm?'

'Trust me.' He drew her close and kissed her cheek. 'It's all in a good cause.'

'I do trust you.' It required only a small tilt of her head—or did he tilt his?—for her lips to brush his.

'My sweet Amy,' he whispered. He kissed her lips again, then a third time. His mouth was so sweet, so tender. She felt herself melting. She slipped her arms around his neck, the ache in her heart turning into a surging warmth.

His tongue searched for hers, found it, caressed it longingly. A thrill of desire ran through her. She was finally learning to trust him. When he kissed her like this, doubts fled like shadows from the rising sun.

Anton's warm hand touched her breasts. She was wearing only a light summer negligée. Her nipples tightened with delight at his touch, pressing into his palm as he cupped her curves. At least *they* were real, she thought, exulting in his touch.

'I want you so much, Amy!' he whispered.

But at that moment, an unmistakable voice floated along the corridor. 'Anton? Have you got lost, darling boy? Where are you?'

'Damn her,' Anton said, with a catch in his voice. He kissed her eyelids. 'She wants us all to go into Antibes to see the moonlight on the sea or some such nonsense.'

'I was about to throw you out, anyway,' Amy said with an effort. She pushed him away with the last of her strength. 'Duty calls. Go where glory awaits you.'

Anton laughed softly. 'Aye aye. Sweet dreams, angel girl.'

He slipped out of her room. Shortly afterwards, Amy thought she heard Lavinia Carron's fluting laugh.

She curled into a ball, feeling his kiss still burning her lips, her nipples still aching at his touch. What she would give to be with Anton for the rest of this night, looking at the moonlight on the sea.

Or some such nonsense.

She had to get a grip on herself. Jealousy was the green-eyed monster that mocked what it fed upon. She would never have dreamed of letting Anton get so close to her—except that it hurt so much to see him being appropriated by Lavinia Carron!

What a mystery the female heart was! She should have been delighted to have the pressure taken off her. Having rejected Anton's advances countless times, in countless subtle and not-so-subtle ways, having convinced herself that he was a heartless rake, what was bringing these tears to her eyes?

CHAPTER EIGHT

SHE would always look back on the rest of that week as one of the most miserable periods of her life.

To begin with, the next morning, Gerda Meyer, the Swiss woman, came down with a violent stomach upset. In light of Amy's unfortunate remarks the evening before about toxins in seafood, it was hardly an auspicious event. Each time Lavinia looked Amy's way there seemed to be an almost perceptible rumble of psychic thunder.

By way of atonement—for the crime, presumably, of not having been summarily fired for insolence—Amy found herself cast in the role of nurse and comforter to Gerda, who was not in any way an easy patient. Her husband, Heinz, seemed to be eager to stay as far away from the bed of suffering as possible.

Bringing Gerda her umpteenth tisane of the day, Amy found the sufferer well enough to be sitting up accusingly, her blonde hair in disarray.

'Why did you have to talk about such horrible things last night?' she wailed. 'You have upset me terribly! What if I have been poisoned?'

'I'm sure it's just a simple tummy bug,' Amy said soothingly. 'It happens in the summertime, especially after eating shellfish.'

'Do not mention shellfish!' Gerda clutched at the tisane and gulped it down. 'Oh, my poor stomach! And I look such a fright,' she moaned, peering into her hand-mirror. 'The least you can do is help me look presentable so I can receive visitors.'

'Of course,' Amy sighed. She fetched Gerda's brush—

silver-backed and monogrammed—and started brushing the heavy blonde tresses into order.

'Where are Lavinia and Anton?' Gerda demanded.

Gritting her teeth at the way the two names had been lumped together as a self-evident pair, Amy replied, 'They've gone for a ride together on the horses.'

Indeed, she had seen them walking off along the hillside together just after lunch, looking very companionable. It was as though she and Anton inhabited different planets today. He had barely spoken to her. His attention had been focused on Lavinia.

'They will be married soon,' Gerda said. 'Please be careful! You are pulling my hair out by the roots!'

'Sorry,' Amy said thickly. 'What makes you say they're going to get married?'

Gerda giggled. 'Oh, Lavinia has made up her mind. And what Lavinia wants, Lavinia gets!'

'You mean Anton Zell has no say in the matter?'

'What would he want to say?'

'He might want to protest.'

'Protest?' Gerda asked in perplexity. 'They are both rich, beautiful and stylish. They belong together. Anyone can see that.'

Amy swallowed. 'Yes. I suppose so. But there do seem to be some differences between them.'

'You mean about the new technology? Oh, that is nothing. A little hitch in the proceedings. She hasn't invited him here to talk about *that*, I assure you, Elsie.'

'It's Amy. So why *has* she invited him here?'

'To propose to him, of course.'

'Oh. These days the women are proposing to the men?'

'Hah! She is as smart as a whip, that one. You know she just got her helicopter licence?'

Amy concentrated on the thick hair. 'Yes, I heard that.'

'Men are like helicopters. You just need to learn which

buttons to push, which levers to pull and, *voilà*, you are flying!' She giggled. 'It will be the wedding of the decade. Help me to put on my housecoat.'

Feeling bruised inside, Amy helped Gerda put on the floral pink geisha gown. Gerda pushed out her monumental bosoms and caressed their curves complacently. 'They are magnificent, aren't they? Yours are all right. Bigger than Lavinia's at least. They're the only thing she lacks—and not for want of trying, either, I might tell you,' she added with a flash of malice.

'I suppose she has all the other advantages a woman could want,' Amy said dully, helping Gerda to tie the sash.

She had to spend most of the rest of the afternoon listening to Gerda boast about her money and her figure—both of which were inherited, apparently, and owed nothing to art. Inside, though, Amy was trying not to let Gerda's gossip-column tittle-tattle weigh too heavily on her soul.

But why should she feel proprietorial about Anton? Just because he had kissed her last night—before that unfortunate interruption? Could she say by that brief moment that he really cared about her? If he went riding with Lavinia— or studying the moonlight with her—it was only business. And *his* business, at that. Wasn't it?

The happy couple returned from their ride looking even more companionable than before. The afternoon had been a hot one, redolent with the smell of herbs and loud with cicadas. Amy had to fight her imagination to stop visualising what might have transpired between them under some gnarled pine tree or in the shade of some olive grove.

She encountered Anton as he was going upstairs to change. His shirt was unbuttoned and among the dark, crisp hair that covered his muscular chest she could see a few torn rosemary leaves.

'I see she's planning to roast you in herbs,' she said tonelessly.

'Roast is right. That's the hottest I've ever been on a horse. How's your day been?'

'Fascinating. I've spent most of it watching Gerda be sick into a Sèvres bowl.'

'That sounds very colourful.'

'You have no idea.'

'You can hardly complain. The poor lady is obviously turning herself inside-out in order to amuse you.'

'Eeww.'

He kissed her cheek tenderly. 'You are a very brave girl. Your gallantry will not be forgotten.'

'There was a young mogul called Zell,' she intoned, 'who smiled as he rode with a belle; they returned from the ride with the mogul inside and the smile on the face of the belle.'

Anton grinned. 'Oh ye of little faith. Wait and see who eats whom.'

But she didn't want either of them to eat the other, she thought with anguish. She wanted everything to be the way it had been before they came here.

But there was no way in the world she could articulate either of those paradoxical thoughts to him. She just had to smile. 'Go get 'em, tiger.'

He hugged her quickly. 'I know this is boring for you. We'll be out of here in a few days. Be patient. You promised!'

Amy pressed her face to his chest, inhaling the delicious smell of his hot skin for a moment, then pushed him away. 'Go and wash. And be sure to pick all the leaves out of your hair, dahling boy.'

At dinner that night, Amy found herself relegated to an even more remote corner of the table. There were extra guests for dinner, mostly quite elderly people, and she was seated on the far side of them. That effectively stopped her from contributing any more unwelcome interpolations into the general conversation—and also prevented her from hearing much of what was said by Anton, Lavinia and the inner circle.

It was a special torture to watch him, from what felt like miles away, apparently having a wonderful time; so handsome when he laughed at Lavinia's sly jokes, so urbane when he spoke. Amy felt more and more like the invisible woman. She shrank into herself, smiling politely at the yarns which the elderly gentleman who was her neighbour seemed to have so many of, but feeling cold and lonely inside.

Once again, she was excluded from the after-dinner fun; everyone went down into Antibes to go to a concert where a famous violinist was performing, but she excused herself, knowing her presence would only irritate Lavinia—who showed no signs of forgiveness—and make it harder for Anton. She felt unwanted, a pariah.

The only other house-guest who stayed was Gerda, who was still feeling fragile. Amy stood her excruciating discussion of her bosom and her bank account until she could bear no more, and crept up to bed.

And though she waited until her poor eyelids grew heavy as lead for Anton to come and kiss her goodnight, he had not returned by 2 a.m. and she fell asleep on the coverlet.

It did not help much when, the next morning at breakfast, Anton told her that he had come into her room very late.

'You were fast asleep,' he smiled. 'Snoring like a lumber mill. So I just kissed you goodnight and left you to get your beauty sleep.'

'Oh, thanks,' she said drily, thinking that kisses didn't count if one was not awake to enjoy them. Nor did it escape her attention that he was dressed to go riding again, long legs encased in jeans and well-worn boots. 'Nice evening?'

'After the concert we went to a cabaret show. It was very dull.'

'Tame, no doubt, compared to your Wanchai strip clubs.'

'Well, the girls are taller. Did Gerda throw up any more?' he asked with interest.

'Unfortunately, the flow has come to an end. But I know everything there is to be known about which bras she pours her boobs into and which banks she pours her billions into.'

'That bad?'

'Worse than you can imagine.'

'Oh, dear.'

'Her money and her mammaries are her only topics of conversation, Anton. If I have to spend another hour in her company, I may strangle her.'

'I promise you, Worthington, you're in line for a medal as soon as we can get away from this morgue.'

'And when will that be? You seem unable to tear yourself away from a certain somebody.'

'Darling, if you think Gerda is bad, you want to try Morticia.'

Amy burst out laughing. 'Oh, that's funny! Gerda says she's planning you to be the next Gomez.'

'Marriage? I doubt that. Lavinia is very happy the way she is.'

'I think she's in love with you,' Amy said, her laughter fading away. 'And she's sexy, clever and sophisticated.'

'So?'

'So, you'd have to have a very good reason to turn her down.'

The smile was more in his eyes than on his lips. 'What if I was only interested in someone else?'

'Who would that be?' she asked, her heart jumping.

'Someone with the face of an angel.'

She was about to reply when a familiar female voice enquired, 'And what is the joke, dear boy? May we share?'

They turned to face the bright eyes and lean brown face of Lavinia. She was once again wearing the jodhpurs and cotton shirt that showed off her figure to such advantage, except that today's shade was peppermint-green.

'Just recalling an old TV show,' Anton said with a smile.

'I never seem to have time to watch television.' Lavinia slapped her kid gloves into her palm. 'Have you had breakfast? Then let's get out on the horses before it gets too hot. There are some absolutely wonderful bridle-paths we can take along the mountainside. And I know a country restaurant where they'll look after the horses for us while we have the most scrummy lunch.'

'Sounds good,' Anton said, with only the faintest hint of weariness in his voice—or was that just his way of pacifying Amy's surging indignation at being left alone all day yet again?

And for the second day in a row, she was treated to the spectacle of Anton and Lavinia riding off into the *maquis*, heads close together.

It all washed over her yet again, that familiar pain at being shut out, unwanted, a sinner not admitted to the golden circle. Her cousins had made her feel like that for most of her adolescence. Now Lavinia Carron was doing it all over again—and it hurt so terribly.

If only Lavinia were a more likeable person, Amy told herself, she would be standing up and cheering at the sight of Anton with a suitable Significant Other at his side.

But Lavinia didn't deserve him!

An appreciative, compassionate woman with the ability to understand Anton's own sad past—that was what he needed. Someone who knew where he had come from and why he was the man he was. Someone who believed in the same things he did and who supported him in his dreams— *that* was what he needed.

Not this rapacious, hard-hearted female who thought only about herself and who surrounded herself with people as tough-natured and selfish as herself. That just wasn't fair.

On the third day of their visit, Lavinia had arranged a cruise along the coast to the Îles de Lérins, the archipelago of islands off Cannes where the Man in the Iron Mask had been incarcerated. Gerda Meyer was now fully recovered from her tummy bug and there was no reasonable excuse to exclude Amy—so she found herself invited to go along. The prospect of finally getting to spend some time with Anton—though hardly alone with him—made her accept, though her better judgement told her to stay home.

The boat, a charter, was a graceful white yacht which picked them up at the port. As they sailed out of the bay towards the islands, a cool breeze picked up, washing away the fierce heat that was already building up.

It was another searing day. Banks of cloud along the horizon promised that the hot weather had to break soon.

The sea was crowded with pleasure boats of all types, though—Amy thought wryly—Lavinia could console herself that hers was the biggest and smartest on the waves.

Lavinia's latest materialisation seemed to be as Bond girl—a very small black bikini which showed her tanned and athletic body, over which she had slung a snow-white nautical jacket and very short white shorts, the ensemble completed with a gold-braided white cap. It would have been ridiculous—if she didn't look so damned good in it.

She was in her element, issuing orders, arranging everything, clearly revelling in being master and commander of the whole ark. Fifteen years ago, Amy thought, Lavinia must have been head girl of some élite college for young ladies.

Tomorrow—thank heavens—she and Anton were leaving for Marseilles and then the flight back to Hong Kong.

That gave Lavinia one more day to clinch the deal, she thought cynically. Unless she was going to wait until the annual general meeting in London at the end of the year. If she was wise, waiting until London was the better plan.

Anton might be tempted by all the wealth and that lean brown body to go with it, but Lavinia probably wanted to be quite sure of her prey.

In her own pink and chocolate Christian Dior bikini and tortoiseshell sunglasses, Amy looked feminine and tranquil. She stayed out of the way, leaning on the polished brass rail and watching the green coastline slip past. At least she was out of that awful stone fortress. The blue sea was purifying and relaxing.

Anton leaned on the rail beside her. 'Your face is peaceful for a change,' he said.

'I love the sea,' she replied.

'Ah, I forgot—a mermaid's natural habitat.'

She smiled. 'I thought I was a monkey.'

'Yes, you're definitely a monkey.'

'Always nice to know one's a monkey.'

'I told you in Hong Kong, the monkey is a very nice sign to be. And monkeys are very good in bed, too.'

'Really? In what way?'

'They know how to enjoy pleasure.'

'And that qualifies someone as being good in bed? Selfishness?'

'I didn't mention selfishness. It's actually just the opposite quality. It's taking delight in being loved.'

'I'm not sure I have that particular monkey quality.'

'I'm doing my best to develop it in you.'

'Lavinia certainly knows how to entertain her guests.'

'Robert left her very wealthy,' he replied. 'She has nothing to do but spend her money in a variety of imaginative ways.'

'You talk as though you don't like her much,' Amy replied, glancing at him. He was wearing only black and yellow Hawaiian baggies. His magnificent physique gleamed in the sun, muscles rippling under his golden skin when he moved. She was so jealous of that body; she hated the way other women looked at him.

'I do like her. But she doesn't always understand that she can't have her way in everything, no matter how rich and clever she is.'

'Yes,' Amy said wryly, 'I can see she's giving you a hard time.'

'She wants me to change direction on the new refineries.'

'Is that what you talk about when you're alone together for hours at a time?' she asked, watching a small sailboat bob past in their wake.

'She seems to think she understands the oil business better than I do,' he said with a smile. 'Robert was happy to sit back and rake in the profits, as you put it the other night. Lavinia has ideas about everything. And with the big stake in the corporation which Robert left her, she can throw her weight around.'

'Could she really cause trouble with other shareholders?'

'She knows a lot of people. And she knows how to get things done. If she persuades enough shareholders that I'm taking the corporation in the wrong direction, there could be big problems.'

'What's the worst that could happen?'

'I could be fired as chief executive officer.'

'But it's your company!' she exclaimed.

He shook his head. 'I own a fifty-one per cent stake. But it's a listed company, and if enough of the shareholders were against me, I would have to step down rather than face a civil war and seeing public confidence disintegrate.'

Amy stared at his face. 'You mentioned buying her out.'

'Yes. If I could persuade her to sell. That's one problem. Another is that Zell is a British company, and under British law, if I buy back shares they have to be immediately cancelled. I can't resell them.'

'What would happen?'

'Well, it's complicated. There would be fewer shares in circulation and so the remaining shares would be more valuable, in theory. But it would cost a lot of money, money that I have earmarked for our expansion in south-east Asia. It would mean delaying my plans for a year, perhaps far longer.'

The Bond girl herself was on deck now, surrounded by her friends. There was a palpable air of excitement about the trim, tanned figure; she looked like a woman who knew exactly where she was going.

'Anton!' she called. 'Darling boy, you're missing the dolphins.'

They both turned. A group of three or four dolphins was indeed swimming alongside the yacht, sleek bodies surging in and out of the waves. It was a thrilling sight. Lavinia Carron's triumphant expression suggested she was personally responsible for the presence of the animals.

On second thoughts, Amy decided gloomily, as Lavinia hooked her arm through Anton's and led him away, the creatures were probably animatronic robots, directed by a remote-control unit in the pocket of Lavinia Carron's very short white shorts.

To avoid the crowds, they sailed to the far side of Île Sainte-Marguerite, the largest of the islands. The yacht moored as near the beach as possible and the dinghy took them ashore.

The white beach was hot underfoot. The whole of the island was covered by a natural forest of Aleppo pine and eucalyptus, whose scented and woven shade offered some shelter from the midday heat.

The weather, however, was now threatening. The fierce heat of the past few days seemed to have charged the atmosphere with violence. A grey haze was in the sky. The endless noise of cicadas was deafening and Amy felt oddly breathless from the heat and the close humidity.

'It's going to storm,' Anton warned.

'No, it's not,' Lavinia said sharply, glancing up at the heavy sky as though daring the heavens to contradict her. 'Breathe deeply, everybody. The eucalyptus is wonderful for the lungs!'

Everyone snorted and sucked the fragrant air obediently. Amy wondered bitterly whether they would stop breathing just as tamely if Lady Carron commanded it.

The plan was that the party should walk through the forest to the port, where they were to have lunch in a restaurant and then visit the Fort Royal, where the Man in the Iron Mask had been incarcerated three centuries ago.

Their hostess led the way.

They set off in a group along the winding, sandy paths through the forest. However it soon became obvious that Lavinia, honed by hours in the gymnasium, had overestimated the physical fitness of her party. Complaining about the heat and the oppressive atmosphere, the less athletic began to lag behind, while Lavinia strode on contemptuously ahead. Within a short while, the party was strung out; and the number of twisting paths became confusing, with no directions to follow. The forest seemed endless, the pine trees identical with one another, each path exactly like all the others.

A rumble of thunder pierced Amy's resentment and released a flood of remorse. She had been walking with Gerda Meyer, who was complaining of the heat, but boredom had driven her to quicken her pace. Now Gerda was nowhere to be seen. Heinz, her husband, was up in the front with Lavinia, obviously believing a footsore wife was not a good enough reason to take his eye off such an important client as Lady Carron.

Amy stopped and retraced her steps. Gerda was as dull a woman as creation had ever put wind in, but Amy felt bad

about leaving her to wander the forests alone like a silly,
bleating sheep.

Walking back a hundred yards or so, she found no trace
of Gerda—or of anyone else. She was completely alone in
the stifling, cicada-loud woodland. A glare of lightning was
instantly followed by a searing crash of thunder so loud and
so close overhead that she almost jumped out of her skin.

A gust of hot wind buffeted her. It was clearly about to
storm, as Anton had predicted. Amy looked up at the turgid
sky anxiously. Sheltering under a tree was not supposed to
be a good idea in an electrical storm, but what if there was
nothing *but* trees? Could lightning tell one identical eucalyptus from another?

Another shattering peal of thunder heralded more wind
and the first heavy, hot drops of rain. Uncertain what to do,
Amy hesitated.

And then the heavens opened and a tempest of rain and
wind was unleashed. Blinded by the onslaught, Amy blun-
dered off the path into the relative shelter of the trees. There
was no point in searching for Gerda now—she would have
to wait until the storm was over.

She snuggled into herself, wishing she were wearing
something warmer; the temperature was dropping fast and
it was turning cold. Damn Lavinia, Amy thought, huddling
up to the rough trunk of a pine tree. She was probably sitting
in a café now with a glass of wine, stroking her 'darling
boy' and chuckling at the fate of the stragglers.

The storm intensified in violence, thunder rolling from
one side of the heavens to the other, the rain lashing down
in curtains that made visibility impossible.

And then a tall, dark figure materialised through the rain,
heading towards her. Her heart jumped into her throat.

'Anton!'

His beautiful white teeth flashed in a grin as he reached
her. He was wearing only his Hawaiian baggies and a cerise

waterproof poncho which he spread over both their heads for shelter. His wet face pressed to hers as he gave her an exuberant kiss. 'Remember Borneo?' he greeted her.

'How could I forget? Where did you get the poncho?'

'Bought it in the port. Lavinia and the others are having lunch already. I came back to find you.'

'You sweet man! I was very pleased to see you. I hate thunderstorms.'

'How did you get so far behind?'

'I was walking with poor Gerda but I just had to escape and she got left behind. I hope she isn't drowning.'

'Her natural resources will keep her buoyant.'

She smiled. 'I hope so.' Thunder pealed across the sky, making her snuggle up against him more closely. His naked, muscled torso was dripping with rain but that somehow made him all the more desirable. The deep pink shade of the poncho was so intimate. 'And you left dear Lavinia to come running back to me? Such a noble man!'

'She's being particularly impossible today. Going on and on about the new technology.'

'She's moving in on you, Anton,' Amy said. 'She wants to show you how knowledgeable she is. What an asset she would be as a wife. And all this lavish entertainment she's laying on—it's designed to show you the wonderful life you could have together.'

'We spend all our time together arguing, Amy.'

'That's the stick to go with the carrot. She's demonstrating that it makes sense to join forces with her. She's chosen you, can't you see that? Fate has thrown twenty per cent of your corporation into her lap. You are an engineering and business genius, the handsomest man in the world according to *Vogue*, and just plain the most eligible bachelor in sight. She's made marrying you her life's mission—and what Lavinia wants, Lavinia gets.'

His deep blue eyes were watching her face with a

strangely quizzical expression. 'I had no idea you felt that way about me.'

'Oh, come on!' she exclaimed restlessly, laying her palm on his powerful naked chest. 'With her twenty per cent and your fifty-one per cent, you'll never have to worry about boardroom battles again. I'm surprised she hasn't spelled it out just as clearly as that.'

'Perhaps she's hoping I would take her without her twenty per cent,' he said gently.

'And would you?' she asked directly.

'I'm much more interested in all these compliments you've just paid me—that I'm handsome, a genius…and an eligible bachelor.'

'You know all that,' she said impatiently. 'Modesty is not one of your virtues.'

'Maybe not. But I'm still somewhat surprised to hear all that coming out of your mouth.'

'Don't be silly,' she retorted. 'Why should you be surprised?'

'I had the impression you don't think very much of me,' he replied, still looking at her with that odd expression.

She gaped. 'Don't think very much of you? What made you think that?'

'Well, every time I try to touch you, you push me away— or run like a rabbit. It's plain you have some violent aversion to being close to me.'

Amy was dumbfounded for a moment. 'Anton, not wanting to become your latest mistress doesn't mean I don't admire you passionately as a human being.'

His eyelids drooped. 'Ah. I'm a genius, but physically unattractive?'

'This is insanity,' she said, half laughing in perplexity. 'Of course you're not unattractive! Haven't I just said you're the handsomest man in the world?'

'According to *Vogue*.'

'And according to every other female who lays eyes on you!'

'Including you?'

He had fenced her neatly into a corner. 'Yes, Anton,' she said quietly, 'including me.'

Her palm was still resting on his chest. He leaned close to her, his warm bare skin touching hers. 'And so you run because…'

'I told you already. Because I'm not going to be your toy.'

He brushed her wet, golden hair with his lips. 'I'm confused. What am I—nice guy or monster?'

'I never said you were a monster. I never said you were a nice guy, either!'

'So what am I?'

'You're a hunter,' she replied.

'A hunter of what?'

'Of whatever you want. Of success. Of women.'

He laughed quietly. 'I thought you'd just been trying to explain how Lavinia was hunting *me*?'

'Yes, that must be a new experience for you. It's usually you doing the stalking.'

'So you think I'm stalking you?'

'Yes!'

'So I can jump on you…and eat you up?'

A rumble of thunder prevented her from replying; and then it was too late. Anton was kissing her with the passion of a man who wanted her desperately. She clung to him, her hungry fingers running across the contours of his naked torso, nails digging in, pulling him closer to her.

Their tongues were tasting one another. Amy's eyes were tight shut but she had never been so aware of who she was kissing—not some faceless figure in a fantasy, but Anton, the man she was growing to love so helplessly, the man she respected and cherished above all others.

She pressed her stomach against his, intoxicated by the naked contact between them. She wanted to tell him how much he meant to her, how frantic she was for his touch. All her caution was melting away like a sugar-cone castle in this tropical downpour.

And then she became aware of a bleating sound, like a lost and very bedraggled sheep.

They turned to see Gerda Meyer staring at them. Her yellow hair hung down in soaked sheets in front of her face but there was no doubt that she could see what was happening perfectly.

'What are you doing?' she demanded in outrage, eyes popping.

'We came to look for you,' Amy said. 'We thought you were lost.'

'I *was* lost,' Gerda said bitterly. 'Everybody just abandoned me. But now it is I who have found *you*, it seems!'

Anton raised an eyebrow at Amy in amused commentary. But Amy did not return the smile. There was no question but that Gerda would report what she had seen to Lavinia— and a disenchanted Lavinia could only spell a great deal of trouble for Anton in the future.

The rain was not yet easing off, but it seemed preferable to brave the thunderbolts rather than try and fit three discomfited people under the one pink poncho, so they walked along the path to the port. Anton tried to hold Amy's hand, but she pulled away from him, anxious not to give Gerda any further ammunition. 'Please don't,' she whispered. 'It's not worth it!'

'Amy, don't pull away from me!'

'Not in front of her! Lavinia can be very bad news for you, Anton. I could never forgive myself if I made things worse for you.'

Gerda, for her part, was evidently bursting for a little private chat with Amy.

She took Amy's arm and drew her aside with a face like thunder. 'What did you think you were doing back there?' she hissed imperiously.

'We were just sheltering from the rain,' Amy said, attempting a desperate defence.

'You were practically devouring him! I have never seen a woman kiss a man so shamelessly as you were doing! Did I not tell you that Lavinia and Anton are going to be married?'

'Lavinia may have told you that that is her plan,' Amy retorted before wiser council silenced her, 'but she cannot speak for Anton!'

'You little fool,' Gerda snapped. 'Do you want to ruin him? Do you really think he could be serious about *you*, a nobody, a junior employee? Do you think you are the first secretary who has fallen in love with him?'

The words bit into her heart like an axe. 'No, I don't think that,' she said quietly.

'The last one was so crazy about him it was embarrassing to everybody,' Gerda went on, shaking the dripping hair out of her eyes. 'You are even worse, getting in the way all the time, like a badly behaved child! All he wants from you is quick sex, can't you understand that? You can have no idea how much trouble you are causing!'

'I don't want to get in anybody's way.' Wisdom made Amy bite her tongue and refrain from saying anything further. The last thing she wanted was to harm Anton. Whatever he wanted from her, and whatever his plans with Lavinia, she cared about him enough not to wish him harmed in any way.

Gerda's eyes narrowed. 'I see now! You think that once they are married, he will install you as his mistress in some lacquered palace in Hong Kong!'

'What?'

Gerda chuckled. 'So, you are not so stupid as I thought!

A business wife in France and a pleasure wife in Hong Kong? Oh, yes, he is man enough for that.'

'Unfortunately, I'm not woman enough for such an arrangement,' Amy replied icily.

'Come, come. You needn't play the grand lady with me, *chèrie*. I am a woman of the world. And I know men like Anton Zell. They want it all—and they always get to have it all.'

Anton Zell can have it all. The fact that she herself had used exactly those words to Anton a few days earlier did not escape Amy. She gritted her teeth. 'I'm not a grand lady.'

'No, but you are not stupid, either.' Gerda's shrewd glance contained a new respect. 'Lavinia is a grand lady. She has money and power. But you have something else, something she will never have. Play your cards right, and it will work. As long as you don't get in Lavinia's way, she may even tolerate you!'

'Tolerate?'

'Empresses sometimes tolerate a concubine—or two,' Gerda said with a malicious smile.

Amy hurried on, leaving the older woman behind. But Gerda's vicious words were stuck in her heart like daggers.

The rest of the afternoon was dark and rainy. Amy could not be sure at what point Gerda Meyer spilled the beans to Lavinia—Lavinia was far too socially accomplished to give any great outward show of outrage—but there was no question that the beans had been spilled. The way Lavinia behaved as though Amy didn't even exist confirmed that.

The downpour and several of the party having been marooned in the forest made for a somewhat subdued evening meal, punctuated by sniffs and sneezes. Amy made sure she avoided both Anton and Lavinia Carron; right now, she didn't want to be alone with either of them.

It rained and blew all night. It seemed to Amy, in bed early, that the dawn would never come. She tried not to think about what might be passing between Anton and Lavinia as the lightning flashed and the thunder rumbled. Anton had said things about Lavinia that showed he was not blinded by her wealth and magnetism. But then, a man did not have to be in love to marry.

A man like Anton needed a strong wife, not a sugar-plum fairy. He might reckon that marriage to Lavinia would give him enough power to accomplish just about anything in life and that it was not necessary that she be a saint into the bargain.

And as for that searing kiss in the forest—he probably reasoned that he could pick many flowers along the way without losing sight of his main goal.

With these and similar thoughts she tormented herself, feeling more wretched and creating uglier monsters until the grey dawn brought relief and she could drag herself into the shower and try to rinse away the pain.

The breakfast-room did not appear to be a very joyous place when she went down. On the other hand, both Anton and Lavinia seemed to be in normal mood and were talking to one another quite cheerfully. Anton wanted to make an early start, so the leave-taking was mercifully brief.

The bags were soon loaded into the car beside the fountain with the snarling lions. Lavinia bestowed a kiss on Anton's mouth that seemed warm enough. Then she turned to Amy, as though suddenly Amy had become visible again. She smiled thinly and said only five words, in a voice so quiet that nobody else heard:

'Don't get in my way.'

Amy said nothing in reply, but the look in Lavinia Carron's eyes stayed with her for a long time—well until they were on the motorway back to Marseilles. The sky appeared bruised and there was still a steady rain falling, drumming on the canvas hood of the Mercedes.

'Stormy night,' Amy said at last, breaking the silence.

'Yes,' Anton replied.

'Well,' she demanded, unable to bear the suspense any longer, 'what happened last night? Did she pop the question?'

Anton burst out laughing. 'Of course she didn't pop the question, you silly girl.'

'Then she'll be waiting until the chairman's report in London,' Amy said decisively. 'She's sweetened you up with boat rides and good food and fabulous entertainment this time. Next time, she'll be carrying the big stick.'

He glanced at her with amused eyes. 'You think she's after my hide?'

'Wait and see,' Amy said gloomily. 'Just wait and see.'

CHAPTER NINE

By the end of September they were in Vietnam.

Amy was getting used to the great Asian cities, with their vast metropolitan centres and immense populations. Saigon's centre was featureless and busy. But once out in the suburbs, it still had the feel of a town with a heart. Instead of the districts of featureless apartment blocks that made up the suburbs of other Asian metropolises, she found charming, dilapidated streets of vintage old buildings that sprawled along the banks of the river.

It was rather like stepping back in time. The streets swarmed with bicycles and scooters. The cars all tended to be vintage models. Even the company car that picked them up from the airport was a forty-year-old Peugeot, rather than the battleship limos of richer cities.

'What a dreamy place!' she sighed happily to Anton in the car. 'Aren't we supposed to call it Ho Chi Minh City?'

'People are tending to call it that now, but it's taken a few years for the name to stick.'

'I love it, whatever it's called,' she said, gazing out of the window. 'It's very different from Singapore or Hong Kong. Some parts look like bits of Paris that have been somehow dumped in Asia and left to soften!'

'Even the colours are different,' he agreed. It was true; the delicate yellows, pinks and lime-greens of the buildings blended in beautifully with one another along the tree-lined boulevards. 'And notice how clean the streets are. The devastation of the war has made the Vietnamese very conscious of their environment. That's one of the reasons I like dealing with them.'

They were not going to be staying in a hotel in Saigon, but in a company villa which the Zell Corporation had bought in the suburbs. She was curious to see what it looked like, since someone at Zell in Hong Kong had told her it was the most beautiful house he had ever been in—in fact, he had become quite dreamy-eyed at the memory.

Their car passed through tall, ornate iron gates and pulled up in a cobbled courtyard. Two maids, delicate Vietnamese girls dressed in black and white uniforms, came out to greet them and help them with their bags.

'This is exquisite,' Amy said with delight as she walked through the house. Indeed, it was more of a small palace than a villa, an intoxicating mixture of French empire and Forbidden City, with rococo mouldings and Oriental antiques, Buddhist silk hangings and dim oil paintings. Her bedroom was vast, with a four-poster bed in the centre of the room, draped with diaphanous voile.

The smiling maid opened the glass doors that led onto the garden. Amy stepped outside, bemused. The walled garden was huge, shaded by great trees with glossy leaves. She could see large and ancient bronze urns meditating among the shrubbery. In the centre was a pond, its surface covered with the pink and yellow flowers and emerald-coloured pads of water lilies. In the still water beneath, crimson and saffron fish drifted in a dream.

She sat on the edge of the pond and trailed her fingers in the water. She gazed at the strawberry-pink house. It belonged to a different era, with empire balconies and arches. Cream marble columns held up the pórtico. The windows and parapets were picked out in the same pale marble. It had been impeccably restored, and given a Riviera flourish, complete with pink stucco and striped awnings.

Anton came to join her. He had changed into jeans and a plain white shirt. He sat beside her on the wall. 'Like it?' he asked.

'I don't know what to say. It's the most beautiful house I've ever seen.'

'It belonged to a member of the French civil government. After the war it was expropriated. I bought it from the Vietnamese government five years ago.'

'You have wonderful taste,' she said.

'Some day I might come and live here,' he said. 'At least part of the year, anyway. I have an ongoing love affair with Vietnam.'

'Then I'll try and love it too.' She smiled at him. The long shadow cast by Lavinia Carron had disappeared from between them. London was weeks away and she was determined to forget about it until the time came.

'Come,' Anton said as a gong sounded, 'they want us to have lunch now.'

The meal was served in the long dining-room from ornate silver tureens, and was bewilderingly delicious. It started with little crab parcels fried in pastry wrappings, proceeded through a succession of elaborate dishes she couldn't even begin to identify—sometimes it seemed to her she was eating French haute cuisine and then the next bite would take her to China—and concluded with a frozen dessert that had a taste that eluded her utterly.

'It's durian ice cream,' Anton informed her. 'Durians are those strange, spiky fruit you see on roadside stalls. The taste is delicious but they heat up the stomach, and the smell is—well, unique. Turning them into ice cream solves the problem.'

'I've never had anything more exotic,' she said honestly. 'I think that was the best meal of my life.'

'You're starting to see why I love Vietnam,' he smiled. 'We'd better get out to the site. They're expecting us.'

The refinery was being built to the east of Saigon, on the coast. The drive there took them through vast rice fields that glittered in the sun, fed by an endless watery network of irrigation canals, waterways and rivers. The countryside was so inextricably mingled with water, indeed, that the commonest means of transport to be seen were sailing vessels of every type imaginable.

They reached the coast after driving through hills of alternating jungle and sugar-cane plantations. The refinery was situated in the ceremoniously named Vung Tao Con Dau Special Zone and it was in the middle of an area of outstanding natural beauty. The Zone, however, was carefully landscaped so as not to spoil the scenery. Rolling green hills surrounded it; a few miles below, the resort town of Vung Tao spread out along a snowy white crescent of beach that reminded her of a huge slice of watermelon—if the sea had been pink instead of deep blue.

The Vung Tao refinery was almost complete. It was one of Anton's most ambitious projects, a plant designed to refine used lubricating oil from the automotive industry and turn it back into something pristine. In an economy like Vietnam's, it was a project that could save millions on oil imports and encourage growth. It represented the kind of thinking that she most admired in Anton—his ability to find solutions for less wealthy clients, saving money and preserving the environment.

Even the colours of the plant seemed positive, a mass of scarlet, green and bright yellow piping that somehow made her think of a huge children's game. The Vietnamese engineers could not have been more hospitable or charming; this was a country of exquisite manners.

Two phases of the plant were running already and they were able to watch the process at work. Wearing the obligatory hard hats, she and Anton walked the length of the plants, the engineers and the interpreters talking enthusiastically about the results they were obtaining.

'Notice something?' Anton asked her, pointing to the

towers. 'No flames. Most refineries burn off waste from chimneys, releasing poisons into the air. We've eliminated that.'

'It's a remarkable achievement,' she said.

In the quality-control lab, a smiling assistant brought two glass beakers for them to compare—one containing black sludge that was the starting point, the other containing a clear golden oil that was the finished product.

'It's hard to believe this can turn into this,' Amy commented.

'Smell the used oil,' Anton commanded.

She obeyed, and wrinkled her nose. 'Not nice. It smells like dirty old engines.'

'Now smell the clean oil.'

'Nectar,' she grinned, amused by his earnestness. 'I think I'll put some behind my ears.'

'Well, at least you can put it in your engine. It's cheaper than imported oil by a long way and it solves the problem of disposing of dirty oil.'

'All our tests on this oil have shown that it meets industry standards, Mr Zell,' added one of the Vietnamese engineers, an older man with gold-rimmed glasses and a white moustache. 'We are very pleased with the results!'

Anton smiled and nodded. But when he caught Amy's gaze, he waggled an eyebrow suggestively. She knew he was hoping to sell more such plants to the Vietnamese and this was a very encouraging sign.

Indeed, as they left the plant some three hours later, he was in a more upbeat mood than she had seen him in for days. 'The man with the gold-rimmed spectacles and the moustache is no ordinary engineer,' he told her. 'He's a senior official in the government's energy programme. It looks like we'll be getting those new orders soon.'

'I'm so happy for you.'

He grinned at her. 'It ain't bad. Hey. Want to go to the beach before we head home?'

'That would be wonderful!'

It was late afternoon and golden sunlight was washing the coastline. The day had been very hot. She felt nothing would be nicer than a visit to the sea.

The driver took them through Vung Tao to a section of beach that was absolutely deserted, more beautiful than any tourist brochure could depict. White sand stretched out for miles, lapped by a gentle sea. Sea birds wheeled overhead. It was heavenly.

Leaving the driver with the car, she and Anton took off their shoes, rolled up their trousers, and wandered along the beach side by side.

'I can see why you love this place,' she said to him. 'It's a slice of paradise. And your refinery is helping to protect it.'

He stooped and picked up a shell. 'Politics have kept their economy from developing the way other Asian tigers have done. Now they can choose their own path to wealth.'

He handed her the shell. It was pink, ribbed on one side and pearly on the inside. 'It's perfect.'

He looked into her face. Here by the sea, his eyes were the deepest blue imaginable. 'It's been a long, hot day. I feel like swimming. Join me?'

'I left my bikini back at the villa! I didn't think we'd be swimming!'

'Don't you ever do anything spontaneous?' he asked.

She looked at the inviting waves longingly, then at the car, barely visible in the distant haze. 'In my underwear? And be wet and sandy all the way back to Saigon?'

'Well, as an engineer, I can tell you that there are multiple solutions to this problem. You can take off your dress, swim in your underwear and go home wearing a dry dress but with no underwear. Or you can take off your underwear, swim in your dress, and go home wearing dry underwear. Or you can take off both your dress and your underwear, swim as Mother Nature intended, and go home in a dry dress *and* underwear.' He laughed softly at her expression. 'I'll leave you to work it out, Worthington. I promise not to look at you, whatever you decide. You shall be as a maiden invisible unto mine eyes.'

'Or I could not swim at all,' she said in a small voice.

He sighed wearily. 'And stay hot and sticky. It's your decision.' He was already unbuttoning his shirt. She looked away quickly. The beach was deserted. She hunted in vain for a chaste rock to disrobe behind.

When she looked back at Anton, he was walking down to the water. He had kept his briefs on, she saw with relief. His muscular, tanned body slipped with barely a splash into the blue water.

The way he'd said *it's your decision* had stung her. She was so afraid that his patience would finally run out with her behaviour—with what he probably saw as her ridiculous prudery.

She stripped off her dress and ran down to the water in her pale blue underwear.

The sea was deliciously cool. She laughed out loud with the delight of feeling the day's heat and grime vanish. She swam out from the shore, her body buoyed on the gentle swells of the South China Sea. What a heavenly place! This was surely the very beach that featured in all those holiday brochures, and somehow never seemed to exist in real life. 'Anton?' she called. 'Where are you?'

Tanned arms closed around her waist. She gasped and squirmed, but his muscular body was far too strong for her.

'You scared the life out of me,' she spluttered, turning to face him.

'Aren't you glad you took the plunge?' he said, laughing.

'It's wonderful!'

'For a moment I thought you were going to sit there on the beach, all forlorn, like Miss Muffet.'

'Don't laugh at me. Men can always strip off and jump into the sea. In case you hadn't noticed, I'm not a man.'

Anton was still holding on to her arms. He drew her towards him so that his face, the most beautiful male face she had ever seen, was close to hers. 'What makes you imagine,' he said in an intimate murmur, 'that I haven't noticed you're a woman?'

'Perhaps I phrased that wrong,' she rejoined in a whisper that was almost as intimate. 'I meant to say *a lady*.'

'Is there a difference between a woman and a lady, Miss Worthington?'

'A lady knows how to behave!'

'Whereas a woman knows how to have fun?'

'That's a typical male attitude. That's what men always say when they want a woman to abandon her principles. *It's only a bit of fun.* But somehow, the fun is all on your side—and the pain is on ours.'

'Not all men are like that,' he said.

She searched his eyes, which were a deep indigo, for the truth. 'I haven't seen any exceptions,' she whispered.

'I'm an exception.' His mouth brushed her eyelids. Her skin, flushed with the sun, felt a million times more sensitive than normal. Her fingers curled, nails digging into his muscular shoulders as she offered her half-open mouth to his.

He claimed it as possessively as if only he, in all the world, had that right. She pressed to him in the cool water, the soft peaks of her breasts thrusting against his chest, covered only by her flimsy bra. It was a kiss more passionate than anything she had ever known. Like a roller coaster thundering down a slope out of control, then swooping up into the air, leaving her stomach behind, so that her heart lurched.

'Anton,' she whispered, 'what are we doing?'

'Isn't it obvious?' He smiled. That the kiss had ignited his passions too was obvious by the deep blue fire in his eyes.

'We can't ever be like this together!' she said.

'Isn't this what we've both wanted, since the moment we met?'

'Perhaps you've wanted it,' she said shakily, 'but God knows I've tried to avoid it in every way I could.'

'Even that day on the island?'

'Even then.'

'What are you so afraid of?' he demanded.

She touched her lips with her fingertips. His kiss had left them throbbing, almost bruised. 'I'm afraid of what you do to me.'

'I thought you wanted that as much as I did.'

'Of course I did. That doesn't mean it's sensible!'

'Or prudent, or moral, or safe?'

'None of those things!' She floated away from him on the billowing waves. 'You said we were doing this to cool off.'

He shook his head wryly. 'You're cool, all right.'

Despite her flippancy, Amy was in anguish. When he'd kissed her like that, her whole body had responded in a way she couldn't control. Even now, she was aching in perilous ways. Her legs felt weak, there was electricity pulsing through her breasts and loins.

She knew exactly what the game was. The cooler she was, the more she aroused the hunter in him. From the start he had seen her as a potential conquest. And now she was not going to be the one that had got away.

As for her own feelings, she was caught in a paradox. She was wildly attracted to him, adored him, but she could not go through another Martin McCallum situation again. Her heart had been damaged almost beyond repair. She was desperately trying to save what was left.

Yet when she felt Anton's desire for her, her whole body sang with joy. She wanted him to see her as a woman, but not as a lover. She wanted this to go on forever just the way it was.

They emerged from the water as the sun was starting to set. She reached up to squeeze the water out of her hair. 'That was lovely,' she said to him, smiling.

His face had changed. He was looking at her body as though in awe. 'Mercy,' he whispered huskily. 'You are so sexy.'

Dismayed, she saw that her flimsy underwear had been rendered all but transparent by the water. She was concealing few secrets from him. 'I'd better get dressed,' she said unsteadily.

'Amy, you're the most desirable woman I've ever seen,' he said quietly. 'I wish I could understand you.'

'I wish you could understand me, too,' she said in a sad voice. Standing there, his magnificent male body still streaming with seawater, he was like some ocean god wanting to claim his bride. If only he knew how she longed to throw herself into his arms!

'There are so many fabulous beaches on this coast,' he said. 'We could go somewhere else tomorrow. Take a picnic, spend the day.'

'The day? The whole *day*? How could you possibly afford to take all day off from your mighty works, oh master? You need to get your priorities straight!'

'You're right,' he replied. 'My priorities have been upside-down for a long time.'

'Meaning?' she asked curiously.

'Meaning I've been neglecting the truly important things in life.'

'Which are…?'

'This,' he replied succinctly.

'What do you mean by *this*?' she demanded.

His deep blue eyes met hers. 'The beach. A sunny day. The woman of my dreams in wet underwear.'

She looked at herself. Her nipples were plainly visible as strawberry peaks under the lacy bra. 'Are those the truly important things in life? This is the latest wisdom from Workaholics Anonymous?'

He laughed. 'Well, maybe it's time I took the cure.'

'Well, I don't have billions to rest my laurels on. I am a working girl. I have to take care of your calls, Mr Zell.' As if on cue, the satellite phone started to buzz from its nest in her dress. 'I'd better answer that.'

He held her wrist, restraining her. 'Let the damned thing ring.'

She met his smiling eyes. 'Are you serious? About to-morrow?'

'Very serious,' he said. He drew her to him and kissed her forehead. His body brushed hers, muscled and smooth. Now her heart accelerated like a locomotive, screaming *danger, danger*.

'You can't kiss me!'

'Why not?'

'You're the boss, I'm the employee. I'm a cat, you're a dog. It doesn't work like that!'

He was amused. He drew a line down her nose with his fingertip. 'Maybe we're both cats, and we just don't know it. Or both dogs.'

'Well, thank you so much for calling me a dog,' she said with mock-indignation.

'You're not a dog,' he said gently. 'There isn't a more beautiful woman than you in the whole wide world.'

She wanted him so much in that moment that it was all she could do to stop herself from throwing her arms round his neck and devouring that erotic, maddening mouth.

They dressed and walked back along the beach to the car, holding hands.

CHAPTER TEN

THEY ate their evening meal at opposite ends of the table, the room lit by two candelabra, which cast a rosy light on their faces. It was the most romantic meal, and Amy's stomach was already populated with a horde of butterflies, so she could hardly taste the exotic dishes that proceeded from the kitchen, one after another.

It was a sultry, still evening. When the coffee had been drunk, Anton rose from his chair. 'I have a present for you.'

Half expecting a repetition of the jade-bangle episode, Amy smiled nervously. 'Really?'

'It was in the house when I bought it. I think it's perfect for you.' He took something from the mantelpiece and handed it to her.

Amy inspected the thing curiously. It was a little wooden box, its sides made of stretched gauze, with four little feet. The lid could be fastened shut and had a hook so that the box could be suspended. It was charming in its simplicity but she had no idea what it was.

'What is it? A little cage for something?'

'It comes from Japan. It's a firefly lantern. Come, let me show you.'

He picked up a painted paper fan and led her out into the garden. Amy exclaimed in delight; the warm darkness was dotted with dozens of tiny wandering lights. They drifted over the pond, especially, their bright glow reflected in the still water. 'That's so beautiful!'

'Let me show you what to do.' He opened the lid of the lantern, then used the fan to deftly tap one of the luminous insects into it. 'It's easy. Try.'

Gingerly, she took the things from him and started hunting the nearest firefly. It was not quite as easy as Anton had made it look. After several wild swats, she learned how to coax the little creature into the box. She snapped the lid shut triumphantly. 'There!'

'Very good,' he said with soft irony, sitting on the wall of the pond. 'Let's see if you can catch enough to make your lantern useful.'

'It's not as easy as it looks,' she said.

'This is what young Asian women used to do on warm evenings,' he said. 'Before radio, before television.'

She tapped another firefly into the box. 'Got you! And what did the young Asian men do?'

'They watched the young women, of course. It's one of the prettiest sights in the world.'

'I hope I don't fall in the pond,' she said, concentrating on a particularly brilliant insect that was drifting languidly over the lily pads.

'At least you'll have a change of underwear handy,' he said ironically.

'You must think me an awful ninny,' Amy said, snapping another firefly into the gauze box.

'No,' he replied. 'I think you're very complicated. I try to see into your mind but usually I can't. I know that there are things that bother you. But I don't know why.'

Amy was silent.

'One of the things that seem to bother you,' he went on after a silence, 'is Marcie. I don't know why. I don't know what you've been told. But it certainly wasn't the truth.'

She had captured another two fireflies in her box and now she stood very still. 'What is the truth?'

'Up until now, I've considered that the truth wasn't mine to tell. But what I've started to feel for you overrides that. So I'm going to tell you what I have no right to tell you.'

She stepped down from the wall and sat beside him, the

little box glimmering like a fairy lantern in her hands. She watched the trapped insects flitting to and fro. 'Go on.'

'Marcie was a fine personal assistant, but she had a drug problem. She'd had it before she came to me. When she started working for me, she was clean. She managed to conceal it during the interview process and she never told me about it. But the stress of the job began to tell on her and after a while it was obvious there was something wrong. I found out what it was. She was using cocaine heavily. I should have fired her then, but I didn't. Instead, I got involved. Not sexually, but in her problem. I made her go for treatment. I gave her leave so she could do rehab, get herself together again. And then I took her back. I told her I would fire her if she went back on drugs. I thought I had solved her problem. It was a mistake.'

'People say she was deeply in love with you,' Amy said in a low voice.

'I think that was part of the problem. That was part of what made it so hard for her to carry on. Without drugs, I mean. But there was nothing I could do for her. I didn't return her feelings. But I don't flatter myself that the problem was just that. I think she'd been an addict for a long time, and the pressure of the job made it worse. Within a few months, I could tell she was using again. She made bad mistakes, did sloppy things that put people at risk. I made her go for a medical. The blood test said it all. So I fired her.'

'She went to Switzerland?'

'Yes. I paid for her to attend an advanced new drug-rehab clinic near Zurich. She's still there. I hope she works her life out. But that's up to her now.'

Amy looked at her box. 'My lantern is pretty,' she said in a quiet voice, 'but it didn't shed much light.'

'Some lanterns are just for looking at,' he said.

'I couldn't see past the end of my own nose,' she said,

mourning her own emotional misjudgements. 'I'm so sorry I said what I did. I thought—'

'What did you think?' he demanded as she broke off.

'Nothing,' she muttered. It was certainly better that he did not know the dark thoughts that had been going through her mind. It was just as well the firefly lantern shed such a dim light; her face was scarlet with humiliation. She wanted to run away from Anton right now, run and not stop until she was a hundred miles away from his presence.

As if sensing her thoughts, he rose. 'I'm going to turn in, Worthington. Coming?'

'I think I'll sit out here in the cool for a little while longer,' she said thickly.

'Don't stay out too late. I think you got a touch of the sun today. You need sleep. Goodnight.'

'Goodnight, Anton.'

There was no goodnight kiss. He walked back into the house. Amy sat turning the glowing lantern in her hands, her mind occupied with many thoughts, not all of them happy ones. She had rushed to judge Anton by her own lights. The fact that she had been so far from the truth said more about her than it did about Anton.

They had rushed to judge her in just the same way. She'd had no defence against the wagging tongues, the sneering eyes of those who thought themselves so much better than she. It had hurt so much.

Now she had done exactly the same thing to Anton, the one person in all the world she most cared about. Did he guess the way her thoughts had run? Had he heard the rumours that the silly nurse in Hong Kong was spreading?

The first thing she would do when she got back, she vowed, was go to her and tell her just how wrong she was. She did not need to give away Marcie's secrets—just tell a foolish gossip how harmful her speculations were.

The little fairy lights revolved restlessly in her lantern.

She opened the lid and shook their prison gently. Like a shower of sparks, the glowing creatures spiralled upwards and dispersed into the dark, velvety Vietnamese night.

She had not believed that Anton was serious about taking the next day off; but she felt his hand shake her gently awake very early the next morning, and struggled upright to accept the coffee and brioche—both authentically French and steaming hot—that he had brought her.

'Rise and shine,' he said, smiling at her tousle-haired confusion. 'We're going to the seaside.'

Within half an hour they were driving through the early-morning traffic out of the city. This time there were just the two of them in the large and dignified old Peugeot. The chauffeur, too, was getting a day off.

'You seem to be having fun driving this old lady,' she commented, sitting sideways in her seat to watch him. 'Isn't it rather a come-down after your pocket rocket in Hong Kong?'

'It's a change of pace, not a come-down,' he said, grinning. 'I'm taking your advice, and getting my life in order.'

She raised one eyebrow. 'Is that what I said?'

'You told me to get my priorities straight.'

'Where are we going, anyway?' she demanded.

'To Bai An,' he said. 'It's one of my favourite places on the coast. We can hire a boat for twenty dollars and tour the islands.'

Bai An was like a landscape out of a dream. When they arrived at the little bay an hour or so later, the early-morning mist was starting to lift. The white crescent of beach was walled with crumbling cliffs. The glassy water of the bay was dotted with innumerable small islands, some no more than weathered spires of rock, others large hummocks covered with tropical vegetation.

'I've never seen anything as beautiful as this,' Amy said honestly. 'I'm not dreaming, am I?'

'I'll pinch you if you like,' he invited, parking the venerable Peugeot near a collection of wooden boats. They got out and Anton negotiated with one of the fishermen to rent a boat. The vessel he chose was a comfortable-looking wooden sampan with a high prow, on which two eyes had been painted.

'What an adorable boat,' she smiled as he reached out his hands to pull her on deck.

Anton helped Amy aboard, his strong arms lifting her as though she weighed no more than a feather. 'You approve?'

'I'm honoured to climb aboard!'

The sampan was in good condition. Her woodwork wore a deep, lustrous varnish. On her high, elegant transom, a little awning offered shade. The sails that were so neatly furled against her mast were a faded red. Down below, her engine was already rumbling like a contented cat.

The owner threw the mooring rope to Anton. With a word of thanks and a wave, Anton took the wheel and began steering the boat out to the islands.

Lost in the joy of the occasion, Amy curled up in the seat and just drank it in. With expert ease, Anton steered them through the maze of smaller islands and fishing boats and out to the larger islands.

A pair of white cranes flapped lazily across their path. Amy had been in the East long enough to know that the birds were auspicious. It was going to be a good day!

An hour later, she was in a state of bliss. If she had any thought in her mind at all, it was that she had seldom been so happy. Not since her early childhood. It had been the most lovely of mornings.

She had changed into her bikini and was lazing on the deck, watching the islands drift by through dreamy eyes.

The same sun that was baking her semi-naked limbs was making each island glow in shades of emerald and gold. Coconut palms and flowering shrubs hung from the craggy rocks. Their sampan was weaving her elegant way through a world where sea surrounded rock and rock surrounded sea, as if in a beautiful dream. They had all this beauty to themselves. It was as if the whole of nature were theirs on this perfect morning, and they its only inheritors.

Anton cut the engines and hauled up the red sail, its wooden battens making it look like a butterfly's wing or a red leaf. They were making their gentle way on wind power alone. It was wonderful to feel the sweet surge of the boat beneath her, knowing that Anton was at the wheel. She glanced at him now. He had stripped to his swimming trunks. The breeze was ruffling his dark hair.

He was the most magnificent man she had ever seen. There was no way to deny that. His body was perfect, not heavily muscled, yet carved as if by a master sculptor. Success had not changed that lean frame of his one iota; she could see the powerful muscles shifting under his bronzed skin, and his belly was flat and taut. His long legs, braced against the movement of the boat, were those of a long-distance runner.

She had been comparing all the men she had known to Anton Zell, she realised. None measured up. No man had ever been as intelligent, as amusing, as physically beautiful.

As if sensing her thoughts, Anton glanced her way and met her eyes.

'I thought you were asleep.'

'Just daydreaming.'

He pointed to the island ahead of them. 'That is Hon Giang,' he said. 'It's bigger than the rest and it has its own private beach. We'll stop there and swim. We'll be there in a few minutes.' He smiled that heart-stopping smile of his. 'You look just like a sleepy cat.'

'Purr.'

'Hungry?'

'Yes,' she said, half-surprised at the sudden rumble in her own stomach.

'We'll have our picnic on the island. Come here. I want you to see the beach as we come into the cove.'

She joined him behind the wheel. He slid a strong arm around her shoulders and drew her close to his side. She could not stop the sensuous shudder from running down her spine. His skin was hot and silky against her. The close contact melted her insides so that she felt like a dab of butter on a nice brown piece of toast, just oozing deep into him… She had a sudden vision of the fireflies, released from their prison, escaping into the humid darkness last night.

'There,' he said. 'Look.'

He turned the sampan into the cove. It was completely deserted. A fringe of palm trees shaded the snow-white sands of the beach. The water, as clear and still as glass, was turquoise blue. Gulls wheeled lazily overhead. Apart from the birds, everything here belonged to them.

'This is the loveliest place!'

'Yes.' His arm had slid down around her waist. His fingers caressed her skin gently. 'Amazing, isn't it?'

Somehow, though she was not aware of doing so, she had rested her head on his broad shoulder. His hot skin burned her cheek. 'I wish this moment would last for ever,' she whispered.

He must have heard her soft voice above the murmur of the sea, because his arm tightened around her. 'It doesn't have to end,' he said.

'Everything has to end.'

'No.' He kissed her neck gently. 'Not everything.'

'Anton, stop,' she pleaded. She was feeling dizzy. 'We've been through this before!'

'And we will go through it again. Until you accept me.'

She looked at him for a moment, and it was like looking over the edge of a high building. It would be so terribly easy to just let go and fall down, down, down. 'Accept you as what? My lover and my boss?'

He looked deep into her eyes. 'No. I'm offering you something much more than that.'

Her heart started to race. 'What are you offering?'

'I'm offering you everything I have, everything I am. I want you at my side, Amy. For ever.'

The world was spinning around her. Fly too close to the sun, she told herself dizzily, and you won't just get your wings singed. You'll burn alive. 'Anton, I am so ordinary. You will grow tired of me very quickly. And then you'll regret those words.'

'Do you think you'll grow tired of me?' he demanded.

She could not lie to him. 'No.'

'Then you feel the same emotions that I do.'

'Anton,' she said, her voice almost breaking, 'it's easy to be infatuated with you. Every woman around you feels it. How can I really believe that you've chosen me, out of everybody?'

His expression grew sombre. 'Amy, what happened to you? What did you go through that hurt you so badly?'

'Just life.' She tried to laugh. 'Let's have a lovely day in the sun, darling man. And stop trying to get me into bed. You'd probably be so disappointed, anyway. No!' She laid her fingers on his lips to silence him. 'Don't say any more!' If she had to listen to him a moment longer, she knew her will would melt like caramel. 'Please, Anton!'

They were so close to the shore now that he had to concentrate on getting the sampan safely beached and secured with the anchor. The boat finally came to rest among the wavelets that kissed the golden shore.

They carried the picnic basket and the towels ashore and chose a place in the shade of a flowering hibiscus, whose crimson trumpets nodded over them. The meal that Anton had packed was a simple one—a freshly baked baguette, some pâté, a cooked chicken and a bottle of champagne in an icebox.

Amy accepted the glass of foaming champagne he poured for her and drank gratefully. The bread was crisp and the cold chicken was delicious. 'You are a very good provider, Captain Morgan. This is heaven!'

'And all ours.'

'Thank you for bringing me here.'

When they had finished eating, he leaned over and kissed her mouth lightly. 'Mmm, you taste of champagne.'

'Because I'm in such high spirits.'

'Oh, dear, that was a feeble pun.' He smiled at her. 'Have you noticed that there are wild bananas and mangoes growing on this island?'

'Bananas and mangoes, hmm?'

'And the rocks are full of clams. I could knock a hole in that boat and then we'd have to live here for ever.'

'On wild mangoes?'

'And each other.'

'Wouldn't we get bored?'

'I would never get bored with you.' He drew his finger softly down the line of her cheek, his fingertip brushing the delicate corner of her mouth. 'Kiss me again,' he invited softly.

'You kissed me,' she pointed out, mesmerised by his proximity.

'Then it's your turn.'

'I can't,' she pleaded. 'Even if I wanted to, I can't.'

'*Do* you want to?' he challenged.

She looked up at his mouth, that mouth she had always thought the most desirable in the world. She felt her heart turn over inside her as she lifted her mouth and kissed him. And then they were in each other's arms.

She had been kissed by other men she'd gone out with, culminating in Martin McCallum, who had been the most experienced lover she had known. But this was different. This was like no kiss had ever been. This was so serious that she felt her body melt in his strong embrace, so sublime that her spirit seemed to soar upwards with wonder.

She could only cling to him. Between kisses, he whispered her name. His mouth was hungry, tasting her eyelids, her temples, the curve of her jaw and sweet line of her throat. Amy knew that nothing in her life had ever been so intense. His body, male and hard against her, filled her with a passionate desire that made her want to devour him, her fingers almost tearing at his muscles, her teeth biting his shoulders, his neck, his lips. But far more than that, there was a spiritual dimension she had only ever encountered in her deepest dreams—the knowledge that it was Anton who was making love to her, Anton, the man she idolised above all others, the man she could never trust.

It was insane, and yet *she* was insane right now. Her erect nipples were making scandalous peaks through the flimsy fabric of her bikini top; the sight of them seemed to drive him wild, and when he began pulling her top off she helped him shamelessly, wriggling out of the garment with a husky laugh.

'God, you're so beautiful,' he whispered, lowering his dark head to claim her. Her breasts were taut, and his kiss was a torment, made so much worse when his mouth closed around her nipples, his hot tongue caressing roughly, sucking, biting.

She arched against him, her thighs parting invitingly. She could feel his arousal, hard and male against her body. She reached for him, her hands wickedly eager, and took possession. He groaned, his eyes narrowing to fierce slits.

'Are you sure this is what you want?' he asked her.

She did not answer with words, but by lifting her parted lips to his mouth.

CHAPTER ELEVEN

Now there was no need of questions or answers. She lifted her hips so he could strip off her bikini bottom, then helped him pull off his swimming trunks.

'Anton,' she murmured as he mounted her naked body, 'oh, Anton…'

The rush of the waves and the whisper of the foam made the music that accompanied their lovemaking. She was staring deep into his indigo eyes as he entered her.

She had dreamed of a wonderful lover so many times, without giving him a face or a name. But she had never met him. Until now. She had never dreamed it could be like this—so gentle, so tender, and yet so powerful. It was as though there, at the edge of the sea, she first realised what her woman's body was made for.

All the time that he made love to her, arousing her to ecstasy, he kissed her face and throat, his soft voice telling her how beautiful she was, how desirable, how wonderful. There was a profound rightness about what they were doing, she felt that in her soul. And at the moment they both reached climax tears spilled from her eyes, sliding down her cheeks to wet his face.

They were both gasping for air at the finish. He gathered her tight against his chest, whispering her name. She held on for dear life, the world still spinning around her.

'I'm sorry if I hurt you,' he said. 'Was I too rough?'

'You were perfect,' she murmured, nuzzling his chest hair blissfully. 'Just perfect.'

He caressed her body tenderly. 'You're exquisite, Amy. So beautiful. I'm the luckiest man alive.'

They drowsed in the shade, cradled in one another's arms. The sound of the waves lulled them, until the growing heat of midday drove them down to the water to swim.

The sea was cool and delicious. It was a flawless day, the sky without a single cloud. Amy watched in fascination as shoals of tiny multicoloured fish nibbled at her toes. The world was different now, and she was different. Her body would never be the same again. Nor would her soul. He had touched her as she had never been touched before.

Anton's strong arms closed around her, holding her close.

'I'm in heaven,' she told him.

'Why did you keep me away for so long?' he asked, kissing her neck. 'You almost drove me insane.'

'I find it very hard to trust people,' she said.

'Why shouldn't you trust me?' His dark hair was slicked back, his passionate face beaded with droplets. 'Why should you doubt me?'

'I suppose partly because I couldn't believe that you really cared about me. I still can't. And partly because I got the wrong idea about you, right from the start...in Borneo, when you kissed me, I thought you were just out to make a conquest. And then, at work...well, people said things...about Marcie...'

'That I had an affair with her?'

'Yes,' she admitted. 'And that she had to leave so suddenly because, well, she was expecting your child.'

His eyes were suddenly angry. 'Who said that?'

'I can't tell you,' she said wretchedly, 'because you'll fire the person concerned!'

'Whoever it is, he or she deserves to be fired,' he said. 'Is that what they think the clinic is all about? And you believed *that*?'

'I'm so sorry,' Amy said miserably. 'Anton, I didn't know what to believe. I was just trying to protect myself!'

He looked into her eyes. 'Amy, please tell me you don't believe that poisonous rubbish any more.'

'I believe in you,' she said simply.

He kissed her passionately. 'Come with me,' he said, 'I want to show you something.' They waded ashore, seawater cascading down their bodies. He led her up the beach and into the green shade of the trees.

'Where are we going?' she asked.

'To a special place.'

The foliage was scented with some spicy flowering plant. As he had predicted, there were wild mangoes and bananas growing on the island. The ripe fruit hung like jewels over the path. Anton pulled branches down so she could pick some of the fruit, which smelled sweet and delicious in her arms.

'We'll take some of these, too,' he said, picking fragrant white and crimson flowers from a vine. As they went on, he held her hand, guiding her over the smooth boulders, holding aside branches that occasionally blocked the way.

At the end of the path was their destination—a small, ancient pagoda that stood half-overgrown among rambutan trees.

'Oh, Anton,' she whispered, 'how lovely!'

'It's a Buddhist shrine,' he said. 'It must be hundreds of years old. It's been almost forgotten—hardly anybody remembers that it's here any more.'

They walked into the temple. The cool interior was decorated with ornate sculptures, the paintings on the walls faded but still discernible. At the back was a stone statue of the Buddha, his serene face smiling.

They stood in front of it together. The floor of the temple was littered with white sand and dried flower blossoms. The domed shape of the ancient structure seemed to capture and amplify the distant murmur of the sea. A deep peace sank into Amy's heart. This was a holy place, whatever one's religion might be.

They laid the offering of fruit and flowers at the statue's feet, then stood there, hands entwined. At that moment, Amy felt that nothing could ever touch their happiness. It was as though they had undergone some sacred ceremony that had bound them together for ever, protecting them from all harm.

'Thank you for bringing me here,' she whispered. 'I'll never forget it.'

They walked back in silence. In the shade of their hibiscus grove, they lay down in one another's arms again.

'Today, our lives start afresh,' he whispered.

'Yes,' she said quietly.

'You've made me so happy today, Amy. I've wanted you ever since you walked into my life, that morning at Kai Tak. I think I felt it even before I saw you, because I should have left for Borneo the day before. But something kept me there, waiting for you. Something told me that I had to meet you. And from the moment I saw your face, I loved you. I didn't think it would happen like this—spontaneously, on a beach in Vietnam. In fact, I didn't really know how it would happen. But I always knew that we would be lovers, and belong to each other completely.'

She looked into the depths of his eyes. 'Anton, forgive me for not trusting you. Things have happened to me that hurt me badly—and—and made it hard for me to give myself. But I have loved you for such a long time!'

His warm fingers cupped her chin and lifted her face so he could kiss her soft mouth. 'My golden girl,' he whispered, 'whatever has hurt you, I will take it away.'

Her eyes closed languidly as he kissed her lips. His mouth was like velvet, so tender and yet so commanding. His arms were so strong as they drew her close to him. No man had ever affected her like this. No man ever would. She whimpered, clinging to his powerful shoulders as their kiss deepened into searing passion. It was as though everything else in the world had disappeared, and nothing was real any more except their two beating hearts.

Kissing her sweetly on the eyelids and mouth, he was slow and gentle this time. He was in complete, masterful control. The muscles rippled unhurriedly beneath his tanned skin. He looked down at her. His eyes seemed to darken with hunger. 'You are so beautiful,' he whispered. 'Your breasts, the swell of your hips…so perfect. I've never touched anything as fine as your skin.'

She shuddered, her back arching, as he caressed her, lovingly, expertly. When he kissed her lips again, her mouth opened under the pressure of his tongue. The maelstrom of passion that she knew so well was sucking her down. She clung to his neck as though she had found herself in a real whirlpool, as though there were real danger that she might be engulfed for ever.

When his fingers found the tender moistness between her thighs, they brought a pleasure that made her senses swim.

He slid down, his mouth seeking her. An attempt at modesty made her try to resist, but her own body betrayed her. Her thighs parted to open herself to him, and her hips rose so that he could claim her secret places with his mouth.

His kiss was gentle at first. But she heard him moan with satisfaction as he tasted her, his tongue sinful and hungry. Amy gasped with pleasure, then could not stop herself from moaning aloud as his strong arms slipped around her hips and pulled her to him.

Over the years she had wondered why it was she could find no man who could unlock her secrets, not even Martin; she had wondered whether she was cold, unresponsive. Unresponsive! The way her body and soul felt right now, she knew that she was every inch a woman. It had simply taken the right man to open up her feelings.

Anton's mouth was hungry and hot, and he seemed to want to devour her, just as much as she ached to be devoured. How heavenly it was to be consumed like this, to be wanted like this! Her fingers threaded through his crisp, dark hair, her heels caressing the strong muscles of his back. Pleasure peaked so intensely that she could not stop herself from sliding dizzily over the edge…and then she was in a world where she had never been, a world where music and colour and passion exploded into one overpowering emotion that was so great, the tears spontaneously flooded her eyes.

He held her until her shuddering faded into stillness, his mouth coaxing every last drop of pleasure from her body.

'Anton,' she whispered. 'Please come to me…'

He obeyed her, gathering her slim body in his muscular arms, holding her so tight that she whimpered with pleasure. He murmured her name softly, tenderly, but spoke no other words. Locked in the passion of their embrace, Amy caressed his body, feeling the power of his man's strength, yet aware of how sensitive his shuddering responses were.

His arousal was as rampant as it had been that morning. She caressed him gently with her fingertips. The velvety skin of his sex was hot, and his arching pleasure thrilled her. He kissed her with fierce passion, his hands cupping her hips, his desire pressing urgently between her thighs.

Amy rolled back and pulled him onto her. Her eyes searched his face intently, searching for the emotion in his eyes.

'You are mine,' he said, as though answering her unspoken question, 'mine, mine. Only mine.'

He entered her body, but far more carefully than he had done the first time. This time he was slow, unhurried, allowing them both to savour the way their bodies united, his sliding deep into her, hers stretching to accommodate him.

When he was fully inside her, he kissed her eyelids and then her mouth. 'I have never felt anything like this,' he told her softly. He was cradling her shoulders in his arms, the dominant weight of his hips pressing hers back against the sand. 'I'll never let you go, Amy.'

Those words were exactly what she wanted to hear. He made love to her with exquisite tenderness and skill, controlling her responses, exciting her, until the pleasure was deep and overwhelmingly delicious. She whimpered his name, her mouth open against his, their kisses growing more abandoned as their lovemaking intensified.

Anton's ragged breathing told her he was as ready as she was. She knew that they were going to the same place together, soon, very soon…

This time her climax was different, a searing sunburst that melted her body and dazzled her mind. Anton crushed her to him, his shuddering in perfect time with hers. Gasping, they clung to one another, their limbs twining until peace descended on them.

He smiled down at her, caressing her breasts and stomach tenderly.

'You're so beautiful,' he told her. 'I want to drink you in with my soul. You are the centre of my universe. You are all I will ever want.'

Amy would always remember that day as the most beautiful of her life. And the remainder of their stay in Vietnam, too, was like a wonderful dream. The lovely villa with the lily pond became their palace, their world. Warm, scented days blended into dark, thrilling nights.

When work called, and they travelled back to Vung Tao for consultations with the engineers, she was at his side, unable to take her eyes off him, this magnificent man who had chosen her, whose every waking thought seemed only to be to please her and fill her with delight. She was so proud of him, of the care he took of his world. She was living in paradise.

Though she was aware that paradise was only leased, that they would soon have to return to Hong Kong and the complexities of their future there, she gave herself up utterly to the moment, and to Anton, as though both were for ever.

They wandered around the charming city of Saigon together, visiting museums and temples, dreamily watching the fleets of bicycles or the groups of people, old and young, performing the stately callisthenics of t'ai chi in the public squares, under flowering trees.

They sat on the tranquil banks of the River Saigon, watching the endless and multifarious flow of traffic, from huge rice barges to tiny little skiffs, threading their way through one another's wakes; and talked endlessly, as lovers did.

They dined at food stalls in the markets and in fancy restaurants. One memorable evening, he took her to the Ben Thanh Restaurant, one of the most famous in Asia, where they had the classic Vietnamese dish, *cha gio*, made from minced crab meat, pork, fragrant mushrooms and bean sprouts, wrapped in a thin rice pancake and then deep fried. The crisp little rolls were utterly delicious, eaten wrapped in a lettuce leaf and dipped in a variety of savoury sauces.

And then, their last night in Saigon was upon them.

'I can't believe we have to go back tomorrow,' she whispered as they lay in bed together.

'What difference will it make?' he asked.

'Things will change.'

'They won't, my darling.'

But she had a dark foreboding. 'You have to be in London soon for the chairman's report. Lavinia will be waiting. You'll start to realise that even though you like me, she has so much more to offer. You'll spend hours with her, just like in France and—'

'Amy!'

'People will be talking about me. The way they did about

Marcie. They'll be laughing behind my back, saying things—'

'Hey.' His caressing hand had been tracing erotic circles on her belly, moving ever lower to the dangerous regions where her reactions were starting to quiver hotly. 'What's got into you, my golden girl? I've never heard you talk like this!'

'Oh, Anton, I'm so afraid!'

'Afraid of what?' he asked softly. His fingers expertly teased her, slipping liquidly across her most sensitive places until delicious pleasure swelled and grew between her thighs.

He seemed to know her every secret. There was no button he did not know how to push, no pleasure he did not completely understand. She had learned more about her body this week than in the previous twenty years. Anton understood her far, far better than she understood herself.

She could only cling to him as he brought her back into that enchanted kingdom of sensual delight, and then led her with utter assurance to another exquisite climax.

Partly because she could not help it, she sank her teeth into his shoulder as he prolonged her pleasure, almost past the point she could bear. She quivered and whimpered, and finally came to rest with her head on his broad chest, his hands gentling her.

'What are you doing to me?' she panted.

'Don't I make you happy?'

'You take me to places I've never been in my life.'

'You do the same to me.'

'But you must have been with so many women. You're so experienced, and I feel so clumsy.'

'You are never clumsy,' he said, crushing her in his arms. 'You are my one true love.'

Amy awoke in the early dawn. There was a rosy tinge to the sky. She was cradled securely in the arms of her lover.

He held her possessively, assuredly, even in sleep. She could hear his even breathing, feel his warm breath on her neck. Her skin smelled of their lovemaking. Her body had never felt like this before. Anton had made love to her so passionately, in so many ways, that it was as though he had dismantled her and then put her together again in a new shape.

She thought about their lovemaking with something bordering on disbelief. She'd had no idea that sex could be anything like this.

Sex. The word seemed so inadequate to cover what he had shown her this week. It was far more than the physical coupling she had always understood by the word. What he had done to her was show her what lay within her own soul. She was changed by it, altered for ever.

It had been a kind of divine madness, a hurricane that had swept through her life without warning. But where would it take her?

An ominous sinking in the pit of her stomach reminded her that within a few hours they had to fly back to Hong Kong.

She was suddenly afraid, very afraid. Her terrified mind was telling her that she was in desperate danger of seeing her dreams crash and burn. It was telling her to run as fast as she could, to fly for her life, before Anton destroyed her heart.

She tried to recapture the deep peace that had filled her in the pagoda on their island. But it eluded her obstinately. There was only anxiety.

Her tension must have wakened Anton. He kissed her face and throat softly, cupping her breasts with his palms. 'Don't worry,' he whispered, as though he had sensed her terror in his sleep, 'everything's going to be all right.'

There was no need of words between them. He made love

to her tenderly, their unhurried movements in complete harmony, until ecstasy and then peace settled around them.

She fell back asleep almost at once, her head cradled in his arms, her cheek pressed against his chest so that she could hear nothing but the deep, steady beat of his heart.

CHAPTER TWELVE

'Do you like it?'

They had walked out onto the terrace of the house. Hong Kong was spread out below them. Anton was looking at her enquiringly.

'It's stunning,' she said. 'You're not seriously thinking of buying it?'

'I've always had my eye on it. It seemed providential when it came up for sale.'

'Well, it's the loveliest house I've seen. But you don't need anything this big!'

The property, called Quilin House, was high on Victoria Peak. With enamelled dragons and other mythical beasts curvetting at the ends of the roof-beams, it was an airy, six-bedroom palace, with a vast balcony commanding a wonderful view of the harbour. It boasted a luxurious pool and parking for five cars in the basement. And it had a stunning natural setting. From the carefully tended garden you could walk straight into forests of bamboo, fern and wild hibiscus on the peak. As they stood on the balcony they were watching kites and hawks gliding on the thermals two thousand feet above the harbour.

She didn't even want to know what they were asking for this property. In Hong Kong, the most cramped apartments commanded a premium.

'Why do you think it's too big?' he asked, looking at her.

She smiled at him. 'Six bedrooms? There's only one of you, remember?'

He put his arm round her waist and drew her close. 'There

are two of us. And what if we have a dozen children?' he murmured into her ear. 'Then it will be too small!'

She kissed him, her heart fluttering. 'I haven't agreed to have *any* children, my lord and master. And you haven't asked me if I want to move in with you!'

'I'm asking you now.'

'You are a crazy man. Why are there dragons on the roof-beams?'

'It's *feng shui*. They guard all four quarters of the house from harm.'

The real-estate agent came out, unfolding her brochure. 'Quilin House has a long history, Mr and Mrs Zell,' she said, beaming. 'The property is unique. As you both know, luxury like this is rare in our city. It's a once-in-a-lifetime opportunity.'

'What was the price?' Anton asked, watching the hawks wheel and glide.

Without batting an eyelid, the realtor named a figure in the high millions.

'Will they take half a million less?'

'They might do,' the realtor said, her eyes gleaming.

'Very good,' Anton said, holding Amy's hand and facing her. 'We'll get a written offer to you in an hour or so. We'll be in London from tomorrow, so I would like an answer today, if possible. I'll give you my number. You can contact me any time. I'll be waiting.'

Amy turned away. She was suddenly remembering something Gerda had said to her in France:

I see now! You think that once they are married, he will install you as his mistress in some lacquered palace in Hong Kong!

At the time, the words had seemed more like a gratuitous insult than a real insight. But perhaps Gerda Meyer was a woman of the world, after all. Perhaps she understood things better than Amy ever could.

Was this not exactly the 'lacquered palace' Gerda had predicted? The most beautiful house in Hong Kong—but in reality nothing more than a golden cage for a kept bird?

After all, he was talking about living together, having children together—but he had not mentioned marriage.

A business wife in France and a pleasure wife in Hong Kong? Oh, yes, he is man enough for that.

And I know men like Anton Zell. They want it all—and they always get to have it all.

Empresses sometimes tolerate a concubine—or two.

Suddenly the magnificent house seemed like a prison to her, a place where all her hopes and joys would slowly die.

In Borneo he had told her clearly that he could never marry, that he had no space or time for women—'the sort of women who want a commitment from a man'. He had told her he was married to his work.

Perhaps he had meant that more literally than she had understood at the time. If he married Lavinia, he really *would* be marrying his work.

As they drove down from the peak, Amy's heart was as heavy as lead. 'I didn't think you were serious until the last minute. Are you really planning that house for—?'

'For us,' he finished. 'Yes.'

'What kind of "us"?'

'You and me. Living together. Don't you like the house?'

'It's your money, Anton,' she said, 'there's nothing for me to like or dislike!'

'Amy, I want us to have a life together from now on. Can't you see that? Don't you understand the way I feel about you? Don't you see how vital you are to me—emotionally, at work, in every way?'

Her heart was beating like a trapped bird against a window pane. Since Vietnam, everything had moved so fast. The pace of work had been hectic—this time, not the practical slog of travelling and touring plants, but the endless paperwork involved in preparing for the corporation's annual general meeting, at which Anton was due to deliver his annual report to a potentially stormy quorum of stockholders.

The report itself, of course, had already been printed—much of the work having fallen to Amy—and mailed to the stockholders. Anton had entrusted Amy with supervising the 'corporate identity' of the report. She had decided that a new look was necessary to communicate the dynamic new direction the corporation was taking. She had worked closely with a cutting-edge team of three graphic designers to produce a seventy-five-page, glossy illustrated report that outlined the global expansion envisaged by Anton while emphasising the solid base of past success from which they were working.

She herself had worked up the tagline 'New Technology, New World', and had redesigned the Zell logo as a blue globe with the green letter Z moulding itself to the sphere. It spoke plainly of Zell Corporation's commitment to ecology and the dominant role it intended to play in recycling technology from now on.

However, taking her cue from Lavinia Carron, she had avoided using *recycling*, 'the least stylish word in the English language', overmuch, and had substituted phrases like *resource renewal*, instead. But the message was clear—Anton intended to take the company ever further into the field of reprocessing that he had opened up with his new technology.

Anton—and everybody else—had been very impressed by the result. The new corporate emblem was going to be adopted and would soon be mounted on the blue tower block. The report was going to be convincing to everyone except the hard-core dissenters.

Anton had already been interviewed by regulars from both the *Economist* and the *Financial Times*, and the forthcoming articles looked set to bring favourable publicity to the new direction.

In the spaces left by this concentrated work, their private life had been even more intense. Like lava flowing at white heat through the veins in rock, it had followed its own course where it could. When the pressure of work gave them a little space alone together, there had been no words; just a fierce desire that incandesced in a moment. Tearing off each other's clothes, making love with frantic passion, falling into an exhausted sleep in one another's arms, waking just in time to wash, dress and rush back to work—that had been the tenor of their days.

Those golden hours on the island, those long evenings in Saigon, were like a distant dream. Though in Vietnam Anton had spoken of getting his priorities right, back in Hong Kong they had been thrown into a maelstrom of activity that left no time to say what needed to be said, or reflect on what needed to be contemplated.

She had never known passion as intense as this, had never known that her body could blaze like a star at a man's slightest touch; but there had also been something terrifying about the speed at which everything was happening. She was beginning to feel like someone driving a very fast car— and the faster the car went, the more the acceleration pushed her against the seat, the less in control she felt.

And now, a few hours before they were due to fly to London, he had rushed her up the peak to look at that palatial house and was talking about buying it for them to live in together.

But not about marriage.

'Anton,' she said in a quiet voice, 'shouldn't we wait until we get back from London before we start taking all these decisions?'

'You know what the property market is like in Hong Kong, darling,' he said. 'If we wait more than a few hours, that house will be sold. Quilin House is one of the most famous properties in the city.'

'There will be other houses. And it's so much money. I know that money isn't much of an object with a zillionaire like you, but you're making an offer of many millions on a house before we've even worked out what we both want.'

'There has been so little time since we got back from Saigon,' he said, the powerful engine of the car throbbing as it snarled impatiently in the traffic.

'That's exactly what I mean,' she replied, looking at him. 'We have no time to talk. No time to plan, let alone just be together!'

He met her eyes with that dazzling smile. 'Do you love me?'

'Yes,' she sighed, 'I love you insanely.'

'And I adore you,' he replied. 'What else is there to talk about?'

'We need to know that what we're doing is really what we want. You're the archetypal bachelor millionaire and I am the latest addition to the company. You know what people will say about us—what they're already saying!'

'What are they saying?' he asked, accelerating through a gap in the traffic jam.

'That I'm your latest—concubine.'

'Do *you* think you're a concubine?'

'I don't know what I am,' she said with painful honesty. 'We know so little about each other.'

'I know all that matters about you. Unless you've kept a dark secret from me?'

'Dear man, I have secrets that I even keep from myself,' she retorted with a wry smile. 'I keep telling you, I may look like an angel, but appearances can be deceptive!'

'I don't think you could deceive me,' he said. 'As for the things my staff might be saying about me, I really don't care. The next person to spread poisonous gossip about me might find him or herself unemployed.'

It was only with difficulty that she had persuaded him not to fire Glynnis, the medical officer who had put two and two together to make five.

'And what about the things Lavinia Carron might be saying about you?' she asked. 'If she gets an inkling that you and I are lovers, she could turn very nasty. And she will be waiting for you in London...darling boy.'

'It has nothing to do with her. Do you really think that I'm so afraid of Lavinia?'

'I don't think you're afraid of anything,' Amy said. 'That's the problem. Your company *is* you, Anton. It comes down to one man, to a much greater extent than with any other company of this size that I know of. It relies on your genius, your ideas, your character. But that also makes you potentially vulnerable. If Lavinia mounts a personal attack on you, you could lose the reins.'

'I can handle Lavinia.'

'You can handle her while she thinks you're going to marry her.'

She waited for him to say something, her heart pounding in her throat. Would he deny it? Would he admit that marrying Lavinia was part of his plan? That installing Amy as his mistress in Quilin House was the other half?

'I don't intend to let Lavinia dictate the company's future,' he said at last.

'Then how will you stop her? She only needs to get a few others on her side. She'll say that you're losing your touch. Making misjudgements that will cost the stockholders money. She'll point to the risks you're taking with the new plants, to your sale of the Marseilles refinery to Henri Barbusse, to your plans in south-east Asia. At the AGM, she'll say those are all bad miscalculations. And in private, she'll tell everybody you've lost your head over an impertinent little nobody—me—who supports you in your wild ventures.'

'But you do support me in my wild ventures. And I adore you for it!'

'You have so much to lose, Anton. The last thing you should be doing is advertising me. And I can't bear the idea of becoming a weapon that unscrupulous people might use to harm you in any way!'

'So I should keep you in the background?' he smiled.

'That's what *taipans* have always done with their girl-friends,' she said, echoing what Gerda had said. 'I'm perfectly happy in Causeway Bay, you have the Wanchai apartment. Living together and buying a huge house is premature. Let's leave it until we're more certain.'

The glance he gave her contained a glitter of anger. 'I've never done this before, Amy,' he said in a quiet voice. 'I never committed myself to any woman, never made promises, never said those words, *I love you.*'

'Anton—'

'I waited half my life for the right woman. And now that you're here, and I am committing myself and all that I am to you, you tell me that you're not certain.'

'I don't know how you can be certain, either!' she exclaimed. 'We love each other madly, and when we make love the world stops turning. But you know as well as I do that relationships are built on more than that!'

'Well, what *are* relationships built on?' he demanded. 'What was your last relationship built on, Amy?'

She fell silent. It had been built on lies and exploitation, but she could not tell him that.

'You haven't even told me his name,' he went on harshly. 'You won't talk about what happened. But I get the feeling that I am being penalised now for whatever it was *he* did to you!'

Again, she had no answer. Perhaps because much of what

he said was true. She *was* penalising Anton for what Martin had done to her. But her very inability to tell Anton what had happened to her made her afraid that everything was moving too fast. She wasn't ready. Like a wounded doe, she needed time and patience before she could come out of the thorny thicket where she had buried herself so deeply. If only Anton could see that!

And if only he could understand that her needing time did not mean she didn't love him! On the contrary, she adored him with every fibre of her being. Nor did she doubt that he loved her just as passionately. But did she love him so madly that she was prepared to become his mistress— and perhaps have his children—and have to watch him marry Lavinia...and know she would never be his wife?

Their jet took off at five in the afternoon. As it rose swiftly over the city, Amy saw the Zell Corporation tower flit under their wings. But in the sunset, the blue windows were now blood-red.

She thought about her arrival in this city, the first time she had seen that glass tower. It had only been a few short months earlier, yet a whole lifetime had been compressed into that time. So much had happened to her; she was hardly the same woman who had been on that other flight.

It was typical of their lives at this moment that the only quiet time they had together was on an airplane. And even here, Anton was brooding over his laptop, assimilating the latest information as it came in, so that he could give his stockholders the latest news.

She curled up on the seat next to him—once again, there were only two of them in the spacious cabin—and passed him the whisky and cola that had become their sundown ritual, the crystal tumbler to be shared by both of them.

'Are you ready to face the stockholders?' she asked.

'Dividends are higher this quarter than ever before,' he commented. 'They ought to roll out the red carpet for me.'

'Or the guillotine.' As in commercial airliners, soothing jazz was drifting out of the speakers, designed to allay the terrors of take-off. She snuggled up to him and rested her golden head on his shoulder.

'Tired?' he asked.

'It's been a long day.'

Anton pushed the table aside, shutting his laptop. He pulled a blanket over them both, put his arm around her and drew her close.

'I contacted the real-estate agent and told her we wouldn't be putting in an offer until next week,' he told her.

'I'm sorry,' she murmured. 'I know how you wanted to buy that house for us.'

'It may still be there when we get back. But as you said, there will always be other houses.'

'I love you so much,' she said, stroking his face. 'I hate you to be disappointed in me. But we have nothing to lose by taking things slow.'

'And what do we have to lose by taking things fast?' he asked with a smile that she could feel with her fingertips.

'You might regret having committed so much to me,' she replied. 'You might want your heart back.'

'And will you give it to me?'

'I will give you anything you want.'

The Lear jet was soaring up into a clear sky that darkened from violet into ultramarine. Below them, in a glittering, twilit sea, islands were scattered like jewels. The smoky music of the saxophones was peaceful.

Under the warmth of the blanket, his hand caressed her stomach. 'I only want you. The rest of it can go hang.'

'You've got me. But I'm afraid of the trouble I may cause you.'

Anton kissed her lips tenderly. His kisses were always so

erotic; no man had ever kissed her in this way, not taking, but giving, a velvety caress that was so sweet. She felt his hand slide under the waistband of her pants and move downwards.

'You've lost weight,' he accused.

'I'm just sucking in my tummy,' she whispered.

He kissed her lips again, then her eyelids. 'Don't worry about anything. We were meant to be together. And as soon as you let me, I'm going to buy you a beautiful big house where we can lock the doors, draw the curtains, turn out the lights and...'

His hand had slipped into her panties now. His fingertips caressed her soft curls, sliding between her thighs to where she was already wet and waiting for him. He cupped the warm mound of her sex in his possessive palm.

'And?' she asked, her breath catching in her throat.

'And do this.' The touch of his fingers on her sex was, as always, shockingly intense, bursting on her senses the way a honey-sweet grape burst in the mouth.

One of the things she most loved about Anton was the way he knew how to touch her, any place, any time, in any number of ways, and fill her soul with delight. His caress was rhythmical, expert, making her response grow and swell like a tropical wave.

She reached her own hand between his legs and found his arousal, thrusting passionately towards her. Panting with desire now, she explored, finding the way in through zips and pleats until she could wrap her fingers around him. He was hot and thick and long, and she wanted him desperately inside her.

Kissing hungrily, their mouths locked together, they manoeuvred in the wide seats until she got him exactly where she wanted him—pressing on top of her, his manhood thrusting between her yielding thighs.

It was so delicious, so fulfilling, to feel him slide into her body, stretching her, filling her, taking the love deep into her soul. Their lovemaking was slow and exquisitely prolonged, each searching for every corner of pleasure in the other, each wanting to give every possible ounce of fulfilment; until, with a rush like an ocean wave, their climax swept them both up into heaven.

She lay satiated, drugged with his love, her head cradled on his chest. Out of the window, she could see a velvety sky spattered with diamond stars. At these moments, there were no doubts for her. She was alive and on this planet only to be with Anton. Nothing else mattered, or ever would.

That was the power of sex. It was anti-thought, anti-caution. No doubt Mother Nature had planned it that way to ensure the continuation of the species, no matter what obliteration threatened!

CHAPTER THIRTEEN

IT WAS a long flight. Through the dark, star-spangled night they made love again, slept, then made love yet again. It was, Amy thought, by far the best way anyone had yet discovered to pass an intercontinental flight. She wished that they might never have to land back on earth again.

But the red glow of dawn appeared at last and coming back to earth could no longer be postponed. Britain appeared in the distance as a dark and rumpled mass of cloud that looked like a huge counterpane.

As they descended through the cloud layer, however, the illusion of softness was soon dispelled. It was December weather in northern Europe. Darkness closed in, lit only by lurid flares of lightning. Turbulence shook the Lear as strong winds battered the jet. Amy watched apprehensively as heavy ice formed swiftly at the windows. It became perceptibly very much colder. When the Lear finally descended from the maelstrom it was to find itself above a city lashed by a snowstorm, bathed in a dim and unearthly grey light.

'Well,' Anton said, hugging Amy, 'time to face the music. Buckle up!'

The landing at Heathrow was made in driving snow and violent cross-winds that made the Lear stagger and seem to stall in the air. Amy clutched Anton's strong arm for comfort as they bounced down the runway. Why was it that so many of their moments together had been marked by storms and rain?

The reality of London was dark, bitterly cold and very snowy. In the taxi to the Ritz, where they were going to be staying, Amy switched on the satellite phone and at once the calls began to pour in. With every passing minute, the intimate warmth that had been built up so deliciously between them during the night flight was giving way to the endless clamour of work.

The great hotel, however, with its atmosphere of a French château somehow magically dropped in the middle of Piccadilly, was a welcoming monolith. With its Christmas lights and cheerily illuminated windows, it resembled an ocean liner looming out of the whirling flakes of snow.

Their suite was breathtaking, bearing witness to the refurbishment that had restored every tassel, every gleaming piece of furniture and every crystal in the chandeliers to their original Louis XVI style. Watching the snowflakes whirl against the windows from within the glowing luxury of a room like this was delicious.

Amy half expected to see King Louis himself—or at least Napoleon—reclining on the ornate four-poster bed. But it was wonderfully empty and she sprawled on it happily with the newspapers that had been thoughtfully provided.

At huge expense, Anton had booked the famous Marie Antoinette Suite here at the Ritz for tonight's reception. The glorious room, one of the most famous venues in London, would make an opulent setting for Anton to entertain the several dozen major stockholders in advance of tomorrow's AGM, which would be held at a modern conference room overlooking the Thames.

While Anton talked on the phone, she opened the *Financial Times*, expecting to find an article in advance of tomorrow's stockholders' meeting. It was there, all right, but its tone made her sit up, frowning.

'You'd better read this, darling,' she said.

Anton read the article carefully, starting with the headline, NEW DIRECTION FOR ZELL CORPORATION QUESTIONED BY SHAREHOLDERS.

When he'd finished, he passed the newspaper back to her.

'It doesn't say who any of these supposed shareholders are. I don't take that too seriously.'

'Well, it's obvious who one of them is,' Amy said. 'Though, as you say, it doesn't quote her name.'

'You can't blame everything on Lavinia, darling,' Anton said with a smile. 'It's just a journalist picking up a possible story, that's all. They'll be singing a different song after the AGM.' He glanced at his watch. He was scheduled to meet Lavinia Carron for drinks before lunch. Ostensibly, she was welcoming an old friend to London, but Amy feared it would be the first clash of sabres between them. 'I'm guessing you have no desire to rekindle the flames of friendship with Lavinia?'

'I never want to see her again,' Amy said. 'I'm sure she's behind that story, my darling. It's a shot across your bows.'

He came to sit beside her, took her face in both his hands, and kissed her carefully on the mouth. 'Don't worry about a thing.'

'I can't help worrying,' she replied, searching his eyes with her own. 'She wants your money or to be your wife, Anton!'

He laughed. 'Sit tight, angel. What are you going to do while I hobnob with Lavinia?'

'I'll do some shopping.'

'OK, we'll meet for lunch at the Savoy Grill—I feel like something quintessentially English. One o'clock, Miss Worthington. Don't be late!'

She had told Anton that she was going shopping but the truth was there was almost nothing she needed. Her life in Hong Kong was so pampered and the shopping there was more than adequate for her relatively undemanding tastes. Of clothes, cosmetics and accessories, she already had more than she could use.

And the sinking feeling that persisted in the pit of her

stomach would not have allowed herself to spend on luxuries, anyway.

Books, however, were another matter. The prospect of losing herself in a sea of the latest books was very alluring indeed. Belting herself into a coat, she headed purposefully out to tour the large book emporiums of the city.

It was very cold. As so often, London seemed to have been taken by surprise by heavy snow. It was piled in dirty mounds, uncollected, on the traffic islands and pavements, or spread in slushy marshes that the traffic sprayed on hapless pedestrians. It was also, however, very beautiful; the great parks were stark snowfields where nobody had yet ventured to leave footprints, and each famous building, monument or statue was decorated with white caps on any horizontal plane where the stuff could adhere.

Amy roamed the bookstores, buying things for Anton as well as for herself. Exciting new books were about the only Christmas present she knew he would enjoy. Heaven knew when they would have time to read all the volumes that soon accumulated in piles on the counters, but she could always dream of a peaceful future where she and Anton would have time to please themselves and nobody else.

She tried not to think of what might be passing between Anton and Lavinia as she paged through the glossy books that still smelled of new paper and fresh ink. For all his light-hearted assurances, she was aware that the next few days were going to prove a watershed for Anton. She was not so prone to melodrama as to cast it as a battle for one man's soul—but one of the reasons she had persuaded Anton not to make an offer on Quilin House was that deep down inside, she knew that there was going to be a winner and a loser. And she knew she was going to be the loser.

Because she knew that love did not conquer all. Love was conquered by many things—by money, by expedience, by power. And Lavinia had them all on her side.

All she herself had was the miracle that Anton had fallen in love with her—one snowflake out of so many others. One snowflake that would melt as soon as it was touched by the breath of reality.

She bought so many books that there was no way she could carry them all, so they were sent to their suite at the Ritz. And then it was time for her to hurry across to the Strand to meet Anton at the Savoy.

The front of the hotel was crowded as always with Rolls-Royces and limousines trying to get their occupants as close to the entrance as possible. A uniformed commissionaire hurried out to her cab and ushered her in under the shelter of a large black umbrella.

The restaurant was crowded but she saw Anton at once, sitting at a banquette alone, his chin resting on his clasped hands. Her heart sank at his pose—she could tell at once that something was wrong. The drinks with Lavinia had evidently not gone well.

A waiter ushered her to the table and she settled down opposite Anton, trying to smile brightly. 'Sorry I'm late— the traffic's awful.'

Anton looked up at her. For the first time since she had known him, his eyes seemed empty and cold. That, more than anything, chilled her to the bone. She reached out for his hands.

'Darling, what's the matter? Did the meeting go badly?'

He pulled his hands away from hers. 'Why didn't you tell me?' he asked in a quiet voice.

'Tell you what?' she replied in shock.

'Why did I have to hear about that from Lavinia Carron, Amy?' His face, always so handsome and alive, looked like a mask of anger and pain. 'Couldn't you have told me before?'

'I don't understand what you're talking about,' she replied urgently. 'Whatever Lavinia has said to upset you so much is a lie, I can promise you that!'

'I don't think so,' he said flatly. 'I think it's you who have lied to me.'

'I have never lied to you,' she flashed back at him.

The waiter, who had been hovering with the menus, discreetly vanished at this point, though they barely noticed. The elegant restaurant, with its light wood panelling and snowy linen surmounted by bunches of pale yellow roses, seemed to be spinning around Amy.

'When you first came to me,' Anton said grimly, 'I asked you directly whether you had had an affair with Martin McCallum.'

'Oh,' she said, realisation hitting her like an arrow thudding into her heart, the shock spreading through her body, paralysing her.

'You flatly denied it,' Anton went on. 'I asked you if that was why you were so eager to leave McCallum and Roe. You denied that, too.'

'Anton, those questions weren't ethical at that point, and you know that. You had no right to ask them.'

'But you chose to answer them,' he pointed out with ineluctable logic. 'You answered them with lies.'

'Yes,' she said hopelessly, 'I lied to you.'

'We became lovers, Amy. You've had months to tell me the truth. To correct those lies. But you never did.'

'I warned you,' she said quietly. 'There are things about me that I hide even from myself. I'm not an angel. I'm very sorry that Lavinia was the one to tell you. I should have guessed she would make enquiries about me and find that out. Of course she would use it.'

'She didn't have to look very far, Amy. McCallum and Roe are one of the companies she owns shares in. A lot of shares. Of course the boy would take her into his confidence.'

'Of course he would,' she said drily. 'I have been a fool.'

Anton's eyes never left hers. 'I've been the fool, Amy. I allowed myself to believe things about you that I haven't believed of any other human being—that you were honest, that you were pure, that you were different from all the others.'

'Those are the things I believed about you, too,' she said dully.

'I even persuaded myself that we were the same inside,' he went on. 'We'd come from the same pain, we'd travelled the same route. I thought we believed in the same things, about people, about the world.'

'And don't we?'

'I don't think so, Amy. I could never lie to you the way you have lied to me. I asked you those questions during the interview because I was afraid that you'd had an affair with your last employer. You lied to me.'

'And yet, within hours of taking me on, you were telling me you wanted a ''special relationship'' with me, Anton,' she shot back. 'You kissed me on the lips in Borneo.'

'I did not expect or plan to fall in love with you!'

'Nor did I expect or plan to fall in love with *you*, Anton. Don't you remember how I tried to avoid it? Have you forgotten how angry you used to get with me when I wouldn't just jump into your bed?'

'Why didn't you tell me the truth?'

'For what it's worth, I always planned to tell you about Martin. I knew that there were things in my past that might upset you. That was why I was trying to put the brakes on—until I could get the chance to talk about them.'

'Somehow that chance never came.'

'Don't sound so bitter,' she begged. 'It never came because our life together is so hectic. People in love need time and space to learn about each other. You cannot find the truth about someone just through sleeping with them. If there isn't ever a moment to relax together, how can there be communication?'

'I see. So the fault is mine.'

'The fault is mine,' she replied. 'I'm just trying to tell you why I never got around to telling you about Martin. The only time we have ever had together that we weren't travelling at the speed of light was in Vietnam. And that time—' Tears filled her eyes suddenly and she could not speak for a moment. 'And that time,' she went on, brushing the wetness off her cheeks with shaking hands, 'was so precious and beautiful. I didn't want to even think about my life before you. I couldn't bear to bring up such ugly things.'

'I wish you had. It might have made a difference.'

'I'm sorry, Anton,' she repeated. 'Yes, I had an affair with Martin McCallum and I wish it had never happened.'

'It's much more than that,' he said, his eyes darkening. 'You're still hiding the truth. The truth is that you got pregnant. Didn't you?'

The room was spinning faster and faster now, the yellow roses blurring into the panelling, the elegant light fittings dazzling her aching eyes. 'Anton—'

'You got pregnant and you used that to try and force Martin McCallum into marrying you. And when that didn't work, you terminated the pregnancy. As callously and as cynically as that. And you tell me not to be bitter?'

'Anton, I can't stay here,' she heard herself say. 'I have to go.'

She rose. A deadly wave of dizziness rushed into her brain. She had to clutch the table to stop herself from falling.

Anton had risen, too. He faced her across the table, his mouth compressed into a hard line, his normally tanned face pale with emotion. 'Haven't you got anything to say?' he demanded.

Conversation around them had halted and people at neighbouring tables were staring curiously. She was aware of everything through a spiralling haze. She knew only that she had to get out of Anton's presence before she fainted or was sick all over the Savoy's snowy white linen.

'No,' she whispered. 'I haven't got anything to say, Anton.'

She clutched her bag and stumbled out of the restaurant. The alert waiter was waiting with her coat. 'Can I get the commissionaire to call you a cab, miss?' he asked her in concern.

Not trusting herself to speak, she just shook her head. She made her way frantically through the noisy crowds in the lobby.

And then she was running blindly into the whirling snow.

She found herself back in Piccadilly, at Green Park. She was not sure how she had got there. The vast white space of the park drew her in, though she was already icy cold and shivering.

Snow banks were piled high. The paths had been shovelled at some point but the heavy snowfalls had all but obliterated them again. The snow had also mocked the bare trees by piling every branch and twig with a glittering foliage of ice crystals.

Amy walked through the park, finding a wilderness in the heart of the bustling city. Soon, the loudest sound in the world was the beating of her own heart. The only life was the clouding of her breath in the icy air. Flurries of snow twirled and fluttered down constantly.

Her mind was largely a blank. She wasn't rehearsing what she might say to Anton when he finally returned to her—there was nothing to rehearse. There was only the truth. And the truth would come out of her in its own way, whether she tried to put it into clever words or not, no matter how she tried to phrase it.

She saw nobody in the park. Her frantic heartbeat began

to slow as the icy cold sank into her flesh and bone. Shuddering now with the severe drop in temperature as the afternoon closed in and it grew dark, she turned her steps back towards the Ritz.

The sparkling façade of the great hotel was like a beacon in the gloom, the famous name spelled out in lights. It was like another world, a glittering ocean liner from which she had fallen into deep, dark waters.

As she walked into the lobby she mingled with the people from this other world, men in evening dress, women in gowns of silk or sequins. Curious eyes glanced at her, a snow-stained waif coming in from the cold, who scarcely seemed to belong here; but she didn't care; she wanted only to get to her room and find Anton.

She entered a world of pink serpentine columns and rich woods, of gold leaf and luxurious carpets in peach and blue and yellow, of chandeliers that dripped glowing crystals. The smell of snow in her nostrils was driven out by the mingled scents of a dozen famous perfume houses. She was trembling with the cold.

And then she saw Anton. Anton and Lavinia Carron, walking through the lobby towards her. His arm was linked in hers. He was wearing evening clothes, she was in a long dress of pearl lamé with her dark hair lifted off her face. They were easily the handsomest couple in the lobby of the Ritz tonight, the king and queen of all these beautiful people.

Gasping for breath, Amy tried to flee, but there were too many people to allow for escape. The press of the crowd brought her up face to face with Anton and Lavinia.

Anton's eyes blazed wide as he saw her. 'Where the hell have you been?' he greeted her savagely.

The shock and the pain of that almost made her legs give way. 'Walking,' she replied.

'Walking? In the snow? Are you insane?'

'I suppose I must be,' Amy replied. Lavinia's violet eyes were mocking, triumphant. How sweet it must be to see her rival, bedraggled and half-frozen, in the lobby of the Ritz!

Anton grasped her arm and half pulled, half led her into an alcove where there was a measure of privacy. Lavinia followed, still smirking.

'You look like death warmed over,' Anton said, lifting Amy's face with a firm grip on her chin and staring into her eyes. 'Why did you run out of the Savoy like that?'

'I had nothing more to say at that point,' she replied, pushing his hand away from her face.

'And now?' Anton demanded in a growl. 'Have you got anything to say now?'

'Not in front of that woman,' Amy retorted, not even deigning to look at Lavinia Carron.

Lavinia's simper faded at the enmity in Amy's tone. 'Are you going to let her talk to me like that, Anton?' she demanded angrily.

'Amy,' Anton said tersely, 'all I need to hear from you is a yes or a no. Is it true or isn't it?'

'I can't talk to you here,' she retorted, 'least of all in front of *her*.'

'She is the one who found out these things about you,' Anton said grimly. 'She is the one who enlightened me. If you want to say anything, then you should be able to say it in her presence.'

'And if you can't understand why I cannot say a word in her presence, then you are not the man I fell in love with,' she retorted through chattering teeth.

'*You* don't love him,' Lavinia hissed, leaning forward with bared teeth. '*You* want to drag him down to your pathetic level. You can offer him nothing except ruin!'

'I do love you, Anton,' Amy said, ignoring Lavinia's outburst. 'The question is, do you love me?'

'I loved someone,' he said heavily, and in the shadows

under his eyes she suddenly saw the pain that he had gone through. 'But I don't know where she is any more.'

'She never existed,' Lavinia said with a brusque laugh. 'Like all these people who appoint themselves custodians of the so-called environment, she liked to pose as a saint, but the truth is something else. Someone who used her pregnancy to blackmail her lover, and then aborted it to get revenge on him, cannot claim any moral high ground! She deserves no consideration whatsoever!'

'And someone with a mind as loathsome as yours should keep her mouth shut,' Amy retorted hotly, acknowledging Lavinia's presence at last. 'How dare you talk about blackmail? Aren't you blackmailing Anton right now? All *you* love is money, Lavinia. You said it yourself in Antibes—nothing else matters to you except lots and lots of money in your bank account.'

Lavinia turned to Anton, her nostrils flaring. 'This is the woman you spent all afternoon scouring London for,' she said harshly. 'She destroyed Martin's happiness. Are you going to let her destroy yours?'

'That's enough from both of you,' Anton said quietly. He glanced at his watch. 'We are due to meet the major shareholders in five minutes. I take it you don't intend to be there, Amy?'

The reception at the Marie Antoinette Suite! She had forgotten all about it. Her snow-soaked clothes weighed heavily on her.

'No,' she replied. 'I can't be there.'

'Do you intend to come to the AGM tomorrow?' he demanded.

'Do you want me there?' she asked, meeting his eyes.

'No,' he said flatly. 'It's probably better if you stay away.'

Amy felt as though her heart was stopping. She could hardly breathe. So it had happened, just as she had always feared it would—had always known it would. Lavinia had won and she had lost. As Lavinia sneered at her now, Amy was unable to even cry.

Anton looked into her eyes one last time. His expression was unfathomable, dark. Then he turned, and, taking Lavinia by the arm, led her towards the Marie Antoinette Suite.

CHAPTER FOURTEEN

THE old house had once seemed so huge to her. Now she saw it as just a simple white cottage with a slate roof and a smoking chimney, nestling among a thicket of birches. The garden, which had once been a terrifying forest through which she had run madly with pounding heart, relentlessly hunted by her enemies, was now revealed as a ragged shrubbery of laburnums, rose bushes and laurels.

But the smell of the house, of wax and wood-fires, was just as she had always remembered it. It filled her with so many memories, some bad, some good, some happy, others irreparably sad.

The heating of the cottage depended on the iron boiler built into the fireplace. It was another cold and snowy morning, and the fire was burning low, so Amy piled more logs into the grate. She nursed the fire until it was blazing and she could hear hot water gurgling through the pipes of the old radiators. The chill began to come off the air.

She went into the kitchen and put on the kettle. While it boiled, she contemplated lunch. For the past few days, her life had been this—concentrating on the simple tasks of making a fire, brewing tea, planning a meal. Nothing more, nothing less. It was about all she could cope with. A broken heart did not allow anything more demanding.

As she washed vegetables, she heard the sound of a car coming up the lane. It was a red family estate, driving slowly and carefully because of the thick snow. She did not recognise it—the cottage had few visitors these days. She watched from the kitchen as the car pulled up next to the garage. A woman and a child got out. The child ran to the cottage. The woman paused to lock the car, then followed.

At last Amy saw who it was—one of the twins, her cousin, Jamie-Lee.

She dried her hands and went to open the door for the visitors. The child, a four-year-old boy named David, jumped into her arms.

'Hi, Aunt Amy!'

'Goodness, you've grown, Davie,' she said, hoisting him in her arms. 'Hello, Jamie-Lee. I've just put the kettle on.'

'It's so warm and cosy in here,' Jamie-Lee said, hauling off her parka and hanging it on the coat rack beside the door. 'You've turned it into a home again.'

'Your dad has gone for a walk down to the village to buy a newspaper and some pipe tobacco,' Amy told her cousin.

'I know,' Jamie-Lee said. 'We saw him as we crossed the bridge. But it's you I wanted to talk to, Amy.'

'OK,' Amy said cheerfully, though a cordial tête-à-tête with her cousin was hardly customary—nor a particularly welcome idea right now. 'I'll pour the tea.'

There were some of the child's toys in a cupboard. Amy got them out so he could play while she and Jamie-Lee sat on either side of the fire. Jamie-Lee was a thin blonde woman with feathery hair. She had married a doctor and lived some two hours' drive away, so she had evidently made a special journey to be here. She seemed nervous, her thin shoulders tense under the expensive cashmere cardigan, her mouth compressed.

'What did you want to talk about?' Amy invited.

Jamie-Lee drew a deep breath. 'I've come to make my peace with you,' she said in a brittle voice. Amy said nothing, cradling the teacup in her hands and watching the flames lick around the logs. Jamie-Lee swallowed and then went on. 'We were loathsome to you, Amy. All three of us. We did and said horrible things to you. When I remember what we were like, I feel sick. You were all alone and you had just lost your parents. You needed us to be kind to you, needed your family to help you, but instead we—'

In the silence, the flames crackled. Still Amy said nothing. It was not her job to help her cousin out with whatever it was she wanted to say.

Jamie-Lee's fingers were shaking and the teacup rattled against the saucer. 'We were talking about it the other day. We were all so ashamed of what we did to you. I know the others want to talk to you themselves, but when I heard you were staying with Dad I decided to come over and apologise to you. I'm so sorry, Amy. More sorry than I can say.'

To her surprise, Amy saw that her cousin's eyes were brimming with tears, her pale lips working painfully. She reached out her hand. 'Don't cry, Jamie-Lee. It was all a long time ago.'

Jamie-Lee put down the cup with a clatter and grasped Amy's hand, sobbing. 'Please say you forgive me,' she begged, 'please say that, Amy.'

'Of course I forgive you,' Amy said, 'though I'll never know why you all disliked me so much.'

Jamie-Lee gave a laugh that was halfway to a sob. 'Oh, of course you know why!'

'I promise you, I don't.'

'Well, because you were so much prettier and cleverer than any of us, of course,' Jamie-Lee said, wiping her eyes. 'You were so talented and we were such mugs. And Dad thought the world of you. You showed us up for what we were.'

'I see,' Amy said quietly.

'And all the boys fancied you like mad—they never even looked at Sally-Ann or me. And then you started winning all those scholarships and bursaries and things. You got honours for sport *and* academics. The teachers adored you, and it was always me or Sally-Ann at the bottom of the pile.

You even started your periods before we did. We were so insanely jealous. And you grew breasts before we did and all the boys were crazier about you than ever—'

'You'd better stop,' Amy said as her cousin's voice rose, 'I don't want you chasing me round the garden with the carving knife again.'

Jamie-Lee gave that half-sob again. 'It's taken me all these years to crawl out from under that inferiority complex, Amy. If it had just been me, I think I would have worshipped you. But there were three of us, you see, and so we ganged up on you. The tall poppy effect, you know. Trying to cut you down to our size. But you just kept growing taller and taller, and the taller you grew, the smaller we felt. When you arrived in our little world, everything turned upside-down. But I finally realised something important.'

'What was that?' Amy asked gently.

'You gave me a wonderful example,' Jamie-Lee said simply. 'I had someone to look up to. I learned from you—to work hard, try my best, to achieve. I wouldn't be the person I am today without you.'

'Well, I hardly—'

'I'm serious,' Jamie-Lee said. 'You're such a good person. So in control of your life. I still envy you like mad, but it's under control now. You have had three wonderful jobs in a row. And now you're in Hong Kong, working for Anton Zell. We're so proud of you; a top job overseas for a wonderful boss, travel, money, excitement—you deserve it so much.'

Amy smiled painfully. 'I'm not so sure it's all it's cracked up to be,' she replied. 'And I don't think I'll be going back to Hong Kong any time soon.' She was feeling shaky. She took the cups back to the kitchen to make fresh tea.

Jamie-Lee followed her. 'What are you talking about?'

'I lost the job.'

'But—why?'

'I concealed some information during the interview process.'

'Professional information? About your qualifications?'

Amy sighed. 'No, something personal. About my private life.'

'But, Amy,' Jamie-Lee protested, 'they're not allowed to bring up your private life during an interview.'

'This job was special.' The last thing she wanted to do was talk about Anton to Jamie-Lee, but her cousin's wide blue eyes were fixed on her. 'The employer was—special. He grew to be special to me, I mean. And I think I did to him.'

'You fell in love with Anton Zell?' Jamie-Lee gasped.

'It's an occupational hazard,' Amy said wryly.

'But—what happened?'

'Things didn't work out.'

'Why?' Jamie-Lee persisted, taking the second cup of tea that Amy gave her.

'Let's just say that perhaps I'm not as good a person as you imagined,' Amy said painfully. 'And I'm certainly not as "in control of my life" as it seems.' She glanced at the little boy playing with toy soldiers on the carpet. 'And you can't envy me a tenth as much as I envy you now,' she finished quietly.

Her uncle returned from his walk just before lunch. He had stayed out longer than usual, probably warned by Jamie-Lee that she wanted time alone with Amy. Retired and grey-haired now, Jeffrey Cookson presented a comfortable figure with his cloth cap and his pipe dangling from under his moustache.

He was carrying a pink newspaper which Amy recognised as the *Financial Times*. He took it from under his arm, unfolded it and passed it to Amy.

'Some news about your boss, my dear,' he said laconically. 'I'm going upstairs to wash.'

Alone by the fire, Amy turned to the article. It was on the front page. The headline read, Zell Buyback Has Impact on Share Prices.

Her heart beating fast, she read the text.

The Zell Corporation's recent buyback of a major block of shares, formerly owned by the late Sir Robert Carron, is now widely perceived to have enhanced shareholder value. ZellCorp share prices surged after news of the buyback was announced at the stormy recent stockholders' meeting.

At the current share price of 134p the dividend yield is 8.9%, and since the dividend appears safe the shares are proving attractive to income investors, though capital growth may be limited as company CEO Anton Zell takes ZellCorp into new areas over the next two years.

Zell denied that the aim of the buyback was simply to give a short-term boost to his company's shares.

'There were differences of opinion on the direction the company should be taking,' he explained, talking from his Hong Kong office. 'In the end, it came down to a crisis of confidence. The simplest solution was for us to buy back blocks owned by dissenting elements. This has proved expensive, especially since our requirement for capital expenditure is set to be high as we expand into new areas. But we now have a free hand to develop the way we want to, and the remaining shareholders have seen the value of their shares substantially increased, which will enhance their confidence in management.'

Lady Lavinia Carron, the principal beneficiary of the buyback, is back in France; however, she made a brief statement today through her financial advisor, Heinz Meyer. 'We disagreed with Mr Zell about his new operations and on several other fundamental issues. He refused to listen. We got our money back. That's all. The improvement in the share price is immaterial to us. We believe Zell paid too much for his own shares and expect to see a substantial drop in the share price as soon as the public realise their confidence in this man is misplaced.'

Lady Carron received a multimillion-pound cash sum for her shares. However, her prediction that the ZellCorp price is set to fall soon is unlikely to be borne out in reality, as demand for the shares is now very high.

The imminent implementation of exciting new technologies, including advanced recycling refineries and the laminate plate system, has rocketed ZellCorp into the forefront of the petrochemical industry. The market has interpreted the buyback as a highly positive signal from ZellCorp and there is considerable market interest in this company.

The rest of the article dealt with the details of the new technology including a sidebar about the Korean shipbuilding licensing deal, and a photograph of Anton taken at the Ritz during the AGM.

Amy laid down the paper, staring into the flames. Her heart was still thudding. So things had not turned out as she had anticipated. She had been too afraid to read the papers since leaving London. She had simply assumed that Lavinia would carry the day and that Anton would shortly be announcing his engagement to her.

But it hadn't happened that way. The bitterness so evident in Lavinia's Press statement bore out the newspaper's report that the stockholders' meeting had been 'stormy'. She had not, after all, carried the day. Whatever deal she had offered, Anton had had no intention of bargaining down his position.

Now Lavinia was back in France and Anton was in Hong Kong. And she was here in Northamptonshire. Their lives had collided passionately and then had gone on their own ways.

Amy rose, restless and agitated, and went into the kitchen. She would give a great deal to have seen Lavinia's performance at the AGM. The venue which she had expected to be the scene of her triumph had turned into her Waterloo.

She would give a great deal, too, to have seen Anton's performance. She had made many mistakes of judgement about Anton Zell. She had assumed that he would let expedience rule his life, the way other men did. But he was not like that.

He was not that kind of man.

She busied herself with preparing lunch for herself and Uncle Jeffrey. But her mind was busy with so many brilliant and fiery images, images of Anton she had locked away until this moment: Anton making love to her, filling her like a sail in a hurricane; Anton making her laugh till she was weak; the deep core of peace she had felt with him as they stood in that temple on an island off the coast of Vietnam.

Her heart filled with tears and restlessness, she laid out the food for her uncle. She sat with him while he ate but could not touch anything herself. Her stomach was in a knot. He did not ask why Jamie-Lee hadn't stayed for lunch, nor about the reason for her visit.

That was his way. Jeffrey had never asked her directly about the reason for her sudden departure from Anton's employment. Perhaps because he was not her real father, he had always kept out of her private life. Yet when she'd needed somewhere to run to, he had asked no questions, had just opened his door to her.

She felt he had always known more than he said about what happened to her, but he did not pry. One day she would be able to explain some of the dark places in her life to him; but not today, not yet.

The snow had stopped falling and the sun was peering

uncertainly through luminous cloud, so after lunch she decided to go for a walk in the woods alone. As a girl, it had always been her refuge, her place to think.

It was early January—almost a year to the day since she had walked into Anton Zell's life, and he into hers.

In the summer, the woods were a deep-dappled place of rustling leaves and teeming bird life. It was strange to walk through them now and see the sky above, criss-crossed with bare twigs, and hear no sound but the crunch of her own boots in the snow.

There was much to think about. It had been such a strange day. Twice in quick succession, her expectations had been transformed. People had behaved as she had never expected they could or would.

She had never anticipated that any of her cousins would ever feel guilty about the wretched childhood they had given her, let alone that she would hear Jamie-Lee, always the ringleader, apologise with tears in her eyes.

And then, the news of Anton's buyback had come as an even greater shock. She knew that Lavinia had seen herself as Anton's consort and could only imagine the huge effort she had made to achieve that goal. Anton could have staved off the crisis by a dozen means. What had happened that awful evening at the Ritz, after she had left, and Anton and Lavinia had walked into the Marie Antoinette Suite together? She would never know.

But somehow, Amy felt that article in the *Financial Times* had rounded off her understanding of Anton; just as Jamie-Lee's apology had rounded off her understanding of her cousins, and had closed the door on a dark and unhappy chapter. Understanding why her cousins had been so resentful of her had helped her understand herself, too.

She had always been such a high achiever, so determined to be at the top, to be the best at everything. Perhaps she, too, had been unbearable to them, as they had been to her.

But where had it led her, that relentless urge to excel? Into two disastrous experiences. She had become personally involved with two employers in succession. Both relationships had ended in catastrophe.

Hardly the great professional triumph that Jamie-Lee perceived.

And it was painful to see herself through Anton's eyes—as a woman who habitually slept with her bosses, who lied about her past relationships, who concealed what she was under a cloak of hypocrisy.

Of course Martin McCallum would have told Lavinia the story his own way, absolving himself of all blame and making her out to be a monster; and no doubt the story would have improved further as Lavinia relayed it. But the truth was that she had been terribly stupid with Martin and was still paying for it now—would pay for the rest of her life. Because she had lost the one man she had ever loved. The only man she ever could love.

There was a pool at the heart of the wood, fed by a little stream that trickled down from the hills. She reached it late in the afternoon. In happier summers she had swum here, cooling off in the clear water. Today parts of the pool were iced over and its heart was a deep turquoise blue. The sun had set low and was turning crimson through the trees.

Amy sat on a boulder and looked into the aquamarine depths of the pool. It was so still here, in the heart of the woods. Nothing stirred. No creature moved, no wind blew. It seemed to Amy that after so much travel and noise and colour and movement, she had finally reached some still point in her own life—a centre, around which everything else revolved.

In this still place, the decision formed in her heart out of the silence. Retreat and despair were not the answer. She would not accept that it was all over.

She was not that kind of woman.

In this silent moment of her busy life, Amy prayed for the strength to go back to Anton. To find him and tell him the truth about herself. Whatever he decided to do, whatever he chose to believe, she would tell him that she loved him truly and deeply and would never love another man as long as she lived.

She would go back to Hong Kong and look into his eyes once again. Perhaps he would reject her. She would accept that pain if it came. But she would not accept defeat.

She loved him. That was all there was.

The silence was broken by a distant sound, perhaps the cracking of a twig. Amy opened her eyes. She had thought herself alone in the woods. But through the silvery trunks of the trees she could see a figure approaching. It was a tall man, whose outline was so painfully familiar to her that she felt her heart leap into her throat.

Anton stepped into the clearing. Against the muted colours of the snowy woods, his eyes were the deepest blue imaginable, the colour of a warm tropical sea.

'It's almost our anniversary,' he said.

'How did you find me?' she whispered.

'I followed your footprints through the woods,' he replied. 'They were the only ones. Yours are the only footprints in my heart, my beloved Amy. Can you forgive me?'

'Oh, Anton,' she said. She held out her arms and he came to her swiftly.

How wonderful it was to be enveloped in that strong embrace again. She lifted her joyful face to his, accepting his warm kisses with ecstasy, with rapture.

'Please tell me you'll give me another chance,' he begged, crushing her even tighter in his arms. 'Please tell me you forgive me for being such a fool, my beloved.'

'We have both been fools.'

Their kiss seemed to last forever. When the world stopped spinning around them, he looked down into her eyes. 'You are the most precious person in my life. Can you pardon me for the terrible words I said to you?'

'If you tell me that you don't believe the things Lavinia told you about me!'

'Not any more. I didn't sleep the night you left, just lay with my own thoughts, realising that it was impossible that the Amy I loved could have done any of that. It was during the meeting itself that it came to me, suddenly, what a madman I had been. I'm so sorry I took so long to find you. You hid yourself well. I had to go straight to Hong Kong after the AGM because of the trouble Lavinia caused. I only got back last night. You know about the buyback?'

She nodded. 'I read about it just this morning. I didn't know before. I just assumed that you and Lavinia—'

'Morticia will have to find another Gomez, my darling.'

She laughed unsteadily. 'She made you pay for rejecting her, my love. I'm sorry about that.'

'It was worth every penny—because now we are free. We can do things our way. And I have some promises to make to you, Amy. One is that our lives will never move at the speed of light again. There will always be time and space for just us. No matter how far we travel, no matter what goals we set ourselves, nothing will matter more than we do. You are the most important person in my world and you always will be.' He kissed her tenderly. 'I will always listen to you and hear the words that you say. Will you come home with me, Amy? Your house is waiting for you, my angel, with dragons to guard all four quarters.'

'You bought Quilin House!'

'Actually, *you* did,' he smiled. 'The house is in your name, beloved.'

'But Anton…why?'

'For one night in London, I thought you didn't exist any more,' he said. 'No night has ever been as dark and terrible as that. Not even when they locked me in the cupboard as a child. When I lost my faith in you, I lost myself. I want to atone for that. I want to show you that I will never again distrust you. I want you to come back to Hong Kong with me and live in your house. It will always be yours, even if you decide not to make me that happiest man in the world and become my wife. But I hope that eventually, you will be ready to marry me. Quilin House is my gift to you, and my apology.'

Another still place, another calm centre, thousands of miles away from that frozen pool.

They stood side by side in the pagoda, holding hands, as they had done once, months before. The ancient shrine was filled with peace. The distant sound of the sea threaded itself around the old stones as though weaving a garland around their blessed happiness. The smile on the face of the statue was serene and beautiful.

As before, they had laid offerings of wild flowers and fruits on the floor of the shrine.

'I never told you how much I loved you,' Anton said. 'If I had done that, perhaps you would have trusted me more.'

'Perhaps I didn't trust myself,' she replied quietly. 'I could never have willingly terminated my pregnancy. But when I had the miscarriage, it seemed to me that it was my fault. I felt such deep guilt for so long. I felt I was to blame somehow.'

His fingers tightened around hers. 'It was an accident of nature,' he replied. 'Only a mind like Martin McCallum's could have believed otherwise.'

'I'm so sorry you had to hear it, warped and twisted like that, from Lavinia. It must have hurt you so terribly.'

'I could never really believe it,' he replied. 'I knew it was wrong, it had to be wrong. You were not the sort of woman who could have behaved in the way she described.' He turned to her, his face serene. 'You are the best and most beautiful person I know, Amy. I am so proud that you're going to be my wife.'

'And you are the only man in the world,' she replied simply. 'There is no one like you.'

'I've brought something for you,' he said, reaching into his pocket. 'I hope you will accept it this time.'

She knew what it was, even before he held it out to her—a hoop of the deepest, greenest jade, carved with the muscular body of a living dragon.

'The first time I offered it to you,' he went on, 'I think you thought I was trying to mark you as a trophy, a conquest. But I was trying to say the opposite, my love—that you had conquered me, and could wear me on your arm, your own tame dragon.'

'It's so beautiful and alive, just like you. But it will never be tame.' She slipped the cool, precious thing onto her arm and then kissed the warm velvet of his lips. 'I'll never take it off.'

The floor of the temple, as before, was scattered with silvery sand and the flowers that the wind had blown in, as though in mute worship. The domed roof over their heads was filled with the murmur of the sea. Once again, Amy knew that they were in a sacred place, beyond all religion.

'Thank you for bringing me here,' she whispered. 'It's so beautiful.'

'Yes,' Anton replied. 'The world is a beautiful place. I want to spend the rest of my life making sure it stays beautiful for you—and for our children. One of the many reasons I adore you is because you want that, too. I could never love anyone who just didn't care.'

They kissed, with the tenderness of complete love.

Then they turned and walked back down the path, under the drooping boughs of wild hibiscus and ripe fruit that hung like jewels over their heads, back down to the beach, to where their boat was rocking at anchor, waiting to take them onward.

ACCEPTING THE
BOSS'S PROPOSAL

BY

NATASHA OAKLEY

Natasha Oakley told everyone at her primary school she wanted to be an author when she grew up. Her plan was to stay at home and have her mum bring her coffee at regular intervals – a drink she didn't like then. The coffee addiction became reality and the love of storytelling stayed with her. A professional actress, Natasha began writing when her fifth child started to sleep through the night. Born in London, she now lives in Bedfordshire with her husband and young family. When not writing, or needed for 'crowd control', she loves to escape to antiques fairs and auctions.

Find out more about Natasha and her books on her website www.natashaoakley.com

CHAPTER ONE

SHE'D made a mistake.

Jemima knew it the minute she saw what the woman on the reception desk was wearing. Kingsley and Bressington might sound like some staid turn-of-the-last-century law firm, but the reality was completely different—and the woman on the reception desk embodied exactly that.

She wore a rich brown T-shirt which hugged the kind of yoga-toned body that always made Jemima feel vaguely depressed. Dramatic turquoise jewellery picked out an exact shade in the receptionist's vibrant skirt and brought out the colour of her eyes. Her look was overwhelmingly young…fashionable…and a world away from Jemima's borrowed suit. Its aubergine colour might be perfect with her carefully straightened red hair, but it was entirely too formal for Kingsley and Bressington.

Nor was she quite sure how she could dress any differently tomorrow. Even if her own wardrobe wasn't restricted to jeans and easy care fabrics, she was two children too late for that kind of body conscious clothing.

Jemima glanced around the acres of white walls, taking in the abstract paintings and sculptural plants in huge stainless steel pots. What the heck was she doing in a trendy place like this? If she didn't know she'd be letting Amanda down she'd turn tail and run now. Fast. This wasn't what she'd wanted at all.

Instead she made herself stand firm. She could hardly balk at her first placement and this was about so much more than one temporary job. This was about standing on her own feet, recovering her self-esteem, making a new beginning... All those trite phrases that everyone instinctively churned out when they were confronted by the rejected half of a 'now divorced' couple.

That she believed they were right was probably something to do with the British 'stiff upper lip' thing that was buried deep in her psyche. She twisted the gold chain at her neck. God forbid she should break down and cry. Or curl under her duvet and refuse to emerge until the world had settled back to the way it had been before. She had to be strong. For the boys. Everyone said so...

Jemima took a shaky breath and waited for the receptionist to finish her telephone call. She'd already been cast an apologetic 'I'll be with you in a moment' look and watched with growing fatalism as the receptionist tapped her acrylic-tipped nails impatiently on the glass table while she explained why she couldn't transfer the caller to the person they wanted.

She could do this. She *could*. Jemima made herself stand a little straighter and concentrated on exuding confidence. What was it Amanda had said about 'transferable skills'? All those years of PTA involvement had to amount to something. Not to mention her degree, secretarial qualifications...

'I'm so sorry to have kept you waiting. Can I help you?'

Jemima jerked to attention, a small part of her mind still free to speculate on whether the receptionist's long hair was the result of nature...or extensions. 'Jemima Chadwick. I'm Jemima Chadwick. From Harper Recruitment. I'm here to temp for Miles Kingsley and I'm to ask for...' She pulled her handbag off her shoulder and started to rummage through Visa slips and assorted pieces of screwed-up paper. Somewhere in the depths of her bag was the small notebook in which she'd written all the details Amanda had given her on Friday afternoon.

Somewhere…

'Saskia Longthorne,' the receptionist said with authority. 'She deals with all temporary staff. I'll let her know you're here.'

Too late. Just too late Jemima pulled the piece of paper out of her bag and looked down at the words she'd scribbled.

'She won't keep you a moment. If you'd like to take a seat?' There was the faintest trace of a question in her modulated voice, but Jemima had no difficulty in recognising a directive.

She balled the piece of paper up in her hand. 'Th-thank you.'

Jemima turned and went to sit on one of the seats. They were set in a semi-circular format around an unusual shattered glass coffee table and were the kind of low-slung design that required the same impossible skills as climbing in and out of a sports car. She perched uncomfortably on the edge in a vain effort to stop her skirt from riding up.

This morning she'd been hyped up for the challenge of re-building her life. A new beginning—and this temporary job was merely the first step. But now she was actually here…all that beautiful confidence was evaporating. Everything about Kingsley and Bressington made her feel uncomfortable. It was all so far outside of her personal experience it hurt.

But then, that was the idea. Amanda had been adamant that she ought to test her new skills in several temporary vacancies before she looked for a permanent position. She should see what kind of working environment she preferred, push the boundaries a little… As Amanda had said, she might surprise herself with the choices she'd make.

At least, that had been the theory. Sitting in Amanda Symmond's comfortable Oxford Street offices, it had seemed like a very good idea, but right now she'd give up practically everything to be at home and loading her boys into the back of her Volvo for the school run. Safe. Doing what she knew.

As the minutes slipped by, Jemima sank back into her seat and stopped jumping at the sound of every footstep.

'Jemima Chadwick? Mrs Chadwick?'

She looked up at the sound of a masculine voice. 'Yes. That's me. I…' She struggled to pull herself out of the deep seat while still clutching her handbag. 'I'm sorry…I was told to wait here for Saskia Longthorne,' she managed foolishly, looking up into a pair of intensely blue eyes. 'She deals with temporary staff and—'

'Saskia's been held up, it seems. So, as I'm passing…' He held out his hand. 'Thank you for helping us out. We do appreciate it.'

Jemima transferred her handbag to her other shoulder and held out her own hand. 'You're w-welcome.'

His hand closed over hers in that double handshake thing. The one that was supposed to convey sincerity, but was usually a sign of exactly the opposite. Tall, dark, handsome…actually, very handsome…and completely aware of it.

Everything about him was clean-cut and expensive. His suit was in a dark grey with a faint blue stripe in the weave and it fitted his muscular body as though it had been made for him. Perhaps it had. Jemima didn't know how you judged these things.

It was easy to get the measure of the man himself though. Smooth and sharp. Too smooth…and too sharp. It wasn't by chance he'd selected a tie in a cold ice-blue, a colour that matched his incredibly piercing eyes.

'I'm Miles Kingsley. You'll be working with me.'

Jemima felt her stomach drop and disappear. *This was absolutely not what she wanted. He* was not what she wanted. All the way here on the tube she'd been praying that Miles Kingsley would be a comfortable kind of man and easy to work for.

Amanda had told her that she'd never had a complaint from any temp about working for Miles and, in her mind, she'd pictured him as a controlled, sensible, mature man. Someone not unlike her late father, in fact. Perfect for a woman dipping one very nervous toe back into the job market.

But there was nothing 'comfortable' about this man. He was a cocksure thirty-something who clearly felt he was God's particular gift to the world.

Perhaps Amanda hadn't understood quite what she was looking for in her first job? Or perhaps Amanda had simply decided to drop her firmly in the deep end and see if she swam. That was the trouble with going to an agency owned and run by the sister of your best friend. People who thought they knew you well were all too apt to make decisions they considered to be in your best interests…without reference to what you actually did want.

'I'll take you up to where you'll be working and by then I'm sure Saskia will be free to take you through our procedures.'

'Thank you.'

'Nothing too out of the ordinary, I imagine.'

And then he smiled. A perfect balance of casual warmth and glinting sex appeal. Jemima clutched at her shoulder bag. This was going to be hideous. Miles Kingsley might possibly have hidden neurosis somewhere, but if he did it was deeply buried.

How could any one individual be so completely without…? She searched for the word. So without self-doubt? That was it. He was so darn sure of himself. And all that confidence seemed to suck away what was left of hers. Perhaps she ought to ring Amanda now? Tell her she couldn't do this job?

Jemima frowned. But how pathetic was that? She'd have to go home and tell her mother she hadn't been able to do it. How did you do that? How did you tell a woman who'd been a senior civil servant until she'd taken early retirement that you couldn't manage a simple temp job? Then she'd have to tell the boys…

And she wanted them to be proud of her. Wanted them to see her taking control of her life again. It would be good for them. Everybody said so.

Miles turned and crossed to the reception desk. 'Felicity, would you hold my calls for the next five minutes or so. And would you let Saskia know I've collected Jemima on my way through.'

'Yes, of course.'

Jemima watched as the receptionist became a pool of hormones at his feet. Assuming she did have hair extensions, one more flick of her lustrous locks and they might fall out. Though, to give him his due, Miles Kingsley didn't appear to notice. Perhaps because ninety-nine point nine per cent of women he met did the same.

'This way,' he said, turning back to her and pointing up the wide glass and steel staircase.

Jemima gave the receptionist a tentative smile and turned to follow him.

'Have you been temping long?'

'No. Not really.' *Or, in fact, not at all.* Probably better not to mention that, though. Jemima clutched at her shoulder bag and swallowed nervously.

'To the left here,' he remarked, pointing down a corridor, 'you'll find a staff recreational room—which is a grand way of saying it's a pleasant place to have a coffee break. Saskia will show you around later and introduce you to the other support staff. We're a tightly knit team and I'm sure they'll all be available to help you, should you need it.'

Jemima nodded.

'This way.' He stepped back and held the door open. 'Do you know much about what Kingsley and Bressington do?'

'Not a great deal,' she replied stiffly. Amanda had concentrated on it being a 'fantastic place to work', and 'I've got temps queuing up to go there. Give it a try and see what you think'. Clearly the smooth and efficient Miles expected she'd have been given a little more information than that.

She let her eyes wander about the total unexpectedness of the place. From the outside it looked like any other Victorian building in the street, but inside…Inside it had been gutted and everything chosen to ensure maximum impact. Small, but perfectly formed, it was all cutting edge and very modern. Intimidating, actually. But that was probably intentional. Anyone hiring Kingsley and Bressington to manage their public persona probably wanted to see something high-tech, stylish and controlled.

'But you've worked in public relations before?'

Jemima shook her head, feeling as though she were letting Amanda down. She watched the slight frown mar his forehead and wondered, not for the first time, whether Miles Kingsley was the kind of man who'd be satisfied with her newly acquired secretarial skills. As if she didn't know he wasn't.

'There are various aspects to what we do. Some of our clients are large corporations and we track and manage their image in the press, both here and abroad.'

She struggled to suppress the rising tide of panic. A six month post-graduate secretarial course hadn't even begun to touch on anything he was talking about. Somehow she didn't think he'd be particularly impressed that she held a Qualified

Private and Executive Secretarial diploma—albeit with a distinction.

'Others are individuals, predominantly working in the media. Many find themselves in a particularly sensitive place in their lives when they first come to us.'

'I see.' Another door, another corridor. It wasn't that the building Kingsley and Bressington occupied was particularly large, it was just it was painted in similar shades of cream and it was difficult to get your bearings. There was only so much limestone and travertine a girl could take.

'Confidentiality is an absolute prerequisite,' Miles continued, 'as I'm sure you realise.'

Confidentiality was something they'd covered in her diploma course. It was nice to know there was at least one part of this job she was going to find easy. 'I wouldn't dream of repeating anything I learn from working here. I'd consider that very unprofessional.'

'Excellent,' he said, holding open the door for her. 'I know Amanda wouldn't have sent you to us if that wasn't the case. This is your office.'

Jemima stepped through into a room that had obviously been designed to have a *wow* factor. Yet more shades of cream blurred together as a restful whole and made the burr walnut desk a focal point. The computer screen on it was wafer-thin and the chair she recognised as being a modern design classic. A Charles and Ray Eames styled, if not original, chair upholstered in soft cream leather.

'We rarely keep our clients waiting, but if there's any delay I'll rely on you to keep them happy until I can see them.' He turned and pointed to some chairs clustered around yet another shattered glass coffee table. 'Ply them with tea and coffee. Make sure they feel important.'

Jemima felt the first stirrings of a smile. Maybe Amanda

had known what she was doing when she had sent her here. She knew a lot about making other people feel important. Being a satellite to other people's bright star was what she did best. In fact, a lifetime of practice had honed it into an art form.

She glanced back towards the door and noticed the twenty or so black and white photographs grouped together on the wall. Dramatic publicity shots all autographed with love and messages of thanks.

Miles followed her gaze. 'Some of our clients,' he said unnecessarily. 'You can see why discretion is imperative.'

She certainly could. Her smile widened as she recognised the chiselled features of an actor who'd scarcely been off the tabloid front pages in recent weeks. His particular 'sensitive place' was a pole-dancer from Northampton—allegedly.

And Kingsley and Bressington had to find a way of spinning that into a positive, did they? She couldn't quite see how that would be possible. If Miles Kingsley could restore that actor's persona as a 'family man', he was a genius.

The door opened and a young and stunning blonde in impeccably cut black trousers burst in, an A4 file tucked under her arm. 'Miles, I'm so sorry. I was caught on the phone and couldn't get away—'

'Jemima had been in reception for over fifteen minutes.' His voice sliced smoothly over the other woman's words.

'Felicity has just buzzed me. I'm so sorry.'

'It's not a problem,' Jemima interjected quickly, unsure whether the apology was for her benefit or for Miles's.

'If you'd like to come with me now, I'll take you through everything.' The other woman adjusted the file under her arm. 'I'm Saskia Longthorne, by the way. Come through to my office….'

She was halfway to the door before she'd finished speaking.

'Jemima might like to hang up her jacket? Put her bag down?' Miles suggested in a dry tone.

He'd strolled over to the walnut desk and had picked up a large black diary and was leafing through the pages. Jemima glanced over as he looked up. His eyes were astonishingly bright against the minimal colour in the room. At least that was her excuse for the sudden tightening of her throat.

'I'll see you again in a few minutes.' He picked up the diary and carried it across to the wide double doors that, presumably, led to his own office.

Good grief. Jemima let out her breath in one slow steady stream. Miles Kingsley was a sharp-suited nightmare. No other way of looking at it.

Saskia seemed to understand what she'd been thinking. 'I know,' she said, walking over to a tall cupboard. 'Miles is a walking force field. You can leave your jacket and handbag in here.' She pulled out a hanger and handed it across. 'It'll be perfectly safe, but there's a key to lock it if you prefer. Zoë always did that…and then kept the key somewhere in her desk.'

'Zoë's the person I'm covering?' Jemima asked, self-consciously slipping her jacket off and putting it on the hanger.

'Her husband's job was transferred to Hong Kong. Just for six weeks, but Miles was as irritated as hell. He thought he'd finally found a PA who didn't seem to want to get pregnant, when Zoë announced she had to be off anyway.'

Saskia accepted back the hanger and popped the jacket into the cupboard. 'Not exactly a "baby-man" is Miles. More wine bar and whisky on the rocks, if you know what I mean.'

That figured, Jemima thought.

'Zoë's lovely so he's holding her job open for her. We mustn't take long over this,' Saskia said, pushing open the door to the corridor. 'He'll want you back quickly. Obviously do put down nine thirty as your start time for today on your time sheet as it's my fault we're a little behind.'

* * *

'Jemima, I'm going to need you to book a table at The Walnut Tree for this lunchtime,' Miles said, opening the door to his office, presumably by magic since he had a file under one arm and a mug of black coffee in his other hand.

Jemima tucked her handbag away in the tall cupboard and glanced down at her wrist-watch. Officially she wasn't even supposed to be here yet, but this morning the tube had been kind and the boys cooperative. He was lucky she was here. Jemima hurried across to her desk and jotted down 'Walnut Tree'.

'I've arranged to meet Xanthe Wyn and her agent there at one,' he said, putting the file down on her desk. 'If that's not possible you'll need to contact Christopher Delland to let him know the change.'

'Okay.'

Miles took a sip of his coffee and then raked a hand through his dark hair. 'Actually, confirm it with him anyway. Xanthe is notoriously difficult to pin down. His number is in…' He trailed off as her fingers had already pulled the appropriate card out of the strangely old-fashioned card system her predecessor had favoured.

'Excellent.' Miles flashed her that mega-watt smile that no doubt managed to melt the hardest of hearts, but didn't do anything for her but irritate. Given the choice she would so much rather he left the charm offensive until after ten o'clock when she'd had a chance to wake up properly. Not to mention grab a coffee for herself.

Jemima flicked the switch that would boot up her computer. There was something in the gene pool of men like Miles Kingsley, she thought, which meant they had a deep inner belief that they were somehow special. That when they said 'go' everyone around them would naturally follow. A leader of leaders. It was in the way he moved, walked and owned the space in which he stood.

If he thought one smile would mean she didn't notice the extra ten minutes at the start of the day, the additional twenty minutes at lunch time and the fifteen or so at the end, he was going to be disappointed when she presented her time sheet on Friday.

'Thanks, by the way, for staying late last night.'

'You're welcome,' she said stiffly, finding it annoying to be thanked for something she was busy resenting.

'Amanda didn't say anything about you being fluent in French, but it was extremely useful. Phillipe Armond said your accent is perfect and he was very impressed.'

Jemima smiled through gritted teeth.

'It looks like we're going to get their business. So thanks for that. I'm going to fly to Paris to meet him for lunch some time next week. His secretary will ring you with the arrangements.'

She nodded and picked up the enormous pile of paper that had appeared in her in-tray overnight. If only he'd disappear back into his office. She desperately wanted to grab a coffee before getting started on this lot. She really couldn't be late again tonight.

'Did you have a good evening?'

Jemima looked up incredulously. She'd not left Kingsley and Bressington until twenty past six. Then she'd had to stand up on the tube all the way home, apologise to her mum, who was going to be late for her bridge evening, listen to Sam read, search out Ben's missing football sock, put another load of washing through the machine…

What did he think her evening was like? Miles Kingsley really had no idea how the other half lived. 'Fine, thanks,' she said, keying in the password.

'I went to see the new production of Noel Coward's *Private Lives*. It's not my favourite play, but it was excellent. That reminds me,' he said, finishing off the last of his coffee. 'Send some flowers to Emma Lawler at Ashworths for me. The address is in that box. I've got an account with Weldon Florists. Ask for Becky.'

Jemima flicked through the 'A' section and pulled out the 'Ashworths' card. She couldn't quite believe he was asking her to do this. One would think he'd manage to send his own girlfriend some flowers and not have to get his secretary to do it for her.

'Not roses. Try for something more…'

'More what?' Jemima asked, her pencil hovering over the pad.

Miles flashed a smile. 'Neutral. Tell Becky it's the end of a beautiful friendship. She'll know what you mean.'

Good grief. Was he really ending a relationship so casually? 'And what message do you want?'

Miles picked up his file. 'The usual. Thanks for a nice evening and I'll be in touch,' he said cheerfully, putting his mug down on her desk. 'When you've got a second, I'd love another coffee. No rush.'

Miles rubbed a tired hand over the back of his neck and listened to the high-pitched panic on the other end of the phone. Some days….

If the blasted woman, and that was putting it mildly, had done as he'd advised there wouldn't *be* a picture of her in the *News of the World*. He let his long fingers idly play with the paper-clips he kept in a small Perspex box. She'd been in the business long enough to know the kind of caption she'd get if she got caught without make-up—so what had possessed her to go out like that? It was hardly rocket science to know there'd be one or two paparazzi, at least, who'd be hanging about on the off chance of their getting something.

Well, it seemed they'd hit the jackpot. No editor alive

would have been able to resist pictures like that. He sat back in his chair and mouthed 'coffee' at Jemima, who was coming in with the morning mail.

Did his temporary secretary ever crack a smile? The woman seemed to be perpetually frowning. Or perhaps it was just him that had that effect on her? Jemima was efficient enough, but she wasn't like Zoë and the sooner she was back from Hong Kong the better. Given a choice he really would prefer a bit of humour in his working day.

'Lori,' he interrupted the distressed woman on the other end of the phone, 'there's nothing we can do about pictures that are already in the public domain. I know we've got an injunction out on the topless photographs you did when you were twenty, but this really isn't the same situation and I—'

Miles frowned in irritation as she launched off again. Her famously husky tones transmuted into something quite uncharacteristic. Lori obviously needed to vent her spleen somewhere and he was a safe pair of hands.

'It's not the same situation at all. Lori, you need to keep a low profile at the moment. You and I both know how this works. Give it a couple of weeks and they'll be after the scent of someone else's blood—'

He watched as Jemima came back in to the room carrying his coffee. She'd eased off slightly on the formal clothes since her first morning, but she was still the most 'old before her time' woman he'd met in a long time. She dressed like a woman between forty and fifty and yet he was sure she was younger than that. She could be anywhere between twenty-five and thirty-five.

Miles studied her intently. She probably would look dramatically more attractive if she did something with her hair other than tie it back in a low pony-tail. It was the most amazing colour. A natural redhead. His mouth curved into a sexy smile. It wasn't often you met a *natural* redhead.

'Lori, it'll be two weeks at worst.' He picked up his pen and started to doodle on the A4 pad in front of him—large abstract boxes which he shaded in with swift strokes. Then he wrote 'Keira', around which he put flourishing curlicues. 'If any member of the royal family do anything remotely newsworthy it'll be less than that.'

Jemima placed his coffee in front of him and he looked up to mouth his thanks. It irked him that he couldn't get any real response out of her. She didn't talk about anything personal. Not her husband, nor her children. Nothing. She didn't even seem to have any kind of social life. A question as to what she'd done the night before had elicited a blank look.

And she didn't seem to like him much. Every so often he would catch her watching him with those big green eyes and her expression wasn't complimentary. She seemed to be on the verge between contempt and amusement. All in all, he wasn't sure what to make of her.

He turned his attention back to Lori. 'Just make sure you don't give any kind of statement to the press. Do you understand me? It's very important.'

Miles finished his call and flicked through his mail. There was nothing there that particularly caught his attention and his eyes moved over the doodles he'd drawn on his pad of paper—*Keira*. Keira Rye-Stanford. Now she was one very…sexy woman. That wraparound dress she'd worn last night had seemingly been held together with one very small bow. Just one pull would have…

He stood up and walked over to the door between his office and the outer one. 'Jemima.'

She looked up from the computer screen, a small frown of concentration on her forehead. 'Yes?'

'Would you arrange to have some flowers sent to a Keira Rye-Stanford at—' he pulled the name of her art gallery out from the recesses of his memory '—at Tillyard's. You'll find the address in the directory.'

'Keira Rye-Stanford?'

He could hear the censure in her voice, as though she were reminding him he'd sent flowers to someone entirely different three days earlier. 'That's right.'

'What would you like to send?'

Miles conjured up an image of Keira—a Celtic beauty with a soft Irish lilt and a very seductive glint in her blue eyes. She was a woman who probably received flowers often. And that meant one needed to be creative.

He smiled. 'A dandelion.'

Jemima looked up, her pencil poised on her pad. 'You want to send a dandelion?'

'With a message:

Roses are red, Violets are blue,
This is a Dandelion, but it's for you.

Ask them to wrap it in cellophane with a big bow and deliver it to the reception desk at Tillyard's.'

'A dandelion?'

'Trust me,' he said with a wink as he headed back towards his office, 'it works. Every time.'

Jemima finished writing his message and thumped her pencil down on top of the pad.

He stopped. 'Do you have a problem with that?'

Jemima's green eyes flashed, but she answered smoothly. 'If the florist does, I'll let you know.'

'She won't. She'll just charge me the earth,' he said, shutting the door to his office.

What was Jemima's problem? Anyone would think he was asking her to pick the blasted dandelion herself, instead of picking up the telephone and calling a florist he had an account with. Becks would think it a giggle. He could guarantee she'd make a first rate job of it. Keira would receive a disproportionately large cellophane-wrapped weed tied together with a classy ribbon. Perfect.

His telephone buzzed and he picked up the receiver with a casual, 'Miles.'

'It's an Emma Lawler. She's says it's personal.' His temporary secretary's voice was bland.

'Thanks, Jemima. Put her through.' Miles sat back in his chair and waited for Emma's breathless voice to speak before he said, 'Did you get my flowers?'

CHAPTER TWO

'PLEASE come tonight. It'll be fun. Alistair's best man is going to be here—and he's single.'

Jemima closed her eyes against Rachel's voice. Why did she do this? *Why did everybody do this?*

'You'll like him.'

'I'm not interested in getting involved with anyone else,' Jemima protested weakly, carrying the phone through to the lounge and curling up in one oversized sofa. *Been there, done that and burnt the T-shirt*. The man who could get under her defences was going to have to have more ability than Houdini himself.

'Just because Russell is a complete arse it doesn't mean all men are.'

She knew that, of course she did. Not that Russell was an 'arse', as Rachel put it. If he had been it would have made everything so much easier. He was a nice man—who didn't love her any more. He was very sorry about it, but…

He just didn't. Simple as that, apparently. He'd sat down opposite her in the kitchen one Sunday afternoon and explained that he needed time apart. Time to think about what he wanted from life. Of course, in the end he'd decided he'd rather have a blonde account executive from Chiswick called Stefanie.

How had that happened? Had he woken up one morning and suddenly realised he felt nothing for her? Or had it been something that had come on gradually, almost without him noticing it? Jemima shook her head as though to rid herself of those thoughts. Dissecting every part of their marriage like that was the surest way of going insane. Sometimes she felt as if she was hanging by a thread anyway.

'I'm not trying to pair you up, really. He's not your type.' Rachel's voice seemed to radiate happiness. 'We just thought it would be a nice way of you two meeting before the wedding. The boys are with Russell this weekend, aren't they?'

'Yes.'

'Well, then,' Rachel said, as though that settled everything. 'No point sitting in on your own. Alistair is cooking—so you don't have to worry about food poisoning.'

Jemima gave in to the inevitable. 'Do you want me to bring anything?'

'Just you. Come early. I've been dying to show you the Jimmy Choo sandals I've chosen to go with my dress. I've had to take out a second mortgage, but they are to die for and since I'm only going to do this once…' She broke off. '*Hell,* I'm sorry. That was really insensitive of me.'

The contrition in her friend's voice brought a smile to her face. 'Don't be daft.' Her finger followed the shape of the agapanthus leaf design on the sofa fabric. 'Alistair's lovely and I'm sure you're going to be very happy together.'

'I really should try and engage my brain before I speak. It's just this wedding stuff is all-encompassing. I don't seem to be able to think about anything else at the moment. It's all dresses, bouquets, flowers, table settings…I'm really sorry. And I haven't even asked you anything about your new job yet. What a cow I am!'

'There's not a lot to tell.' Jemima idly twisted the navy-blue tassel at the corner of the cushion. 'I've only done a couple of weeks.'

And I hate it. I hate being away from the boys. Hate missing meeting up with my friends. Hate my life being *different* from the way I planned it. No point saying any of that. There was no way Rachel would understand how she felt about working at Kingsley and Bressington.

'Are the girls you're working with nice?'

'Girls' was just about the only way to describe them. Jemima thought of Saskia with her board-flat stomach, Lucinda with her exquisite and very large solitaire engagement ring, Felicity with her nails...

'Everyone's very friendly.'

'But?' Rachel prompted. 'Go on, tell me. I can hear it in your voice. How's it going really?'

There was going to be no escape. 'Everyone's incredibly friendly,' she said slowly. 'Just a little young, maybe. I feel a bit like Methuselah.'

'You're only thirty,' Rachel objected. 'And so am I, for that matter! Nothing old about being thirty.'

Jemima smiled. 'Well, I reckon the average age of the female staff is about twelve. Thirteen at the outside. And I don't think there's a woman in the building apart from me who doesn't have prominent hip-bones and the kind of skin that doesn't need foundation. It's all a bit depressing.'

Rachel gave a cackle of laughter. 'You should be used to that. Growing up with Verity as your sister must have been really depressing.'

'You'd think so,' Jemima agreed, 'but honestly, Saskia makes even my sister look fat. They all sit around at lunchtime telling each other they're completely full on a plate of lettuce and make me feel guilty for eating a cheese sandwich. At least Verity moans about being hungry.'

'You're wicked. What about the guy you're working for?'

'England's answer to Casanova?' Jemima said with a sudden smile. 'He's nice enough. Very calm in a crisis, obviously brilliant at his job and completely full of himself. Yesterday he got me to send a dandelion to this poor woman he'd met at a party the night before. Says it works every time…'

Jemima trailed off as she watched her ex-husband's silver BMW drive up the road.

'Did it work?'

'Rachel, I'm going to have to go. I've just seen Russell arriving. I'll see you tonight.'

Jemima finished the call and called out, 'Ben. Sam. Daddy's here.'

She glanced across at the mantelpiece clock. He was five minutes early. He'd now sit in the car until it was *exactly* ten. She hated the way he did that. Why couldn't he be like other absent fathers and gradually drift out of their lives? It would be so much easier if he simply disappeared.

Guilt slid in—as it always did. *She shouldn't have thought that.* She didn't mean it. It was *great* that Russell didn't let his boys down. Turned up when he said he would. *Great* that he paid everything he should—and on time. Really, really *great*.

Jemima uncurled from the sofa and threw the cushion across to the armchair. It just didn't *feel* so great.

'Ben. Sam.' She walked to the foot of the stairs and shouted again. 'Ben? Did you hear me? Daddy's here.'

Ben appeared, shuttered from all emotion. Almost. His eyes were over-bright and his body was stiff. 'I don't want to go.'

She hated this. 'I know, darling,' she said softly.

'I want to go to the football tournament.' Ben walked slowly down the stairs. 'Everyone's going to be there. Joshua's mum is going to take a picnic.'

'I know, but Daddy has been looking forward to seeing you. He loves his weekends with you.'

The front doorbell rang. Jemima glanced at her wrist-watch. *Exactly* ten o'clock. Not a minute before, not a minute after. Russell was so…*damn* reasonable.

She looked at Ben as he picked up his bag. 'It'll be fun when you're there.' What a stupid thing to say. That wasn't the point. Ben was eight years old and he wanted to play football with his friends. *Of course* he did…

'You'll be okay.'

He nodded.

'And you'll have a really great time.'

Ben put his backpack on his shoulders. 'What are you going to do, Mum?'

'Me?' *What was she going to do without them?* Cry a little… Miss them a lot… The same as every other weekend they spent with their father. 'I'm going to spend the day trying to decorate the bathroom, maybe get some tiles up, and then I'm going to go and have supper with Rachel and Alistair. I'll be fine.' She forced a bright smile and wondered how convincing she was. 'It's not long. Just one night and you'll be home again.'

The doorbell rang again.

'Will you go and hurry Sam up for me?'

She watched him climb the stairs and counted to ten before she opened the front door. It didn't matter how prepared she thought she was, seeing Russell always felt strange. In the space of a millisecond she remembered the first time he'd kissed her, the proposal in a felucca in Vienna, the way he'd cried when Ben was born…

Russell looked good. Clearly he'd decided to keep up his gym membership and she liked the way he'd let his hair grow a little longer. Jemima wrapped her arms protectively around her waist. 'Ben's just gone to find Sam. They're all ready.'

Russell nodded. 'There's no hurry.' Silence and then, 'How are things?'

'Fine.'

Another pause. 'That's excellent.' He rattled his car keys and looked uncomfortable.

He always did that too, Jemima thought. *What exactly did he think she was going to do?* Cry? Scream at him? He flattered himself. She was a long way past that. 'You?'

'Yes, well, we're fine.' He stood a little straighter. 'Stef's just got a promotion…'

'That's…great.'

'She's heading up a team of three.'

Jemima nodded. She was proud of herself for being so grown-up and dignified. But why exactly did Russell think she'd be interested in the career progression of the woman he'd left them for? *No*, she corrected swiftly. The woman he'd left *her* for.

'Daddy!' Sam hurled himself along the hallway. 'It's Daddy!'

The change in Russell was instantaneous. The smile on his face gripped her heart and screwed it tight. He reached down and caught the tornado. 'Hiya, imp.'

'I've lost another tooth.' Sam pulled a wide grin, showing a huge expanse of pure gum.

'Did the tooth fairy come?'

Ben pushed past. 'There's no such thing. It's Mum. No one believes in the tooth fairy any more.'

Above his head Russell met her eyes. Jemima gave a half smile, then a shrug. 'Have a good time.' She reached out and touched Ben's head. 'I'll see you tomorrow.'

Then she had to watch the three of them walk to the car.

She really hated this.

Still.

How many weekends had it been now? Was there ever

going to be a time when it didn't feel as if part of her was being ripped out of her body when she saw her sons walk away? She felt exactly like a piece of string which had been pulled so tight it had started to fray.

Miles locked his Bristol 407 and sauntered over to the three-storey Victorian house where Alistair and Rachel had bought their first flat together. It was nice. High ceilings, plenty of original features, good area…and that oh, so rare commodity—outside space in the form of a tiny courtyard garden.

Normally he really enjoyed his visits to their home. Every so often it was pleasant to spend an evening where there were no demands placed on him, no expectations. They were a calm oasis in a life that was becoming increasingly pressured. But…

He pulled a face. Truth be told, he wasn't entirely looking forward to the next few hours. An evening spent discussing weddings wasn't exactly high on his list of favourite things to do with a Saturday night. But hey…

He reached up and rang the bell. If his old school friend had finally decided to take the plunge, the least he could do was be there to see it. The poor beggar probably only had a year or so before their country place in Kent was filled with bright plastic toys and the first of several mini-Mackenzies. Grim.

The door opened suddenly and Rachel met him with a bright smile. 'I thought you'd be Jemima,' she said, glancing up the tree-lined street. 'I wonder where she's got to. I bet her car is playing up. She was coming early to look at my shoes.'

'Would you like me to look at your shoes?' he asked lazily.

Rachel turned back to him. 'You behave or I'll make you wear a pink floral waistcoat! Go on in.'

'For you—anything,' he glinted, leaning forward to place a light kiss on her cheek.

'You'll find Alistair in the kitchen doing something clever with the duck.'

She shut the door behind him and Miles shrugged out of his tan leather jacket and threw it over the oak church chair they kept in the hall. 'So, tell me, will I fancy the bridesmaid?'

'Quite possibly—' she grinned up at him '—but I doubt it'll be reciprocated. She's a woman of taste and discernment. Actually, I don't think I have any friends who would deign to join your harem.'

Miles smiled and wandered through to where Alistair was stirring something in a small saucepan. He looked up as his friend walked in. 'Talking about Jemima?'

'He wants to know whether he'll fancy her,' Rachel said, leaning over to see how the sauce looked. 'Should it be that lumpy?' Then, as the doorbell rang, 'That'll be her. Excellent.'

Alistair watched her leave with an expression of amusement and turned back to his sauce. '*Lumpy!* Just about escaped with her life. Miles, grab yourself a drink.'

Miles sauntered over and poured himself out a large glass of red wine from the bottle on the side. 'You?'

'Got one,' Alistair said, with a nod at the glass by his side. 'How's work? I saw Lori Downey's double page spread and thought you might be having it tough.'

Miles grunted and took a mouthful of the full-bodied wine. 'This is nice.'

'Rachel and I got it in Calais last month. Our car was so laden it's a wonder we weren't stopped.' In the hallway they could hear the mumble of female voices. 'Sounds like Jemima's here at last.'

Miles perched on a high bar stool, feeling more relaxed than he had done all week. He set his wineglass down on the side and idly started stirring the sugar in the bowl. 'I've got a Jemima temping for me at the moment. Amanda sent her to me.'

'Good?'

'She's fine.'

Alistair smiled. 'Damned with faint praise.'

'Something like that. You can't fault what she does when she's in the office, but she arrives at the last possible moment and leaves as soon as she can. Doesn't talk. Doesn't socialise with the girls.' Miles picked up his wineglass. 'She dresses like her mother and obviously thinks my florist bill is too high.'

'Can't blame her for that. Rachel thinks your florist bill is too high.'

The voices from the hall became louder.

Miles watched as Alistair carefully decanted his sauce into a jug. 'That doesn't say much for Rachel's judgement. Are you sure about marrying her?'

Alistair laughed. 'One of the most attractive things about Rachel is that she prefers me to you. Go easy on the futility of marriage stories tonight. Jemima's been through a traumatic divorce. Russell left her with a house to renovate and two boys to bring up on her own. She's a bit brittle.'

'So I'm not even allowed to flirt with the bridesmaid—' He broke off as soon as the door opened, but he could see from Alistair's face that he thought they may have been overheard. He felt a vague sense of sympathy. If he knew anything about women—and he did—Rachel would have her fiancé's kneecaps for that *fauxpas*.

'Miles—' Rachel's voice sounded ominously clipped '—this is Jemima. My bridesmaid.'

He turned round, ready to pour oil on troubled waters…and felt his smile falter. It was as if he'd stepped through a portal to an alternative universe. *Rachel was standing with her arm tucked through Jemima Chadwick's.*

And, stranger than that, Jemima Chadwick as he'd never seen her before.

Her red hair was a riot of curls and she was dressed in a

simple linen sundress. She looked crumpled, curvy and surprisingly sexy. He felt that familiar kick in the pit of his
abdomen that was pure reflex. It was all a bit surreal.

'This is Miles Kingsley. Alistair and Miles were at school
together and, scarily, have known each other for something
like thirty years.'

Somehow he couldn't get his mouth to work. Thoughts
were whizzing through his head, but they didn't stay still long
enough to know whether they were worth putting words on.
Even a simple hello seemed to elude him.

Alistair leapt into action, clearly motivated to bonhomie by
the 'brittle' mistake. 'Absolutely right. Miss Henderson's
class. Aged five. Abbey Preparatory School, Windsor. What
can I get you to drink, Jemima?'

She moved further into the room. 'White wine would be
lovely. Thank you.'

Jemima Chadwick.

Here.

And looking so different. Smelling of…roses. Her red
curls still damp…

Miles found that his mind was thinking in expletives. It was
almost unbelievable that Jemima Chadwick could have transformed herself so entirely. The woman who'd left the office
on Friday evening bore very little resemblance to the one
who'd arrived for dinner tonight.

At work she looked…bland. Completely invisible, as
though she didn't expect to be looked at. In fact, very *married*.
His eyes flicked to her ring finger. Nothing. He'd not noticed
that. He hadn't noticed she had legs like that either…

Miles took a sip of wine and tried to recall exactly what he'd
said about his temporary secretary to Alistair…and then he
winced. Thank God he could trust Alistair not to land him in it
when he realised they'd been speaking about the same Jemima.

Damn. This couldn't be happening to him.

What was the probability of Jemima Chadwick being Rachel's bridesmaid? It had to be zillions to one. Except, of course, she was Rachel's friend and Amanda was Rachel's elder sister. *Damn it!* It wasn't so much improbable as extremely likely.

Alistair poured out a glass of wine. 'Miles was just saying he's got a temporary secretary working for him at the moment who's also called Jemima.'

Miles felt his stomach drop. It was the same feeling as when your dinghy was about to capsize and there was absolutely nothing you could do to stop it. He was going over. It was inevitable.

'That's quite a coincidence. It's not a particularly common name, is it?' Alistair continued, sublimely oblivious to the missile he was hurling in their midst.

'I heard.' Jemima looked directly at Miles. Her green eyes were steady, like lasers. 'She dresses like her mother.'

Miles's head jerked up.

It was like receiving a swift left to his chin. So quick he hadn't seen it coming. It hadn't occurred to him that Jemima could have heard what he'd said about her. In his adult life there'd probably only been a handful of occasions when he'd wanted the ground to open up and swallow him whole. This was one of those occasions. It was up there in number one slot along with the time his mother had given a television interview explaining that he'd been conceived in a moment of 'peace and meditation'.

Rachel reached out for her own wine. 'Jemima's just started temping. Perhaps she ought to work for you, Miles.'

This was getting worse. Miles's eyes searched out Jemima's, a desperate apology in his own.

He watched the indecision as it passed across her green

eyes. Then she gave a half smile and held out her hand. 'It's lovely to meet you.'

His sense of relief was overwhelming. 'And you,' he said, stretching out his own hand. 'Jemima…?'

'Chadwick.'

It was fascinating to see the sudden spark of laughter light her eyes. What was it they said about still waters running deep? 'Jemima Chadwick.'

His hand closed round hers. On the whole he thought she'd made the right choice. It was far easier to pretend they didn't know each other. He was more than happy to go along with that. And, at the first opportunity, he'd apologise.

'The man she's working for sounds worse than you, Miles,' Rachel said. 'Apparently he sent some woman a dandelion. Or rather he got Jemima to do it.'

Miles watched a red stain appear on Jemima's neck and gradually spread to her cheeks. It seemed that fate had struck a blow for equality. 'Sounds fun,' he said, releasing her hand.

The flush became a little darker. 'I'm told it works every time,' she shot back quickly.

'He sounds a jerk,' was Alistair's observation. 'Shall we go out to the garden? We've set everything out there as it's a nice evening.'

Miles led the way outside, not sure how he was feeling any more. Honesty compelled him to admit that Jemima carried the advantage in the cringe stakes. The things he'd said about her to Alistair were completely out of order—regardless of whether she'd overheard them. His mother would have him flayed alive for comments like that. As long as Jemima did her job properly there was no reason why she should social-ise or dress differently. No reason at all.

Nevertheless it was a mystery to him why someone who could look as…downright sexy as Jemima, would go to work looking like everyone's image of the worst kind of librarian. Why do it?

Her work clothes were too safely conventional, but the difference was mainly due to her hair. How had a nondescript pony-tail become a riot of curls? She looked as if she'd stepped out of a pre-Raphaelite painting. All curves, cleavage and abandonment. Perhaps better not to allow his mind to go too far down that particular avenue. Single mums were absolutely out of bounds. Too much baggage. Far too many responsibilities.

He took the seat opposite her, the little devil on his shoulder prompting him to ask, 'So, you're temping?'

Jemima shot him a warning glance, but he didn't care. With Rachel listening in, she'd have to answer him. Who knew what he might find out about her? If you were going to have an excruciatingly embarrassing evening, you might as well turn it to your advantage. Salvage whatever enjoyment you could.

'Yes.'

'As a secretary?' he continued blandly.

It was worth it for the flick of those green eyes. 'Yes.'

'Are you enjoying it?

Jemima reached out and took a breadstick. She snapped it in half. 'No.'

'Why's that?'

She looked at him and shook her head as though she were warning him off.

'It's because it's her first job,' Rachel chipped in.

First job. Now that was interesting. Miles let his eyebrows raise a fraction and watched with complete enjoyment the blush that heated her face.

Alistair picked up his wine and stood up. 'I'm sure that's right, Jemima. It's a huge lifestyle change for you. Your hair looks great, by the way. I've not seen you leave it curly for months.'

Jemima self-consciously touched her hair. Miles watched

as she twisted one strand around her forefinger. She had no idea what that simple movement of one finger was doing to him. 'I didn't have time to straighten it. I had an argument with a paint pot and the paint pot won.'

'It looks great,' Alistair said as he headed back towards the kitchen.

Rachel nodded. 'I keep telling her.' She looked at Miles. 'She won't listen. She thinks it looks more sophisticated straight.'

He wasn't about to enter that debate, but he was in no doubt which he preferred. 'It's a great colour,' he said softly, willing her to look at him.

She wasn't having any of it. 'It's red,' Jemima said, picking up her wineglass. 'And the bane of my life.'

Did she really think that? It was unbelievable. He watched as her fingers played with the stem of her wineglass. Nice fingers. Short, tidy nails with no polish on them. That was more in keeping with the Jemima Chadwick he knew.

'So,' he said after a short pause, 'you're in your *first* job…?'

'After my divorce.' She looked at him then and there was no mistaking the warning light in her green eyes. 'It's a shame I'm not enjoying it more, isn't it?'

His lips twitched. 'Why aren't you?'

'My boss is very…smug. Do you know the kind of man I mean? Very difficult to take seriously.'

Her green eyes were…incredible. Why hadn't he noticed them before? Tiny flecks of topaz worked out from dark irises. Two weeks—ten days—sitting in his office and he hadn't noticed. He was slipping.

And she thought him *smug*—apparently. Miles smiled. He probably deserved that. Even so… 'When you've had a little more experience, perhaps you ought to consider working with me. I must speak to Amanda about it.'

Her eyes narrowed and Miles waited to see what she would

do next. She took her time and snapped off another piece of breadstick before saying, 'I don't know whether I'd be interested. What is it that you do exactly?'

'Public relations.'

She wrinkled her nose. 'That's a form of professional lying, isn't it?'

'Jemima!' Rachel exclaimed, shocked.

Miles laughed and raised his glass in a mock toast. *Round one to the lady.* How surprising. He took a sip of his wine and placed the glass back on the table. 'So, Jemima,' he began and watched with enjoyment the way she tensed, 'how do you know Rachel?'

'We were at university together,' Rachel answered for her. 'Jemima and I met during freshers week and ended up sharing a house together in our second and third years. Do you remember the house we had first?' she asked, turning to Jemima. 'I swear it had mould in the corner of every room. It even smelt damp.'

'What did you study?' Miles asked.

Those green eyes flashed up at him, clearly resenting telling him anything. It added a little spice to the evening.

'English and French.'

'We both did,' Rachel chimed in. 'Except, of course, Jemima got a first, whereas I got a 2:1.'

Which rather begged the question—what the blazes was she doing working for little more than the minimum wage in a temporary secretarial job? It was none of his business, but his curiosity was piqued.

And, if he was honest, a little more than that. 'So how come you're temping? I'd have thought a first in English and French from Warwick would have led you in an entirely different direction.'

'She meant to be an editor. But then she met Russell and…' Rachel shrugged '…everything changed.'

'So…you gave up everything for love?'

There was a toss of that incredible hair and then she met his eyes. 'I gave up everything when I had my first son,' she corrected him firmly. 'Not that there was much to give up. I was only twenty-one and hadn't had a chance to get started on anything.'

'And now you're picking up where you left off.'

'Hardly,' she shot back with a flash of those incredible eyes, her resentment shimmering across the table towards him. 'When I left off I'd just got a job as an assistant editor with a small educational publisher. Now I'm a temporary secretary. If life's a game of snakes and ladders I've just gone down that really big snake on square twenty-four.'

Alistair was wrong. Jemima Chadwick wasn't *brittle*, she was angry. It seemed that life had hit her particularly hard. Alistair had described her divorce as 'traumatic', but then Miles had never witnessed a divorce that wasn't.

In his circle the accepted opinion was that ex-wives were avaricious and bled their former spouses dry. This was the flip side of that, he supposed. His smile twisted. Jemima had been left with no career to speak of and two children to bring up alone. That was tough. No wonder she was angry.

Rachel topped up Jemima's wine. 'I still think you ought to think about—'

Alistair interrupted by carrying out a large platter of salmon. 'Nigella Lawson swears this is the easy way to entertain. Just fork up what you want. The duck may be a disaster so I wouldn't hold back.'

Rachel stood up and cleared away her central table decoration to make space. She looked around for somewhere to put it.

'Put it behind me,' Jemima suggested. 'It won't get knocked round here.'

Rachel handed over the stunning arrangement of white hydrangea, viburnum and tulips. 'Thanks.'

'You know this is gorgeous. You could do something like it for the wedding,' Jemima suggested, deliberately steering the topic of conversation into a new direction.

In her opinion, Miles Kingsley had spent long enough enjoying himself at her expense. Even talking about weddings was preferable to the continual haemorrhaging of her private business. She pulled back her chair and placed the flowers carefully on the ground. 'All these tea lights are very romantic too.'

Rachel sat down eagerly. 'I was wondering about that. I think it would work really well with our theme—' she sat back to add gravitas to her announcement '—which is going to be…medieval.'

Medieval. That wasn't what Rachel had been talking about for the past four months. 'What happened to "nineteen-forties Hollywood glamour"?'

Miles moved his chair. 'Am I supposed to be understanding any of this?'

'I find it better not to try,' Alistair said, resting an arm along the back of Rachel's chair.

His fiancée smiled at him. 'We've managed to get Manningtree Castle. They've had a cancellation and slotted us in. It's going to be beautiful.'

And an incredible amount of work, Jemima added silently. Manningtree Castle was probably the most romantic place on earth to get married, but it wasn't a package deal by any stretch of the imagination. As far as she could recall from their initial research into the options, Manningtree Castle provided little more than the Norman keep itself and a grassy field with permission to erect a marquee.

'Where's Manningtree Castle?' Miles asked.

Jemima glanced across at him. 'Kent. It's not so much a castle as a bit of one.'

'And it's not far from where Rachel and I bought our cottage. A couple of miles. No more than that,' Alistair added. 'They're booked up a good eighteen months in advance so we were surprised when they called us to say they'd had a cancellation for the weekend we'd enquired about.'

'Can't you just imagine all those tea lights in the stone alcoves?' Rachel's eyes danced with excitement. 'Or even big church candles. It's going to be stunning.'

'But your invitations—'

Rachel brushed her friend's objection aside. 'We'll just have to resend them.'

Not to mention hire a marquee, find a caterer and local florist to decorate the keep, Jemima thought dryly. She sat back in her chair and made a determined effort not to let what she was feeling show. In her opinion, three months before a wedding was far too late to be changing the venue.

Jemima gave half an ear to her friend as she continued to lay out her artistic vision of a medieval wedding with a distinctly twenty-first century twist. No mention of the halter-neck dress in soft white satin she'd chosen four weeks earlier. What was happening about that?

She wanted to be excited for Rachel, she really did, but it all seemed rather pointless. So much effort for one day…

She speared a piece of salmon from the central platter. She was being selfish. Just because her marriage hadn't been the happy ever after she'd hoped for wasn't a good enough reason not to enter into someone else's excitement. It was just difficult to summon up much enthusiasm for all this nonsense. That probably made her a horrible person, certainly a lousy choice of bridesmaid, but if she didn't say it aloud, just thought it—that wasn't *so* bad, was it?

Jemima glanced across at Miles and caught him watching her. She had the strangest feeling he'd been able to read her mind. That was impossible, of course, but…there was a definite look of…something in his blue eyes.

She turned back to concentrate on her salmon, feeling slightly shaken. Perhaps she'd been imagining it? On the other hand, perhaps they shared a mutual cynicism for big white weddings? She couldn't believe he'd be particularly interested in the finer details of how Rachel intended to decorate the marquee.

Jemima risked a second look. He was listening to Rachel and, whatever his opinion of it all was, he was making a reasonable job of looking fascinated. He really was impossibly handsome. Strange how two eyes, a nose and a mouth could look so different from one person to another. He had a good chin too. Her mum would say it was strong and characterful, but what she particularly liked about it was the small indentation in the centre. It was kind of sexy.

Grief. What had made her think that? Jemima pulled herself up a little straighter. There was nothing sexy about a man who knew he was sexy. If that made any sense. Miles was too gorgeous. No woman wanted to be with a man who spent more time looking in the mirror than she did.

Actually that was unfair. Miles didn't seem a vain man. He just was drop dead gorgeous. An accident of nature.

She really shouldn't blame him for that. It wasn't his fault any more than it was Verity's that she'd inherited the enviable bone structure and the ability to survive on half a grape.

'Jemima?'

She heard her name and looked up to find Rachel looking at her.

'You're off with the fairies. What are you thinking about?'

Thinking about? 'Um—' Jemima hunted for something to say '—um…' Opposite her, Miles's eyes were alight with laughter. Please God he didn't know *what* she'd been thinking.

She cast about for something likely. 'Um…I was wondering what you were going to do about your dress? Surely it's too late to change it now?'

Rachel smiled. 'I was worried about that, but I rang the designer the second I heard Manningtree Castle was available. It's not a problem. And she's caught the vision absolutely.' She gave a delighted laugh. 'I'm so excited. It's going to be perfect.'

'As is my duck. I hope.' Alistair began to gather together their plates.

Rachel picked up the central platter. 'It had better be. He started soaking the apricots last night and he'll be very sulky if it hasn't worked.' She followed Alistair back into the kitchen and Jemima was left alone with Miles.

'Liar,' he said softly.

Jemima looked up. 'Pardon?'

Miles's eyes glinted with wicked amusement. 'You were not wondering about Rachel's dress.'

A smile tugged at the corner of her mouth. 'Did it show?'

'Not to Rachel, it seems. You live to daydream another day.' There were gales of laughter from the kitchen. Miles looked over his shoulder and then turned back to her, saying quietly, 'Do you think she's going to ask me to wear tights and a tunic?'

'If she does,' Jemima whispered back, 'you can console yourself that it's only marginally worse than a russet-coloured waistcoat made from the fabric of my bridesmaid dress.'

The look of complete horror that passed over his face made her laugh and she was still laughing when Alistair and Rachel returned.

'What's so funny?' Rachel asked as she put a warm plate in front of each of them.

'Nothing.'

Miles cast Rachel a baleful look that was intended to charm. 'Are Alistair and I going to be wearing tights?'

'Absolutely not,' Alistair said, putting his masterpiece in the centre of the table. 'I don't have the calves for it. Now this…is Duck Breasts with Blackberry and Apricot Sauce.'

'Do please notice the elegant presentation,' his fiancée teased, looking up at him. 'Particularly the apricot halves, watercress and blackberry garnish. It was very fiddly.'

The look of love and affection that passed between them suddenly made Jemima feel lonely. Most of the time she managed perfectly well, but just occasionally it spread through her like ink in water.

Rachel sat down. 'You know, Alistair, I think you've got great calves. What about wearing tights?'

CHAPTER THREE

THE Duck Breasts with Blackberry and Apricot Sauce was a triumph, but the Poached Figs with Macaroons and Mascarpone Alistair had lovingly prepared for dessert was less successful. He was entirely philosophical about it and was threatening to invite them all back for a retry later in the month.

Jemima stirred brown sugar crystals into her coffee, surprisingly relaxed. This was so much better than staying home to decorate the bathroom, which had been her original plan for the evening. She'd almost forgotten the trail of 'welkin blue' footprints she'd left spread across the new vinyl floor when she'd tripped over the paint pot lid. She'd even managed to forget that Alistair thought she was 'brittle' and Miles had said that she dressed like her mother.

She sipped the dark liquid and let the flavours travel over her tongue. *Brittle?* Did she really come across as brittle? She didn't want to be seen as brittle. She hadn't known Alistair thought that about her. Rachel had never said.

It was probably true, though. No one knew how painful a divorce was unless they'd firsthand experience of it. It felt as if…you were being physically ripped in half. There was no other way of describing it. Her whole life, everything she'd invested in and worked for, had been shredded as though none of it had mattered. Anyone would be a little 'brittle' after that. *Wouldn't they?*

'Mint?'

She looked up to find Miles was holding out a plate of gold-wrapped mints. Jemima took one.

'Rachel? Do you want one?'

'Thank you.'

Jemima slowly unwrapped the foil-covered mint and let the conversation swirl around her. Miles Kingsley had turned out to be good company. At work he seemed…well…a complete caricature of what she'd imagined a playboy would be like.

It offended her that he seemed to select his dates with no more care than you would make a decision between a chocolate with a cream-filled centre and one with a nutty coating. Even more offensive was the way he discarded them days later, with as little thought.

It seemed the chase was what interested him. Winning. It was as though he were playing some complicated game of his own devising, and when he'd won he lost interest.

Not surprisingly, it wasn't that simple. Miles was a much more complicated man. She'd wanted to dislike him, but she'd not been able to. Jemima spread out the foil wrapper and gently smoothed out the creases.

Maybe it was no more than that she disliked being at Kingsley and Bressington so much that it coloured her opinion of anything and everyone there. Tonight she had to admit that Miles had been fun. Kind, too. If discussing the various merits of a chocolate wedding cake over a traditional fruit one had bored her, it must surely have pushed him close to the edge.

In any case, she thought, smoothing out the final crease, his erudite endorsement of an assortment of cheeses and warm bread in favour of any cake had her vote.

Miles's low laugh made her look up. 'I haven't seen

anyone do that since school,' he said, holding out his mint wrapper to her.

Jemima looked back down at the perfectly smooth gold square and back into his laughing blue eyes. A hard lump seemed stuck in her throat.

He had the most amazing eyes. *So sexy*. She felt like a rabbit caught in the glare of oncoming headlights. She couldn't look away. Couldn't speak either.

'I used to do that,' Rachel said, spreading her own wrapper out in front of her. 'It always used to rip, though.'

Alistair leant back in his chair. 'That's because you rush it. Jemima's got patience.'

Finally Jemima managed to find her voice, albeit a huskier one than usual. 'Jemima's got two boys who need amusing when they go out to Sunday lunch. I make a pretty good job of putting After Eight Mint envelopes inside each other too.'

She took Miles's wrapper and carefully eased out the creases. She was aware of Miles's soft laughter and Rachel's cry of irritation when her wrapper tore. Jemima kept her eyes focused on the gold paper until the last crease disappeared and she was left with a shiny square.

'Beautifully done,' Miles said softly.

He made even that sound seductive. No wonder he had women falling over themselves to go out to dinner with him. Like lemmings on a cliff…

Daft. She didn't like to think how dreadful they must feel when he didn't phone, didn't make any effort to contact them again.

Alistair reached out for a mint. 'So, what kind of wedding will you have, Miles? When the time comes.'

'Shotgun,' he answered quickly amid raucous laughter. '*If* the time comes.'

Rachel screwed up her foil wrapper in exasperation and

placed it on her plate. 'It'll come. Some woman will sneak up on you and you'll be up the aisle before you know it.'

'She'll have to be SAS trained,' Miles said lazily. 'I think I've got my defences in place.'

He wasn't joking. Miles clearly enjoyed his life exactly as it was, Jemima thought. As long as there were women out there foolish enough to risk their hearts spending time with him, he'd probably go on enjoying it. Why wouldn't he?

Jemima glanced down at her wrist-watch and noticed with surprise how very late it was. The candles dotted around the courtyard had come into their own, but it was beginning to feel cold. She rubbed at her arms.

'Are you getting chilly?' Rachel asked. 'Perhaps we'd better move inside.'

She shook her head. 'It's late. I ought to be going home.'

'Now?'

Jemima held out her wrist to show her watch. 'It's nearly eleven. It's going to take me half an hour to get back.'

'You can't go yet. I've not shown you my shoes,' Rachel protested.

'You can't go before she's done that,' Alistair concurred. 'Miles, more coffee?'

Within minutes she'd been taken to the guest room and Rachel had carefully shut the door. 'Sit on the bed,' she said, opening the wardrobe and reaching up to the top shelf.

Jemima sat down on the deep red eiderdown. Rachel carried the shoe box over and perched next to her. She opened the box as though it contained a live thing. Inside, loving packaged in tissue paper, was a pair of exquisite shoes. They were the colour of rich clotted cream and had seriously pointed toes. Not exactly medieval, but Jemima could see why Rachel had fallen in love with them.

'Are they comfortable?'

Rachel laughed. 'Don't be daft. They're beautiful.'

There was a rap on the door.

'Don't come in,' Rachel shouted, hurrying to put the shoe box back at the top of the wardrobe.

Alistair's voice sounded through the closed door. 'Come on out of there, you two. Miles is about to leave.'

'I'm just coming.' She smiled across at Jemima. 'I can't believe I'm getting married. Can you believe it? I'm so excited.'

Jemima smiled back, but was relieved when Rachel turned away to open the bedroom door. It was hard to keep up the façade that any of this mattered. In reality, married life had nothing to do with the choice of shoes.

As Jemima picked her handbag from off the bed she heard Rachel say, 'Miles, do you really have to go now?'

'I'm afraid I do.'

'Me too.' Jemima appeared in the doorway.

'You're both very boring,' Rachel said, tucking beneath Alistair's arm.

Miles picked up his leather jacket from the hall chair and shrugged himself into it. His black jeans and thick black T-shirt had been sharp, but the jacket took it up another notch. Jemima looked away.

He was actually, she thought, a terrifying kind of man. Too gorgeous to be real, more like someone who'd been air-brushed to perfection.

Instinctively she smoothed down the hopelessly creased linen of her dress and immediately hoped he hadn't noticed. She glanced up at him and caught the wicked glint in his eyes—whatever that meant.

'It was lovely to meet you, Miles,' she said hurriedly, aware her voice sounded slightly breathy.

The glint in his eyes intensified. 'You, too.' He leant forward to kiss her cheek. 'Unexpected, but…lovely.'

It was no more than a peck, but Jemima hadn't anticipated the way it would feel. His hand was strong and warm against her arm and his lips seemed to burn on her cheek. When he stepped back it was as much as she could do not to raise a hand to her face. She glanced over at him, wondering whether he'd noticed anything, hoping he hadn't, but female enough to be irritated when he seemed not to have.

'Thanks for a great evening,' he said as he kissed Rachel before turning and placing a casual slap on Alistair's left shoulder.

Jemima forced herself to move. 'It was fun.' She reached up to kiss Alistair's cheek. 'And the food was delicious.'

Alistair smiled down at her. 'Not the figs.'

'Agreed,' Miles said as he opened the front door. 'The figs need work.'

'I'll ring you,' was Rachel's parting shot. 'I'll arrange another evening when we can all get together.'

'That'll be good,' Miles said, stepping out on to the pavement.

Jemima followed. As the door closed she took a deep breath and stopped to rummage through her handbag for her car keys.

'You survived,' Miles remarked.

She glanced up to find him standing a few feet away from her and her stomach flipped over at the lazy laughter in his blue eyes. Whatever it was he had, he really should bottle it. It was intoxicating. 'So did you.'

'But I was saved the shoe ordeal. Are they particularly medieval, would you say?'

Jemima choked on an unexpected laugh. 'I think a twelfth century peasant might have struggled with the three-inch heels, but…' She smiled. 'Rachel's going to look beautiful…which, I suppose, is the idea.'

He made a noise that sounded remarkably like a 'humph'. 'Alistair will think she looks stunning if she turns up in jeans.

He can't believe his luck she's agreed to marry him.' He pulled out his own car keys from his jacket pocket. 'I'm inclined to think they'll be all right, buck the statistics, don't you? They seem good together.'

Jemima glanced back at the blue-painted front door. 'Yes. They are,' she said slowly, turning back to him. 'Really good together.' Then. 'I—I'm sorry I said anything about the dandelion. I shouldn't have—'

'You're apologising to me?' he interrupted, seemingly surprised. Then he smiled. 'It worked, you know. Dinner date on Friday. Keira rang as soon as the delivery hit her desk.'

Jemima's eyes widened. 'Good grief.'

The lines at the sides of Miles's eyes crinkled. 'Wouldn't have been so successful with you, then?'

'Absolutely not!' Jemima smiled up at him. 'I'd probably have sent you back a daisy. Can't think of a rhyme at the moment, but I'm sure I'd have come up with something suitably scathing.'

The blue eyes took on a deeper glint. She loved the way they did that. It made her feel irresponsible, somehow.

'That would have been irresistible.'

He was only teasing—but he was *very* sexy. Jemima looked away. It was going to make Monday morning a bit difficult. She'd preferred it when she'd been able to keep him in a nice, safe mental box marked 'temporary boss—self-assured philanderer'.

'Where are you parked?'

It took a moment before she understood what he'd asked. 'Oh, not far. Just down there.' She nodded down the pavement.

'I'll walk you down.'

'There's no need, I—'

'It's late,' he said, cutting across her, 'it's dark and even my mother would think it okay to accept.'

'Your mother?' Jemima said, confused. What had his mother got to do with anything?

The lines at the edges of his eyes crinkled. 'You don't know?'

She shook her head. *Didn't know what, exactly?*

'My mother's Hermione Kingsley. I would have thought Rachel would have told you. Most people can't resist it.'

Jemima knew she looked blank for a moment and then she clicked who Hermione Kingsley was. Serious journalist and staunch feminist. Perhaps the most famous single parent of them all... Her thought processes clicked up another gear. 'In that case, you must be...' she said slowly.

'Exactly.' He nodded, his eyes once again alight with laughter. 'A social experiment and the most public product of a sperm donation bank.'

Jemima wasn't quite sure what her reaction should be. She hadn't expected he'd say anything like that.

'She tells me it's something to be proud of and I like to think she put a great deal of effort into her choice of donor.'

'I imagine you do,' she replied a little primly and he burst out laughing. 'W-what?'

Miles shook his head, still laughing. 'And you really hope she washed her hands after...'

'I didn't say that,' Jemima protested, her own lips twitching.

'At least you don't have to feel guilty about letting me walk you to your car. Even my mother believes that personal safety has to take precedence over higher ideals of equality.'

'I suppose if your mother approves.'

His answering glint had her stomach twisting itself into knots. It really was no wonder he could get away with sending a dandelion. She had the strongest feeling he could get away with practically anything.

Her car really was only a few paces down the road. Jemima stopped next to her battered Volvo. 'This is it,' she said self-consciously.

Not by so much as a flicker did his eyes give away his

opinion of her car. That took some skill, as it was a complete rust heap. She put her key in the lock and turned it.

'Look,' he said after a short pause, 'I'm really sorry about…earlier. I was out of order.'

Jemima looked over her shoulder. 'That's okay.'

'It isn't. It was crass.'

She straightened up. 'Okay, it was crass,' she agreed with a smile, 'but you didn't know I was standing in the doorway.'

'No, but… Just how much of what Alistair and I were saying did you overhear?'

He looked more uncomfortable than she'd ever seen him. *Not so pleased with himself this time.* It was funny. 'Pretty much all of it.' Miles groaned and Jemima laughed. 'I got the bit about my clothes looking like my mother's—'

'You look lovely tonight,' he cut in softly.

Her stomach flipped over and all of a sudden she didn't want to laugh any more. This felt dangerous. She couldn't cope with it. She didn't know the rules of the game and it made her feel scared. 'Stop it!'

'What?'

'You can't resist flirting, can you? Does anyone ever take you seriously?'

He said nothing—and it was immensely satisfying to feel back in control.

Jemima swallowed. 'Where was I?' she asked, trying to re-capture the light mood. 'Oh, yes, I heard the bit about my arriving late and leaving early. Not wanting to socialise—'

'You got it all,' Miles said, holding up his hand to stop her. 'I'm really sorry. I had no business talking about you like that.'

He seemed genuine. Jemima shrugged and turned back to her car. 'Don't worry about it.' His words had hurt, but not as much as he might imagine. She'd never valued the way she looked. How could she when she would always be in the shadow of a super-model sister. 'I know I don't fit into the Kingsley and Bressington image.'

'I was out of order.'

She turned in time to see Miles thrust an agitated hand through his dark hair. 'Your timekeeping is fine. You're always there by nine-thirty and don't leave until six. That's exactly what we asked for.'

'I did tell Amanda. It's because the boys need to be—'

'It's fine,' he cut her off firmly. 'Nine-thirty is fine.' He frowned and then asked, 'Will you be in on Monday?'

'No choice. I promised Amanda I'd stay for the duration. She thinks it's all good experience for me.' On Friday when she'd posted her time sheet back that had been a grim prospect, but it didn't feel so bad any more. 'Besides,' she added with a sudden grin, 'she told me on Friday afternoon how pleased you were with my work. Now, unless you were lying to her...'

His crack of laughter made her feel terrific. She didn't want to think why. She opened the car door.

'Jemima?'

She turned. 'Yes?'

'Why didn't you tell Rachel we'd met?'

Jemima smiled. 'Same reason you didn't, I imagine—just too complicated.'

'True.'

She climbed into the driver's seat. 'One or the other is going to need to ring Amanda, though. If we leave it to chance she's bound to say something to Rachel and then we'll look very stupid.'

'I'll do it.'

'What will you say?'

'Don't know.' Miles rested his hand on the car door, preventing her from closing it. 'The truth usually works best. Might have to be a little sparing with it, but basically I'll stick to the truth.'

Jemima laughed again and put her keys into the ignition. Miles took that as his cue to shut the car door and then he stepped back on the pavement, clearly waiting until she drove off. She just prayed that this was one of those occasions when her Volvo started without trouble.

Please, she murmured. *Just start*.

Somehow it wasn't a surprise when the engine turned over without firing up. Jemima closed her eyes and sent up a tiny arrow prayer, then tried the engine again.

Of course, it shouldn't matter at all that her car was failing in front of Miles Kingsley. It *didn't* matter. Of course it didn't. It was just…

If there was any justice in the world she'd have twisted the ignition key and her old Volvo would have risen to the occasion and purred away into the distance.

'Problems?'

Just life. *Her* life. She couldn't even make a stylish exit. Jemima pinned a smile on her face and wound down the window. 'It's a little temperamental. Sometimes is doesn't start straight away. I'll give it a little rest and try again in a minute.'

'Sounds like the battery's flat.'

Yep, it sounded like that to her. You didn't need to be a mechanic to know that the battery sounded as dead as a dodo. 'I'm sure it'll be fine. Don't bother waiting. If there's a problem I can ring for a taxi.'

'Try it again.'

It seemed he wasn't going anywhere. Jemima twisted the key again and the silence was deafening. Sometimes it helped if she pumped the accelerator, but mostly what helped was the downhill run she had from her house. Once it was going it was usually fine.

Of course, she could always suggest he gave her a push. Sometimes that worked well… There was a part of her that wished she had the audacity to do it. The mental image of an impeccably dressed Miles Kingsley pushing a battered old Volvo had a certain appeal. But if it didn't work she'd be left blocking the road and, worse than that, her temporary boss would then get the opportunity to see how difficult she found reverse parking…

This was so mortifying, though why it felt so *particularly* mortifying she didn't know.

'It doesn't sound like it's going to work.'

'No.'

'Have you got any jump-leads?'

Now that would have been sensible. Jemima had a mental picture of the shelf in the utility room where she'd left them. *Why* hadn't she brought them? She always did if she was doing anything longer than the school run.

But tonight she'd been so late. That last little bit of wall in the bathroom had needed painting and it had been so tempting to finish before she went out. If she hadn't left it so late to get ready she probably wouldn't have tripped over the paint lid, wouldn't have needed to grab a shower and, therefore, wouldn't have forgotten the jump-leads. Strange how one seemingly innocuous decision could set you up for disaster.

'Unfortunately not,' she said, bravely climbing back out of the car. 'Have you?'

He shook his head.

Stupid question. Why would he have jump-leads in his car? Miles Kingsley probably drove a top of the range BMW or a flashy-looking Porsche. Jemima shivered as much from embarrassment as cold. What she really needed was Miles to go away and leave her to it.

Jemima looked back down the road towards her friend's flat. Perhaps Rachel had jump-leads? It didn't seem likely. She wasn't sure that Rachel knew how to open the bonnet of her car, but Alistair was the kind of man who would have jump-leads.

'Are you going to go back inside?' Miles asked, turning to follow her gaze.

Together they watched the bedroom curtains close. Jemima forced a smile. 'No. I can't face waiting for the AA to tow me home. I think I'll just ring for a taxi on my mobile and deal with it all in the morning. The boys aren't back until four. I've got plenty of time.'

It seemed like a great plan to her, but Miles didn't look convinced. 'Where do you live?'

'Harrow,' she said, turning back to look forlornly at her car. It was going to cost a lot of money to take a taxi, particularly at this time of night—even assuming she could find a driver who wanted to go that far out of central London.

'I'll give you a lift.'

Jemima whipped round to look at him. 'I—I couldn't ask you to do that.'

'You didn't.' Miles nodded at Alistair and Rachel's flat. 'They've gone to bed and I can't leave you waiting in the street for a taxi—'

'Your mother wouldn't like it,' Jemima quipped, unable to resist the thought that had popped into her head.

'You've got it.' He pulled his car keys from his jacket pocket.

Jemima hesitated.

'If I minded I wouldn't have offered. I'm staggeringly selfish. Consider it an opportunity for me to salve my conscience for having been so rude to you.' He started to walk back towards Alistair and Rachel's flat.

Why was he doing this? Driving her out to Harrow had to be the last thing he wanted to do. Hell, this was so embarrassing. She wanted to curl up in a ball and howl, only that wasn't an option.

With one last look at her Volvo, Jemima followed him back along the pavement. Perhaps she should just ring the AA? But they'd take a while to get to her and Miles would probably insist on waiting with her. So that would be equally embarrassing—and the prospect of ringing the AA for the third time in six months *really* didn't appeal. They'd probably be irritated because it was palpably obvious she needed to do something about replacing the car. It was dying—and she knew it.

Jemima bit her lip and tried to decide what was the least embarrassing option open to her. In her next life, she decided, this kind of thing was not going to be allowed to happen. She was going to be effortlessly elegant, thin, possibly blonde…

'Coming?'

'Yes.'

Miles's car was showroom perfect—as she'd known it would be. It was also old—*very* old—and she hadn't expected that. Cars weren't high on her list of interesting things, but for this particular model she might make an exception. It was truly a classic.

'It's a 1962 Bristol 407,' Miles said, watching her. 'Don't say it…'

She looked up questioningly.

'I know.' His mouth twisted into a wry smile. 'The ultimate Boy's Own accessory.'

Now that he said it… Jemima smiled. 'It's even older than my car.'

Miles opened the passenger door. 'But greater loved.'

Despite everything she felt a bubble of laughter start somewhere in the pit of her stomach. Being with Miles was an exhilarating experience, Jemima thought as his Bristol 407 pulled away from the kerb. Before the boys, before Russell…before life had robbed her of optimism…she might have been tempted by him. It felt exciting being with someone like him, as though anything could happen and probably would.

She smiled in the darkness. Even before the boys, Miles would never have been seriously interested in a woman like her. Or even un-seriously, since that appeared to be all he did. He was the kind of man Verity dated. They'd look great together…

But even Verity hoped she'd meet someone one day who'd be able to see beneath the beautiful veneer and love her. Just her. It was strange that Miles was so adamant he'd never marry. Most people hoped that one day they might find someone to share their life with. *Didn't they?* Jemima glanced across at his handsome profile. It was unusual not to want to find a soul mate. Didn't he feel a need to be loved and share his life with someone?

'Why are you so negative towards marriage?' she asked suddenly.

He turned his head to look at her, before refocusing on the road. 'Did it show? I was making a special effort to be positive.'

Jemima laughed. 'I know. I heard the instruction, remember. I'm "brittle".'

She felt his smile. 'And are you?' He glanced across at her.

Yes. No. No one ever asked her that outright. She'd spoken without thinking and she didn't know how to answer him. She was just 'poor Jemima'. The lame duck that everyone had to rally around. 'You tell me.'

'Evasion,' he said softly, his eyes still on the road.

Jemima took a sharp intake of breath. Was she 'brittle'? Surely she was stronger than that? She was holding it together, doing really well under the circumstances. She sighed. 'I think I'm walking wounded.'

He looked at her and smiled and, all of a sudden, it didn't seem to matter any more what people were saying and thinking about her. The air in the confines of the small car seemed rarefied and she felt light-headed.

Jemima looked down at her hands, white against the dark linen of her dress. She wasn't good at this one-to-one with an attractive man. She didn't understand how the game went.

And he was attractive, that small voice whispered. Very. She'd known that since her first morning at Kingsley and Bressington. Miles Kingsley was scarily sexy—and way, way out of her league. She sighed and gave a tentative smile. 'I'm trying to support Rachel…but I just can't summon up any enthusiasm for confetti and white ribbon. It doesn't seem particularly relevant to anything any more.'

Miles looked across with another smile. It was perfect. Warm, but not pitying. It was like a shot of whisky—supremely comforting.

'I feel guilty, though,' she continued, hurriedly looking away. 'Rachel was my bridesmaid and she put in more effort than I'm doing. We spent hours poring over magazines. We even made an ideas scrapbook. How sad was that?'

She heard his smile rather than saw it. It was in his voice. 'Rachel must have known you were going to find it difficult when she asked you to be her bridesmaid.'

'I suppose.'

'In fact, are you a bridesmaid?' Miles looked at her. 'Do you return to virginal status after a divorce or do you become a matron of honour?'

Jemima felt another laugh well up inside her. 'That's your problem. You've got to do the speech.'

'Thanks for that!'

She slipped her foot out of her flat pump and rubbed the back of her right heel with her toes. 'It's probably better to make me a "bridesmaid" since Russell's going to be at the wedding.'

'Your ex?'

She nodded. 'It's bad enough I'm still using his name. We've been divorced just over a year and were separated for eighteen months before that.'

'So why do you?' he asked, his hands moving easily on the steering wheel.

'It seemed simpler to have the same name as my boys. You know, less confusing at the school gate.'

He nodded his understanding, but she wasn't sure whether he thought it a good enough reason. She wasn't sure whether it was either. 'Anyway, Alistair and Rachel asked if I'd mind if they asked him. Rachel's known him since university…' Jemima drew a breath. 'So he's coming…with Stefanie.'

'Couldn't you have said you did mind?'

She gave a hard laugh. 'I could, but then Russell would have known I was uncomfortable about him being there…and I couldn't have that. In fact, everyone would have known I'd said I minded and then they'd have felt sorry for me.' She turned to look at him. 'I've had enough of that. I must have heard every possible connotation of "poor Jemima" going.'

'It's a tough deal to be bringing up two children on your own.'

'Russell helps. He's really good.' A familiar sense of gloom spread through her body. She hated the way everyone said that. What was so good about walking out on your family? 'And he's great with the boys. Spends as much time with them as he can.'

It was me he left. That small voice bit into her self-esteem. Russell had enjoyed everything about his life—but *her.* She wasn't about to tell Miles that. She hadn't told anyone how…destroyed she felt by that. The person who had promised to love her until she died had taken a sledgehammer and smashed her to smithereens. *How did you stick yourself back together after that?*

'It's not the same though, is it?' Miles indicated to move

lanes. 'The ultimate responsibility is yours. I imagine it's the same difference as running a company and being employed by one. The emotional investment is completely different.'

Put like that her sense of crushing responsibility seemed entirely reasonable. She turned slightly in her chair. 'So, what's your excuse? Why are you so lacking in enthusiasm about marriage? You didn't say.'

Miles glanced across at her. 'I've got no problem with the ideal; it's just I don't believe it's achievable. Two people in a monogamous relationship which lasts fifty years plus…?' He shook his head.

'People have done it.'

'Perhaps. I don't know.' He smiled. 'People change. Circumstances certainly do. Apart from anything else, we all live a great deal longer now and I'm not convinced it's possible to find one person who will be a perfect fit for an entire lifetime.'

Jemima thought for a moment. What he said sounded plausible—but *bleak*. Did he really believe that? It sounded like something Hermione Kingsley might say in one of her strident columns. 'Maybe not "perfect", not all the time…but don't you think it's possible to evolve together? If you value what you have enough…' That was what she believed.

'Wouldn't it be simpler to accept that one person might be right for a period of your life, and then someone quite different for a different period?'

No. It was such a cold and isolated way of living. She couldn't accept that. Jemima frowned. 'What about children? Don't you believe they do better with stability?'

'Ah.'

She looked at him curiously.

'Now you've found the rub to my argument. In many ways I had a great childhood. Materially privileged, great schools…' Miles broke off and glanced across at her. 'You're going to need to start directing me on where I should be going.'

'Oh.' Jemima thrust her foot back in her shoe. 'Straight on here. Take the third exit at the next roundabout. We're nearly there.'

Miles glanced across at her and his eyes crinkled. 'The trouble with my argument is that I know I wasn't very interested in my mother's principles as a child.' He focused back on the road. 'It was all fine, no doubt, but I desperately wanted to have a dad. Of course, in my case, it was all a little extreme.'

'A little,' Jemima agreed, wondering how difficult it had been for him to have grown up with a mother who was so public about the circumstances of his unconventional conception.

He paused while he negotiated the roundabout. 'I wonder… If I'd been conceived in a more usual way…'

'Yes?'

'I don't think I'd have been remotely concerned about my parents' marital happiness. I think I'd have simply been happy to have someone on hand to play cricket with and produce on Parents Day.'

Jemima felt a rumble of laughter. 'That does rather blow your life plan out of the water.'

'Only if I have children.' His eyes flicked across at her. 'It's not my intention. I like things exactly as they are. Why change it?'

No children. Ever. Miles might be right in his assessment of the realities of modern day living, but she preferred to believe it was possible to spend a lifetime loving one person. Hope in the face of experience. 'It's the third turning on the right.'

'This one?'

'That's it,' she said, and a few seconds later, 'The one with the burgundy door.'

They pulled up outside and Jemima felt conscious of the

peeling paintwork and the generally unkempt appearance. 'Thanks. I appreciate you bringing me home,' she said awkwardly.

'It's no problem.'

All at once she felt as if she was seventeen again, coming home after a date. Jemima bent to pick up her handbag, not quite sure what she should do now. It felt *awkward*. Should she ask him in for coffee? Or not? What was the correct thing to do when your friend's best man was also your temporary boss?

But he had gone out of his way and driven her home…

And he could always say no… Probably would.

Take a deep breath and ask him.

It was just coffee.

In the end she took it in a rush. 'Do you want a coffee before you drive back?'

CHAPTER FOUR

It wasn't as though asking Miles in for coffee would turn this evening into any kind of a romantic interlude. It was nothing more than common courtesy.

Jemima gritted her teeth and waited for his answer—the inevitable no. Of course, he'd say no. It was a long way back into central London—assuming, of course, Miles lived in central London. He might not. He might live somewhere closer, like Pinner or Ruislip...

'Coffee would be great.'

Jemima's eyes widened in shock. 'R-right.' *Coffee was easy. She could do coffee.*

'It's not as though I've anywhere I need to be.' Miles smiled and her stomach flipped over like a pancake. Whoever his mystery sperm donor had been, he'd donated some seriously good genes to the pot.

His smile made her forget she was the mother of two boys, forget that her Victorian semi needed a new roof, forget that her bedroom had a scary damp patch in the corner by the window. All these things seemed to vaporise and she was left with a breathless excitement.

'That's not what you told Rachel,' she managed.

'Implied,' Miles corrected. 'Like you, there's only so much

confetti and white ribbon I can stomach. Once you'd made
your break for freedom it seemed sensible to follow on behind
you. Good job, too, since it's given me the opportunity to play
Sir Galahad.'

Jemima felt for the door handle.

'Hang on. I'll help you out,' he said, climbing out his side
and walking round.

Jemima couldn't remember the last time a man had opened
a car door for her. Miles made it seem such a natural, con-
temporary thing to do. 'Thanks,' she said as he shut the passenger door.

'It's a shame to have to go back in to town tomorrow,
though. It's going to take up most of your Sunday.'

She shrugged. 'It doesn't matter.'

Miles's eyes narrowed astutely, but he didn't say anything.
Jemima wondered what he was thinking. He couldn't possibly
understand how lonely she felt on the weekends her boys
were with Russell. It was like an ache. She was always wondering where they were, what they were doing. The days
stretched out endlessly and, despite the hundred and one jobs
she had to do, she found she was listless.

Jemima glanced up at the peeling paintwork on the front
door and wished she'd done something about that on one of
her 'weekends'. 'It's a work in progress,' she cautioned.

'What?'

'The h-house,' she clarified, searching for her keys. 'It's a
bit of a mess.'

'You're renovating it, aren't you?'

'Well, that was the plan,' she agreed, fitting the key into
the lock. 'Progress is a bit slow.' That was a bit of an under-
statement. If it wasn't for the generosity of her family, it
would have all but ground to a halt.

'I imagine it's difficult with children around,' Miles said neutrally.

Jemima glanced across at him in the dark. It *was* difficult with the children around, but there was so much more to it than that. More even than the lack of money. It was surprisingly difficult without someone to bounce ideas off. Every decision seemed momentous. Even choosing tiles for the bathroom.

She knew, of course, that against the wider context of world poverty and social injustice how she decorated her bathroom didn't rate as anything more than a dot. Nevertheless it felt important.

The door opened on to the original Minton tiled floor and Jemima stepped inside.

'The floor's great,' Miles observed. 'You were lucky to find a place where it's in such good condition.'

'I know. It's one of the reasons we bought it. That and the fact there's a good primary school at the end of the road,' she added.

'We?'

'Russell and I. He was really great about us having the house when he left,' Jemima said with determined cheerfulness. 'He didn't want the boys to have to move. You know, Ben was settled in school and Sam had only just had his bedroom decorated…'

She was rambling. She knew she was. Jemima bit her lip and made a conscious decision to stop. Miles wouldn't be interested.

'Is he going to deal with the roof?'

Jemima turned back to look at him, her eyes wide with surprise. 'Of course not. It's my responsibility now.'

No one had ever asked anything like that before. It made such a change for someone not to be impressed at how 'great' Russell was being about everything. She was just a little tired of being grateful to the man who had torn her family apart for no other reason than that he'd felt bored.

'How far have you got with everything else?' Miles asked, his shoes loud on the tiled floor.

Jemima pulled a face and switched on the light further down the hall. 'See for yourself.'

Miles said nothing. He didn't need to. Jemima was acutely aware of how much still needed to be done. There was still painted woodchip paper in the hallway and even gloss paint over what she was sure would be original tiles in the fireplace in the sitting room.

'It's coming on,' she said bravely. 'The kitchen is basically finished and I've just had a new bathroom fitted in one of the upstairs bedrooms. Maybe I'll think about re-roofing the house next.'

If she won the lottery, she added silently. Or accepted yet more help from her family.

This was embarrassing. Why the blazes had she asked him in for coffee? Jemima caught sight of herself in the hall mirror and ran a despairing hand through her red curls. She looked a mess too. Like some kind of Muppet.

They walked through to the kitchen, with its sleek maple units and dark worktops. Her eyes instinctively turned to the one thing that was different—the small puddle on the central island. Her eyes moved upwards to take in the damp stain on the papered ceiling and she watched a single drip fall down. 'Oh—'

'Damn,' Miles finished for her.

'Something like that,' she agreed, dropping her handbag. For a moment Jemima couldn't decide what to do and then she hurried into the redundant bathroom and returned with a red plastic bucket. *Perfect. Just perfect.* First the car, now this. 'Why does this always happen to me? I ricochet from one disaster to another.'

'It happens to everyone,' Miles replied with infuriating calmness. He slipped off his jacket and threw it carelessly across one of the high bar stools. 'It's one of the joys of owning property, but it's usually better than it looks.'

Jemima plonked the bucket on top of the worktop and then searched for some kitchen towel to wipe up the water already there. 'In my experience, it's almost always worse,' she muttered.

He didn't seem to be listening. His eyes were fixed on the stain on the ceiling. 'Have you got something sharp to make a hole? I reckon you ought to let the water out and contain the damage.'

'Pardon?'

'It looks like it's collecting up there. Water always finds a level,' he explained patiently. 'It'll spread and become more of a problem if you leave it until you can get hold of a plumber.'

Spread. Just great. Of course, she knew water always found its own level—it was just she hadn't connected that fact with a leaking ceiling. Jemima went back out to the old bathroom and rummaged through her tool box. She picked out a bradawl. It probably had a very specific use in the hands of an expert, but it also looked like the kind of thing that would be excellent for making a hole in a papered ceiling.

'Do you want me to do it?' Miles asked as she returned.

'No.' Jemima slipped off her shoes and climbed on to the central island. 'If there's got to be a hole in my ceiling, I'll do it.'

'Fair enough.'

His voice was so bland that she looked down at him. 'I know your mother would be proud,' she said.

Miles laughed.

'This isn't funny.'

'It's not bad from where I'm standing.'

Jemima ignored him, shut her eyes and pushed hard. It took a fairly stiff twist before she managed to make a hole. Almost immediately, water started to trickle down into the bucket below. With gritted teeth, she used the bradawl to make the hole bigger.

'That'll do it.'

'It's wrecked the ceiling paper,' Jemima observed as she looked at her handiwork, feeling a sudden unexpected desire to cry. She really didn't want to do *that* in front of Miles. It would be the final indignity and he must already think she was a walking disaster area.

'That's cheap to sort.'

She climbed down and drew an irritated hand across her eyes. What was the matter with her? She didn't usually allow the house to get her down. She only felt like crying because she was so tired. In the morning this would all look so much better…

'It's slowing down.'

'Is it?' Jemima asked doubtfully, looking back up at the damp mess of her ceiling.

'I know it looks like a lot of water at the moment, but I'm fairly sure it's not going to be a major problem. How long ago did you have your bathroom fitted?'

'The plumber finished a couple of days ago.' She couldn't believe it! Two days. *Damn it!* It just wasn't fair…

'Then it's probably no more serious than he dislodged something while he was doing the job. Give him a ring on Monday.'

'And you're the expert?' Jemima said, finally irritated by his…*smug* calmness. Everybody was always so good at making light of problems that weren't their own.

'Not specifically in plumbing, but in renovating houses.' His blue eyes glinted as though he knew exactly what she was thinking. 'I'm on my sixth.'

'Sixth?'

'House,' he said with a smile. 'In ten years. Do you want to check upstairs? I doubt there'll be anything to see, but you ought to look.'

She hated that he was right. She should have thought of that for herself. Jemima put the bradawl down on the worktop and padded barefoot across the kitchen and up the stairs. The bathroom looked as chaotic as she'd left it. The welkin blue footprints were still on the vinyl floor waiting to be cleared up, but there was no sign of any leak.

She took a deep breath and returned to the kitchen.

Miles looked up as she walked in. 'Well?'

'Nothing.' She glanced up at the ceiling. 'You wouldn't know anything had happened.'

He smiled, the blue eyes crinkling at the edges. 'That's good. It's unlikely to be an expensive job. So, what about that coffee?'

Jemima found she automatically turned towards the kettle. She filled it with water and flicked the switch before asking curiously, 'Do you really renovate houses? I mean personally?'

His smile intensified. 'You really don't think a lot of me, do you, Ms Chadwick?'

'Apart from the dandelion thing, I haven't thought about you at all,' she responded quickly. More reflex action than anything else, but as soon as the words had left her mouth she wished she hadn't said them. The poor guy had given her a lift home, had stayed while she sorted out the latest disaster to hit her life…

She glanced across at him to find he was laughing. 'I'm sorry—that was rude.'

'Why do you find it surprising I renovate houses? It can be very profitable.'

She looked over her shoulder to find he'd perched comfortably on one of the high bar stools. He might be wearing jeans, but they weren't the kind she recognised and they certainly hadn't come from the high street. 'Well…' She frowned.

'Go on, I can take it.'

Jemima looked across at him and smiled in defeat. 'You

don't exactly come across as a handyman. I can't imagine you spending hours stripping wallpaper or tiling.'

Miles laughed. 'I'm not bad, but I tend to buy in these days, more than do it myself.'

'Nice to have the choice.'

'That's what I think,' he agreed with a smile and her stomach flipped. The realisation hit her that she liked being with him. So often when she was talking to other people she felt as if she was playing tennis by herself, but with Miles every ball came back with spin. It felt a little dangerous, certainly exciting.

Jemima turned away and put a teaspoon of coffee granules into a mug. 'Is instant okay?'

'Fine.'

He even managed to make that sound as though he meant it. Kingsley and Bressington had beautiful coffee—expensive, rich and freshly ground. Jemima straightened her shoulders and tried not to think about it. 'You do know black coffee stains your teeth?'

'So I'm told.'

Jemima felt her mouth curve into a smile. She almost didn't mind about the leak. How did Miles *do* that? In the space of one evening he'd gone from a temporary boss she didn't much like to someone who felt like a friend. Almost. He was too unsettling to be something as comfortable as a friend.

She put milk in her own coffee, followed by a sweetener, before she turned round to find he was watching her. She passed him his coffee with a hand that shook slightly.

'Thanks.'

Miles made her feel self-conscious. It was something in his expression. Something she didn't quite understand. Something that made her breath shallow and her voice sound as though it were catching on cobwebs.

'I—I did wonder whether I could take that out,' Jemima said, looking at the old chimney-breast, 'and make a big family room in here.'

'Nice idea, but it'll be too expensive—'

'Oh, not now. Later on. When I've got a better job than working as your temporary secretary.' She paused to sip her coffee and watched him over the top of her mug. His eyes had started to laugh again and she felt her own mouth curve in response. It was automatic. An involuntary response. He made her feel alive and, she realised with a shock, she hadn't felt like that in months. Perhaps years. There was always so much to do. So many responsibilities. Most of the time she just felt tired.

But this evening…

With Miles…

'It's a phenomenally expensive thing to do. That chimney stack goes up three floors and you'd have to take it out all the way up. You'd be better off putting a conservatory type extension out the side here.' He stood up and walked over to the window.

It gave Jemima a perfect view of how fantastically he filled his designer jeans. In a formal suit he looked intimidating; in more casual clothes it was far worse. You could really see how muscular his thighs were and how tight his buttocks. She swallowed.

What was happening to her? *Never* in her entire life had she thought about a man the way she was thinking about this one. She'd always gone for the safe option. She wasn't the kind of girl who'd ever have coped well with the style of casual dating Miles favoured. She thought about consequences and weighed every decision she made carefully. That was *who* she was. It was ingrained in her personality as though it were carved there.

And Miles was who he was. Different from her. Shaped by his background as certainly as she'd been by her own.

Even if Miles were to look up and notice her... Jemima smiled even at the possibility of the possibility. She'd be terrified. Totally and utterly terrified.

Jemima sipped her coffee to hide her face. Miles seemed to have the uncanny knack of being able to read her mind and it wouldn't do for him to get an inkling of where her thoughts were taking her now.

He turned to look at her. 'If you've got the space to push the house out sideways it would link the kitchen and breakfast room together, besides bringing in so much more light. I've seen it done and it looks incredible.'

'You really do know about this renovation thing, don't you?'

His mouth pulled into a crooked smile. 'Frustrated designer.'

'Really?' Jemima wouldn't have thought he'd been frustrated in anything he wanted to do. He had the aura of a man who habitually succeeded in everything. It was interesting to think he might have been thwarted in something. Unbelievable, really.

He walked back towards her. 'I did my degree in Industrial Design.'

'How come you went into public relations?' Jemima asked, genuinely curious.

Miles shrugged. 'Seemed sensible at the time.'

'No, really,' she prompted. Miles didn't easily talk about himself, it seemed. He either turned the conversation or he gave a flip answer which made everyone laugh and forget about all about the question they'd asked. Was that a conscious technique he used? Her eyes narrowed astutely. 'I'd like to know.'

He appeared to hesitate for a moment and then he shrugged. It was a kind of victory. 'Oh, I gave design a chance. I set up a company out of a caravan in the Lake District with a friend from university. Dan and I came up with some fantastic ideas, but not surprisingly found it difficult to get anyone to take us seriously.'

He still smiled, but he seemed more guarded. She sensed he wasn't used to failure and he didn't speak about it easily.

'We were both twenty-two and very inexperienced. Not to mention that I came with an image that didn't inspire much confidence in the design world.' He shrugged again. 'In the end Dan decided he needed to eat and the idea folded.'

'That's a shame.'

Miles smiled. 'I couldn't blame him for that. I had an allowance paid into my bank account every month. Dan was on his own.'

Miles sounded as if he really minded. It surprised her. She'd been silly to think he was invincible and impenetrable to hurt—no one was. 'And then?' she asked after a moment.

'Then I sold my soul to the devil.' He smiled. 'Public relations was an obvious choice for someone with my background. I've been dealing with the media since I was in my mother's womb.'

She wasn't sure what to say. 'You're good at it.'

The blue of his eyes intensified as the laughter returned. 'Professional lying…?'

Jemima bit her lip. 'Sorry about that.'

'Don't apologise. I deserved it.'

'Yes, you did,' she said, cradling her hands around her mug. 'I wonder what Amanda will make of us not saying anything. It would have been much simpler to own up that we'd already met.'

He shook his head. 'I'd never have lived it down. Alistair would never have let me forget it.'

Miles watched as Jemima uncurled her hands from her mug. She really did have beautiful hands. They didn't need long nails and brightly coloured varnish. She looked fresh…and real. That was it. It had been a long time, he realised with a pang, since he'd spent any time with a woman who hadn't dressed to impress him. Or if not him specifically, men in general.

Jemima simply didn't care. Miles smiled, watching the way she was concentrating on the warmth her mug gave off. If anything she was reserving judgement on whether she liked him. That really did make a change.

Normally he was the centre of attention. He knew that he had to do the barest minimum to get a woman to accept a dinner invitation—assuming she was single and heterosexual. But Jemima…

He rather fancied he'd be whistling in the wind if he tried to get her to take him seriously. She was more concerned about her ceiling and what that might mean to her bank balance. He watched as she looked up at it and he could almost read the thoughts passing through her head.

Then she smiled at him, quite suddenly, and he felt the air freeze around him.

'It seems to be stopping. There's no point standing about in here. It's all a bit depressing. Let's go into the sitting room.'

'Okay,' he said, picking up his jacket.

She led the way back into the hall and along to the main reception room. 'Of course, it's a bit depressing in here too. Every time I sit in here I'm reminded of how much there is to do.'

The sitting room was exactly as he'd expected it would be. He'd seen many Victorian semis which had been 'improved' in just such a way during the sixties and seventies. The ceiling was covered with thick Artex, which would be both expensive and messy to remove, the walls were painted woodchip and the carpet was predominantly brown with overblown yellow roses on it.

Jemima followed the line of his gaze. 'My son thinks they look like cabbages.'

'It's all cosmetic stuff. Great the fireplace surround has survived.'

'Yes,' she agreed, curling up in one of the comfortable sofas like a kitten. 'It's a shame about the tiles.'

'You should be able to get the paint off. It would have been a disaster if they'd been chipped off.' Miles took the sofa opposite. He scarcely knew Jemima—didn't know Russell at all—but he felt a spurt of anger when he thought of the situation she'd been left in. The house had enormous potential, but it was a money pit.

It was a wonder she hadn't cried when she came home to discover she'd taken two steps forward and one back. It must be heartbreaking. And she'd faced it all with determination and a toss of that incredible red hair. It was courage…and he admired it.

He smiled as he thought of her, barefooted, bradawl in hand. Unconsciously sexy. It seemed he'd often thought that about her tonight. She was a woman without artifice—and he'd begun to think they didn't exist.

Miles sipped his coffee, watching her. Jemima had the most amazing skin. It was clear, almost translucent, with a smattering of freckles across her nose. Every other woman he knew would have covered them up with some magic concoction from Estée Lauder. But not Jemima…

Sun-kissed. *Sexy*. She had no idea how much he wanted to kiss her right now. He smiled. Probably just as well.

His eyes followed the line of the mantelpiece. There were photographs of two boys, both dark-haired. Handsome. The elder had serious green eyes, very like his mother's. The younger was full of fun. He looked uncomplicated, as though life didn't trouble him much.

Jemima's voice cut in on his thoughts. 'The photographer said "sausages".'

'Pardon?'

She nodded at the photographs. 'That's why he's laughing. Apparently it's very funny when you're five.'

'Which is which?' Miles asked, turning back to look at her.

'Ben is the elder. He's eight. Sam is five.'

Miles stood up and walked over to have a closer look. He had to keep remembering Jemima Chadwick was a single mum—with responsibilities. It put her firmly out of bounds. If a single mum was in the market for a no-strings relationship she shouldn't be.

Personal freedom was all well and good, but he knew first hand how it felt to be dragged through a series of short-term father-son relationships. How it felt to be without a secure base. Never quite knowing which 'special friend' his mother would have introduced into his home each holiday.

Occasionally, very occasionally, he'd like one or another, but their involvement in his life had always been brief. Miles didn't consider he had much of a code of honour, but, for what it was worth, this was his. He'd *never* let himself get involved with a woman who had children. It wasn't fair on the children.

Miles picked up the photograph of the elder child. Ben, wasn't it? He looked like a sensitive boy. Intelligent.

Not unlike how he'd looked as a child, he thought, taking in the guarded expression. Ben would find his father leaving him difficult to deal with. He knew it as certainly as if he'd been told. It was a betrayal, and betrayal dug deep. How could a child be expected to understand the full ramifications of adult emotions? The whys and the wherefores?

Even now, as an adult himself, he didn't really understand it all. No doubt a psychoanalyst would have a field day if he allowed them to delve into his motivations. He put the picture of Ben back down on the mantelpiece.

However tempted he might be, Jemima Chadwick would

remain unkissed. His eyes followed along the mantelpiece and he gave a cursory glance at the next cluster of photographs. Lots of smiling groups—more snapshots than formal portraiture. Presumably they were of extended family? Parents?

And…

He didn't quite believe what he was seeing. He looked closer, then over his shoulder. 'You know Verity Hunt?'

Was it his imagination or did Jemima curl up more tightly on the sofa? 'She's my sister.'

Verity Hunt? Jemima's sister? Miles looked again at the photograph, almost prepared to disbelieve her.

'Younger sister,' Jemima continued, as though it were nothing out of the ordinary. 'Imogen is the eldest. She's a homeopathic vet. Married, three children, three ponies, a house in Cheshire and a Danish au pair.'

'Sounds perfect,' Miles managed neutrally.

'I don't know about perfect, but it's a great place to go during the summer. She takes us in each year for a holiday. I've promised the boys we'll spend at least a week with them before they go back to school in September.'

Miles took a moment to look more closely at the picture of Imogen and her family. Of the two sisters, she was the most like Jemima, but she lacked the stunning hair. In any other circumstances her strawberry-blonde would have been dramatic. Against Jemima's vibrant mane it looked washed out and colourless.

Verity was completely different again. She had a gamine look and a smooth shining curtain of carefully highlighted chestnut hair.

Jemima pulled her legs in closer. 'Do you know Verity?'

'No.' He crossed back to the sofa and sat down. 'At least I've met her at a couple of parties, but I can't say I know her. We certainly don't handle her PR…but you must know that.'

It wasn't appropriate to say, but what he remembered most about Verity was that he'd thought her less beautiful than her photographs—something that wasn't uncommon with models. They had amazing bone structure and the camera loved them, but that didn't necessarily translate into a real beauty. Not the kind you wanted to find curled up under your duvet, anyway.

Nevertheless, she must be a difficult act to live up to. The homeopathic vet too. How hard was it to see your life disintegrating around you when your siblings were living the dream?

'I wondered whether you might know her. We don't look similar. Obviously.' Jemima smiled and he thought she looked sad. 'She's lovely. Both my sisters are.'

If Verity Hunt was so lovely, the question that begged to be asked was—why didn't she help with re-roofing the house? The sister with the three ponies and the Danish au pair didn't look like she was strapped for cash either.

Miles glanced across at Jemima. There was no way he could ask her that. It would be treading on far too personal ground. Her whole body language had mutated from that of a kitten to something entirely more wary.

'Verity lives abroad for most of the year,' Jemima continued tonelessly. 'She has a flat in Manhattan.' Then she shook her head. 'No, that's wrong. It's an *apartment*. I never remember to call it that. She also has a smaller place in Milan. It's tiny, but it has the most stunning roof terrace leading off the kitchen. She had an architect who—'

The telephone rang.

Jemima broke off and looked at her watch. Immediately her face paled and she threw the cushion on the floor. '*Oh, God*, I hope the boys…'

CHAPTER FIVE

MILES pulled himself forward on the sofa, draining the last of his coffee. It was too late for someone to be calling casually—well past midnight. Jemima was probably right to suspect the worst.

'Hello.'

There was a short silence. Miles put his mug down on the low 'apprentice' chest which served as a coffee table. He sat poised, ready to leave or to help, whatever was the most appropriate.

Jemima tucked her hair behind her ear. 'I've been out for dinner.' Another pause while the person on the other end spoke and then, 'I must have had my mobile switched off. I'm sorry. What's happened? Are the boys okay?'

It didn't take any imagination to realise she must be talking to the absent Russell. So why was she apologising to him? What for? It was entirely within her rights to turn her mobile on or off as she saw fit. And none of her ex-husband's business any more where she was.

Miles found himself wondering what Russell Chadwick would be like. What kind of man would Jemima have married? And what kind of man, for that matter, would walk away from a woman like Jemima?

Miles watched as Jemima's face took on an expression of

intense worry. *Something had happened to one of her boys*. He felt the low kick of dread as he observed the change in her. Her knuckles were white from the fierce hold she had on the receiver and there were deep frown lines in the centre of her forehead.

In a way he couldn't possibly explain, she suddenly seemed more beautiful. There was a luminosity to her that froze his breath. Just for a moment. Perhaps because he'd never seen what selfless love really looked like on a person.

Jemima would do anything, brave anything, for the people she loved deeply. It was written across her face. In his entire thirty-six years he wasn't sure he'd ever witnessed that kind of love. It was…awe-inspiring. And, in a strange way, it made him feel cheated. There was no one anywhere on earth who had ever felt that kind of love for him. Certainly not his mother. Hermione had her passions, but they'd never been centred around her only son. Currently she was in the Himalayas researching a new book and he doubted she would return for anything less than the news of his death.

Ben and Sam were lucky. They might never realise quite how much.

'I can't. The car's broken down.' Jemima glanced up at the clock. 'Perhaps I can call a cab…'

Miles spoke quietly. 'Where do you need to go?' Whatever it was that had happened, he couldn't drive away into the distance and leave her to deal with it alone. That was impossible. 'Can I help?'

Jemima pulled an agitated hand through her curls and stared at him as though she wasn't sure what she should say. 'Miles, I don't—' Then she broke off, clearly listening to her ex-husband on the other end of the phone.

Miles stood up, waiting.

She glanced across at him, then away, speaking into the phone. 'It's a friend. Hang on a second.' Jemima turned her incredible eyes, now full of worry, back towards him. 'It's Sam. My youngest. He's been sick and wants to come home.'

Miles felt his muscles relax. *Sick*. Nothing too serious, then. Just a little boy who would rather be with his mother. He could remember that feeling. Only his mother had been too busy to stay at home and nurse him. Whereas Jemima…

There was no question but that she'd move heaven and earth to make things right for her son. However awkward she might find accepting another favour from him, Miles knew that she'd do it. And, strangely, there was no doubt that he'd do what he could to help.

Miles felt the stirrings of a smile. *What exactly was he getting himself into?* Somewhere up there someone clearly had an acute sense of humour, he thought as he experienced a momentary pang at the prospect of his precious Bristol 407 carrying a child who might well vomit.

'Do you need to go and fetch him?' he asked quietly.

'Ben's asleep and Russell doesn't want to wake—'

'Tell him we're on our way.' Miles didn't wait to hear what Jemima had to say. He shrugged on his jacket, catching only the edge of her smile. It was still enough to blow him away.

He was going to have to watch it. She was the kind of woman who might well get under your skin and stay there.

Jemima spoke into the receiver. 'Russell, I'm coming now. Tell Sam. Fifteen minutes and I'll be there.' She put the phone back into its cradle. 'Are you sure? I'm so sorry.'

'Don't waste time.' Miles smiled at her. He didn't want her gratitude. It seemed to him she'd spent a surfeit of her time being grateful to other people who may or may not deserve it. And he genuinely wanted to help her. He'd caught only the slightest glimpse of what her life was like…and it was the least he could do.

'No. I'll…' She tucked her hair behind her ears again in a

nervous gesture. 'Right, I'd better fetch an old ice cream tub in case he feels unwell in the car…'

As she disappeared into the kitchen Miles thrust a hand through his hair. *Old ice cream tub?* Alistair wouldn't believe the way his evening was panning out, even if he told him—and he'd absolutely no intention of ever doing that.

Miles waited in the hall as Jemima flew past him.

'I'm going to grab the duvet off Sam's bed. I won't be a second.' She turned at the top of the stairs, stopping halfway up to say, 'Stuff it! I've left the ice cream tub on the island in the kitchen. Could you—'

'I'll fetch it. Get the duvet.'

Another first. Miles couldn't remember ever having spent the evening with a woman who'd ended up thinking absolutely nothing about him. Her attention was entirely focused on her son. Jemima would probably have driven off with the devil incarnate if it would have got her to Sam quickly. He admired her for that.

Miles smiled and walked through to the kitchen. He picked up the empty tub and pulled a face, hoping it hadn't been used for this particular purpose before and wouldn't be this time either. Beside the tub there was a small jar of Calpol. Without reading the label it looked medicinal, so he picked it up as well.

He came back into the hallway as Jemima was hurrying down the stairs with a duvet wrapped into a tight roll under one arm. She'd grabbed a pale green cardigan in soft angora. She looked…charming. Unconsciously charming. He cleared his throat. 'Do you want this?' he asked, holding up the bottle.

'Yes. Thanks. It's liquid paracetamol.' Jemima picked her handbag up from the hall chair. 'It's great for bringing temperatures down. Of course, it'll be no good if Sam's actually being sick…'

Miles held out the ice cream tub, trying not to think about that.

'It's okay. It's got a lid,' she said with a sudden smile, obviously able to read his expression.

The green wool of her cardigan intensified the colour of her eyes. He felt his mouth curve in an answering smile. 'Don't say it.' He stopped her, taking the duvet off her and giving her the tub. 'I don't want to know. That's advanced parenting and I'm strictly the chauffeur.'

Her smile widened. 'You know, I'm really grateful—'

He gave her a gentle push in the small of her back. 'Just go.'

She was lovely. If anyone had told him at the start of the evening he'd be driving through Harrow in the early hours of the morning to collect a sick child for his temporary secretary, he wouldn't have believed it. Miles glanced across at Jemima's profile. It felt right, though.

He wouldn't swap his life with hers for anything. She carried such responsibilities. Where in all of it was time for herself? Did she ever have a moment where she could think about absolutely nothing but herself and what she wanted? Somehow he doubted it and he wished...

Jemima looked across at him. 'What?'

Miles focused back on the road. He couldn't put words on what he was thinking. He didn't really understand what they were himself. 'Where now?'

'Take the second left at the next roundabout and follow the road on. There are a couple of T-junctions, but you need to keep going straight.'

'Okay.' There was silence for a few moments. Miles concentrated on the road, but was acutely aware of Jemima sitting beside him. Every now and again she shifted slightly in her seat, or brushed her hair away from her face. Small, totally insignificant movements, but for some reason he was aware of them.

He swallowed and searched for something to say. *That*

was a first too. Not since he was thirteen had he struggled for something to say to a member of the opposite sex.

It didn't make sense. Any of it.

'It's straight on here.'

Miles changed gear to negotiate the roundabout. 'Why couldn't Russell drive Sam home?' he asked without looking across at her.

'Ben's asleep and he didn't want to wake him. Didn't I say that?'

'I don't know.' Miles frowned. He couldn't remember her telling him that, but he was sure she'd told him her ex-husband had a girlfriend. *Stefanie*, wasn't it? Or maybe he was leaping to conclusions and they didn't live together. It was none of his business, but he really wanted to know.

'Does he live alone?' he asked carefully.

He felt her head shake in denial. 'He's bought the flat with his girlfriend, but…' Jemima paused to consider what she was going to say '…she…isn't particularly maternal, apparently.'

'Then why get involved with a man who has two children?' he asked without thinking.

Jemima smiled and brushed at her hair. 'Makes you wonder, doesn't it? Russell really loves the boys too, so she's on to a loser if she thinks he'll forget about them. He won't. If it's a choice between her and the boys, he'll pick the boys.' She sat back in her seat. 'But I suppose Stefanie didn't know that about him when they got together.' Her eyes flicked across to him. 'They met at work. So she wouldn't necessarily have known what she was taking on, would she?'

Anyone with an ounce of sense would factor that in as a significant risk. Miles made a non-committal response. He could see why Stefanie might not want to drive a sick boy to her boyfriend's ex-wife, but where was the problem with taking care of a sleeping child?

'You take a left at the next junction.'

Miles made the turn. 'Is she at the flat tonight?'

'I don't know. I didn't ask.' Jemima looked at him. 'It wouldn't make any difference. Ben doesn't like her. Russell couldn't leave him with her in case he woke up while he was out. If that happened he'd have a difficult job to get him to stay again.'

Interesting. But still none of his business, Miles reminded himself. He couldn't help but admire the way Jemima had carefully avoided being vitriolic towards her ex-husband or his new girlfriend. That was rare, in his experience. Most people couldn't resist the opportunity to dish the dirt. Human nature, he supposed.

But Jemima hadn't done that. For the second time in a very short space of time it occurred to him how lucky Ben and Sam were in their mother. It clearly cost her to let her boys see their father regularly, but she did absolutely nothing to get in the way of it. Contrast that with his own mother, who'd made it her personal mission to make sure he didn't have a male role model anywhere in his life.

'It's here,' Jemima said, pointing a little way up the wide tree-lined road. 'Just after the next junction. On the left.'

Russell Chadwick might live in a flat, but it was an expensive one. Miles felt a simmering anger when he compared the elegant art deco façade with the run-down family home he'd conceded to his ex-wife. The man ought to be horse-whipped.

Jemima was out of the car seconds after he'd pulled to a stop. 'I won't be long.'

Miles watched as she hurried up the steps and bent to speak into a metal grid on the side wall. She pushed the door open and disappeared inside the entrance.

Miles stood with his back against the bonnet of his car. The street lights were amber orbs in a dark clear sky...and it was cold. He pulled up his jacket collar and tucked his hands into the pockets.

What was he doing here? Saturday night… No, it was Sunday morning. But the question remained the same. What in heaven's name had possessed him to be here doing this? He never…

The door opened and Jemima appeared carrying a small backpack. A man with a young boy in his arms was closely behind her. *Sam's father?* It had to be. Miles stood straight. As they walked down the steps he opened the car door and pulled the front seat forward, turning back to face them.

'This is Russell,' Jemima said as soon as she was close enough. 'Sam, climb in the back and I'll come and sit next to you.'

Russell lowered the pyjama-clad boy to the ground and he scrambled into the back seat. Even in the dark Miles could see that Sam's face was pale and entirely miserable. Miles watched as Jemima smiled encouragingly at her son and leant in to hand the ice cream tub across. The backpack she tucked in the front.

Miles turned his attention to Sam's father. Russell Chadwick looked ordinary. He was of average height, average build and of average colouring. Miles felt a curious sense of relief. God only knew why.

Jemima stood straight. 'Sorry, I should have introduced you properly. Russell, this is Miles Kingsley.'

Automatically Miles held out his hand, his eyes firmly meeting Russell Chadwick's. Unlike Jemima, who appeared to be thinking of nothing but her son, he was completely aware of what Russell was assuming about why he was here and what that must mean about Jemima's relationship with him. Moreover, he was fairly sure the other man didn't like it.

'Miles,' Russell said.

He nodded in acknowledgment.

Russell put his hands in his trouser pockets. 'It was good of you to come and pick Sam up.'

This was probably a clear case of too much testosterone, but Miles didn't like Russell Chadwick one bit. He smiled. 'Jemima only had to ask. She's very special.'

He watched the dawning recognition in the other man's eyes that they had locked antlers as sure as if they were two stags. Miles couldn't remember when he'd disliked a man more.

'Sam's not at all well.'

'So I gathered. I was with Jemima when you phoned.' Miles resisted the temptation to add, *We were about to go to bed.* It wouldn't have been true…and he wasn't sure whether Jemima would play along with it.

Russell shuffled his feet. 'I'd tried to get her earlier.'

It was a gift. Irresistible. 'Yes, we'd not long walked through the door,' Miles replied and put a deliberate arm round Jemima's waist.

He'd intended it to be punishment for the man who'd hurt Jemima so much, a physical act of support, but as soon as his fingers splayed out on the soft curve of her hip he forgot that original purpose.

Russell Chadwick could have fallen down dead on the pavement and Miles wouldn't have noticed. Nothing about her ex-husband mattered. His fingers were alive to the fact that he was touching Jemima. Beneath his hand she was soft and warm.

This close to her, he could smell the soft scent of her perfume, so light it hovered at the edge of his consciousness. He could see the tiny pulse beating in her neck. He was used to being around women, but the effect of the long white column of her neck and the dark burnished copper of her hair sent his libido into the stratosphere.

And then she looked up—her pale face surrounded by that

cloud of red curls, her mouth softly parted and her eyes a shimmering green…

It felt natural. Inevitable. He was going to kiss her. He knew it and the flare in her green eyes told him she knew it too. Miles moved slowly and caught the soft 'oh' she uttered in his mouth. His hands spread out on the linen of her dress, feeling the curves that lay beneath it.

His head was pounding with her name. He could never have expected how amazing this would feel. Her lips were warm and pliant beneath his. It was just a kiss… Not important, he thought as he let his tongue flick out. She was… *Oh, God.*

Who was he trying to kid? There were kisses and there were kisses. Miles pulled her in closer as he deepened the kiss. The temptation was to let his hands slide down over the gentle curves of her buttocks. Pull her in really close.

She was lovely. Really, really lovely.

He heard the soft murmur in the back of her throat, whether passion or protest he didn't know. And then Jemima moved to rest her hands against his chest. Every sinew in his body resisted, but he obediently pulled back to look into her eyes. She was so near he could feel her breath on his lips. *What was she thinking?*

'Sam,' she said huskily, her green eyes darker than he'd ever seen them.

It was a moment before he realised she was talking about her son, sitting feet away in the car. Regretfully Miles moved away. He felt cold without her. Shaken. 'We'd better get him home.'

'Y-yes.' Jemima gave him a half smile and moved towards the car. 'Bye, Russell. I'll see you tomorrow,' she said carelessly over her right shoulder.

It was beautifully done. It would have left Russell with exactly the impression Miles had intended, but…*what had he been thinking of?*

This wasn't a game. Despite every promise he'd ever made to himself about never getting mixed up with a single mother, he'd kissed her. And it was addictive. He knew exactly how it felt to have her soft curves pushed up against him and he knew he wanted more…

But that wasn't going to happen. He wasn't the kind of man who was capable of stepping in to play happy families. He had no experience of one. Nothing to contribute. Miles walked round to the driver's side, climbed in and shut the door.

He'd wanted to help her and yet he'd just made everything extremely complicated. If Rachel got wind of the fact he was messing about with the emotions of her friend she'd be justifiably angry. Alistair had warned him Jemima was brittle. She'd described herself as 'walking wounded' and the last thing he wanted to do was hurt her any more than she'd already been hurt.

Damn it! He should have remembered that… He shouldn't have tried to play stupid mind games with a man he probably wouldn't see again… He shouldn't…

'Miles?'

He looked over his shoulder. Half of Jemima's face was in shadow, but he knew she was smiling.

'Thank you,' she said softly.

Two tiny words and yet they had the power to remove any sense of regret. In the mirror he met her steady green gaze. She'd understood exactly why he'd kissed her…and she was grateful.

'You're welcome.'

Jemima glanced over her shoulder and gave a tiny wave to Russell, who was still standing on the pavement. 'I don't think he quite believes it.'

'Oh, I don't know,' Miles said, glancing in his wing mirror. Russell Chadwick looked like a man in shock to him. Perhaps he'd just been reminded of how fantastic the woman he'd walked out on was. He certainly hoped so.

Miles set the car in first gear as she gave a soft laugh, halfway between a gurgle and a hiccup. *Jemima was entirely surprising*...and she was *very* welcome. In fact, he'd be happy to kiss her any time she liked—with or without the audience. Except, of course, he wouldn't. Kissing Jemima Chadwick was a very foolish thing to do.

'Do you need me to direct you back?' Jemima asked, leaning forward.

Miles shook his head. 'I can remember the way.'

He heard her settle back in her seat. Another swift glance in his rear-view mirror saw Jemima place her arm around her son with the other hand clutching the empty ice cream tub.

'How is he doing?' Miles smiled to himself in the darkness. *Perhaps he didn't want to know the answer to that*.

'Who are you?' A young voice spoke from the depths of the blanket. 'Mum, why aren't we in our car?'

Jemima answered him in a matter of fact voice. 'Because it's broken down again. I had to leave it outside Rachel's house.'

'But who is he?'

Miles let his eyes flick to the rear-view mirror again. For one moment his gaze locked with Jemima's, no doubt they were both wondering whether Sam had seen the kiss. That had been such an irresponsible thing for him to do. The thought that a vulnerable five-year-old might be watching hadn't occurred to him.

Jemima broke eye-contact first. 'This is Miles, Sam. He's Alistair's best friend and he offered to help me come to get you when Daddy rang to say you were not feeling very well.'

'Oh.' And then, after a pause, 'He's got a very small car.'

Miles couldn't help but listen while Jemima explained about classic cars and how some people enjoyed driving really old cars and liked to get together with other people who drove the same sort of old car. It was a kind of club, she said.

He glanced back via the mirror. Hearing his passion put into words like that made it seem rather ridiculous—and he got the feeling she was doing it deliberately. Jemima might have been bruised by her life experiences, but inside she had a wicked sense of humour which was bubbling just beneath the surface.

And he liked the sound of her voice. It was the kind of pitch that sat easily on the ears. She could probably read a telephone directory and make it sound like Wordsworth. It had an innate musicality to it.

In fact, he realised with a shock, he liked *her*. Genuinely...liked her.

Miles pulled up outside her house, reversing neatly into a tight space. He heard Jemima murmur, 'We're home, sweetheart,' as he climbed out and walked round to the passenger side, pulling the front seat forward.

Jemima unwound herself from the tight seating position and stood on the pavement. She pushed back her bright curls as the wind caught them. 'Well, we made it without mishap,' she said, holding up the ice cream tub.

He felt a smile curve his mouth. 'I'm not disappointed about that.'

'I bet.' Then her smile faltered. 'Miles, thank you.' She stopped awkwardly. 'It's really late and I'm—'

Miles stopped her with a shake of the head and a light brush of his fingers against her cheek. He probably shouldn't have done that either. It was those eyes. Truly like windows into the soul—and her soul was beautiful. *She* was beautiful. How had he missed that during the past two weeks?

And she wasn't interested in him. He could see that from the wary look that flashed into her green eyes. In front of her ex-husband she might let him kiss her, but now... It was a clear no.

Salutary.

He didn't think it had ever happened before.

Miles moved backwards. 'Is Sam in his slippers? Do you want me to carry him in?'

'I can manage.' She leant into the car. 'Out you come, Sam. Let's get you into bed.' Her voice was brusque and capable, much more like the Jemima Chadwick he knew from the office.

Sam emerged wrapped in a blanket, his dark hair tousled and his eyes big and shining. Clutched in his hand was the duvet and it was immediately obvious that Jemima wasn't going to be able to carry everything.

'Leave the duvet, sweetheart. Let's get you inside and I'll come back for it in a minute.'

Miles looked directly at Sam. 'Do you mind if I carry you into the house for your mum? Then she can bring in all your things.'

The eyes, just peeking out from the top of the blanket, seemed to consider it for a moment and then a small voice said, 'I don't mind.'

Miles bent down and picked him up. He was surprisingly heavy.

Jemima looked at them briefly and then bent to pull out the overnight bag and duvet. 'Thanks,' she said, shutting the car door. 'How do I lock it?'

'Don't worry about it. It's late, there's no one around and I'll be gone in a minute.'

Jemima rummaged in her handbag for her front door keys. 'Sorry, I should have got these out earlier. I'm keeping you waiting…'

Miles shifted Sam in his arms. 'How are you feeling?' he asked him, thinking he should say something.

'Better.'

'That's good.'

The eyes looked at him steadily. 'I hate being sick.'

'Everyone does.' Miles watched as Jemima hurriedly opened the front door. 'There you go,' he said to Sam as he lowered him inside. Then he looked up at Jemima and felt…tongue-tied.

What did you say to your temporary secretary whose young son was watching and who you wanted to kiss again very much? There was only one thing that could be said. He stepped backwards. 'I'll leave you to it. He looks like he ought to be in bed.'

'I know.' Her hand came out to rest on her son's head, her long fingers moving through the dark curls. 'I don't know how I would have managed without you…'

'It was nothing.' Miles raised a hand in a gesture of goodbye and walked back towards the car. The front door shut before he was even halfway there. He took a moment to look back. His smile was self-deprecating. It had been a strange evening. Very strange.

And Jemima Chadwick….

Without question she was a very interesting woman—and, for entirely different reasons than before, he still wasn't sure what to make of her.

CHAPTER SIX

MONDAY morning seemed to whip round more quickly than Jemima could have believed possible. There hadn't been time to draw breath, let alone decide how it would be best to play the day ahead of her.

Before she knew it she was squeezed into an overcrowded tube carriage and heading into Covent Garden. Commuting wasn't an activity she found particularly conducive to thought, but she was tending towards the idea that the only sensible thing to do was to carry on exactly as before. She could take her cue from Miles as to whether he wanted to acknowledge at work that they had mutual friends.

And the kiss?

Was probably best forgotten.

Sam didn't seem to have seen it. At least he hadn't mentioned any kiss and she thought he would have done if he'd observed anything. So that was good, but it hadn't stopped her thinking about it. Throughout most of yesterday, if she were honest. Jemima smiled to herself. It had been…lovely.

She'd always thought kissing was a little overrated, but that was because she hadn't been kissed by an expert before. When she stopped to think about it, it made sense really that there would be virtuosos in kissing as in everything else. Clearly

Miles Kingsley was one of those. Her insides seemed to curl up at the edges when she thought about how it had felt.

Miles had made her feel…priceless. For those few moments she'd felt spectacularly desirable. Of course she knew it was an illusion. One glance in her bedroom mirror had told her that. In reality she was a slightly overweight mother of two who needed to do some abdominal exercises before she could do justice to any of the clothes in her wardrobe, borrowed or otherwise.

Besides, it hadn't meant anything. It wasn't as though Miles had been overcome with passion. He'd only kissed her to support her in front of Russell. *She could almost fall in love with him for that alone.* Jemima smiled again. It might not be particularly mature, but it had felt fantastic seeing Russell's reaction as they'd driven away. Just the possibility that he might have believed a man like Miles could seriously be in love with her was so funny. Absolutely, delightfully…funny.

Jemima walked round from Leicester Square towards the Kingsley and Bressington building, her stomach beginning to churn in anticipation of… She wasn't quite sure what. It couldn't be the prospect of seeing Miles because she wasn't that stupid. There was nothing about a man like Miles Kingsley that made him right for her even if… Well, if…

She preferred to think her newfound sense of optimism came from a belief in the infinite possibilities of life. Despite the leaky bathroom and the prospect of losing the boys for two whole weeks when Russell took them to Spain on holiday she felt…hopeful.

Of course, it would have been better if she could have conjured up a stunning designer outfit for work this morning. Something spectacular that would have assuaged the wound to her feminine pride caused by the 'dresses like her mother' jibe.

But that wasn't a possibility. She was back in Joshua's

mum's perfectly sensible, if a little dull, redundant work clothes. She couldn't justify it with her conscience to siphon off part of her first pay cheque when Ben needed new school shoes, even though it was so near the end of term and his feet were bound to grow another size before September.

Besides, the whole purpose of taking a temp job this side of the school holidays was that she'd have some money to take the boys out over the summer break and she'd already promised them a trip to Legoland.

But it would have been nice to have bought a new dress. Just one. Jemima allowed herself a small sigh and pushed open the door to Kingsley and Bressington, taking consolation from the fact that she'd allowed herself a little more time than usual to straighten her hair and had made a fairly good job of smearing on a touch of make-up. Nothing so revolutionary that Miles would notice—or comment on. She couldn't bear it if he thought she was taking the kiss thing too seriously and making an effort for him. She'd die of embarrassment.

The door to his office when she got there was, thankfully, shut. Jemima opened the tall cupboard and carefully tucked her handbag towards the back, glad she had a moment or two to settle herself.

'How is he?'

Jemima jumped at the sound of his voice. She whirled round with a gasp.

Miles smiled, leaning nonchalantly against the door frame. 'Sorry, I didn't mean to startle you.'

'I hadn't realised you were here yet,' she said, feeling foolish. He was in another sharp suit. He must own hundreds. This one was more black than grey and the tie was the colour of a ripe Victoria plum. The overall effect was, frankly, very sexy.

'I was in at seven. How's Sam doing?'

'He's fine.' Her voice sounded breathless, even to her own

ears. Her throat had constricted so much it was difficult to get any words out at all. She'd thought Miles in casual wear was more lethal than Miles in a city suit, but she discovered she was wrong.

He seemed even sexier than before—*now she knew what it felt like to be kissed by him,* that voice in her head whispered. More intimidating too—*now she'd been kissed by him.*

Oh…*hell.*

She had to stop thinking like this. Jemima made a determined effort not to let her eyes wander to his lips and tried again. 'I think Sam must have eaten too many sweets because he was fine all day Sunday. Nothing the matter with him at all.'

Much better, she thought, turning away to lock the cupboard door. Cool, calm and composed. That was what she was aiming for.

'I wasn't really expecting you in today.'

Jemima's stomach fell something like three feet and her body temperature plummeted. *Why?* Why wouldn't she be in to work today? Why would Miles think that? Had she embarrassed him by too enthusiastically responding to his kiss? Her mind conjured up an image of the way she'd melted against him…

Oh, God. Please, no. She hadn't mumbled incoherently, had she? Had she seemed too grateful for the attention?

She was going to die of mortification if he thought she thought he'd meant it all seriously. She hadn't for one moment considered that he'd be expecting her not to turn up. She'd promised Amanda she'd stick out the full assignment whatever happened and…

Miles cut across her panicked thoughts. 'Sam looked so woebegone. I thought he'd certainly be off school today and want you with him. If you need to be there for him, just put seven and a half hours down for today regardless and go home.'

Jemima couldn't quite believe Miles had just offered to pay her for a day she didn't work. She'd *never* let him do that. It was kind, but…

Why would he do that for her? He hardly knew her—and the fact that her best friend was marrying his best friend hardly constituted a friendship.

'He's fine. Really.'

'You're sure?'

'Yes.' *He must feel really sorry for her.* Jemima hated the way everyone seemed to feel so sorry for her. She was so…tired of being an object of pity. It irked her that she had been forced to accept so much help. It was kind of everyone, but…

Couldn't they see that only part of the reason behind her trying to build some kind of career for herself was financial? The other part was a desire for independence. She wanted to prove to herself, to her family…to Russell…that she could manage perfectly well on her own.

Miles must have been able to read something of what she was thinking because he added quickly, 'If it would help I could send you home with a couple of audio tapes and you could email everything through later on.'

Jemima shook her head. 'That's really nice of you, but Sam's absolutely okay and back at school.' She nodded as though to emphasise the truth of what she'd said, then walked over and sat behind her desk. There was no need to add that it wasn't an option anyway since her computer, like her car, had given up the ghost.

'I'm glad he's feeling so much better,' Miles said, straightening up and pulling a hand through his hair. She then watched, fascinated, as a smile twisted his sensual mouth. 'I suppose,' he said slowly, 'I'm still haunted by the prospect of him actually using the ice cream tub—'

She went to speak, but Miles stopped her.

'—even if it did have a lid.'

Jemima felt a bubble of laughter form in the pit of her stomach. 'I wasn't going to say that.'

'Really?'

His eyebrows lifted the merest fraction, but it brought her laughter to the surface. 'Okay. No, you're right. I was going to say that,' she conceded. She pulled back a wayward strand of hair and re-clipped it tightly in her simple hairgrip. 'But the lid is important. It keeps—'

'I get the picture.'

Jemima laughed again and leant forward to boot up her computer.

He seemed to hesitate for a moment and then he asked, 'Have you had a chance to speak to your plumber this morning?'

She shook her head, before keying in the password. 'I did try his mobile before I got on the tube but it was switched off. I left a message and I'll give it another go when I go for a coffee break later.'

'If there's any problem with getting him to come back, I've got the number of my plumber with me. He's good. I've worked with him on the last three projects. His name is Steve Baldock.'

Jemima looked up. 'Thanks.'

'It's in my briefcase. Let me know if you want it.'

'I will, thanks.'

'It makes sense to ring the man you used first. If he's to blame he'll have to have put it right without charging you.'

'Yes, I know.'

Miles hesitated, as though he would like to have continued talking. He looked as uncomfortable as she felt. *Strange*. Then he pulled a hand through his dark hair again. 'I suppose I'd better get on,' he said abruptly.

Perhaps he felt uncomfortable about the change in their relationship. He needn't worry. She wasn't about to take advantage of the fact that they had mutual friends.

'I'll grab a coffee, if that's okay? Then I'll get started on all this,' she said, indicating the large pile of files and papers he'd placed in her in-tray some time between when she'd left on Friday and now. 'I missed breakfast this morning. Hopefully the caffeine will stave off my craving for chocolate until lunch time.'

'Was it a rush to get out?'

Jemima stood up. 'It's always a rush in my house. This morning it was a particular disaster because Ben suddenly remembered he'd forgotten to learn his spellings for a test they're having today. He should've done them over the weekend but, of course, he was with Russell.'

'Couldn't he take them with him?'

'He could, but how many eight-year-olds do you know can manage to organise their work like that? Ben forgets about things like homework the minute he walks out the school gate.' She paused at the door. 'I'm going to have to remember to make a point of asking him when I get in. Do you want a coffee?'

'That would be great. Thanks.' Miles stepped back and closed the door to his office. What was happening to him? He couldn't quite believe he'd offered to pay her for a day she didn't work. He thrust a hand through his hair. He hadn't meant to say that; the words had seemed to say themselves.

Jemima had changed, but more worryingly *he* had changed. The truth was he didn't know anything about how eight-year-olds organised their homework. He'd never before experienced the slightest interest in the subject, but he found he was very interested in Jemima. By extension that seemed to mean he was interested in her sons. And he certainly felt an overwhelming compulsion to try and help her.

Why was that? He liked to think he was a fairly compassionate person, but Jemima's problems were just that—hers. He shouldn't be trying to think of ways to make her life simpler. She was a grown woman, more than capable of finding an alternative plumber by herself if she needed one.

Miles frowned and walked across to the window. There was nothing much to see, just a narrow London street typical of the area. He let out his breath in a controlled stream.

He hadn't known what to expect from this morning. From Jemima or himself. How he would feel about working with her, seeing her…

He'd told her that he hadn't expected her to be at work today, but actually that had been a lie. He *had* expected her to be there. In fact, he'd been watching the clock and listening out for her arrival—not consciously, but he'd known the minute she'd walked into the office. He'd heard the door open and had been on his feet.

Jemima, he'd decided, was big on duty. If she said she'd do something then it would have to be something truly catastrophic to make her break her word. She'd come in to work— and he'd wanted to make it easy for her to go home again.

But…offering to pay a temporary secretary for a day not worked was surely taking it all a bit too far.

Of course, he hadn't liked the idea of Sam being sent to a childminder and desperately wanting his mum—and he knew why that was. It was an uncomfortable echo of his own childhood and Sam's small pale face peeking out from a blanket was a haunting image.

But it was none of his business. Jemima Chadwick was a friend of a friend, his very temporary secretary, and her life was absolutely none of his business.

Damn it! Miles turned abruptly from the window and went to sit down at his desk. He picked up his pen and idly started to twist it between his long fingers. Jemima was also a single mother with responsibilities. And that was the one reason above all others why he shouldn't be contemplating any kind of relationship with her.

Miles started drawing straight lines on his pad of paper and then put in the horizontal ones. He needed to focus on how hurt children could get when the adults in their life brought home new partners. *He'd* been hurt when his own mother had done it.

Miles shaded in a couple of the small boxes. He wasn't even particularly comfortable with finding a mother sexually attractive. There was something wrong with that somehow. As though the two things were, or at least should be, mutually exclusive.

But, astoundingly, he was attracted to Jemima. No question about that. She'd returned to her work uniform—but it wasn't as good a camouflage as before. Her hair might be pulled straight and drawn back in a way that concealed how stunning it could look, but he wasn't fooled. Beneath the conventional and dull clothes was someone altogether more interesting.

And he knew what it felt like to kiss her...

The door opened and he had to watch Jemima as she carried in his coffee. He remembered her green eyes wide with surprise and the small gasp she'd made as he'd finally closed the distance between them. Then there was the way her body had felt so soft and inviting, the way she'd responded.

Jemima placed his coffee carefully on the leather coaster—and it was difficult to make his throat work. 'Thanks.' His voice sounded husky.

He couldn't quite place what it was that had made that kiss feel so special. He'd kissed many, many women over the past two decades, but he wasn't sure he'd ever experienced anything quite like it. There'd been a...sweetness about it—and he wanted to kiss her again.

'You're welcome. It's an addiction, though.'

Jemima smiled at him and he felt his mouth curve into an inane grin. 'I know.' It wasn't just the coffee that was addictive. 'And I'm told it stains my teeth.'

Her mouth quirked with suppressed laughter. 'Who dared tell you that?'

'Some people have no ability socially, so one has to make allowances,' he said, loving the sparkle that appeared in her usually serious eyes.

Miles twisted the pen in his hand. There was nothing contrived or artificial about Jemima. How had he missed that? He should have been able to see past the unflattering clothes to notice how beautiful she really was from the very beginning.

'It's quite true that coffee stains your teeth, though,' Jemima said, turning back towards the door. 'I read it somewhere. Did you also know that champagne gives you halitosis?'

'Is that true?'

'No idea. Bit depressing if it is.'

Miles let the laughter warm his eyes. 'Very.'

'Though I don't know why I say that. I don't actually like champagne.'

Didn't she? 'What do you drink?'

'From choice?'

He nodded.

'Pimms, I think. During the summer, anyway.' Jemima's hand was on the door handle. 'Or a nice dry white wine. I'm not particularly fussed about the country of origin or the price of the bottle because I think it's a con.'

'Do you?' he asked with a faint lift of his expressive eyebrows, knowing that she would understand why. He wasn't disappointed. He watched with enjoyment as Jemima bit her lip.

'You're a wine connoisseur, aren't you?'

Miles burst out laughing. ''Fraid so.'

'Oops.' She shot him a mischievous smile. 'I wouldn't have said that if I'd known. That would have been rude.'

'I don't believe you,' Miles said softly, watching for her reaction.

Jemima gave a rich chuckle as she went out and shut the door. It was strange how he'd thought she was so serious when he'd first met her. Despite all the troubles and disappointments of her life, the one thing that had emerged intact was her sense of humour.

Quiet, disciplined, conscientious—all those things were still true, but there was a hidden side of her personality. It was a side he longed to know more about.

But at what cost? Particularly to her. He needed to remember that Jemima had troubles enough without the complication of a man like him wafting in and out of her life. And 'temporary' was all he wanted…or was capable of.

Jemima spread some butter on her toast. The trouble with mornings, in her opinion, was that they happened too early. She needed at least a couple of coffees in her system before she was ready to face the day. She smiled. Better not let Miles suspect that about her.

'Ben. Sam,' she called. 'Hurry up and come downstairs for breakfast. I've made porridge.' She listened to the absolute silence above. 'Grandma will be here in a minute.'

She glanced down at her wrist-watch. At least she hoped Grandma would be here in a minute or she was going to be cutting it fine to get to work by nine-thirty. Her third week at Kingsley and Bressington had flown by. Halfway through her stint there she could almost say she was enjoying it.

Having had no interest in public relations before she'd

started at Kingsley and Bressington she'd developed a healthy respect for it. Certainly a respect for Miles. He was absolutely brilliant at what he did and the hours he put in were punishing.

Unbelievably, she was going to miss it all when it was over. *Miss Miles* too, if she were honest, though she'd seen less of him this week than in the previous two. For much of the time he'd been shut away in his office, emerging only for long working lunches. Yesterday almost the only sign he was in the building was the enormous pile of work he'd left in her in-tray.

Nevertheless there was a buzz about working at Kingsley and Bressington and there was always the prospect of seeing Miles. A five minute conversation with him and her day seemed that little bit brighter. It was probably just as well her time working for him was limited.

'Ben. Can you hear me?' She bit into her toast as the telephone started to ring.

Chewing quickly, she grabbed the phone. 'Hello.'

'Jemima, I'm so glad I caught you,' Rachel began, her voice sounding strained, though that might have been because the reception was so poor.

'Wherever are you?' Jemima asked, frowning. 'You sound like you're in a dishwasher.'

'I'm at the airport.'

'Airport?' She hadn't expected that reply. Rachel never travelled abroad for work, so what was she doing there? Jemima looked up as Ben walked sleepily into the kitchen. She motioned for him to sit at the breakfast bar.

'It's Alistair's dad. He's had some kind of haemorrhage. His stepmother called and said we need to fly out to be there…in case.'

Jemima felt as if she'd stumbled into one of those television adverts where you could freeze time but still be functioning yourself. Everything around her seemed to stop. There was just her moving about as she walked over to put her toast down on a plate. 'Is it serious?'

'Apparently.' The line crackled, making it difficult to hear. 'Jemima, are you still there?'

'Yes, I'm here.'

'He's lost a lot of blood, but I think the concern is that they don't know why it happened. It's going to be a while before we know.'

'How's Alistair?' Jemima asked quickly.

'He just wants to get out to Canada as soon as we possibly can. He's telephoned his mum and let her know…'

Jemima pulled her mind into focus. She needed to think clearly and logically. 'Okay. Right. What do you need me to do?' she asked, sitting down on the bar stool next to Ben.

By the time Rachel had finished speaking she had a list which ranged from asking the next door neighbour if she would push the post through the door to hiring a marquee for the wedding.

'Are you okay with all that?' Rachel asked.

Jemima wrote the word 'medieval' next to the word 'marquee' as a reminder—though she was unlikely to forget. How did you go about finding a medieval-style marquee for a wedding in rural Kent at such short notice?

'Fine,' she said, trying to imbue her voice with confidence. 'I'll work my way down your list. If you think of anything else…' Jemima gave up trying to say anything for a moment because it was obvious Rachel hadn't got a hope in hell of catching what she was saying.

She drew a deep breath and read down Rachel's list.

'Alistair has rung Miles to let him know what's happened,' Rachel said as soon as the line cleared a fraction.

'Miles?'

'Miles Kingsley. His best man. You met him at dinner.'

'Oh, yes,' Jemima said, cursing herself for being all kinds of a fool.

'Do you want his number?'

Dutifully Jemima jotted down the telephone number of Kingsley and Bressington. It would have been so much easier now, would have felt so much more honest, if she'd owned up that she was working there temporarily.

Rachel continued, 'He said he'd help. That's his work number, but I think he practically lives there.'

'Okay, I'll get in contact with him.'

She heard her mother's key in the front door. 'Jemima?'

'Hang on a second,' she said to Rachel. 'In the kitchen, Mum. I'm on the phone.'

The line broke up again, so much that it was impossible to hear what was being said.

'Will you let me know how Alistair's dad is doing?' Jemima said in the hope that Rachel was hearing her better. She ripped off the front sheet of her lined A4 pad and tucked it into the side pocket of her handbag.

'Give Alistair my love.' The reception was truly appalling. Jemima struggled to make sense of the crackling noise at the other end before she gave up and ended the call.

Her mum walked into the kitchen. 'Trouble?'

'Rachel's father-in-law-to-be is ill. I don't know any of the details because the line was breaking up all the time, but they're flying out to Toronto today.'

'Oh, no. So close to the wedding. What a dreadful thing to have happened.'

Jemima glanced down at her watch and picked up her sandwiches from the worktop. 'Is it okay if I'm a little late back? I need to do a couple of things for Rachel at the flat.'

'Of course, darling,' her mother said. 'You'd better hurry

or you'll be late for work. I meant to be here ten minutes ago, but the parking around here is so atrocious.'

'I know.' Jemima went through a mental check of everything she needed to have done and needed to take with her. 'There's some talk of it all being permit parking only, which will help.'

She kissed one finger and placed it on Ben's hair, a concession to his belief that all kisses were too wet. 'Have a good day. Sam,' she called from the bottom of the stairs. 'I've got to go.'

Sam came scampering down the staircase and gave her a quick hug. 'Is Grandma in the kitchen?'

Jemima nodded and watched as he ran through to find her. 'Bye,' she called out as she shut the door behind her. There was no reply. The boys were too busy talking about Ben's forthcoming birthday party. He would be nine—she couldn't quite believe time had gone so fast.

And that was another thing she was going to have to find time to do. Ben needed a birthday present and there was no way she could afford the Xbox she knew he really wanted.

It wasn't as though she particularly wanted him to spend all his free time playing on one, but 'all his friends had one' and she felt guilty. That sharp knife twisted a little more as she felt there was something else she wasn't able to provide for her sons.

Of course, Russell could—and he probably would. That hurt almost as much. Jemima hurried along the pavement towards the tube station. Thank goodness she had this job. She had to keep everything in perspective and keep positive. Things were going to get better.

If she dropped her time sheet off with Amanda tonight she could pick up her cheque personally rather than wait for the post. If she did that the money would be cleared in her account in time for her to use it to buy something for Ben. Maybe, at a stretch, it might even be possible to be the parent who gave the present that would make her son's eyes light up. There'd be no harm in seeing how much an Xbox actually did cost.

It was all going to be fine. Everything was falling into place. Except, of course, she'd also got to make a detour to Rachel and Alistair's flat, not to mention find the time to hire a marquee, book a caterer, a florist and some kind of medieval-type musicians. And all for a wedding that was scheduled to take place in under three months.

Let alone that she wanted to make it perfect. *But poor Alistair*. There was never a good time to lose a parent, but so close to their wedding it didn't bear thinking about.

Somewhere in the depths of her handbag her mobile phone started to ring. She stopped and made a frantic search for it in the dark depths of her bag.

'I gather we've got a wedding to organise,' Miles said into her ear as soon as she answered.

Jemima shifted her handbag to her other shoulder. 'How did you get this number?'

'Alistair gave it to me. I'm to offer my help. As best man he considers it my duty, even though I'm a confirmed wedding phobic and of doubtful use.'

Despite everything, Jemima could feel herself start to smile. 'Did he say that?'

'More or less. Where are you now?' he asked.

Even though she knew, Jemima automatically looked up at the huge sign. 'Rayners Lane. I'm outside the tube station. Why?'

'I thought you might want to take a detour and pick up Rachel's wedding box. Apparently it'll make everything easy.'

'So she says. It's in the kitchen by the kettle.' Jemima walked inside the station. 'I'll go and get it this evening. I can't go now or I'll be late for work.'

'Don't worry, I know the boss. He's prepared to be very understanding.'

What was it about Miles that kept her on the edge of laughter? Moments ago she'd been worried about all the responsibility of taking over the planning of Rachel's dream wedding, but with a handful of sentences he'd managed to twist the situation into something that would be almost enjoyable.

'Does that mean I can start charging you from now? An extra hour on my time sheet…'

'No.' She could hear the smile in his voice. 'But it means I'll buy you lunch while we go through Rachel's exacting requirements.' Then the line went dead.

Lunch with Miles.

How exactly did she feel about that?

CHAPTER SEVEN

MILES felt a vague sense of injustice. No doubt Alistair's father hadn't intended to inconvenience him by falling so ill, but the fact remained that his carefully laid plans to keep his distance from Jemima had come to nothing. And what really bothered him about it was that he was pleased.

He ended his call to Jemima with a feeling of smiling anticipation, and all because she'd agreed to accept his help with booking a few tedious things for an equally tedious wedding. He hated weddings. He hated the ridiculous top hat and cravat he almost always had to wear at them. He hated the long and usually poor quality speeches that made the whole business so interminably lengthy. His own excepted—obviously.

Miles played with the paper-clips in the Perspex box in front of him, letting them rise and fall. He didn't even believe in marriage as an institution. Not really. Why did two intelligent people, who purported to love each other, need a piece of paper to hold them together?

It made no *sense*. His mother was right about that. It was an outdated dinosaur of an institution that belonged... Miles smiled to himself, pleased at the neat symmetry of his thoughts. It was an outdated institution that belonged in *medieval* times.

If he believed Alistair and Rachel had thought of that and were silently laughing he would feel a darn sight better at spending his time trying to book various people who spent their professional lives taking money off other people who thought they'd achieve nirvana if the flowers matched the lining of the best man's jacket.

Miles stood up abruptly and walked through to the small kitchen area. His hands went through the practised procedure of making coffee while his mind tried to analyse why he felt so…

So…

He pulled a distracted hand through his hair. He wasn't quite sure how he did feel. All he knew was that he was ridiculously pleased to be having lunch with Jemima. It felt like a *result*. It made no sense at all, but that was how it felt and the suspicion slid into his mind that all he'd been waiting for had been an excuse to break his decision to keep his distance from her.

And that didn't make any sense at all. There was nothing about Jemima that should draw him to her. In fact, there was a great deal which should have prevented it.

So *why*? Miles returned to his desk and sipped his coffee. The truth was he didn't know *who* Jemima was—and that was fascinating.

The realisation hit him with a sudden force that there were few people, if any, whom he couldn't sum up within the first few minutes of meeting them. But Jemima had him guessing.

There was a…tension between the image she presented to the world and the Jemima he suspected lurked beneath the surface. It was as though she'd got used to hiding behind an image she felt safe with. One that ensured people didn't notice her. *Couldn't hurt her?* Every so often a different Jemima would peek out from behind the façade. The Jemima she would have been if life hadn't acted like a pumice stone.

That was the Jemima that fascinated him—if she existed.

And she might not. He pulled a lever file closer and began to flip through the neatly typed pages. Miles pulled a highlighter pen out of the pot before him and selected a sentence in the second paragraph to shade orange.

It was quite possible his interest in her was entirely altruistic then. He'd had a glimpse of what her life was like and he wanted things to be better for her. Nothing wrong with that.

So what was worrying him? It was just lunch. A working lunch. An hour discussing weddings. Miles smiled. Not that risky then.

The trouble was, when the time came it didn't feel as though his interest in her was altruistic. It felt personal. And it felt very risky from the moment she looked up from the computer screen and smiled at him.

His mouth automatically curved in response—for no other reason than it had felt good to be smiled at. He'd had a pig of a morning and yet one smile seemed to put everything back into kilter.

'Ready for lunch?'

'Two seconds,' she said, turning back and carefully saving everything. 'Do you think I'm going to need an umbrella?'

Miles avoided watching her fingers moving over the keyboard by turning away. 'We're only going a few hundred yards and if there's a sudden shower we can take cover.'

'Okay.' Jemima stood up and walked over to the tall cupboard, pulling out her handbag and a plastic carrier bag. 'Rachel has given us so much to look through.'

Miles said nothing. He was watching the way her simple knee-length skirt moulded beautifully across her bottom. Jemima had great legs too. He remembered them from when she'd stood on her kitchen worktop to make a hole in the ceiling. Long, long legs...

Jemima reached up to adjust her hairclip. He swallowed

and struggled not to notice how the thin fabric of her white blouse pulled tight across her chest.

'Oh.'

'What?'

She opened up her hand to show two broken pieces of brown plastic. 'My hairclip's broken.'

Dark red hair fell round her face and Miles felt a tightening in his groin area. *Very, very risky*, a little voice whispered in his head. 'It looks good loose,' he said brusquely, turning towards the door.

'It doesn't. It looks a mess.' Jemima sighed. 'I've always wanted the kind of hair that was so smooth a hairgrip would slip out. Do you know what I mean?'

Hair like Verity Hunt's. Miles knew exactly what she meant. Hair that could be twisted into something that looked more like a sculpture. *Hair like her sister's.* Although he thought he understood why she wanted it, he also thought she was seriously undervaluing what nature had given her.

'It used to look better when I had layers cut into it. Still—' she shrugged and threw him a warm smile '—it doesn't really matter, does it.'

It suddenly seemed really important that she believed him. The way she looked probably shouldn't matter, but the way she felt about herself certainly did. 'If you want my opinion,' he said as he held the door open for her, 'I'd go for the curls. They're very sexy.'

He closed his eyes briefly. Had he actually said the word 'sexy' out loud? He hadn't meant to do that, but Jemima was certainly looking at him wide-eyed.

'Sexy?'

There was no backing away from it now. He pulled a smile into his eyes, searching for the ground between casual and complimentary. Something that wouldn't have him brought up before a sex-discrimination board. 'I think so.'

She just looked at him for a moment and then she laughed. 'I think men are strange.'

'No question,' he agreed easily. Miles led the way down the stairs. 'Although this should appeal to your practical nature…'

Jemima glanced across at him, a question in her equally sexy green eyes.

At the bottom of the stairs he leant in close to say quietly, 'Just think how much time you'd save in the morning if you didn't bother to straighten it.'

She gave a husky laugh. It ripped through his senses as much as the light rose-scented perfume that hung about her.

'Actually, that's quite a persuasive argument.'

'Felicity,' Miles said, pausing by the reception desk, 'Jemima and I are having a working lunch. I'm on my mobile if you need us.'

The receptionist's speculative glance did absolutely nothing to make him feel more relaxed. As they stepped outside Miles reached up and loosened his tie. It was becoming difficult to breathe, but then the air was muggy.

'So,' he said, making a real effort to keep his voice light and teasing, 'why do you hate your hair so much?'

'Because it's red.' She looked up and smiled—one of those inexpressibly sweet smiles that made him feel as if something intensely precious was being given to him.

'Mainly that, I think. There's no hiding when you have red hair. You always stand out. Wherever you go, whatever you do.'

'Isn't that a good thing?'

She laughed at him, changing the hand she was holding the carrier bag in. 'Only if you like that kind of attention. I leave all that to the other members of my family.'

From the little he knew of Verity Hunt, Miles imagined she

did. Jemima seemed to echo what he was thinking. 'I'm the quiet one. Imogen is a natural campaigner, like my mum. They always seem to be working on some big issue or other.' She smiled across at him. 'Verity is an entertainer. She loves being the centre of everything.'

'And you?'

She laughed. 'Oh, I much prefer to keep in the background. I don't like people talking about me and pointing me out. My dad used to say I was a "facilitator and nurturer" and that I'd get places because I'd slog away at it.'

Miles thought that was a good description of her. Quietly conscientious—but that didn't do justice to the wicked sense of humour she possessed. 'Used to?'

'He died. Three years ago.' Jemima changed the hand she was holding the carrier bag in for a second time. 'He was a fairly formidable man—but very lovely.'

It fascinated him hearing about her family. It began to make it easier to understand why she'd made some of the decisions she had. But if he'd hoped knowing more about her would assuage his curiosity, he was destined for disappointment.

He found the more she told him, the more he wanted to know. It was rather like playing pass the parcel. There was a prize beneath each layer of wrapping paper, but everyone knew the real treasure was found at the absolute centre of the parcel.

Miles reached out for the bag she was carrying and, after a moment's hesitation, she let him take it. 'This is heavy. What's Rachel got in here?' he asked, looking down.

'Her box file.' Jemima laughed, a sudden mischievous light shining in her green eyes. 'And just about every bridal magazine that's been published since Alistair proposed to her.'

'Really?'

'It's serious stuff.'

He peeked in the top of the bag. 'It would seem so.'

Jemima dodged a group of teenage backpackers. 'Rachel's even left me seven pages of detailed instructions. Apart from the fact that I hope Alistair's dad turns out not to be dangerously ill, I really hope she's not away too long. The sooner she takes back control of this extravaganza the better.'

Just that one glance in the top of the carrier bag had him silently echoing her sentiment. 'Considering we're not fans of the whole confetti and white ribbon scenario, we're not the best choice for this assignment, are we?' he remarked, turning the corner and walking down towards the piazza.

She didn't appear to be listening as her attention was caught by a living statue. Miles smiled, watching her expression as the 'Victorian lady' suddenly moved and startled a group of Japanese tourists. 'It's amazing how they do that. How does anyone keep still so long?'

'I couldn't do it.'

'I wouldn't want to. It must be so boring.' Jemima looked up at him. 'You know the boys would love it down here. I ought to bring them one weekend.'

'Why haven't you?'

'I don't know really.' She looked around at the milling crowds, the Italian-style piazza, the jugglers and mime artists. 'I suppose I just hadn't thought of it. I must, though. Perhaps it's something I could do for Ben's birthday.'

'When is it?'

'Saturday week.' For a moment her face crumpled, then he watched as she took control of whatever emotion was gripping her. 'He's going to be nine.'

'Is that what's bothering you? That he's growing up?'

She glanced across at him as he steered her towards the large glass-covered building. 'Of course not. Why did you think that?'

'My mother found it difficult. The passing of one's youth, I suppose…' He trailed off.

Miles watched her swallow. 'No. I don't feel like that. Each stage has been fun.' And then, 'Why do you think I'm upset?'

Miles merely smiled at her. He wasn't about to say that he'd spent the past week surreptitiously studying her. That he could read her expressions effortlessly and gauge her moods. He knew when she was typing something she found boring, when she couldn't read his handwriting, when she was thinking about something else…

And he knew when she was sad. Like now. It had washed over her quite suddenly.

Jemima shrugged. 'It's stupid really. Ben will be with his dad on his actual birthday.' She shot him a brave smile that twisted something inside him. 'It's the first time it's happened since Russell left. Not bad in almost three years, but I'm finding it difficult. It almost happened last year, but since our divorce was so recent Russell didn't push it. This year…' She bit her lip.

His reaction to her words surprised him. For a man with his background, a man whose mother must have been abroad for at least three of his childhood birthdays, he would have expected to feel very little empathy, but his pain surprised him. 'Is Ben having a party?'

'They're going bowling. Ben's really excited about it. He's not talked about much else all this week.'

Miles ran through the myriad responses open to him while the waiter took their order. The temptation was to accept what she said at face value. That was the socially acceptable thing to do. Or he could risk offering a sympathetic platitude or two. Or…he could say what he really thought.

'Hell, that's hard,' he said, as soon as the waiter walked out of hearing.

Sadness flickered across her face and she looked down.

'So are you going to do something special on a different day?' Miles asked, watching her closely. The last thing he wanted to do was to make her cry.

He reached out and played with the sugar sachets in the bowl in the centre of the table. 'You've got to remember I'm essentially very immature, but I'd be inclined to get in first and do something spectacular.'

Jemima looked up on a surprised laugh. 'It does make you want to do that.'

'What's stopping you? It's your weekend coming up isn't it?'

The instinctive response was 'money', but she knew it wasn't that. She wanted to behave well and responsibly. She didn't want Ben to guess how much she was hurting at the thought of not being at his party and not being able to tuck him up in bed on his birthday. He was coming up nine years old, for goodness' sake. She was the adult here. If she let on she was unhappy about it, she'd spoil it for him.

And it was ridiculous anyway, because she was going to see him first thing. She was going to be able to give him his present, see him open it…

'Do something tomorrow,' he said, watching her face.

Miles, Jemima decided, was one of life's problem solvers. Of course, she ought to do something fun tomorrow. She bit her lip and considered her options. First choice would be to take Ben and Sam on that long promised trip to Legoland, but her car was unlikely to make it that far. So…

She smiled. 'I could bring them here. Ben would love the transport museum and the street performers.'

'Would the boys like to see where you work?'

'I—I suppose they would—'

'Why don't you do that too? I'm going to be in work part of tomorrow. Bring them up and show them the office. Let them see where you go each day.'

Miles was a continual surprise to her. Jemima just looked across at him, a little stunned. Day after day she was falling just that little bit more under his spell. She'd never met anyone quite like him.

He was so supremely confident, fearsomely clever...hand-some, naturally...and fun. Being with him was pure fun. Whenever she was with him she felt as though she were a different person. Much more like the woman she wanted to be.

'Okay.' She pulled at a strand of her hair. 'What shall I do? Ring you when we're here?'

'It's probably easiest.'

The waiter walked across with their drinks. Jemima had chosen a tall glass of freshly squeezed orange juice and she took a sip immediately. She would never, ever, have believed she'd be meeting Miles outside working hours, but then this wasn't exactly a date...

Just like this wasn't *exactly* a working lunch either.

'Have you got my mobile number?'

Jemima shook her head. 'Rachel gave me the Kingsley and Bressington one.' She felt a small bubble of laughter in the pit of her stomach. 'I felt daft pretending to write it down.'

He smiled, three tiny lines fanning out at the edges of his eyes.

She watched, fascinated, and then rushed in with, 'Did you ring Amanda and tell her what happened on Saturday?'

The glint in his blue eyes intensified. 'Oh, yes,' he said, drawing the words out.

'What did she say? Actually, what did *you* say? I don't want to contradict you. I'm going to see her this evening.'

Miles picked up his iced water. 'I told her about the dandelion. Since everyone appears to think it was a little naff, I thought Amanda might well agree.'

Jemima bit her lip, trying hard to stop the laughter which was threatening to engulf her. 'Did she?'

'Let's just say I don't think you're going to find the con-versation very difficult at all.'

'Excellent.' Jemima gave up and laughed. After a moment, she wiped her eyes. 'Of course, tonight is the dandelion date.'

Actually that part of it wasn't so funny. It reminded her that, in some respects, Miles was still the man she'd first thought him. He was still the man who played the dating game as though it was, indeed, a game. As though the women he sent flowers to wouldn't care whether he sent flowers to a different woman the week after.

Perhaps they wouldn't. Perhaps it was only her who took everything so seriously. Maybe she was fifty years out of date. *Maybe even as boring as Russell had found her.*

'I hope you're taking Keira somewhere expensive. I think she deserves that after receiving a dandelion.' She kept her voice light. It was absolutely none of her business who Miles saw, but…

Jemima drew a deep breath and then smiled. 'I suppose we'd better get on with the purpose of our lunch.' She pulled the carrier bag on to her knee and lifted out the box file. 'It's a bit daunting,' she said, flicking through the contents of the bag. 'I think I'll leave the magazines in there and go through them this evening by myself. There might be some useful tele-phone numbers and websites in them.'

Miles opened the box file. 'What have we got here?' he said, spreading out a picture of a pink lined marquee on the table.

Jemima put the carrier bag back down on the floor and looked over. 'That's what Rachel doesn't want. It's too girly. We're looking for "medieval", remember. Though, to be honest, I think we'd be better trying to get a basic marquee and adding our own twelfth century touches,' she said seriously.

His eyes lit with laughter. 'Such as?'

She was ready for that one. 'I went to the library and got

a book out on the period,' she said, reaching down and pulling it out from between the February and March editions of *Brides Today*. 'We probably could do something with heraldry.'

Miles turned it over and flicked the pages. 'How efficient,' he slid in lazily.

Jemima pulled out a notepad and headed it up with the words 'To Do'. 'That's why I'm such an excellent secretary.'

Miles laughed as she intended he should, but then he sat back in his chair, watching her. It made her feel uncomfortable, so it was almost a relief when he spoke. 'What *are* you going to do?'

She looked up, her pencil poised. 'About what?'

'Your career. You aren't going to be satisfied working as a temporary secretary for long. What's your long-term plan? I don't believe you haven't got one.'

Jemima smiled and returned to what she was doing. His words were a direct echo of her sisters'. Verity, because she didn't have children, had no concept of mother love and couldn't see there was any conflict of interest. Imogen, because she had a supportive husband who loved her and who had the kind of bank balance which made 'having it all' a distinct possibility.

Not her mum, though. Despite having had a highly successful career herself, her mum was a realist. She recognised that her situation had been very different from the one her middle daughter found herself in—and she was there for her, doing what she could to make things better. Jemima so loved her for it.

'Whatever I do is going to be a compromise,' she said, echoing something her mum had said to her when they'd been discussing the options.

'Between?'

She looked up again to find him still watching her intently.

'Ben and Sam come first. They have to.' He said nothing and she felt obliged to continue. 'That's part of the deal when you have children. I suppose, in the end, I'll settle for something near home.'

'Doing?'

Jemima smiled a little stiffly. She wasn't at all sure she wanted to be telling him all this. 'It doesn't really matter. I want to earn enough to finish the house and pay for some treats for the boys. I'm tired of telling them how sorry I am, but I don't have the money. It's not the earth I'm after.'

Miles looked thoughtful. He handed her back the book on medieval life as the waiter returned with their plates of pasta. 'In a decade or so Ben will be at university. You can't put everything on hold for ten years.'

'I know.' It was what she said to herself. It was *why* she'd gone to see Amanda. And *why* she'd taken a secretarial course.

It had seemed a reasonable compromise, but deep down she knew Miles was right. She did want more. Or, at least, the prospect of more. Being the least successful member of a high achieving family was difficult. But missing the boys' school sports day and never being home in time for tea wasn't an option either.

'So?' he prompted. 'What's your long-term plan?'

It was such a difficult question to answer. Jemima was acutely aware that in accepting the house in lieu of any claim on Russell's pension she had left herself vulnerable for the future.

And while Russell was never awkward about paying his contribution, how long would his girlfriend be happy with him paying out so much to his ex-wife?

And if Stefanie insisted he referred his payments back to the CSA she might find it wasn't worth her working at all, certainly not for the minimum wage. She could end up losing as much as she gained in a vicious catch-22.

Jemima picked up her fork. 'I haven't decided yet.' She looked across at him and forced a smile. 'I think I've become Amanda's project. It bothers her intensely that I've left myself unable to support myself and my children entirely alone. It offends her principles as a card carrying feminist…'

She stopped, suddenly reminded that Amanda's views were very likely to be shared by Miles's mother. Hermione Kingsley was a fierce advocate of financial and emotional independence—whatever the latter actually meant when it was applied to the real world.

Did 'emotional independence' mean you couldn't let yourself love anyone because it was weakness to need any one other person? She'd never be able to truly believe that. Jemima concentrated on eating her pasta.

'Don't let Amanda bully you.'

She looked up, surprised. 'I won't.'

'There must be something out there that'll be a good balance.' He looked thoughtful, and then he smiled. 'Why are you looking so surprised?' he asked, his hand curving around his tall glass of iced water.

'Well—' Jemima searched for a way of expressing what she was feeling '—your mother…'

Miles shook his head. 'Hermione is Hermione. Her views are extreme and I've experienced the consequences of them.'

He must have. Everything he said about his childhood made her feel intensely sorry for him. 'Do you always call her Hermione?' she asked curiously after a moment.

He nodded, eating another mouthful of his pasta. 'Unless she irritates me especially. If she writes about me in her column and the ripples hit my life in any kind of negative way, then I find calling her Mum is very effective.

'The ultimate punishment, of course, will be to make her a grandmother. Although I'm sure she'd turn it to her advantage as long as I've not married the mother.' He smiled across at her. 'Do you want parmesan?'

It seemed an abrupt change of conversation, but clearly Miles was so used to his background that he expected other people to find it as easy to come to terms with. She didn't know quite what to say. His background was so different from hers.

Her mum delighted in her grandchildren, even more since her retirement. She was more of a hands-on grandmother than she'd ever had time to be as a mother.

'You look shocked.'

Jemima shook her head. 'Just can't quite imagine calling my mum "Margaret".' But it was more than that. In all the world there was only Ben and Sam who could call her 'Mum'. That made it special. *Didn't it?*

'Do you want parmesan?' Miles asked again.

She looked at it a little longingly. 'I mustn't.'

'Why ever not?'

Jemima looked at him as though he'd developed two heads. Every day of his working life he was surrounded by stick insects. He must have noticed the difference.

His eyes glinted and his voice was pure temptation. 'Parmesan is an essential. A staple of life. And you've got to try the Apple and Vanilla Tart later.' His mouth twisted into its almost habitual sexy smile. 'It beats Alistair's fig concoction hands down anyway.'

There was a brief moment during lunch where she regretted her lack of willpower, but it was shortlived when she tasted the tart. Jemima's lips closed round the warm puff pastry base with its sweet apple topping and she sighed. 'I'm never going to be thin. I may as well accept it.'

Miles laughed, sitting back in his chair.

'Verity never eats desserts. I think they must be against her religion,' she joked.

'Then she misses out. Try the ice cream with the tart. The combination is terrific.'

Jemima didn't disagree. The cold and the warm mingled in her mouth and she closed her eyes to allow her sense of taste to fully experience it.

'Good?'

'Incredible.' She felt a little self-conscious as she opened her eyes to find Miles was smiling at her, almost laughing, but not unkindly.

'Why is it everything that's bad for you tastes so good?' Jemima rushed on, unnerved by his expression. 'Verity eats everything with chopsticks. She reckons she eats far less that way.'

'It's a cruel business she's in. Most models are emaciated.' Then he looked up with an intensely wicked gleam in his eyes and Jemima braced herself for something shocking. 'Great with their clothes on, not so great without.'

Jemima sent him what her mum would describe as an 'old-fashioned look'. 'And you should know.'

His smile widened and it felt as if a million butterflies had been let loose in her stomach.

How did he do that? She'd forgotten what it was like to flirt and laugh for no reason. Truthfully, she'd forgotten what it was like to have fun. But sitting here in the summer sunshine, the noise and the bustle of Covent Garden going on all around…

She felt more like the woman she'd been when she'd first left university. Anything had seemed possible then.

Miles finished the last of his dessert and reached out for the notepad. 'It's very dull to go out with a woman who's watching every mouthful.'

'I watch every mouthful. The trouble is I'm eating it at the time.'

Miles laughed. 'But you didn't order salad with no dressing or some peculiar combination that's the latest craze. I hate that.'

'I must have tried every diet going.'

'Why?'

Why? Jemima mentally ran through the possible whys. On the BMI index she was coming in at the perfectly respectable top end of normal, but she still felt this…pressure to be thinner.

It was as though she believed her life would be better, happier, more successful, if only she looked…well, thinner.

And that pressure hadn't come from her family. Surprising, considering she had a super-model-sized sister. In the family they all thought Verity looked better a stone heavier.

It was *Russell*. It came as a shock to realise it was Russell's voice she heard in her head. Still. He'd been so keen for her to lose the 'baby weight' she'd gained. Perhaps because he'd already started to be unhappy living with her.

Jemima shrugged the bad memories away. Though some time she ought to think about it more. It made her angry to think she'd allowed Russell to control how she felt about herself.

Miles was reading down the list she'd started. Three weeks ago, if anyone had told her she'd be sitting in Covent Garden's beautiful glass-covered building with a man like Miles Kingsley she'd have laughed.

But here she was. And he didn't look desperately bored. He wasn't glancing down at his watch as Russell had used to do, or making her feel as though she had nothing to talk about but nappies and playschools.

Just possibly, Jemima thought with a new stirring of anger, the problem was with Russell and not with her.

Miles looked up and surprised her watching him. 'Why don't we divide and conquer with all of this?' he said, gesturing down at the long 'To Do' list.

'How would it be if I leave you with tracking down a marquee since, frankly, I don't know where to start with it and searching out possible caterers? And I'll sort out the medieval musicians and the…florist. I might have some contacts that'll be useful,' he said and his eyes were smiling.

Jemima kept a straight face. 'I think ringing Becky is probably a great idea.'

'It'll give her heart failure if I tell her I'm choosing flowers for a wedding.'

'Scare her, more like. You must be ten per cent of her business.' Jemima started putting Rachel's clippings and tear sheets back into the box file. 'What are you going to do if your contacts aren't useful? Realistically, Becky can't do flowers for a wedding in Kent, can she?'

He smiled and she felt as though she'd swallowed something hard and spiky. 'If it all goes pear-shaped I'll call you to fix it.'

CHAPTER EIGHT

MILES flung his jacket across the sofa and sat, staring at the telephone as though it might speak and tell him what to do.

It had been a long and intensely dull evening. Keira Rye-Stanford was all glitz and no substance. She'd looked...amazing. There was no other way to describe her. Tall, elegant, sexy—and delighted to be out with him. So far, so good one would think.

Miles rubbed his hand across his aching neck. *Hell, he'd been bored*. There'd been moments when he'd wondered whether he'd manage to keep his eyes open long enough to end the evening politely.

Lunch with Jemima had felt like a five minute highlight of the day, whereas dinner with Keira had felt like a five hour endurance course.

And, when he looked at it logically, he didn't know *why*. Keira was a great idea, Jemima a dreadfully bad one.

Keira was an alluring, independently wealthy career woman who didn't have a genuinely romantic bone in her body. Jemima was 'walking wounded' from her divorce, had two dependent children and an irrational belief in living happily ever after.

Miles smoothed his hand across the taupe-coloured suede

of his sofa and debated whether eleven was really too late to ring Jemima. He wanted her to know…

What?

He frowned. What was it that he wanted her to know? That he was home by eleven? That he was home alone?

He stretched back on the sofa and debated the wisdom of ringing her. All he needed was an excuse, some…reason for calling. His eyes lighted on the scribbled note he'd left on the coffee table and he reached for his phone. If she'd gone to bed she'd have switched her mobile off and he could leave a message for the morning. Safe enough.

Miles tapped in her number, so convinced she wouldn't answer, that he was surprised when she did. 'Jemima!'

'Yes.'

'Are you awake?' Miles closed his eyes. *Daft, daft question!* Of course, if she'd answered the phone she was awake. What kind of idiot was he?

'Miles?'

And she didn't even recognise his voice. It was getting better and better. 'Miles Kingsley.' He cleared his throat. *Damn!* He felt…like an adolescent schoolboy.

What was he trying to achieve here? Jemima didn't *need* to know he'd found a group of musicians who were prepared to play at the wedding. Not tonight.

It was merely his need to hear her voice that meant he had to call her. 'I've just got in and I thought I'd try and catch you before…'

Bed. Not a good thought. Miles thrust an agitated hand through his hair, his mind inevitably starting to imagine what Jemima might wear in bed. Seamlessly he went on to wonder whether her freckles covered every inch of her body. Or, more intriguingly, whether there were areas they didn't?

'…before you went to sleep,' he continued, his voice slightly deeper.

'I'm awake. I've just finished ironing all the school uniforms for Monday. How did your dandelion date go?'

How to answer that? Keira had worn a dress that was designed to make sure a man thought about what it would be like to take it off. She'd listened attentively to everything he said, had moistened her lips and tossed her hair. But, undeniably beautiful though Keira was, he hadn't been remotely tempted by her. He'd dropped her outside her Chelsea house and walked away without a backward glance.

'No, don't tell me,' Jemima continued, without him needing to say anything. 'I can gauge it all by the type of flowers you get me to send her on Monday.'

Miles sat back on the sofa, hoping that a nonchalant posture would somehow transmute itself into his voice.

'Does she know that's the form?' Jemima asked. 'A cactus and it's all off, two dozen red roses and I'll need to buy a hat.'

Her voice was full of teasing laughter and he felt the boredom of his evening evaporate. Jemima did have the sexiest voice. It coated her words like warm chocolate over fruit. It relaxed him. *Seduced him.* 'Buy a hat?'

'For the wedding.'

'Ah,' he said, understanding. 'You know, I've never sent a woman a cactus—'

'Yet,' Jemima cut in swiftly.

Miles laughed, although there was a part of him that felt piqued. *Didn't it bother Jemima at all that he'd spent the evening with another woman?* And, if not, *why* not?

He'd spent the better part of the evening thinking about her. He'd wondered whether she'd told Ben and Sam about their trip into town. If she still felt sad at the thought of missing

Ben's party. But, most of all, he'd wondered whether she was thinking about him at all…

Less than a minute into this phone call and it was crystal clear she hadn't given him a moment's consideration.

'A cactus isn't a very persuasive plant,' he said smoothly.

'And a dandelion is? Goodness, Miles, you know the wrong women.'

It was an opinion he was beginning to share. What would Jemima say if he asked her out to dinner—right now? This moment? The answer came swinging into his mind with the velocity of a cricket ball at the Oval. *She'd say no.* There wouldn't be a moment's hesitation.

If he asked Jemima out on a date he'd have his first slap-back since Jenny Baymen told him he couldn't take off her bra. He'd been fifteen then and his technique had lacked sophistication.

But…

Miles shifted his position on the sofa and made the conscious decision to make it clear that he had a real, bona fide reason for ringing her. Something that had absolutely nothing to do with the fact that he'd not been able to forget how green her eyes were or how pale her skin. Or that he remembered, absolutely, how it had felt to kiss her.

'I wouldn't rush to get the hat,' he said, uncomfortable and shifting his position yet again. *It had felt so good to kiss her.* It would be even better if he could kiss her when she was lying down beside him, warm and sleepy. If he could reach out and touch her…

'Not a good evening, then. How very disappointing, and after such a promising start.'

Women never teased him, Miles thought with a slow smile. If Jemima had asked him in for 'coffee' tonight he wouldn't have left her standing on the doorstep. He would have taken her inside and started a detailed exploration of just how far her freckles covered that pale, almost translucent, skin.

Miles shook his head, mystified by how he was feeling. *Jemima?* The intensity of it was frightening and entirely unexpected.

But the really tragic thing was that when Jemima asked him in for 'coffee' she really did mean coffee.

The truth was she was as unimpressed by him as he was by himself. For the first time in his adult life he felt as though he'd met a woman who could see past the façade—and she thought him shallow.

He sat forward and rested his elbows on his thighs. 'Whatever my evening was like, it was probably better than yours if you spent it looking through bridal magazines.'

She gave a rich chuckle. 'You've got me there. Did you know you can buy silver-plated yo-yos with the words 'you make my world go round' engraved on them?

'Actually, no.'

'Apparently it makes a great gift for a page-boy.'

'Would it?' he asked, marvelling at how steady his voice was.

'I can't see it either,' she agreed easily, 'but I've done brilliantly with the marquee. Or I think I have.'

Miles stood up with the phone tucked under his ear and walked across to the kitchen to fetch a beer from the fridge. 'I hope it's got turrets and a flag waving on the top or Rachel's going to be disappointed.'

'That's just it. It hasn't.'

Miles poured his beer into a tall glass and walked back to the sofa. 'What have you done?'

'Well, it suddenly occurred to me that the people who were to have had that weekend at Manningtree Castle had probably reserved something.

'While you were out of the office this afternoon, I did a bit of digging, found out who it was, and I've agreed to take over their booking. What do you think? Good idea?'

'Clever.' *No more than he expected from her.*

'It's large and white and we'll have to add the medieval touches ourselves, but it's a marquee and Alistair and Rachel are running out of time.'

'Now all you need to do is find a caterer who fancies roasting an entire pig over a spit.' Miles sat back and waited for her reaction.

'Don't you have contacts for that?' she asked silkily.

It was so good to be home. So good to be talking to Jemima. 'I know. It's such an odd place to have a huge gap in my address book.' Miles sipped his beer. 'But I have pulled all kinds of strings and pledged a ridiculous amount of money to Great Ormond Street Hospital in order to hire a group of baroque musicians called Solstice.'

'How did giving money to Great Ormond Street Hospital help?'

'You may well ask.' Miles pushed off his shoes and sat back more comfortably. 'One of the violinists is the daughter of a paediatrician who just happens to be the boyfriend of the sister of Hugh Foxton. And Alistair and I went to school with Hugh.'

There was a moment's stunned silence and then, 'Good grief!'

Miles laughed. 'Impressed?'

'Very.'

There was a momentary sense of exultation and then he realised that he no longer had an ostensible reason for speaking to her—and he wasn't ready for her to go yet. 'Have you spoken to your boys about tomorrow?' he asked abruptly.

'Not yet. I thought I'd make it a surprise, but I've already packed a picnic so we don't waste any time in the morning.'

Miles pictured a few rounds of sandwiches, the kind she

brought into work each day tightly wrapped in cling film. Then he imagined Jemima and her boys struggling to find somewhere to eat them. In a just world she'd have been able to take them to a restaurant, money no object.

She seemed to take it all in her stride, but it angered him that she had to think like that. Pinching and scraping for every blasted thing while Russell wafted in and out of his sons' lives like Santa Claus bringing gifts.

'Have you planned your day?' he asked, frowning.

'Not really. I thought I'd see what the boys want to do. They might be happy enough wandering through the market.'

No. The thought burst within him. He wanted better than that for her. Better than a day left to chance with one eye on what everything cost. This had to be a fantastic day. A day that Jemima would love to give her boys.

The kind of day he'd missed out on himself. Where would be the harm in that? It wasn't as though he would be really involving himself in her family. But he could help her. She found his ability to network and the myriad contacts he had amusing, but one phone call…

Miles transferred the phone to his other ear. 'Jemima?'

'What?'

'If you don't have anything fixed for the afternoon I thought I might ring a couple of people and call in a favour or two.'

'Miles, I—'

He could hear the doubt in her voice. 'It's just an idea. I'll talk to you about it tomorrow.'

'You don't have to feel—'

He stopped her. 'Just concentrate your mind on finding someone who specialises in cooking over an open fire and I'll come up with something I think Ben will enjoy.'

And that was where it would stop, he promised silently. He needed to refocus on how impossible a relationship would be with Jemima. Only…it was becoming more and more difficult to remember that.

'Do you really work here, Mum?' Sam asked the following morning, pushing his face close to the glass entrance doors of Kingsley and Bressington.

'Yes. You'll see where in a minute.' Jemima pulled him back and nervously touched her wildly curling hair. She should have straightened it like normal. She only hoped Miles wouldn't think she'd left it curly because he'd said he thought it looked sexy.

Although she had. Obviously. Which was sort of fine as long as it wasn't *obvious* to him that she had.

'There's a man coming,' Ben said, standing to one side of her.

Sam pressed forward. 'That's Miles. I went in his car when I was sick.'

Jemima felt her stomach clench. She was being ridiculous, but her mouth was dry and her hands clammy as she watched him walk towards the doors, effortlessly sexy in denim jeans and blue T-shirt.

Her reaction to him was as instant as a puppet's to the jerking of its strings. Jemima smoothed down her fitted cotton blouse and tucked her hands into the pockets of her own jeans. *Heaven help her*.

'Hi,' she said breathlessly as he opened the door for them to come in.

'Hi yourself.' And for a moment Miles looked at her.

She felt more self-conscious in that moment than she'd done in her entire life. Every instinct was to fluff her hair and hold her stomach muscles in tight. *What was he seeing when he looked at her like that?*

Then he turned away. 'So, you must be Ben,' he said with an easy smile in her son's direction. 'I've already met Sam.'

'I went in his car,' the younger boy chirped in, his grin wide and toothless.

Jemima placed a hand on Sam's head and steered them inside. Ben looked round, clearly overawed by the dramatic interior.

'Cool,' he said, looking at the staircase that seemed to float upwards. 'This is so much cooler than Dad's office.'

Above his head Miles met Jemima's eyes and smiled. 'You'd better see where your mum is working. It's upstairs.'

Sam slipped his hand inside hers as Jemima led them towards her temporary office. She was aware of Miles shutting and locking the door before he followed on behind.

'I work through here,' Jemima said, showing the boys the stunning interior of her office.

Ben's eyes instantly focused on the computer as she'd known they would. 'Does it have games on it?' he asked.

Jemima caught Miles's soft laugh. 'I shouldn't think so. I haven't had time to play games while I've been here.'

'Mine does,' Miles interrupted and she turned round to look at him. He grinned unrepentantly and walked over to open the door to his office. 'Do you want a go?'

Neither Ben or Sam needed to be asked a second time. They lost all sense of nervousness as they realised that they'd finally come into contact with a grown-up who knew that, *of course*, they'd want to have a go.

Jemima watched as the three male heads crowded round the screen. Then Miles looked up and smiled at her and she felt breathless again.

She stepped back into the comparative safety of her own office, trying to remember all the reasons why she would never be able to trust any man ever again. And, most particularly, why she couldn't trust this one.

'They're quick on the uptake,' Miles said as he joined her.

'Yes.' Jemima rubbed her hands down the legs of jeans. 'I

think it's something they're born with these days. Ben seems to know instinctively how to work my mobile phone better than I do and I've spent ages reading the instructions.'

Silently Jemima counted to ten. She had to keep a perspective on things. It was only because it was a Saturday and the Kingsley and Bressington building was empty that it felt so strange.

Miles was just being kind.

'Tea? Coffee?' Miles asked as he walked over to the kitchen. There was nothing different about him. He still looked as though he was completely comfortable and in control of his world. The difficulty was with her.

'Um.'

He smiled at her. 'I think they may be a while.'

'Yes. Sorry.' She took another deep breath. *Oh, stuff it!* This was horrible. 'Were you working? I can call them off any time and you can get on…'

'It's fine. I've done everything I need to do today.'

Which naturally made her worry he'd been hanging round waiting for them to arrive when he really wanted to get off home. *She just wasn't good at this.* Whatever *this* was.

She followed Miles into the small kitchen. 'I can't believe you have games on your computer,' she said, struggling for normality.

He laughed.

'So when you've been shut away in there and I thought you were working you've actually been trying to increase your top score?'

Miles winked at her and her stomach flipped over. 'Tea or coffee?'

She pulled one twist of hair straight in a nervous gesture she'd had since childhood. 'Coffee. Please.'

'Nice hair, by the way,' Miles remarked, turning to lean on

the worktop. 'Very…sexy.' And his voice deepened in a way that made her believe he might really find it sexy.

Jemima could feel the blush spread across her face. She felt as if she was going to combust. What was happening here? Was it her? Or him?

'It's lovely.'

'Th-thank you.'

And then he reached out and touched one copper corkscrew. Jemima stood motionless, her heart hammering against her chest as though it were contained in far too small a space. She couldn't breathe. She couldn't think.

There must be some smart clever comment she could say in a situation like this. Something light and sophisticated, but for the life of her Jemima couldn't think of it. She looked up helplessly into his eyes, eyes that had become impossibly dark.

All those clichés she'd read in books became instantly understandable. His eyes really *were* like two deep pools you could drown in. It all made perfect sense.

Flashes of what it had felt like when he'd kissed her played across her mind. Was she imagining it now, or was he looking at her as though he might do it again?

She felt scared and excited by it. She wanted him to kiss her. She didn't want him to kiss her. Her indecision lasted as long as the possibility.

Very, very slowly Miles let his hand fall to his side and he turned away, concentrating on making the coffee. Jemima felt as though she'd been sluiced in ice-cold water. He'd deliberately backed away from her and it felt like a rejection.

'I received an email from Alistair this morning.'

Jemima swallowed hard, trying to dislodge the hard lump stuck in her throat. 'Did you?'

'You can read it yourself, but…' Miles broke off to pour

the coffee into two mugs '…it seems everything is looking better than it did.'

'That's…great.'

'Alistair asked me to let you know. I don't know why he couldn't have sent it through to you directly—'

'M-my computer's not working at the moment.'

'Ah.'

Miles handed her a mug of coffee. 'Thanks.'

'I'm a bit muddled as to what is actually going on,' he said, pausing to take a sip of his own, 'but Alistair's dad is about to have, or has just had, an operation to remove a small tumour.'

Concentrating on what Miles was saying helped to calm her. She was reading far too much into what had been a casual gesture. Jemima followed him back out into her office and sat opposite him on one of the chairs. 'Is that connected to the haemorrhage or something different?'

'You'll need to read the email yourself. It was obviously dashed off in a hurry, but I think so. I think the tumour hit the artery—which could turn out to be a good thing, I suppose, if it means they can cut it out before it's had a chance to spread.'

In the nearby office there was a loud cheer. 'They seem happy,' Miles remarked.

'Yes.' Jemima made a huge effort to relax. 'They loved the tube ride in as well. I probably don't really need to do anything else.'

Miles put his mug down on the shattered glass coffee table. 'I forgot. I've arranged something for your afternoon. I only hope Ben will like it. I don't have much experience of nine-year-old boys.'

'Except having been one yourself.'

'Except having been one myself,' he echoed, turning back

to her with a warm expression in his eyes. It made her feel unaccountably shy, all the more so when he handed across a plain white envelope. 'I think I'd have liked this.'

'What is it?' Jemima asked, holding out the envelope.

'Open it.'

With one more questioning glance, Jemima flicked open the unsealed envelope and looked down at tickets for a Thames river cruise and… 'What's this?' she asked, looking across at him, bemused.

'I've hired a private capsule on the London Eye.'

'Yes, I know, but—'

'It means you have a capsule to yourself and priority boarding. That's one thing I do remember about being nine. I hated having to stand in line waiting for things.' He smiled. 'Actually I've not changed much. I still hate waiting.'

Jemima didn't know whether she ought to cry or to laugh. She didn't know whether she ought to accept it either.

She'd looked at tickets for the London Eye months ago and decided it really was too pricey. How much had Miles had to pay to get a private capsule?

Miles pulled a hand through his hair and stood up as though he sensed her indecision. 'Hopefully I've timed it right so you've still got time to have your lunch.'

'Thank you.' Jemima carefully folded the tickets and put them back in the envelope.

'It's a shame we didn't think about it earlier because Ben could have asked some of his school friends along. You can have up to twenty-five guests, I think—'

'Miles.' She stopped him and he turned to look at her. Jemima held the envelope out helplessly as though she didn't quite know what to do with it. 'This is lovely, but…how much did this cost you? I really didn't mean you to—'

'I told you, I was owed a favour. It's nothing.'

'But—'

'And anyway, it's not for you, it's for Ben's birthday. Just have a good time.'

Miles turned away as though what he'd done for them was completely insignificant. *But it wasn't.* It really wasn't.

Inside her head sparks were flying. She wasn't sure what she thought about anything any more. What she was thinking had to be *impossible*.

But then she thought about the way his eyes had darkened when they'd looked at her earlier. The way she'd been so sure he was about to kiss her.

What did any of it mean? She was so out of practice at reading the signals. And she'd hardly ever been *in* practice. Russell had been her first serious boyfriend and he'd been more in love with the success of her family than her.

A man like Miles Kingsley? Attracted to her? It wasn't possible.

'Mum?'

Jemima turned to look at Ben standing in the doorway. 'There's a wicked picture of a sailing boat on this computer.'

She turned automatically to look at Miles.

He was looking at Ben. 'It a Najad. Forty-six foot. Swedish.'

'Is it yours?' Ben wanted to know.

Miles laughed. 'I wish. One day, perhaps. Are you interested in sailing?'

A shadow passed across Ben's face. 'I used to be, when I was a bit younger. We had a Heron, but Stefanie doesn't like sailing and Dad sold it.'

'Stefanie's your dad's girlfriend, right?'

Ben nodded.

'Perhaps you'd come out with me in my dinghy? You know, some time? If your mum's happy with that.' He looked across at her.

Jemima thought she wanted to cry, but when she looked at Ben's face she knew she wasn't going to. She didn't understand why Miles would do that for Ben, but she was absolutely sure she could trust him not to carelessly hurt her son. She didn't know how she knew that for certain either, she just did.

Jemima looked at Miles. 'Come with us today?' Then she hesitated, amazed she'd found the courage to ask him. 'I...I mean, if you're not too busy this afternoon, that is.'

Oh, help.

Miles started to shake his head so she rushed on, 'It seems a shame for just the three of us to go on if there's space for twenty-five.'

Jemima felt as though her face must be shining with embarrassment. It was almost as though she'd asked him out. She wanted to curl up into a ball. He must be so embarrassed. He'd tried to be kind and she'd completely got the wrong end of the stick and...

'On one condition.'

Jemima looked up at him. Slowly he smiled and her mortification faded. 'I get to buy you lunch.'

Lunch? Whatever she'd thought he'd say, it hadn't been that. 'You'll come with us to use tickets you got us,' she said slowly, 'as long as I let you buy us all lunch?'

'That's about it. Do we have a deal?'

'We've brought...' *sandwiches*, she finished mentally. What was the matter with her? The lines at the edges of his blue eyes deepened and she fell that little bit more under his spell. 'We'd like that.'

What was it he wanted from her? They were such *different* people. She had to be imagining what she thought he was thinking. *But what if she wasn't?*

Miles had a philosophy of life that was completely incompatible with hers. She couldn't change—and, she suspected, neither could he. But there were these moments when he looked at her when all those differences didn't seem to be very important.

It was so daft. Miles dated amazing women. Women as beautiful as Verity, as confident as Imogen and as successful as her mother. It was inconceivable…

She couldn't even put words on the idea that had taken up residence in her head. Why would Miles be attracted to someone as…*normal* as her?

CHAPTER NINE

'MUM, isn't pepperoni the best topping on pizza?' Ben asked, bringing Jemima back into the concrete present. 'Miles says it's beef and chilli—'

Miles winked at her. 'Or ham and pineapple. Everyone loves that.'

'Mum,' her boys said in unison, stretching that one syllable into something with at least three. 'Tell him it's pepperoni.'

Jemima sat back, a smile tugging at her mouth. She couldn't remember the last time she'd taken the boys out to eat anywhere. It was just too expensive. She knew that Russell did it fairly regularly, whenever Stefanie wanted some peace and quiet, but…this was such a rare occurrence for her—and it was all the more special for that.

Special, too, because Miles was there to share it with her. He made everything seem easy somehow. For a man who hadn't had much contact with children, and claimed not to want it, he made it look effortless.

Miles looked over the top of his menu at her, the expression in his eyes making her feel as though she were entirely composed of marshmallow.

'It's going to have to be your decision,' Miles said. 'But I want you to know I fully intend to bear a grudge if you decide against me.'

Jemima laughed as her sons immediately started canvassing for her vote.

'Why don't we have the one that's got a mixture of toppings on it?' she suggested, her negotiating skills honed by experience. 'Then we can try a bit of all of them and give them a mark out of ten.'

'Like a cake picnic,' Ben said.

Miles lifted an eyebrow in her direction. 'What's a cake picnic?' he asked.

The boys fell over themselves to tell him. Ben leant forward eagerly. 'We choose a cake each and cut it into three bits—'

'It's cool,' Sam said with a wide toothless smile. 'You get a bit of all of them.'

'Mum always picks shortbread.'

Miles looked across at her and his eyes were laughing. 'Does she?'

'Particularly if it's been dipped in chocolate,' Jemima agreed, keeping a straight face. 'And Ben always has a chocolate éclair.'

'And the cream drops down his top,' Sam said, 'because he doesn't lean over the plate.'

Ben looked stormy, but Miles forestalled world war three with a quick, 'Okay, I get it. Pizza picnic it is.' Then he folded the menu and asked the boys, 'Who wants what to drink?'

Ben looked at his mum for guidance.

Miles also turned to her and she tried to answer as nonchalantly as possible. 'We tend to either have something to eat and ask for tap water, or we have a drink and nothing to eat.'

This was where people usually said something sympathetic—and made her feel worse about it. When they were with their father, she knew, Ben and Sam could have anything they wanted.

Miles said simply, 'Sounds like a good plan.' Then he smiled and looked at her. 'But…since this is a special occasion. What do you think?'

Jemima swallowed hard. 'I—It's your money,' she managed.

When the waiter brought across a tall glass with Coke in it, Ben couldn't quite believe his luck. 'This is the best birthday treat ever,' he said and his younger brother nodded in full agreement.

'Well, it's not often you get to be nine. In fact,' Miles said, 'I've only done it once.'

Ben and Sam dissolved into giggles—and it was a state Miles pretty much kept them in.

Jemima enjoyed watching them. *All of them.* And she found she could relax. For the first time since Russell had decided to walk out on their marriage, she wasn't totally re-sponsible for the success of the day. Of course, she *was* re-sponsible. She knew that. They were her children.

But it was different with Miles there. Better. *Much better.*

When he suggested they walk to the London Eye rather than take the tube, she didn't have to worry about working out the route in her A-Z. She merely had to follow, confident that when he led them down tiny side roads Miles knew exactly where he was going.

It might not sound like much, but it *felt* revolutionary. Sam had been only two and a half when Russell had decided to leave and, from that moment, Jemima had been 'it'. Every sleepless night, every illness, every decision she'd made for them had been her responsibility alone.

'Did you know,' Miles said, as they boarded their capsule, 'that one thousand, seven hundred tonnes of steel was used to construct the Eye?'

Ben and Sam looked at him.

'Which means it's heavier than two hundred and fifty double-decker buses…and can carry fifteen thousand visitors every day, which is more than enough to fill Concorde one hundred and sixty times over.'

The boys were suitably amazed. So was she, but for very different reasons. Miles was so…unexpected.

How had he guessed that Ben loved facts and figures? That his favourite reading was the kind of huge tome crammed full of a thousand and one things no one else knew and probably wouldn't need to. Jemima smiled. Miles had set out to make this day magical for Ben and he was doing just that. It was also magical for her.

Sam came and tucked his hand into hers as they started to climb higher, but Ben was peering out of the glass from the very beginning.

'Why do they call it a flight?' he asked Miles and she tried not to laugh as her usually articulate boss did his best to answer to the satisfaction of a nearly-nine-year-old.

Strange, but she didn't think of him as her boss any more. Their relationship had changed irrevocably since dinner with Alistair and Rachel. Jemima turned on the bench to look at him, watching the way his T-shirt stretched over his toned torso. *Heart-stoppingly handsome*, she thought—and way, way out of her league. But there were moments when he looked at her when she was sure…

Her smile twisted. Even if she had done all those abdominal crunches after Sam was born, how attractive would she really be to a man like Miles who had his pick of women? It didn't seem particularly likely and, truth be told, she wouldn't be happy in the kind of relationship Miles advocated.

She was naturally monogamous, she supposed. She wanted to build 'family' and make things secure for the people she loved. *Was that so wrong?*

As Sam ventured over to join his brother, Miles came to

sit beside her on the wooden seating. 'Good idea?' he asked, his eyes indicating the glass capsule they were in. 'Do you think they're enjoying it?'

Jemima couldn't believe he was experiencing a moment of doubt about it, but his blue eyes seemed to be waiting for an answer. 'It's brilliant. They're loving it. Thank you.'

Then he smiled and she wondered whether it was doing her heart any permanent damage to keep beating so erratically. For thirty years she hadn't experienced the slightest difficulty, but since meeting Miles it had been behaving very peculiarly.

'Are you?'

She nodded, feeling unaccountably shy.

'Come see,' he said, holding out his hand.

Slowly, her heart pounding, Jemima put her hand inside his. She'd seen a movie once where they'd talked about looking down and not knowing where one hand left off and the other began. It felt a little like that, except that she knew which hand belonged to whom. His hand was dark against her fair skin. It was more that she felt as if it belonged there.

Jemima tried to pretend that nothing had changed, but she was too honest a person not to know she was falling in love with Miles. Little by little. Despite the paralysing fear of being hurt again, she knew she was sliding inexorably closer to the point where there would be no way back.

She didn't want to be in love with him. *Or did she?* Surely at thirty the idea of giving way to unrequited passion, particularly when you were responsible for two young lives, was a bit ridiculous. And, if it wasn't unrequited, what then?

What was Miles thinking? She looked up at him, trying to read what was going on in his head. It seemed so…*unlikely* that he should be feeling anything like she was.

But there *was* that look in his eyes—just sometimes. The expression that made her feel hot and cold at the same time. Excited and scared.

And now he was holding her hand. Miles led her over to where she had a perfect view of the River Thames snaking through the city. It was an amazing thing to see, curiously beautiful and everything it was hyped up to be, but it was the feel of his fingers interlocked with hers that filled her senses.

'There's Buckingham Palace,' Miles said, pointing.

Jemima took a shaky breath. 'There's so much green around it,' was the only thing she could think of to say in reply.

She felt him smile. 'Not a bad back garden,' Miles agreed.

'It's amazing to see the whole city laid out like this,' she said, conscious of the fact that he was still holding her hand. There was no reason for him to be holding it, other than that he wanted to.

Did he want to?

'Have you been on the Eye before?'

She shook her head. 'I thought it would be a little like the Ferris wheel in Vienna, but it feels so different…' Then she stopped as a memory started to ache like an old wound.

She didn't want to think about that. Not now. It was years since she'd been in Vienna with Russell. She didn't want to think of him now.

'Bad memories?' Miles asked, watching her face.

Her mouth twisted. 'Actually, no. Good memories turned bad.'

'Difficult to forget?'

'You can never forget,' she said brusquely. 'I know I've been divorced a year and everyone seems to think I should be over it by now, but no one *gets over* something like that. It's such a stupid thing to say. You can't just erase all the memories and pretend none of it happened.'

Jemima made a half-hearted effort to take back her hand, but Miles refused to let her pull away. 'Do you…still love him?'

'No,' she said quickly and then, more slowly, 'No, I don't, but I did.' Her eyes searched for understanding. 'And…he's the father of my children. It's not as though I can draw a line beneath the whole experience and re-invent myself.'

Miles moved his thumb gently across the palm of her hand, sympathetic and erotic at the same time.

'When you've been…badly let down by someone you trusted, it's always inside you. You think you're fine and then something happens and you…remember.'

'Like now?'

Jemima shrugged. 'Russell proposed to me in Vienna.' *She shouldn't be saying all this.* Not to Miles. Everyone said that the first rule of 'getting back out there' was that you never talked about your failed relationships…

But what if you hadn't had so many failed relationships? What if there'd only been the one? And what if it had been the largest part of your adult life? *How was it possible not to talk about it?* Almost every memory she had since the age of eighteen involved Russell or Russell's children.

Miles was frowning.

'He proposed on the Ferris wheel?'

'In a felucca,' she said with a shake of her head. 'It's a horse-drawn carriage.'

'Yes, I know.'

'It was supposed to be very romantic because I'd really wanted to go in one, but—' and she bit down on a laugh as she remembered the farcical elements of the ride '—it started to rain halfway round and we had to stop while the driver put the hood up.'

The frown disappeared from his forehead. 'Probably an omen.' Then he reached out and slowly, very slowly, stroked her cheek. Jemima felt her breath freeze. The felucca hadn't been romantic—but this was. This was incredible. It was the kind of thing that only happened to other people.

'I'd like to kiss you,' Miles said quietly. So quietly she was almost unsure of what she'd heard.

'W-would you?' Her voice sounded cracked and dry.

'You're beautiful.' She shook her head in denial and he smiled. His hand moved so that his thumb could lightly brush against her lips. 'Why do you find that so surprising?'

Jemima could have recited all the things Russell had filled her head with when he'd wanted to justify his decision to leave. Miles couldn't have noticed that she was focused entirely on her children, that she wasn't spontaneous and that she took life too seriously.

Miles smiled and pushed back a red curl from her forehead. 'I need to bring you back here. You ought to see London when it's lit by electric light.'

A *date?* Was that what he was meaning? Jemima swallowed nervously. Miles *was* attracted to her. She wasn't imagining it. The air thinned around her and she struggled to think of anything beyond that.

'Look, Mum,' Ben said from the other side of the capsule. 'Look down here.'

Miles let his hand drop and Jemima walked over to look where her eldest son was pointing. Far below on the ground there was a clown with exceptionally long arms and big white hands.

Sam pushed his face up against the glass and peered down. 'He looks funny.'

'Yes,' she agreed, looking up to catch Miles watching her. A *frisson* of awareness passed between them. It was really happening.

And he wanted to kiss her. That thought stayed swirling

around in her head—exciting and scary at the same time. *Miles* wanted to kiss her.

She was aware of everything he said, everywhere he moved. She noticed the way he rested a hand on Ben's shoulder as they stepped out of the capsule, exactly as she might have done herself. Ben normally would have shrugged someone he didn't know well off. But he'd looked up and smiled. Miles couldn't know the incredible compliment he'd been paid. But she knew.

She thought about that as the four of them walked towards the pier and watched the boat dock that was to take them on their river cruise. She felt Miles inadvertently brush against her and glanced up at him. He smiled and there was nothing she could do but smile back. She felt as if she was in freefall.

Jemima knew she only took in a fraction of the sights. Somewhere amongst all her memories of the day was Miles's voice pointing out the famous landmarks as they passed and her boys' excited questions.

'That's the Houses of Parliament.'

'Why does it have green striped blinds and red striped blinds?' Ben wanted to know. 'Is it because they ran out of material?'

Sam yawned and sat down next to Miles. Without thinking, Miles stretched out his arm and tucked the young boy in close. 'Tired?'

'I'm never tired.'

Jemima watched her son instinctively curve into Miles. *How had he managed to get them to trust him like that?* In the space of one afternoon he'd absorbed himself into her family, made them trust him. Made *her* trust him.

Slowly Sam's eyes closed and Miles looked across at her. 'He's tired.'

Jemima nodded. 'We'd better start for home. It'll be quite late by the time we get back.'

'The tube's not far from here.'

This incredible day was over.

As they approached the pier, Jemima reached down and picked up her backpack, still full of the uneaten sandwiches. Miles took it off her. 'I'll walk with you to the tube.'

Jemima said nothing. She didn't quite trust her voice and wasn't sure what she'd say anyway. Her mind was one large exclamation mark. She needed time to think and to consider what was happening.

She couldn't quite believe…

Why would Miles Kingsley…?

'Ben—' she called her son, who was staring up at the London Eye '—keep with us.'

'Sam's got his energy back,' Miles observed seconds later, a smile in his voice.

Away from the gentle motion of the boat, Sam seemed to be back to a full quota of energy. 'Yes.'

The two boys ran slightly ahead, stopping every now and again to point something out or, rather less pleasantly, pick something up off the pavement. By the time they reached the tube station, Ben was fifty-two pence better off and Sam thirty-one pence from all the loose change they'd collected from the ground.

Jemima stopped. 'Thank you,' she began awkwardly. 'For today. It was…'

Miles stopped her with a gentle touch on her mouth. 'You're welcome.' His smile twisted and Miles turned to look at Ben. 'Happy birthday. Thank you for letting me share your day with you.'

Ben came closer, hesitant suddenly. 'Will you really take me sailing?'

'If your mum is happy with that,' Miles said, with a glance up at her. 'We'll arrange something.'

His eyes were the blue of the darkest midnight sky and, Jemima thought, if this one moment was all there was it would be enough. *Almost*. And with that thought came the realisation that it was too late to be cautious. She already loved him. She loved him—and if she continued the way she was, she was about to get very hurt.

Miles put the phone down with mixed feelings. Of course it was great news that Alistair's dad was doing so well and that his doctors were confident they'd successfully removed the tumour. Alistair had sounded buoyant, a complete contrast to how he'd sounded a week ago.

It was great, too, that Rachel would be flying back to the UK immediately. Excellent. He frowned and walked over to look down on the street below. With a mere nine weeks to go before the wedding it was just as well. He and Jemima had performed miracles, but he would be pleased to hand the organisation of it back to the bride herself.

He didn't like weddings. Had never liked them. Miles pulled a tired hand across the back of his neck. So *why* did he feel this sense of disappointment?

It didn't take much introspection before he knew the answer to that. With Rachel back holding the reins, he'd no longer have any excuse to persuade Jemima out to lunch. *Damn*. If the woman wasn't interested, she wasn't interested. What was the matter with him?

He knew the answer to that too. In the space of a month Jemima had altered everything. He wasn't quite sure how; he just knew that she had. And he was fairly certain it wasn't that she wasn't interested, it was more she was running scared.

Miles walked across to the connecting door and looked across at Jemima's empty desk, then at the clock. She'd taken a late lunch, had slipped out while he'd been out of the office himself. By the time she returned he'd be out at meetings. All, he was sure, quite deliberate.

He turned back to sit at his desk, his fingers idly playing with the paper-clips. Jemima wanted the promise of 'for ever'—and he couldn't say that. He didn't see how anyone could. He made a rapid calculation. Suppose he lived until he was eighty. Quite possibly longer, given modern health care. That meant a conservative estimate of forty-four years. *Forty-four* years with one person. It wasn't *possible*.

He wasn't prepared to make Jemima promises he knew he couldn't keep, but neither was he contemplating something temporary either. Jemima could set the pace. He had no problem with that—or, at least, not much.

Miles stood up and picked up his briefcase. What he was offering was a completely open-ended relationship. They could share their lives as long as it made them happy. He frowned. But Jemima had two boys in tow and how that fitted in with his unwillingness to risk becoming important in a child's life he wasn't quite sure. The emotional pull of his own childhood memories made him uncomfortable. But then, even if his relationship with Jemima finished, it didn't mean he need drop all contact with her children. He would be responsible…

Miles opened the connecting door and was startled to see Jemima. It was as though every time he saw her he was a little stunned by his reaction to her.

She turned. 'I thought you'd be gone. You'll be late for your meeting.'

Her hand moved to tug at a copper curl, then coiled it round her forefinger. Miles felt a smile tug at his mouth as he recognised the outward sign that she wasn't comfortable around him. There was some satisfaction in that.

'Alistair phoned.'

'I—I know. I mean I've spoken to Rachel and she told me

about Alistair's dad. She rang while I was at lunch.' Jemima shut the door of the cupboard and went to sit at her desk. 'It's good news, isn't it?' she said brightly. A little too brightly, perhaps?

Miles nodded, watching her. 'Sounds like it. Although I doubt he'll make it over here for his son's wedding. I doubt they'd let him fly even if he felt up to it.'

'No.'

Miles shifted the grip of his briefcase. 'Did Rachel say what time she's expecting to get back to the UK?'

'I don't think she knows yet. She plans to get the first available flight.'

Which meant tomorrow was still an opportunity for him. Ben and Sam were with Russell. It was Ben's birthday, so Jemima wouldn't want to be alone. 'Shall we drive down to Manningtree Castle tomorrow?' he asked as casually as he could. 'Take the last opportunity to check everything we've arranged is going to work in that setting. Besides, I've still not seen it and I'm curious.'

Jemima bent down to pull a file out of the bottom drawer of her desk. 'I'm sorry. I've said I'll drive over to Rachel's as soon as the boys have left. She's desperate to know what we've done.'

'Right.' Miles smiled, if not easily, at least with the appearance of it. Some sixth sense told him he had to take the pressure off. Take it slowly. Inch by inch… 'It's a pity because we could have stopped off for a pub lunch somewhere, but I'm glad you're not planning on spending the day alone.'

She looked up and bit her lip.

He might be imagining it, but Miles wondered whether part of her was already regretting turning him down. He certainly hoped so. 'Wish Ben a happy birthday for me.'

'Yes. Yes, I will.'

Miles opened the door to leave. 'Have a good weekend.'
'You, too.'

He closed the door softly behind him. Miles smiled. Next weekend would be different. He'd take Ben sailing, perhaps invite Jemima and Sam to join them at the club later. There were possibilities.

Ben was good, Miles thought, watching the boy duck down without being warned as the boom swung across after a jibe. He enjoyed his company. Genuinely. He enjoyed teaching someone to sail who was so receptive.

And he liked knowing Ben's mother was on the bank. Miles looked into the distance and saw Jemima sitting on a bench watching them. Her hand was raised to shade her eyes from the sun.

'Perhaps it's time we headed back,' he suggested to Ben.

'Do we have to?'

'We can come again—' Miles smiled and knew he meant it '—but I'm getting hungry and we've got to pack the boat away and have a shower before we can have our picnic.'

'Mum's made tuna rolls.' Ben shifted on the seat. 'And we've got lemon drizzle cake.'

It sounded perfect. Bizarrely. It was beginning to feel like a privilege to join their tightly knit circle. Who was he kidding? It *was* a privilege. A chance to experience the kind of family life he'd wanted as a child.

Miles turned the boat into the wind and zigzagged his way back to the bank. Jemima was on her feet immediately, her hand holding on to Sam's and one arm lightly resting on his shoulder as they waited.

'Mum,' Ben called out, 'I did better than last time. Did you see us nearly go over?'

The summer breeze caught at her curls and Jemima

reached up to push them away. 'I saw.' Then she looked at Miles and smiled, intimate and warm, and he felt as if he was going over himself.

He *cared* about her. His smile twisted. That was rather a revolutionary concept for him. He wasn't sure he had ever cared about anyone before. At least not so it was uncomfortable for him. But he cared about Jemima. And he cared about the people she loved because she loved them.

'Can Sam help sponge down the insides?' Ben wanted to know.

Jemima shook her head. 'I want Sam to help me set the picnic out.' She smiled again at Miles. 'We'll get everything out of the car and meet you at the tables. Over there.' She pointed towards the cluster of picnic tables on the other side of the lake. 'Is that okay?'

It was more than okay, Miles thought. It was great. He tried hard not to watch Jemima walk away. He didn't want Ben to notice how much he enjoyed seeing the way the filmy fabric of her summer dress blew about her legs.

'I've taken the bungs out,' Ben said, bringing him back to earth with a vengeance.

'Good.'

'Can we come sailing next Sunday?'

Miles shook his head. 'You're with your dad, but the weekend after that—if your mum is okay with it.'

By all that was reasonable the prospect of taking a nine-year-old sailing every other weekend should have had him hurrying in the opposite direction. Miles smiled, knowing he wouldn't change these Sundays for anything.

'Let's hurry up and get our showers. I'm hungry.'

'Mum won't let Sam eat all the crisps,' Ben observed. 'We need to put everything away properly.'

Miles laughed. Together they pulled the boat into position

and put the sails into the sail bag. Then, when it was neatly covered, they walked towards the shower block.

By the time they'd arrived at the picnic tables Jemima had laid everything out. 'Do you want a coffee?' she asked as he approached, lifting up a flask. 'I've remembered to leave it black this time.'

Miles took the bench opposite her. That way he could watch the expressions that passed over her face. 'Thanks.'

She poured it into a plastic mug and handed it across to him with the kind of smile that had the blood pounding in his head.

'Miles, do you think dogs go to heaven?' Sam asked beside him. 'Mrs Randall says that dogs do, but goldfish don't—'

'Sit down to eat your sandwich, Sam,' Jemima instructed, passing Miles a plate. 'Ben, please eat a roll before you start on the crisps.'

Miles sat back and enjoyed it all. He loved this…the opportunity to be part of a family. *Jemima's family.* Somehow he'd become interested in every aspect of Jemima's life. In her boys. In her worries.

He loved her shy smile. The unexpected laughter that lit her green eyes. He loved the way she pulled at her hair when she was nervous. The way she smiled at him as though they were part of an exclusive world.

In fact, he couldn't remember ever feeling more…content.

Rachel sat on one of the bar stools in Jemima's kitchen, the list of things to check in the last two weeks before the wedding in front of her and her hands cradling a mug of hot coffee. 'So, let me get this straight,' she began incredulously.

Jemima turned to look at her, comfortably resting her back on the worktop.

'Miles has taken Ben sailing *three* times since I got back from Canada.'

'Four, if you count today,' Jemima said with a glimmer of laughter. 'Every other weekend.'

Rachel's eyebrows almost disappeared up into her hairline. She shook her head in disbelief. 'In a little dinghy?'

'I don't know much about sailing, but Ben says it's called a Heron. I think that's what Russell had, so I expect he's right.'

'On a little lake?'

Jemima smiled. 'It's quite a big lake.'

'Miles doesn't do lakes.' She shook her head. 'He's a serious sailor. He goes down Chichester way and sails over to France for lunch. You don't honestly believe he's doing it simply because he likes Ben, do you?'

'He's a friend—'

'Miles doesn't do *just friends* either. Come on, Jemima, you're divorced, not brain-dead.'

Jemima put her mug down on the worktop. 'I know he likes me—'

'Yes, he *likes* you. He also raises the temperature of a room just by looking at you.'

Jemima shook her head. 'That's nonsense.'

'So—' Rachel took a sip of coffee '—why do you think he bothered to introduce you to that literary scout?'

'Because Eileen was overloaded with work and was looking for someone who could read and write a report on what they'd read quickly. Miles knew I'd like to work from home. There's nothing odd about that.'

Rachel gave a despairing squawk. 'And you don't think it's because he fancies the pants off you?'

'A little. Maybe,' she conceded.

'*Maybe?*'

'Rachel, what do you expect me to do?' Jemima asked, finally irritated. 'I don't do affairs. I've *never* done affairs. I met Russell when I was eighteen and he's the only man I've ever slept with.'

'Slime-ball,' her friend interjected loyally.

'I've got two children to look after. I'm not about to jump into bed with a man like Miles. Am I?' she asked, picking up her empty mug and walking across to the dishwasher.

'Why not?'

Jemima stopped, turning to look at Rachel. 'Why not?' she repeated incredulously. 'Because I don't *do* that kind of thing.'

'You mean you *haven't* done that kind of thing,' Rachel corrected. She held up a hand. 'I know Miles isn't a great long-term bet, but he's…fun.'

'Fun,' Jemima repeated.

'And I'm not suggesting you make a habit of leaping into bed with men because they're fun, but I reckon Miles is just what you need right now. He's clever, sexy-looking, not going to take the whole thing too seriously… Fun.'

Fun. Jemima was sure that 'fun' was exactly how Miles saw it as well. And she was tempted. Of course she was tempted. But…

She didn't understand affairs. Sex shouldn't be something casual. *Should it?* It had to mean something. What was so wrong with wanting to make a commitment to one man and to spend the rest of your life with him?

And that was the point, really. She was in love with Miles. Even Rachel would admit that beginning an affair with Miles if you were in love with him was a bad idea. He went for temporary—the right person for right now, and she wasn't cut out for that kind of life.

Jemima placed her mug carefully in the dishwasher. 'I don't do that kind of fun.'

'But you could,' Rachel said, her eyes watching her friend above the top of her mug.

'Don't be ridiculous. Look at me, Rachel.'

'I'm looking.'

'I lost my hip-bones some time around the age of twenty-one and I've got stretch marks you could use to design a board game. It's not going to happen. There's no way I'm going to get undressed in front of Miles.'

'But if he doesn't mind—'

'And how would we know that until it was too late? It's not going to happen, Rachel. Even with the light off,' she added as she saw her friend was about to speak. 'Hush. I think I hear them.'

The doorbell rang almost immediately and Jemima went to answer it.

'We're back,' Miles said, both hands on Ben's shoulders.

'We nearly capsized thirty-nine times! It was wicked.'

Jemima looked up into Miles's laughing blue eyes. 'Thirty-nine?'

'Takes skill, that.'

Whenever she was with Miles she wanted to smile. From behind her she heard running feet on the stairs and Sam hurled himself down the hallway. 'We've been painting the drawers in my bedroom.'

'Have you?' Miles said, reaching out and touching a strand of Jemima's hair. 'Let me guess. Blue.'

'Welkin Blue,' Jemima said. 'Left over from the bathroom. It's supposed to be the colour of a summer sky.'

Miles smiled down at her. 'It looks lovely.'

'Put her down, Miles,' Rachel said as she came to stand behind Jemima. 'There are people watching.'

'Just getting the paint out of her hair.'

'So I see.'

He calmly released Jemima's hair. 'One son returned without too much damage.'

Jemima didn't know how he managed to sound so cool. She felt hot and flustered. Knowing Rachel was watching them for the slightest sign of anything made her feel self-conscious and jumpy.

'Why don't you go through to the kitchen? Get yourself a coffee…or something,' she said, hardly daring to look Miles in the eye.

As soon as he had taken Ben through to the kitchen, Rachel leant forward and gave Jemima a light kiss on the cheek.

'What?'

Rachel grinned. 'Nothing. Nothing at all.'

CHAPTER TEN

MILES felt peculiar as he stood in the banqueting hall of Manningtree Castle. Really quite nervous—and he wasn't sure why that would be.

Candles flickered everywhere and the soft light created the kind of romantic setting that wouldn't have been out of place in a Hollywood version of *Robin Hood*. Flowers were studded through intricate swags of dark green foliage and atmospheric music wafted down from the gallery above.

It was incredible how everything had come together in such a short time. Rachel was going to have the wedding day of her dreams.

Miles reached into his pocket to check for the ring. It was still there. He must have checked for it at least half a dozen times in the last few minutes. He'd no idea why. This was his fourth outing as best man, so one would have thought he'd be icily calm and a real pillar of strength.

Instead he felt as if he was the one about to sign his life away. Alistair, by contrast, looked completely cool. He'd been happily chatting to the eighty or so guests who'd assembled dutifully on dark red velvet chairs and he looked like a man who was thoroughly enjoying himself.

'Okay?' Alistair asked, looking across at him.

'Shouldn't that be my question?'

His friend merely smiled.

Miles glanced down at his watch. 'The girls are late.'

'That's their prerogative...' And then the music changed. 'Here we go.' Alistair turned to watch his bride walk over the polished floorboards towards him.

Miles swivelled round as the wedding guests all stood up as though they were one entity and he let his breath out in a steady stream. He was so nervous. And he didn't have the faintest idea why. Anyone would think *he* was the one getting married, instead of which...

He stopped thinking as Rachel came into view, but it wasn't the bride that had caused this cessation of all normal functions. It was Jemima. She looked...unbelievable. Beyond beautiful.

Miles smiled, feeling a strange mixture of pride and *care* for her. He knew how nervous Jemima had been about today. She didn't like being in the limelight, so this was always going to be difficult for her, but there was more to it than that.

She hadn't had to tell him how apprehensive she was about so many of her university friends coming to the wedding. For many, if not most, this was the first time they'd have seen her since her divorce. She had pride, his Jemima.

His.

That was how he thought of her now. Her worries had become his worries. He had this overwhelming need to make life better for her. Easier.

But, looking at her now, he couldn't imagine she'd ever need anything from him. She looked confident and breathtakingly lovely. Her rich copper hair had been left loose with the front sections twisted back and held in place by small white flowers. His eyes travelled lower to the simple column dress in an unusual russet brown and skimmed over the curves of her body. She'd told him she thought she looked ridiculous and that if there was a strong wind she might take off because of the sleeves. It was a description that didn't come close to doing justice to the fine gauze-like fabric, slashed from the elbow and elegantly falling to ground level.

She was stunning. And he felt a little in awe of her.

Jemima stepped forward and took Rachel's artfully natural bouquet and added it to her own. Miles wondered whether she'd had a chance yet to notice where Russell was sitting. He knew. His eyes had instinctively searched him out. Russell was sitting on the bride's side, six rows back.

Miles wondered, too, what Russell was thinking when he looked at Jemima. He felt nervously in his pocket for the ring as the short civil ceremony moved on. If memories crowded in on Jemima, surely they'd crowd in on her ex-husband too.

These were such new feelings and thoughts for him. In some kind of abstract way he'd always known that people came with a past. He'd known that specific incidents and even the general tenor of his childhood had shaped the man he was now. But…he'd not really been interested in any one other human being to want to know what had formed them.

Jemima was different. He was fascinated by her. She was reserved, self-effacing, witty, strong, beautiful… There were so many facets to her personality. She endlessly surprised him. In fact, she was like no other woman he'd spent time with. He loved being with her. Loved saying something that brought a burst of laughter. Loved making her blush.

And she never bored him. He reckoned she never would. Even after a lifetime. *Lifetime?*

Miles turned to look at Jemima, a little amazed by where his thoughts had taken him. She was so still. Her hands were clasped loosely on the bouquets she was holding and her eyes were focused on her friends. She hadn't looked at him. *Why* hadn't she even glanced across in his direction?

'The ring?'

He'd almost missed his moment. Miles pulled it out of his

pocket and handed it over. He'd been to scores of weddings over the past decade, but this was the first time he really listened to the promises the bride and groom were making. Understood what it *really* meant when Alistair slipped the gold band on Rachel's finger. Big promises, but it was actually quite beautiful.

Instinctively he glanced across to where Jemima was standing. She'd made those same promises to Russell. Had made them with the intention of keeping them. What was she thinking now? Was she reminded of her own wedding? Hurting?

Looking at her face, he thought not. She looked poised and strong. No one seeing the outward Jemima would guess she felt anything but pleasure at her friends' wedding. She was doing well, but he knew, because she'd let him glimpse beyond the capable façade, how much more complicated her emotions were.

His eyes wandered over to where Russell was sitting, presumably with Stefanie beside him. The man had made a poor trade, he thought. Why would any man choose a petulant-looking imitation blonde, who didn't seem to like his children, over Jemima?

But thank God he had, otherwise Miles knew he would never have had the opportunity to get to know her, learn to love her…

Love her. He *loved* Jemima.

That should have come as a blinding revelation, but it didn't. Miles smiled slowly. *Of course,* he loved her. In the end it was as simple as walking from one room to another. He loved her.

And it felt terrific.

Suddenly 'for ever' didn't seem quite long enough. *And what did she feel about him?* Was it very arrogant to think she might love him too?

And then the ceremony was over. Miles reached out and took hold of Jemima's hand, threading it through his arm for the short walk across the banqueting hall. She looked up and smiled at him, the first time since she'd arrived.

'I'm glad that's over,' she whispered quietly. 'It went well, though, didn't it?'

'Now, as long as the marquee holds up we're on the home straight.'

She laughed. 'Oh, heck, and it'll be my fault if it doesn't. If ever I get married again I want to do nothing but turn up. This is too stressful.'

'I'll remember that.'

Jemima looked up at him and then away, but he'd caught the glimmer of something in her eyes. *What did it mean?* Then she moved away in order to help Rachel manage her long train as she walked down the stone spiral staircase.

The next three hours were strange. In many ways they were predictable. There were the endless photographs on the tulip lawn with the castle as a dramatic foil. Yet more had been taken on the Tudor bridge which spanned the dry moat. Then they moved seamlessly through a champagne reception and on into a wedding breakfast comprising six courses with a very twenty-first century feel.

What was strange was how much of a spectator he felt, despite being so involved in what was happening. He felt as if he was on the sidelines watching, waiting for his real life to start. And real life could only happen when he'd been able to speak to Jemima.

His speech as best man was everything Alistair and Rachel had hoped it would be, but it was Jemima's calm green eyes he looked at for approval. It was her slow smile that warmed him. He was anxious to know how she was doing, eager to be near her, but there was little possibility of that. Despite preferring to leave the limelight to others, Jemima was continually surrounded throughout the long afternoon.

In the end she found him.

'My feet ache,' she said, coming to stand beside him. She lifted up the hem of her dress and revealed matching shoes with viciously pointed toes.

He wondered how women could squeeze their feet into that tortuous shape and spared a moment to think how glad he was that male fashion hadn't evolved that way. 'That's twelfth century footwear for you.'

Jemima gave a gurgle of laughter. 'They'll be going soon. Have you done anything about Alistair's car?'

'It's all under control. I've organised rose petals to be put in the air vents and streamers practically everywhere else.'

He turned to look at her, loving the way her copper hair framed her beautiful face.

'I even managed to dissuade Alistair's young cousin from putting stones in the hub-caps and fish in place of the rose petals. Can you imagine how awful that would smell?'

'And how long it would have lasted,' Miles added. Then, 'Are you tired?'

'Shattered. My face aches from continually smiling and I'm longing for a cup of tea.'

Miles laughed and reached out for her hand. 'Come and find five minutes quiet. They won't leave for a good half an hour yet.'

She hesitated, he thought, but then she let him lead her away from the hubbub of noise and along by the lake. 'It is beautiful here,' Jemima remarked, looking out across the lake. 'I would never have changed my wedding venue so late in the day, but I can see why Rachel felt she had to do it. There's something rather special about standing where kings and queens have been entertained.'

Miles moved to stand beside her. He had to tell her what he was feeling. And he had to tell her now. It wouldn't wait.

There was a moment's silence and then he said, 'I love you.' His voice was quiet and his eyes were focused far in the distance.

He felt her turn to look at him and he moved so that he could see her face. He noticed the small pulse in her neck and her wide eyes. His smile twisted at her surprise.

'I love you.' Miles swallowed, searching for the words that would convey to her exactly how far he'd travelled in the past three months. 'I didn't know… I haven't ever felt…'

Words never failed him. But now, when they really mattered, he couldn't find them. There was so much he wanted her to understand. He pulled an agitated hand through his hair. 'I love you,' he repeated, reaching for her hands and holding her listless fingers in his firm grasp.

'You love me?'

'And I want you to marry me. I want for ever.'

He'd said it. The words he'd thought he'd never say to anyone. He wanted a future with Jemima as his wife more than he wanted his freedom. He knew with complete certainty that she was the woman he wanted to spend the rest of his life with. That if she said no his life would always be a pale imitation of what it could have been with her beside him.

He looked into Jemima's face, searching for some reaction other than surprise. He found it in the soft shimmer of tears that covered her green eyes.

'Miles, I—I can't.'

His mouth moved soundlessly and his body felt cold.

Jemima pulled her hands away and covered her trembling mouth. 'I'm so sorry, Miles.'

'Why?'

She shook her head as though she didn't want to explain, but then the words were drawn from her anyway. 'I never thought…' Jemima moved nearer. 'You said you didn't believe in marriage,' she said, almost accusing.

'I know. I didn't.' His eyes willed her to understand, to feel how much he loved her. Would always love her. 'I've never felt like this before. I've never been in love, so it took me a while to understand what I was feeling. And…then, today, I listened to the promises Alistair and Rachel were making and…I want that. I want to know you're going to walk the rest of your life beside me, loving me, supporting me.'

Jemima's hand felt for a coil of her hair and twisted it round her finger. Her green eyes were full of fear and pain. 'When I married Russell I really believed it would be for ever. I thought he was a steady kind of man who really loved me.'

Miles went to speak, but she stopped him.

'You…you're not safe enough for me. I've got two boys—'

'I know, I—'

'And I'm not brave enough. I can't risk them being hurt…and I can't risk being hurt myself. I'd always be wondering why you were with me. Whether you'd met someone you found more attractive, more amusing, more… Well, more.'

Miles felt as though something had reached deep inside him and had taken hold of his heart and was squeezing it with long, tenacious fingers. 'Jemima, I love you.'

He watched with an acute kind of pain the moisture well up in her eyes and fall in soft tears down her cheeks. Miles went to move, but she held him off. 'I'm so sorry. Really s-sorry.'

And then she walked away, back along the lakeside path. Miles remained still for a moment, too wounded to move. Loving, he realised, came at a cost. Until this moment his understanding of rejection had been entirely cerebral, but if Jemima had experienced a fraction of the pain he felt now…

He would wait for her, he thought with quiet determination. Slowly he would win her round, make her love him enough to be prepared to risk anything.

'What's happened?' Rachel asked, looking anxiously at Jemima's tear-stained face.

'Nothing. I'm sorry. It's nothing.'

'Is it Russell?'

Jemima shook her head.

Rachel looked past her and saw Miles coming out of the woods. 'Miles?'

'It's nothing, really,' Jemima said, summoning up a brave smile. 'I'm being ridiculous. Are you and Alistair about to leave?'

'We were,' she said, still looking concerned. 'Alistair was going to look for Miles and then we were going back to the cottage to get changed. But if you're upset we can—'

Jemima reached out to hug her friend. 'I really hope you'll both be very happy. I'm just feeling emotional. It's nothing. It's been a very emotional day,' she said, pulling back and smiling bravely.

It was amazing to Jemima that Rachel believed her. Even more amazing that her over-bright smile appeared to fool everyone else as well.

Inside she was falling apart, piece by piece. All she wanted was solitude where she could begin to unpack the emotions that were building inside her. *Miles loved her.* If she hadn't known that was an impossibility she might have been more prepared. But that he loved her enough to *marry* her… There was no amount of preparation that would have made her ready to hear that.

It was a fairytale. It was the knight on horseback climbing up the tower to rescue his princess. Or the foreign prince waking his love with a kiss. It was everything she'd ever dreamed of…just there within her reach. If she only had the courage to reach out and take hold of it…

As soon as she'd waved Alistair and Rachel away, Jemima quietly slipped back into the woodland. Perhaps if she hadn't been so sure of Russell she might feel braver now. But…

She had been sure of him. She'd skipped through her

wedding day with the confidence of someone who knew she'd be happy for the rest of her life.

And yet… It had all come down to a rainy Sunday afternoon when she'd been told she'd become boring. That the man she believed loved her no longer found her physically attractive…

'Jemima.'

She turned to see Russell standing there, almost as though he'd been conjured up by her thoughts.

'May I…talk to you?'

Jemima felt too empty to care whether he stayed or whether he went. He probably wanted to ask if he could have the boys longer over the summer. No doubt his mother wanted them to visit her in Devon.

Russell must have taken her silence for tacit agreement because he sat down beside her. He cleared his throat with a dry cough. 'You look lovely.'

She looked across at him, surprised. 'Thank you.'

Russell looked down at his hands and cleared his throat again. He seemed tense and nervous. Jemima waited for what would come next.

'Stefanie…'

She was too tired, too heart-sore to sit here while Russell talked about Stefanie. She didn't *care* any more what they did. She just wished she didn't have to see them or think about them.

Again that irritating dry cough. 'Stefanie is pregnant.'

Jemima turned to look at him. 'Pregnant?'

'Four months.' Russell nodded. 'Not planned.'

'Oh.' What else could she say? It didn't seem quite appropriate to say 'congratulations'. She didn't quite know why he thought he ought to tell her. It was nothing to do with her any more…

Except, of course, that the baby would be a half-brother or sister to Ben and Sam. Even so, she thought it was his responsibility to tell them the news. Ben would hate it. Sam would probably be pleased.

'I…er…'

Jemima looked at him curiously.

'Are you and Miles…?'

She found that she was getting impatient with this whole conversation. She had so much else to think about. It was none of Russell's business whether she and Miles were or weren't. He could hardly expect they'd be able to sit companionably side by side discussing their respective love lives.

'I'm sorry, I…' He stood up restlessly and then sat down beside her again. 'I hated it when you got pregnant with Sam,' he said suddenly.

Jemima couldn't quite believe what she was hearing.

'I love him now. Of course I do. But I found the whole pregnancy difficult. You know, the antenatal classes, the house being full of baby things. It was worse with Sam because I knew what was coming. And you were always so tired—'

Jemima cut him off. 'I don't think I need to hear this,' she said, standing up.

'Jemma.' His voice stopped her. 'If I could do things differently, I would.'

Jemima turned and her dress swooshed on the path.

Russell's eyes looked up bleakly. 'I've made a mess of everything, haven't I? I suppose there's no way…no way back…?'

Any way back? To her?

'Is there?'

No. There was no way back. Jemima moved to sit beside him. It was strange how 'little' he seemed to her now. Not the handsome, strong man she'd thought she'd married, but a little boy. Confused, frightened by responsibility. She was sad for him.

She reached out and touched his hand. 'You're with Stefanie now. That's the choice you made.'

A muscle flicked in his cheek. 'I suppose…'

'She's not like you, Jemima. I—' he smiled sadly and then found the word he was searching for '—miss you. Does that sound strange?'

Jemima wasn't sure whether it did or didn't. In a way, she understood. She missed the dream she'd had. As she looked at Russell, she realised that she'd spent nearly three years of her life mourning the loss of that far more than the man himself.

'We had some good years.'

'Yes.'

She felt almost as if she was talking to one of her sons rather than the man she'd once thought she'd spend her life loving. 'And we share two fantastic boys. But we have different futures ahead of us now.'

'You don't love me?'

'No. No, I don't.' And she really didn't. Searching inside herself, there was no sense of regret. When she looked at Russell she felt…nothing.

'Miles is a lucky man,' Russell said, putting his arms around her and holding her. It seemed rude to push him away, so Jemima stayed still.

Vaguely she heard the sound of footsteps and then Miles's voice sliced through the air. 'I'm sorry. I…'

'Miles!' Jemima pulled away from Russell and looked up into Miles's eyes. They were bleak, as though his soul had been ripped out of him. For a moment she didn't understand the expression on his face and then she felt as though she'd been torpedoed. Miles thought… He thought…

'I didn't realise Russell was with you,' he said with quiet dignity. 'I'm sorry.' Then he turned to walk away without waiting for her to say anything.

Oh, God, please, no.

Jemima sat, stunned. She'd never heard such a raw edge of pain in anyone's voice. Not even hers. Her limbs were slow to respond. She wasn't sure what she ought to do now. She only knew that Miles was hurting—and she had to find him.

'Russell, I'm going to have to go,' she said, standing up. 'I'll talk to you about the boys next week, but I've got to go…'

She trailed off and walked briskly down the woodland path. She came out on to the tulip lawn and looked around her. She couldn't see him anywhere. She slipped off her high-heeled shoes and almost ran across the soft grass.

'Jemima.' Alistair's second cousin stopped her.

'I'm looking for Miles. Have you seen him?'

'No. Oh, yes, he was going towards the marquee.'

It was the start of a horrible fifteen minutes. Miles seemed to have vanished. He wasn't in the marquee or even back at the castle. It was almost as though aliens had landed and he'd been plucked from the earth.

Jemima stood listlessly looking at the Tudor bridge, finally accepting that he'd gone. Home? Possibly. Most of the guests had either left or were on the point of leaving.

He was hurting. It was almost unbelievable that she could have the power to hurt a man like Miles. *She had that power because he loved her*—loved *her*—and in her fear she'd thrown that love back in his face. Had hurt him. She picked up the front of her dress and walked purposefully towards her hired car. He loved her.

And she loved him. Not like she'd loved Russell. That had been…different somehow. Maybe it was because they'd been so much younger, but…

This felt scarier. She'd thought her fear was because she was too scared to risk her heart on another relationship, but actually it was because she knew she wouldn't survive Miles falling out of love with her.

But then she'd seen the pain in Miles's eyes as he'd seen

Russell holding her. It had changed everything. Every thought in her body was that she needed to get to him, talk to him…

The journey back to London seemed to take for ever. She didn't even have a very clear idea of what she intended to do when she got there. The traffic slowed to a snail's pace as she reached the outskirts of town and she felt more impatient than she'd ever done before.

She didn't even think about how strange she must look still dressed in her bridesmaid's dress when she stopped for petrol. It was as though she was running on pure adrenaline.

And all the time she was planning what she should do. She could phone him, but she didn't think she could say what she wanted to without being able to see his face. She had to see him. And it had to be tonight.

Although she'd never been to his house, she had his address on a piece of paper tucked inside the front pocket of her handbag. It meant she had to drive to Harrow first.

What if he wasn't at home? Well, if he wasn't she'd have to phone him then. But only if he wasn't home.

'Jemima!' her mum exclaimed, looking up as she ran through the lounge. 'I didn't expect you back yet.'

'I know. I…' Her fingers fumbled with the front clasp of her handbag and she pulled out the piece of paper. 'Are the boys okay?'

'They're fine. Fast asleep.'

'Mum, I've just made the most terrible mistake. I…' Her voice cracked and her mum smiled.

'Miles?' she said gently.

'I've got to go and find him.'

'Good idea.' Her mum settled back into her armchair. 'I'll stay with the boys, so don't hurry back.'

In a whirl of russet fabric, Jemima tore out of the house. She was so focused on what she was doing that she didn't notice that she drove up a bus lane and twice cut up the same black cab.

It was only when she approached Miles's house that she felt any sense of nervousness. She was used to seeing him in her own home, even against the stylish backdrop of Kingsley and Bressington, but this was money. Money as Verity lived it. It felt a little strange.

She parked the car and managed to find change for the meter. His house was tucked away in a small mews—double-fronted with its own garage. She remembered now that he'd told her he'd bought it because it had a place to keep his precious car.

Jemima picked up the hem of her dress and walked towards the blue front door. *She could do this. She really could.* Her heart was pounding but she was filled with an uncharacteristic exuberance.

Without giving herself time to think any more about what she was going to say, or what Miles might say to her, Jemima pushed the bell. Then she waited, her ears straining to hear the sound of his footsteps coming to answer the door.

There was silence. Perhaps he'd decided not to come home. Perhaps…

And then the door opened.

He looked dreadful. He'd changed from his wedding clothes and he looked…broken. She'd never imagined Miles could look like that.

She wasn't sure how to begin to explain why she was here. It had seemed so simple back in Kent. She loved *him*, not Russell, and she wanted him to know that. Russell was her past, not her future.

Miles didn't ask her in. He seemed confused that she was there, braced to be hurt. She understood how that felt.

Jemima moistened her lips. 'I…'

'Yes?'

'I came to tell you… I…' She broke off again and cursed herself inwardly for not having worked out exactly what she was going to say.

'Yes?'

'I came to tell you I'm sorry. That I…'

Miles stepped back into his house as though she'd hit him. He seemed to expect that she'd follow, so she did, shutting the door behind her.

She'd never felt so nervous in her entire life. What if Miles had only asked her to marry him as a momentary impulse?

But what if he was hurting?

Jemima moistened her lips. 'Miles.'

He'd picked up a whisky tumbler and took a sip. 'Can I get you anything? Wine? Tea? Coffee?'

It was difficult to speak to him when he was like this. Everything was making it seem harder to say what she needed to, even their being in his starkly beautiful home rather than somewhere familiar to her.

'Miles.' She moistened her lips again. 'I came to tell you—'

'That you're taking Russell back?' His voice was thick with pain and Jemima lost her English reserve.

'No.' She shook her head. 'No, I came to tell you that I love *you.*'

It was as though something snapped inside him. She heard the sound of his glass being put down roughly on the table and then she felt his hands tenderly cradling her face.

'Say that again,' he instructed, looking deep into her eyes.

It was easier this time. Her smile was tremulous. 'I love you. And—'

But she didn't get a chance to finish what she was saying because he was kissing her with a desperation that was incredibly erotic. His voice was husky as he said her name and Jemima let her hands snake up to bury themselves deep in his dark hair.

It was going to be all right. Not just all right—it was going to be incredible. She felt tears of relief start in her eyes.

'I thought I'd lost you.'

Jemima didn't pretend to misunderstand. 'To Russell? No. I love you.'

She heard the soft groan he made at the back of his throat and then he was kissing her again. His mouth was warm and tasted of whisky and her body responded as though it were liquid heat. She'd never experienced anything so instantaneous. So…mindblowingly sexy.

There would be time later, much later, to tell him about Russell's new baby. All about their conversation in the wood. For now it was enough that Miles was holding her as though he'd never let her go. More than enough.

Miles pulled back and stroked his thumbs gently over her tear-stained cheeks. 'You taste of salt.'

'You taste of whisky.'

He smiled then, that twisting sexy smile that made her feel light-headed. 'I was depressed.'

'That's a very bad reason for drinking whisky. You need taking in hand.'

'I know.'

Jemima took a deep breath and looked into his glinting blue eyes. 'Will you marry me?'

Slowly, very slowly, Miles traced his thumb across her lips, his face inexpressibly tender. 'You're asking me to marry you?' he said, his voice thick with wonder.

Her stomach was churning with a mixture of nervousness and excitement. 'Will you?'

'Try stopping me.'

EPILOGUE

JEMIMA stood outside the church and experienced a moment of intense panic at the enormity of what she was doing. Her heart started to beat erratically and her legs felt like blancmange. *She couldn't do this.*

What if Miles changed his mind five years down the track? What if he woke up one morning and realised he didn't love her any more? What if he'd already realised he was making a terrible mistake and was standing at the front of the church now wishing he wasn't?

'Ready?' Rachel asked, smoothing one wayward curl back off Jemima's forehead.

'I'm scared.'

Her friend looked at her and then asked gently, 'Is that nervous scared, or scared scared?'

Jemima's hands started to tremble. 'I'm scared this is the wrong thing.'

'For you, or for him?' Rachel asked sagely. Then, in spite of the hand-tied bouquet of white roses, she took hold of Jemima's cold hands. 'Look at me, Jemima.'

Slowly Jemima brought her frightened eyes away from the arched church door and looked into Rachel's unusually calm and sensible ones.

'This is *Miles* you're marrying. There's nothing to be scared about.'

I'm marrying Miles. Jemima repeated Rachel's words in her head and felt the fear recede as quickly as it had come. *Miles.*

'I've seen you make some daft decisions. Not many, but some,' Rachel said with a smile. 'This isn't one of them.'

No, it wasn't. It absolutely wasn't.

Rachel released her fingers and Jemima looked down at the engagement ring Miles had chosen for her, but it wasn't the beauty of the princess cut diamond she saw. She saw instead the amazing man who'd given it to her.

And she saw the expression in his eyes when he'd presented it to her. They'd been standing in a capsule on the London Eye on a balmy late August evening, the city lights dramatic in the night sky.

It had been one of those golden moments, the kind you knew you'd remember until the day you died. He'd pulled the small velvet box from his pocket and had told her he loved her, the woman she was and the woman she'd become.

She'd been a little scared that day. Part of her had been worried that if she allowed herself to be too happy it would hurt more when it was snatched away. And Miles had known that, had understood why.

Jemima passed Rachel her simple bouquet to hold and twisted her engagement ring off her finger, transferring it to her right hand for the ceremony.

There'd been moments during their engagement when that fear had risen to the surface. Days when she'd been so sure Miles would look at her and realise she wasn't what he wanted.

Like the day when Sam had ridden his bike slap bang into his prized Bristol 407 and made a horrible scratch along the right passenger door. Jemima smiled wryly. *She'd been certain Miles would leave her then.*

Then there was the time when he'd been left kicking his heels outside Ben's classroom because Russell had unexpectedly been able to make parents' evening after all. *She'd been terrified he'd leave her then.*

Jemima took back her bouquet from Rachel and smiled. 'I'm marrying Miles.'

'And he loves you,' Rachel said, adjusting the single white rose amidst the copper curls. 'Very much. Your sad times are all behind you.'

No more sad times. It was something Jemima thought of all the way down the aisle. Such a short distance and yet it felt so far.

She was vaguely aware of the music that heralded her entrance and the faces of close friends and family. Her mother was a blur of soft dove-grey and Hermione a more noticeable figure in burgundy, but mostly she saw Miles waiting for her, Ben beside him.

Miles turned to watch her. Tall, dark, handsome…actually, very handsome…and *hers*. Rachel was wrong. There would be sad times. But there'd also be happy times, exciting times…

And there'd be Miles.

Hers. *For better, for worse. In sickness and in health. Forsaking all others.*

And she believed him. Absolutely.

It meant that when Miles promised to love her until she died she knew he'd keep that promise, whatever the future held for them. It was the time for *doubting* that was over.

And when Ben, as best man, solemnly passed over the gold band and Miles slid it on her finger, Jemima felt a sense of peace.

'*…pronounce you man and wife. You may kiss your bride.*'

Jemima looked up into his blue eyes and she knew he meant it when he said softly, 'I love you, Mrs Kingsley.'

Her own eyes twinkled up at him. 'Then you'd better kiss me.'

His hands cradled her face and he did just that, his lips saying more than the words of the church service. Then he reached down and touched Ben on the head. A simple gesture, but it was something Jemima knew she'd never forget.

Just as she wouldn't forget the sight of the traditionally painted Gypsy caravan pulled by one horse as it came round the corner towards the church.

She looked up at her new husband, a question in her eyes.

'You said different,' he said, reaching down to hold her hand. 'Good idea?'

It was strange how close laughter and tears were, because Jemima suddenly felt as if she wanted to cry. 'Brilliant idea.'

'No ghosts, then?'

She shook her head. 'No ghosts.'

Then Miles smiled and it came as a blinding revelation to her that he'd been worried there might be. She reached up and touched his face. 'I love you.'

'Just me,' he said with mock severity. 'No one else.'

Jemima shook her head and held up her left hand. 'I promised.'

His eyes took on their customary glint. 'I'll hold you to that,' he said, leading her towards the Gypsy caravan that would take them to their reception. 'I love you, too. And I really love your "something blue". Very sexy. Are brides supposed to be sexy?'

Jemima smoothed out the ice-blue silk of the elegant but simple dress she'd chosen to be married in. Then she looked up, a mischievous twinkle in her own eyes. 'Just wait till you see what I'm wearing that's white,' she said, teasing. 'I think you're really going to love that.'

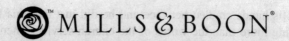